Vicious THRONE

MJ CROUCH

Copyright © 2024 by Calamittie Jane Publishing

All rights reserved.

No part of this book may be reproduced in any form or by any electronic or mechanical means, including information storage and retrieval systems, without written permission from the author, except for the use of brief quotations in a book review.

This a work of fiction. Names, characters, places, and incidents are the product of the author's imagination or are used fictitiously, and any resemblance to actual persons, living or dead, business establishments, events or locals is entirely coincidental.

Cover created by Deranged Doctor Designs.

A Calamittie Jane Publishing Book

VICIOUS THRONE: GILDED EMPIRE

Chapter 1
Mari

I was fucking done.

Sick of white walls in a room I didn't know and unfamiliar sheets on beds that weren't mine. Sick of people coming in and out of our rooms and the incessant beeping that was driving me slowly insane.

Beep. Beep. Beep.

Yet everything faded when Greyson's eyes opened for the first time.

It had been two days of silence, two days of Nate and Dominic bitching every time their bandages were changed and me snapping at them to get over it. Two days of avoiding being treated myself until there was no other option but to allow it. Two days of pretending that the men who *were* awake weren't at odds with each other.

Two days of praying to gods I didn't believe in to spare Greyson. To spare us all.

Thank fuck they listened.

"Mari," Grey croaked, and I felt my heart crack down the middle. I heard shuffling around me, happy mumbles that shut off the moment Dominic realized Nate was trying to talk to him.

"You're awake."

"What happened?"

I carefully fed a straw between his dry lips, letting him drink as much water as he needed, not ready to answer him.

"You nearly died," Dominic snarked from his side of the room. "I had to carry your ass out with a bullet in my leg."

"It was a through and through. Don't be such a baby." I didn't bother to look at him, too terrified to take my gaze away from Greyson.

Would he disappear if I did? Would I wake up and all of this would be a dream? I couldn't handle either of those options.

"Died?"

"Blood loss," Nate said from his side of the room. He and Dominic had instinctively taken the outer beds that were closest to the doors. I knew they were bookending so Grey and I were protected if anything went down, and it warmed my heart to see them working together even that much. Dominic had been damn near arctic since we'd arrived. "Your bullets were through and through, too, but one nicked your neck."

"The artery?" Grey's eyes were tight. We both knew what an artery wound looked like and the recovery time for it. Time that we didn't have right now.

"Not quite, but very, very close. You're lucky you're alive."

Grey's hand squeezed around mine, and I let myself sink into that feeling. Let myself press my forehead to his knuckles as if they alone could ground me.

He's here. He's alive. He's safe. For now.

But outside the walls of the hospital, chaos was still reigning.

Fingers brushed back my nasty hair. "Are you okay?" Grey asked.

Before I could even attempt to answer, Dominic snorted. "She refused to get treated until I sat on her, but she's fine now."

Grey's eyebrow lifted, and I whipped around to glare at Dominic.

"You sat on her?"

"Absolutely. Face down, ass up." Dominic waggled his brows like an idiot, but the small smile on Greyson's lips made it worth it. They could make fun of me all they wanted as long as they were all alive.

"The city?"

"Fine for now," someone else answered. All four of us tensed, and I saw the flash of metal in Dominic's and Nate's hands before I turned to the newcomer at the door.

Despite helping us to the hospital and keeping us safe, Two-Bit had been absent the past few days. Allowing me the space to focus on my family, first and foremost. Seeing him now, I knew that was over.

Fact was, a war was waging outside those walls, and I was the general.

"Has he moved?"

"No," Two-Bit said. "He's been quiet."

It wouldn't last. It never did.

Two-Bit looked past me at Greyson, cataloging every injury in the span of a blink. "You alive?"

"With one more hole than before, yeah. Are my memories fucked, or did you get us out?"

"That was real."

"So, you're an ally." Greyson said it more like a question than a statement, and Two-Bit smiled.

"In more ways than one."

I so didn't want to deal with head games after the week I'd had. "Tell me who you are, what you want, and what I owe for your help," I said bluntly.

"You owe me a conversation—that's it. As for the rest, I am the leader of the 48th Street Vipers."

"But that's not all you are." It was Nate who said it. Was this yet another thing he knew that I didn't? He gave me the slightest headshake, telling me he was just as in the dark, but I recognized that he was going to have to spill his secrets soon too if we had a chance of survival.

"No, not all," Two-Bit admitted.

It hit me then as I saw the way he held himself so differently from the plain, easy-to-overlook way he existed inside of our meetings. He stood with something like power, confidence, and that fucking God complex so many of them had.

"Holy shit, you're a Fed." If I hadn't seen him in action myself, I'd never have believed it. That was a testament to Two-Bit's acting.

"That's not all he is." Griz, his second, walked in behind him and locked us all in. The four of us tensed even more, but no one moved.

Two-Bit tipped his head to the side and smiled, though it was strained and uncomfortable. "My name is Dante. I believe you've met my father, Rafael Osorio."

"Jesus fucking Christ," Grey whispered behind me.

It said a lot about my current mental state that I wasn't even surprised at the news. *Another cousin.* I had so many questions but decided I needed answers from Rafael, not Two-Bit. Dante. Whatever the hell his name was. At least I could trust Rafael to some degree. I didn't trust cops, no matter what flavor they were.

"Why did you step in? If you're a Fed, it would have made sense for you to let us die. We're not exactly good Samaritans." That was an understatement if I'd ever uttered one.

Two-Bit—because I couldn't acknowledge him as anything else—shrugged. "We're family."

Which he'd known for how long and done nothing about? No, that wasn't it either. "Are the Vipers all yours?"

I desperately needed him to say no. He grimaced. "Most. There are some who are old-school Vipers, but for the most part, they're all agents."

Saying nothing, I turned to Griz. The bastard grinned. "Not a Fed, but not a civvy either."

Fucking great.

"Motherfuck," Dominic grumbled.

What a mess. The idea that teams of federal agents were walking their way through my city made my skin crawl.

"Are you here for us or Cash?" I asked finally.

"Cash, actually." *Thank fuck for small miracles.* "Despite your illegal dealings, you're kind of a low-level issue for us. You keep the city clean. You force your business partners to do the same. It's admirable."

I rolled my eyes. "Don't make me seem like a saint, cousin."

"Never said you were. I just said what you're doing is admirable. Admirable enough that you're not really on our radar."

The warning was crystal clear. *We have the information we need to take you down. We're choosing not to.*

"But Cash is," Grey prompted, readjusting himself until he was sitting up. I tried to move off the edge of the bed where I'd been planted, and he dragged me back until I was pressed against his side, head tucked under his chin. Not the most dignified, but with his heart beating under my ear, I wasn't going to complain.

"The FBI and the DEA have a joint task force for Mr. Beckstrom."

"The drugs," Nate said softly.

Two-Bit's eyes flashed to him. "Your brother is acting as an import partner to one of the cartels, and while we know they have other partners, he's one of their biggest. It's important we shut that down."

He didn't mention the Osorios, so I had to assume this partner was someone else. But I noticed the narrowing of his eyes, the stiffness of his shoulders. It was plain to see this was something Rafael's son wasn't going to tell me.

"Why help us if you're here for Cash?" I asked, settling back into Grey's arms.

"Because you are the closest thing we have to an ally. You can get rid of him."

"Have you been paying attention?" We'd been working for months to unravel the Aces and every hit we landed didn't seem to be enough. He'd had over a decade to plan his war, and every turn we took made it obvious we were playing catch-up.

"You're failing because you don't have the support to take him out head on. We are willing to give it to you."

"Bullshit," Dominic spat. "Since when do Feds trouble themselves with gang wars?"

"This isn't a gang war. It's the only way to ensure a dictator doesn't take over a major point of access to the country."

"National security shit." Dominic's sarcasm was thick, but Two-Bit still nodded.

"Essentially, yes. Cash needs to be removed from power. We have the money and the tools to make it happen, but we don't have the foothold. He has too many people watching us to get close."

Sighing, I held his gaze. "Be straight with me. What do you want? Am I supposed to turn him in or something? Because asshole or not, I'm no snitch."

Two-Bit and Griz laughed, the latter taking over. "We're not asking you to be a witness. We're asking you to be a weapon."

"So, you see the three-headed snake, and you want me to be the sword that chops them all to pieces. Is that it?" They said nothing and I nodded. "How typical of the government. You put your resources up, but not your people. God forbid your little soldiers end up in a tiff they can't get out of, so you ask mine to instead."

"He needs to die," Two-Bit said.

I didn't disagree, but I wasn't going to say that to a Fed. Not when I had no clue just how far he was willing to go if I said no. Could he arrest me? He'd already insinuated that he had the leverage. If I declined playing God, would he take me in? What about my men?

Greyson squeezed my shoulder weakly, knowing where my thoughts were. "What exactly are you offering?"

"To look the other way," Two-Bit said carefully. "Tools and weapons as needed. Ammunition, money, safety for some of your people. You, included."

"You're giving me a get-out-of-jail-free card."

"One that you desperately need. Don't forget, if you end up in jail, you're dead. The Aces have more of a foothold in the system than you could ever imagine. The fact that he survived was a miracle." Two-Bit pointed to Dominic, who grunted like it didn't matter, but I saw him glance at Nate with the barest flash of appreciation. After all, it had been Nate's men who'd saved him while he was inside. It went a long way toward Dominic's hard-won forgiveness.

"So, you'll turn a blind eye to everything that we do if we kill him. What's the catch?"

"There isn't one. At the end of the day, either Cash ends up dead, or you do. In which case, my deal is null and void. If you survive, you're free to move on as if nothing happened. This isn't exactly an easy mission, and we knew the bribe would have to be enough to entice you to risk it."

God help me, it was. I didn't want to work with the Feds, but we needed allies. We needed safety and protection, more than I could give us with Cash chipping away at the foundation of my empire. Still, the Feds were going to be the last fucking place I turned.

No use surviving if the rest of the city leaders killed me thinking I was a snitch.

"We'll need some time to discuss," Nate said carefully, hoisting himself out of bed.

He stood tall and proud, a barrier between us and them, but I saw the wince he was trying to hide and could practically feel the ache of his wound. Had it been anyone else standing in front of us, I'd have told him he was a fucking idiot for moving when he didn't need to. But we had to be a united front from here on out. We couldn't let the world see a single crack.

Griz and Two-Bit looked at each other before the bigger man stepped into the hallway. "Take some time to think about it, but just know we don't have forever. This needs to end fast."

With a nod to all of us, Two-Bit headed for the door.

"Thank you." The words were ripped out of my chest, but looking at Nate standing there, Dominic lounging back on his bed, and feeling Grey's skin warm underneath mine, I couldn't help but say it. He didn't have to save us. Hell, he probably shouldn't have.

Even if he did it because he wanted something from me, he'd kept my family alive when I couldn't. That deserved gratitude and the respect of considering his proposal, at the very least.

Two-Bit inclined his head and left the room, shutting the door behind him. The second we were sealed off from the rest of the world, our shoulders lowered, and we all seemed to relax. Greyson's hand was shaky as it stroked my greasy hair back. "Are you really all right?"

"I'm fine," I promised. Nate paused as he passed me, leaning over to press a kiss to the back of my head and hissing through his teeth when he straightened up again.

"Lie down, moron," Dominic snapped. "You'll rip your stitches."

"Okay, Mom."

"You wish your mom was this gorgeous."

Nate laughed, then grabbed his stomach with a wince. "Shut up."

Dominic didn't laugh with him, and it was obvious there was still tension there. Confessions needed to be made and discussions to deal with anger, but I saw the slow thaw in their interactions too. Dominic understood that we were better together. He could hate Nate if he wanted, but it wouldn't last. He was already halfway to forgiveness, even if he didn't want to admit it.

I heard the rustling of sheets behind me and Nate's half-pained, half-relieved sigh. Were his burns hurting him? It wasn't all that long ago that he'd run into a burning building for me, and then he'd been shot. I felt like his bad-luck charm, though I doubted he'd agree.

After deciding to corner him with the doctor later, I snuggled deeper into Greyson's side as he reclined us again. Bone-deep exhaustion made my eyes sandy and dry.

"We should discuss his proposal," he said.

"Not today," Nate said, his voice getting further and further away. "She hasn't slept since we got here."

It was true. I'd had some catnaps here and there, plus falling asleep upright in the one shower they'd forced me into that first night, but that was it.

A hand on my hair, a soft, slow sigh, followed by, "Later, then."

Grey hauled me against him until my nose was pressed to his neck like he knew that was what I needed. The scent of him, the sound of my men talking quietly, the reminder that we were all together. All safe. It was everything to me, even if I wasn't sure how to make it last.

Chapter 2
Nate

Mari slept like the dead in Greyson's arms. The three of us lapsed into silence the moment her breathing evened out, and I'd closed my eyes to listen to those soft inhales. She'd been run so ragged that Dominic and I had discussed sedating her. Thank God Grey woke up when he did.

Even as removed as I still felt from my family, I couldn't help but be grateful.

We were alive, Mari was safe, my brothers were here, and I was free.

Cash wouldn't let me go. I knew too much. Worse, he'd come after Mari even harder because I'd abandoned him. But I wasn't sure that mattered. I would do whatever it took to make sure that we stayed safe, even if it cost me my soul.

Her breathing hitched, and I was smiling before I even opened my eyes, knowing she was awake. I didn't expect her to be turned over, staring right at me. "We need to talk."

The darkness under her eyes made my chest tight. I was used to her full of life, not this pale imitation of my Mari.

"Take a shower first, angel." She needed to wash away the fear that still clung to her. I could see the fight in her, desperate to refuse, but Dominic cut her off.

"Seriously, *mariposa*. You stink. We'll watch the invalid."

"You're all invalids." There was the rub. We'd all been shot—not that she seemed to remember the graze on her arm—and we'd terrified her. I couldn't imagine what that had been like for her. Watching her hurt was bad enough, but she'd watched all three men she loved go down. That was going to have repercussions.

"We are, and we can take care of one another. Now, go. Get clean. We'll survive the next ten minutes."

Mari narrowed her eyes. "Five."

"Twenty."

"That's not how negotiations work, Dominic."

"It is today. If you can't take care of yourself, we'll do it for you. And I can promise you won't like my way."

She darted her eyes between Greyson and me, looking for support she wasn't going to find. She needed to relax, but if the basest form of self-care was all we got, I'd be okay with that, too.

"Fine," she snapped, hauling the dinky duffel bag over her injured shoulder. I knew from the burning glare she sent us that it was intentional. *Stubborn woman.*

We hadn't brought our people here, wanting to stay under the radar. With Greyson in such an uncertain condition, we had to be as close to ghosts as possible. Hence our current suite at the University Med Center instead of a private suite at Seattle General and shitty clothes a nurse had bought us from a local thrift store. Cash wouldn't find us injured and unprepared.

The door shut quietly behind her, and all three of us cringed. A quiet Mari was a dangerous one.

"Any chance there's a shower for me too?" Grey asked with a wince.

"If you're looking for a sponge bath, your nurse just left," Dominic joked, even as the two of us crawled out of our beds and over to Greyson. It was instinctive, and thankfully, Dominic didn't make an issue of me helping. He did keep his distance, though, making sure no part of us touched. We'd fucked our girl together before, but God forbid he got my cooties now.

Christ, this was a mess.

"She's going to freak," I warned quietly when we stood in front of the bathroom door. Mari was going to panic the second she heard us.

Dominic sighed. "Yeah, I know."

He'd barely finished knocking when the door whipped open, and Mari's wide eyes found ours. "Is he—?"

We must've caught her just as she'd climbed in because her hair was still mostly dry. Beads of water slid between her breasts and down her body until my mouth watered as I followed the drops to the promised land. Christ, I needed her on my tongue.

"God*damn*," Dominic growled, obviously on the same page as me. "You should be illegal."

"I'm fine. I just need a shower, *reina*," Grey interrupted, elbowing Dominic in the stomach. "Can I join you?"

The breath she let out was unsteady, but it firmed up immediately as she pulled him into the room and shut us out.

"Lucky bastard," Dominic muttered under his breath, moving to his own bag to change. I snorted, then froze when I saw his shoulders tighten.

Dominic's anger was a living, breathing thing between us, and now that Mari was gone, I expected him to lash out with it. We needed it, honestly. A way to repair the damage I'd caused.

Instead, he shook himself off like a bird flicking water from his wings and changed.

Another time, then.

When it was obvious Mari and Greyson were still showering, I called the nurses in to strip and replace the sheets. We'd allowed Dr. Grant, whom we'd brought over from Seattle General, and the nurses we knew to help Greyson, but we watched every move they made with predatory suspicion. After that, we'd bandaged ourselves, handed out our own medicine, and even ordered food to be discreetly delivered to a fake name. Nothing was left to chance, despite the doc vouching for the staff. There were just too many ways we could get screwed here. I couldn't wait to leave.

The bathroom door opened just as lunch arrived, and Mari helped a weary-looking Greyson back to bed and started to rewrap him.

"You need to eat," Mari said, piling his plate high once he was a proper mummy. "You have to regain your strength."

Grey hauled her in for the world's softest kiss and smiled. "Thank you, baby."

"Whatever," she grumbled, taking the plate I'd made her with an appreciative smile and settling in. "Talk, Nate."

"I walked out of the Aces."

"Permanently?" Mari asked, acting like my answer didn't matter, when we both knew it mattered a lot.

"Yes."

"You have no allegiance to them anymore?"

"No." I said it firmly, watching the entire time. The slight hitch of her shoulders that told me she was happy, but there was no other acknowledgment. Not from her, anyway.

Dominic leaned forward, food forgotten. "You're a big shot in the Aces. Your brother's the fucking leader. Why change your position when you could be set for life if he wins?"

"Because you're my family."

He snorted, turning away and taking a vicious bite out of his sandwich, and the ache in my chest grew stronger. What did it say that I missed the asshole who'd been my friend?

"What can you tell us?" Grey asked, and I found it easier to talk past the ingrained fear of Cash than I expected.

I gave them everything. Every location, every warehouse, every dealer on the street. Conversations I'd overheard and plans I thought my brother was making. Cash's addiction and how bad it was, his tasting process before he took anything, the way he skipped certain foods because they made him uncomfortable. Eventually, we moved on to the Aces that I'd found skimming, the ones that I knew weren't loyal enough, and the ones that I knew could be turned if possible.

By the end, I'd laid everything Cash-related at their feet, and it felt so fucking good to be free of that burden too.

"Where do the shipments come in?" Mari asked, having long since abandoned her food to pace. "There's no way Micah would let them in the port."

Grey looked up from the tablet he'd had in his jacket at the wake, which had luckily survived the ambush, waiting for my response. It felt good to be able to ease their anxiety for once.

"He doesn't," I promised, shifting to reach into the pocket of my jacket hanging on the back of my chair.

Dominic looked like he'd jump out of his chair and tackle me. "What are you getting?"

"Proof."

Pulling out the phones I'd stuffed into my pocket the night of the funeral, I set them all in a line, listing as I went. "This is a clone of Cash's phone. My original phone from when I lived here. Then the phone that replaced it. This one tracks some of his most-used cars, which he uses for shipments, with a backup, in case I ever lost the first one. The last is for past contacts."

Mari stared at them inscrutably, opting not to ask about the final one. It showed more trust than she knew, and I appreciated it. "Are any of those traceable?"

"No, they're all ghosts. Cash didn't even know I had more than one."

"How can we trust you with that shit?" Dominic eyed the phones like they were all bombs.

"You're welcome to take a look at them if you want," I said, sliding them across the table. "I have nothing to hide."

"Not anymore, you mean."

"Dominic," Mari warned quietly before turning back to me. "Where are the shipments coming in?"

"Tacoma." It was the only place less than an hour away from Mari's port that wasn't run by one of her allies.

Grey frowned. "That's not as easy to get into."

No shit. I'd put more bodies in the ground than I'd expected to get Cash a slot at that place. "He needed someplace you wouldn't look."

"What else?"

Thinking back on everything I'd said, I realized there was still more—though I was sure there would *always* be more—but I hesitated. They knew the moles Cash had placed in the other leaders' empires, but I hadn't told them about the one in ours. Mari was already so fragile, so hurt. I didn't want to make it worse, but it wasn't my decision.

"You have a mole too."

All three of them tensed, and when it was obvious Mari wouldn't, Grey asked, "How high up?"

"High." There was no mistaking the desperation on my angel's face. She didn't want to know this, not right now. Her fingers shook where she clutched her shirt. "Are they a danger right this second?"

Not wanting to lie, even inadvertently, I took time to consider it. Did I think the traitor in her midst would move against her right now? No, but soon. Very soon. "You have a little time."

"Then let's table it." I could see how much she couldn't deal, so I agreed. When she was ready, I'd tell her, and we'd hunt them down together. "Was that it?"

"O'Bannon."

"What about the Irish fuck?" Dominic asked, balancing his chair on two legs. He'd gotten increasingly angry the longer I talked, but I couldn't change the past. I could only help them clean it up so our family had a future.

"He sided with Cash," Mari guessed. I nodded, but she wasn't surprised. "He's never really been on my side. We'll deal with it later. Right now, we need to make a move."

The loud smack of Dominic's chair legs hitting the floor stole our attention. "I don't want to be the bearer of bad news, but nothing he told us matters now. Cash will be scrambling to move everything out of our reach."

"Maybe not," I said. It was possible Cash assumed my loyalty was still with him, or that I'd keep my mouth shut to keep my mother alive. And one look at Mari leaning by the window said she'd already considered that. "Cash knows losses are inevitable. He'll assume we're going to hit some of his empire. In fact, I can guarantee he's planning on it, and he'll have a trap ready."

"So, we either hit one or all, no in-between. The quicker we take everything down, the less likely he'll retaliate against our most vulnerable people."

Because that was where he'd strike. He'd hit the weakest links and move up from there, if only to kill morale.

Mari tapped her fingers on the counter, falling silent as she thought through everything. I could practically see her mind working. Plans and fallback options, consequences and what a worthy sacrifice would be.

Finally, she looked back at me with a mix of sadness and

compassion. "There's no way to avoid it. We need to move your mom."

The fact that it was the first part of her plan was telling. She cared. She loved me. She'd forgiven me. It was more than I'd hoped for.

"I know."

"I'll go with you," she offered, sharing a quick glance with Greyson. "Dominic can stay here."

"Don't worry about us." Greyson squeezed her hand before turning to me. "The only thing you didn't mention was Cash's cartel contact. What do you know?"

"Nothing." It was the one secret my brother truly hid from me, and I had been searching for years to figure it out. "Maybe Two-Bit—"

Mari slashed her hand through the air. "There's no way he'll give it up, if he even knows. We'll need to find some other contacts to figure it out. Maybe Rafael will know."

"I may have a solution for all our problems." I snatched one of the phones and sent off a text before I could second-guess myself. *Please don't let this backfire.*

"Which one's that?" Mari asked.

"The past."

* * *

It was nearly two a.m. when we pulled into the parking lot to find Shady Oaks overrun by trucks as big as tanks and an army of men outside.

"I assume the men loaded down with high-caliber weapons are friends of yours," Mari drawled, hand drifting toward her gun just in case.

For a moment, my heart tripped, wondering if Cash had made his move before I could. Then I saw the tactical gear, the flash of the rifles, and the head of someone I knew almost as well as I knew myself.

"Something like that."

"Fucking mercs." I laughed when she rolled her eyes.

In the time since I'd moved away from black ops, I hadn't spoken a single word to any of my contacts. That was the deal the company had given me.

Sever your connection, and we'll let you move on. Open your mouth and die.

For as long as I'd been out, I'd done exactly that. Mostly, it was self-preservation, but part of me didn't want to be involved. Didn't want to be reminded of everyone I'd lost and what I'd done. I knew it wasn't going to be easy to see the men I'd worked with before, but if facing my demons got Mom safe, I'd do it.

"Is it weird that I'm excited to see this little part of your life?" Mari asked.

I parked the car and turned, taking in the faint smile on her lips that had been absent for the last few days. I couldn't help myself; I had to taste her.

Wrapping a hand in her hair, I pulled her halfway across the center console until I could take her mouth. Her lips were sweet, the taste of her just as addictive as ever. Like a lifeline, she clung to my arm, giving as good as she got. "I'll show you anything you want to see," I said, pulling away.

"I know." The door slammed behind her as she waited for me in front of our SUV.

"Black!" a deep voice bellowed across the busy parking lot the second I opened the door, and I found myself smiling despite my nerves.

Losing my team had been awful and was still something I struggled with, but seeing Eagle here reminded me of the good times. Playing cards around a fire, celebrating a successful mission, waking up in the middle of the night to their fucking snores. He wasn't a part of it, necessarily, but he'd always been something close to friendly.

We met in the middle of the parking lot, hands out to shake.

Edward "Eagle" Finn was a giant, with skin as dark as rich, wet earth, eyes to match, and a presence that seemed to vibrate around him.

"Eagle," I said after he patted me on the back with his huge mitt of a hand.

"Black." I was man enough to admit he was handsome, just like I could admit I didn't like him looking at my angel. He'd locked on to Mari immediately, and I had to swallow the urge to drag her close and put my claim on her, but he saw. He always saw. Eagles had the best vision.

He smirked at me, clearly enjoying my territorial moment, before holding a professional hand out to her. "Edward Finn, ma'am."

Mari had to tip her head back just to meet his eyes. "Marianna Marcosa. Thanks for coming."

"Anything for Black. Whatcha been up to, bud?"

"Oh, a little espionage. No big deal." Mari's answer was dry, but her eyes were warm with laughter when she looked at me.

Eagle's eyebrows rose when I didn't contradict her, then he laughed loud and deep. "Why am I not surprised?"

"Because it's a very Nate thing to do," Mari answered. "Where are you taking Marjorie?"

"We've got a few black sites that no one can get into. One of them is a hospital about this size. Same comfort level, too. It's typically where we house older agents who have too many secrets and no filter to keep them in anymore, so she'll have company and safety."

He said the last bit for me, and some of the guilt I'd been carrying slipped away. Choosing to commit your parent was a hard enough decision, but at least at Shady Oaks, I could see her.

That wouldn't be the case now. She'd be in completely unfamiliar territory, far away from me, and I couldn't help but wonder if that made me a shit son.

"She deserves the best," Mari said, picking up speed when she saw my mother huddled by the front door in a blanket.

At first, Mom's eyes glazed over me, but then she jerked her head back with a small cry. "Nate."

"Hi, Mom." I leaned down to hug her, knowing that I might not have another chance to do it. If things didn't end well with my brother, these could be our last moments. I was so fucking grateful that she remembered me right now.

She pulled back and looked me over. "You're not sleeping. You need to rest, Nate."

"I know, Mom. We've had a rough time lately."

At *we*, she turned to Mari, and I saw the faintest hint of recognition before she grinned. "You got her back, then?"

"He did." Mari's smile was just as big, and suddenly, I was grateful for the space we were about to have. Those two together would get into some trouble.

Mom winked. "I hope you made him work for it."

"I did."

They didn't hug, just squeezed each other's hands with a sense of camaraderie I'd never expected them to feel.

With their moment over, Mom turned back to me. "Your brother?"

"I left." Not going into the gory details was an easy choice. Just because she didn't always remember didn't mean she wouldn't worry.

"They're moving me so he can't keep using me as leverage."

Thank fuck she was coherent today. I couldn't imagine moving her on a day when she was struggling with reality. "Are you okay with that?"

"I want you happy and away from him. If that means I'm stuck in a hole somewhere, that's fine."

"Not a hole," Mari promised, glaring at Eagle in warning. "You'll be taken care of."

Taking her word as law, Mom reeled me in for a hug that felt more like goodbye than I wanted it to. "I'm proud of you. For everything. It hasn't been easy, but it seems like it was worth it."

"Thanks, Mom. It is."

"It's time," Eagle said, quiet but firm. "We need to get out of here before anyone realizes what we've done."

Four trucks had been backed up to the building, each one identical. Three of them were already filled with agents, and the fourth stood open, waiting for my mother.

"I'll see you soon," I promised.

"I think I'll like a change of scenery," she whispered as her nurse took her arm and helped her to the vehicle. She smiled sadly, her eyes starting to go distant as the door shut behind them, punctuating what I hoped wasn't the end of our story.

I would see her again. I would be a better son. I just had to get through Cash first.

Eagle stood beside me, and the three of us watched as the trucks pulled out. Each one was bookended by two SUVs full of enough security to take down a small army.

"I'll leave you two to talk," Mari said, quietly slipping away. I watched until she was locked inside our vehicle, needing to know she was somewhere protected if she wasn't within reach.

"Your mom will be safe," Eagle promised, but I wouldn't have called if I didn't think he was capable of that.

When the trucks vanished, each one heading in a different direction, he cleared his throat. "I was told to offer whatever assistance I could. Weapons, intel, bodies. You let me know."

The offer was genuine, but it had enough strings to hang me with if I let it.

Eagle walked me toward the SUV, stopping before I got in. "If I can offer you a shred of advice? Avoid using the company's resources if at all possible. I'll help on my own as much as I can, but if you want to stay out, they should be a last resort. The price you'd have to pay for help this time would be too much for anyone."

I looked at Mari, head dipped to text something on her phone, and I knew he was right. The company didn't care about any allegiance but the one I had to them. They'd rip my family away if I let them.

I wanted Mari, my brothers, and the family we'd built, not a life of missions and death and surviving without actually living.

"I'm going to try not to," I said. "But I'll do whatever it takes to keep my family alive."

"Even if it means going back to the life you tried so hard to get out of?"

"Even then."

Chapter 3
Mari

"Are you sure you're going to be okay?" All three men were at the door to the hospital suite, watching me. Greyson needed to take a break and get out of the room but was refusing a wheelchair, so Dominic had agreed to be his leaning post.

They could've gone alone if we were at Seattle Gen, where we had a whole floor blocked off to ourselves, but we weren't. So, Nate was waffling between going with them as a bodyguard and staying with me for the same reason.

"I'll be fine. I've got to make a call."

All three of them winced.

I'd taken a week to sit with Two-Bit's news, to let it sink in. Our recovery took precedence anyway, but the information was always in the back of my mind. It wasn't learning about another cousin that bothered me; it was the fact that he'd been hiding under my nose the whole time.

A fucking *Fed* to boot. Christ, I'd never live it down.

Nate walked over, tipped my chin up, and kissed me softly before pulling back. "Do you want me to stay? I don't mind, even if it's just for moral support." His face was so open now that he'd told us everything. Things weren't perfect and they wouldn't be for a long time, but I was just happy he seemed to have less on his shoulders.

"No, go with them. I'll be fine." I tapped the gun lying next to me on the bed, but I refused to get snarky. This was the first time we'd been separated since Grey's surgery, and it made all of us antsy.

Nate moved away, just for Grey and Dominic to take his place. I stood, making it easier for Greyson to dip down and kiss me too. "Be careful."

"You too."

As soon as Greyson had his kiss, Dominic passed Grey over to Nate and hauled me into his body. "You'll stay in here with the door locked until we come back. *Do not* open it for anyone but us. I don't care what they say. You wait until we get here. Got it?"

Any other day, I would've argued that I was capable of making my own decisions, but Dominic took the opportunity from me when he kissed me stupid. We were nothing but teeth, tongues, and the need to connect. When he finally let me go, I was breathing heavily and my brain definitely leaked out of my ears. "I mean it, *mariposa*. Lock the damn door."

My lips were still tingling when they shut the door behind them, three sharp raps reminding me to lock it up.

In the time we'd been at the hospital, I hadn't really considered my libido. I liked sex and the connection it brought, but I'd had more pressing matters to think about. Now that Greyson was mostly out of the woods and we were working on getting back to the real world, that low-level need my men instilled in me seemed to flare back to life.

Maybe I can convince Dominic to have a quickie in the bathroom later. I needed all of them again, but there was no way Grey or Nate was up to sex yet. They needed more time to heal. I was sure Dominic could carry the weight of responsibility happily until they were.

Chuckling to myself, I took my gun to the window and sat on the bench seat before dialing the number. It rang twice before he picked up.

"Mari." There was obvious relief in my uncle's voice, and I hoped it wasn't the last time I heard some sort of softness pointed my way. "Where are you?"

"Safe. Did you know you had another son?" I didn't see the point in beating around the bush.

Rafael's sigh was loud over the line, but he didn't ask how I'd found out. I had a feeling he knew exactly who had spilled the beans. Which, I guess, answered my question.

"Is Christian aware?" I'd never met any Osorios besides Rafael and the Wolf, so I didn't want to assume that my cousin knew. I'd barely known about my father's actions when he was alive.

"He is," Rafael admitted. "It's part of the reason we don't get along very well."

I wasn't aware they weren't on good terms. "He doesn't like that he has a half brother?"

"The boy was the product of an affair."

Was it the disrespect of his mother's marriage that bothered Christian, or was the problem that Two-Bit—Dante—was a potential rival for his birthright? "Ah."

"I wasn't around the boy when he was younger."

The boy, not Dante. Interesting way to keep himself distanced from his youngest child.

"Because of your wife?" Most mafia wives knew their husbands were cheaters because the generations that raised them had been too. Absolute devotion like my men gave me was abnormal in our world. This conversation made me all the more grateful for it.

When someone made you their whole world, it was hard to believe they'd ever turn their back on it.

"Because I felt awful that he existed. She left because of him." The heartache in his voice told me who he meant. His wife. "She could have handled the affairs in general—and had more than once—but creating a child with someone else was too much. She walked away, and Christian never forgave me."

"You never saw Dante?"

"No. Guilt kept me away, and his mother raised him as long as she was able to."

"But not the whole time?"

"She moved to the States and died young. Overdose. I wasn't aware she was into drugs when we were together, not that it would have mattered. By the time I found out she was gone, Dante had disappeared."

"How hard did you look?" He had the resources to search the world twice over. I didn't believe he couldn't have found Dante if he'd wanted to.

"I looked into his family, but when it was obvious they didn't have him..."

He'd left him there.

Anger burned in my gut. It was common knowledge that foster care in the States was rife with abuse. The man had more than enough money to give his sons separate households if that was what they'd needed, and he'd done *nothing*.

"You're a piece of shit."

"Your mother would've said the same thing. I should've fought harder to find him, but I was a coward. I didn't want him to implode the peace I'd finally found. Christian's anger didn't help."

"Don't blame your son. They were your decisions."

"They were, and I regret them."

He sounded so sad and defeated, so unlike what I expected from any mafia man. Marriage was an heir's requirement to secure alliances and power; it rarely had to do with love. I assumed Rafael's was the same, but what if it wasn't? Did that make his cheating worse? Did it absolve him of abandoning his son to a corrupt system?

I'd expected this conversation to change things, but I hadn't expected it to adjust how I viewed the man who'd saved my life. I wasn't sure I could look at him the same again.

"Do you regret getting married?" I eventually asked, needing to know how far the changes went.

"I regret hurting the person I loved more than anything, the one I vowed to protect. I regret hurting my son. But I'd live it all over again if it meant I could love her as long as I did."

Son, not *sons*. *Wife*, not *ex-wife*. I had no doubt that he still loved her, despite the fact that she was long gone, and I didn't know how to reconcile that with what he'd told me. Had his marriage meant that much to him? Had his *family*?

So much of mafia life meant sacrificing happiness for the good of the family, and I'd always assumed marriage was the same. A sacrifice you made because you had to. Empty vows that meant nothing because there wasn't mutual respect and admiration behind them.

My father certainly hadn't proven my feelings wrong.

Then again, what about Antoni and Shara? What about Aislynn and Cameron or Tennessee and Moore? There was love there, even if it was new and unexplored. They'd built lives together and embodied the vows they'd spoken.

What about my men? Did I expect them to change down the line? Did I think they'd leave me and find another they didn't have to share?

No, I didn't. I had them forever, even if we didn't have an official commitment. Maybe it wasn't so hard to believe that Rafael could have loved his wife at one point too. He'd just loved her too late.

"You're not calling me about my mistakes or my son."

"No."

"I heard about the wake."

"I assumed you would." I didn't need to explain more; he knew what I wanted. The same thing I'd always wanted. The same thing he and Emmanuel had dangled over my head, just to snatch it away. Help. Allies. A way to save my fucking city.

Rafael's silence was pointed and clear. He knew what I wanted and, once again, it didn't matter.

"Why show up if you aren't going to help?" I snarled, suddenly so fucking angry I thought I could scream. Yes, he'd saved my life, but other than that, had he actually helped much?

"I can't give you any more help than I already have." That was always his answer. It would always *be* his answer. I'd known it was coming, but it still pissed me off.

"By that, you mean skulking around my city occasionally?"

"Keeping you safe," he corrected. "I'm honor bound to stay, just as I'm honor bound to leave. I can't give you anything else without upsetting the balance. I'm sorry."

"You can. You're just a coward. If the Wolf doesn't command you, you don't move."

That rubbed him wrong, and his voice got heated. "What would you like me to do, Mari? Fight my father for you?"

"I'd like you to try. You say I'm so important to you, yet you're comfortable standing on the sidelines while we're being ambushed."

"Because I can't!" he yelled. "Not without risking my legacy. I'm not even supposed to be here anymore."

So, Emmanuel *had* called his son home. Two-Bit's warning was real. "Your legacy is more important than my life? Than the lives of the people in my city? Money and power and drugs matter more than people's lives?"

"Of course not, but there are other things to consider. It isn't easy to walk away from your birthright, *tesorita*."

Isn't it? If Cash were a better option and it meant the people in my city were safe, I would walk away from everything my father had built in a heartbeat. If I knew that Cash would let us live, I'd disappear from Seattle forever to live a life of peace with my men by my side.

That was the problem, though. Cash *wouldn't* let us live, and the people I'd sworn to protect *wouldn't* be safe. I'd be trading a leader for a death-dealer.

Taking a breath that did nothing to calm me down, I tried again. "You're concerned about Christian's legacy. I get it, I do. But this is about more than him. More than you or me or even the Wolf. People will *die* if Cash gets ahold of Seattle. Not just some, a lot. He'll slaughter anyone who looks at him wrong or sees something they shouldn't. Once I'm gone, he's going to be too powerful to oust.

"He's too unstable to live as it is. It'll only get worse once he has no clear target to take his anger out on. Just because it's my city doesn't mean the ramifications won't fuck everyone over. If Cash wins, he'll have the Feds on your ass as fast as he can, just to prove he's got the power to manipulate them. Killing him now will protect your legacy."

"Marianna."

He was going to say no again. "Look, I know it's hard to step out from under the Wolf's shadow when he holds so much power, but who do you want to be, Uncle? The man on the throne one day, or the man who risked it all to save lives? Which one will sons be prouder of?"

Rafael's bitter laugh hurt my ears. "You say that like I'm a good man, *tesorita*. I'm not. I'm selfish and vain. Foolish, even. My family matters most to me—"

"*I'm* your family."

"You are, but you aren't all of it. I need to think of my son."

"*Sons*," I hissed because I was pissed, and honestly, he deserved it thrown in his face because I doubted anyone truly had.

His actions were what had led to his divorce. His actions were what had estranged him from Christian, and in choosing to bury his head in the sand about it all, he'd left a child alone. In the dark. Even if I needed his help, I wasn't sure I could ever forgive that.

Dante had needed him once too, and Rafael had let him down, just like he was letting me down.

"None of us are good people, Uncle. It's not ingrained in us to be good. We were born into a life of bloodshed and death, and that's never going to change. But this isn't a selfless act. People dying is going to bring too much attention to the city, to imports, to our world. Cash is a risk to everyone, whether Grandfather believes that or not. Ignoring it is a fool's game."

"He's your problem, Mari. Until he becomes ours, my hands are tied."

Disappointment hollowed out my stomach, and I forced myself to sit up straight. To remember who I was.

I'm Marianna fucking Marcosa, and I run this city. If he doesn't want an alliance, then fuck him and his bullshit family.

When I spoke, my voice was controlled again. "I won't force you to help, but I'm telling you now, this isn't over. I'll make whatever alliances I need to save my city, even if it means teaming up against you."

"Mari—"

"If you aren't on my side, then you'd better not stand in my way, Uncle."

He sighed, and I could feel the defeat in it. "I understand. Do whatever you need to do."

I hoped he knew how fucking stupid he was being. He was throwing away the rest of his life on a man who didn't truly care about his family. If he had, Dante wouldn't have grown up alone. He'd have been there with the Osarios the whole time. The Wolf was nothing but a power-hungry asshole, and my uncle was going to figure that out one day. I just hoped it wasn't too late.

"Good luck, *tesorita*."

"Goodbye, Uncle." The wedge between us dug deep as I ended the call and tossed my phone away.

Chapter 4
Mari

That night, I woke up with the sheets stuck to my skin and a gasp caught in my lungs. Impulse made me reach out my fingers, sliding gently over Greyson's chest. I had to feel him breathe.

Inhale. Exhale. Inhale. Exhale.

He's okay. He's alive. He's safe.

Echoes of the nightmare held me captive. The sight of blood leaking down his neck, of him crumpling to the ground. The sight of his body still and lifeless on the hospital bed day after day. Hour after hour.

Anxiety had ruined every night of sleep I'd attempted since we were ambushed, but I knew it was more than that. Dominic, Nate, and I were headed back to the real world tomorrow, but Grey wouldn't be joining us. His blood loss had been severe, and Dr. Grant wanted a bit more recovery time before he fell back into the thick of it with us. It was the right thing to do for him, but leaving without him made my skin crawl. Could I protect him if he wasn't by my side? I didn't know. Hence the nightmares.

Knowing I needed to resettle myself, I quietly took a shower. The water was boiling as I scrubbed my skin raw, but even when I was done, my mind wouldn't rest.

There was a gnawing in the pit of my stomach that told me to cling to Greyson. To hold him closer. The urgency that had drawn me to propose pulsed inside me, desperate and needy for something concrete. Something tangible to say I was his and he was mine.

I got dressed quickly, pulling out clothes for him and strapping weapons on myself. The med center was secure and, without an emergency room, shut down for the night. No one was getting in or out without a badge, but I wasn't stupid enough to go without protection.

Armed, I sent a few texts. Everyone responded immediately that things would get sorted. *Good.*

Putting away my phone, I leaned over the bed and pressed my mouth to his.

Greyson woke immediately, leaning into the kiss even after I moved away. Before he could ask why I was up, I slipped a hand over his mouth.

Quiet.

He nodded and threw off the covers carefully. We dressed him in silence, checking periodically to make sure the others still slept. I strapped a gun to his side, but I knew I'd make sure I was the one firing if it came to that.

It wasn't until I was helping Grey off the bed that I saw the faintest sliver of an eye from Dominic. I froze, caught, but he just stared until he intentionally closed his eyes and rolled to give us his back.

At that moment, I felt the biggest rush of love for him. For all of them.

We were a family. We loved one another, but this was just for Greyson and me, and Dominic knew it. Even though I knew he was going to worry about us being alone, he wouldn't intrude. I'd have to make it up to him later.

My arm around Greyson, we headed out the door, careful to shut it silently. In the hall, we found the wheelchair the night nurse had brought, and Grey pouted.

"I'm not getting in that thing."

"It's just for now," I promised. "You have somewhere to walk in a minute. *Please.*"

He didn't want to. I knew that, but he slid into the chair anyway. For me. It made me love him even more.

"Where are we going?"

"We have something we need to do."

Grey didn't ask anything else as we took a slow, purposeful path down the hall. The twists and turns took us to the very edge of the floor, and I could feel Grey's curiosity. We took the last turn to stand in front of a large door, the stained glass illuminated by candle flames within.

I'd never been inside the chapel. My prayers for his soul had been said bedside with his hand in mine. But tonight, I'd go in. We'd both go in.

And we'd come out different.

"You planning to save my soul, *reina?*" Greyson joked, but I could see some of his anxiety bleed away. He knew why we were here. He knew what I wanted.

The gleam in his eyes told me he was excited about it too.

Moving so I could kneel in front of him, I twined our hands together. "Marry me, Greyson."

His lips twitched, and those beautiful brown eyes of his

brightened with laughter. "I feel like we've been through this before."

"So you know my answer." When he just watched me, I dropped my gaze. "You tried to die on me."

The words hurt to say, like razors in my throat, and he stole one of his hands back to run it through my hair, pulling me in until my cheek rested on his thigh. "I would never."

"You did, and I spent three days wondering if you would wake up."

"Such confidence in me."

Didn't he get it? Didn't he see what I did? Time was a resource we didn't have. We were going into war, and I'd be damned if I did it without him as my husband. I couldn't bring him home yet, but I could do this for the both of us.

"I don't want to lose another moment when we've already lost so much, Grey. Marry me. Tonight. Right now."

I pulled his ring out of my pocket, the one they'd removed for surgery. Most of the hours he slept, I'd stayed up polishing it. Praying I'd get to put it back on him again.

"Are we always going to do these things backward?"

"Probably," I admitted. "Does it bother you?"

He caught my hand in his, bringing it to his lips. "No. It doesn't bother me."

"Good. Say yes, Greyson."

Even tired and anxious for what tomorrow would bring, his smile still lit me up. "What about the others? Should they be here?"

Probably, but this wasn't for them. "We'll tell them tomorrow."

This was for Greyson and me. It had been a lifetime coming.

"Dominic's going to shit a brick." There was no mistaking the smugness in his voice, and it made me snort.

"Are you two going to compete over me for the rest of our lives?"

He wound his hand through my hair and pulled me up until he could brush his lips over mine. "Don't kid yourself. Nate will join too. Does it bother you?"

"Not at all." As long as the four of us had a forever to look forward to, I wasn't sure I cared what the hell they did.

"You ready for forever, *reina*?"

Relief nearly took me to my knees. "More than ready."

I didn't argue when Grey clicked the brakes on the wheelchair and slowly stood up on unsteady legs. He'd been walking here and there, but the blood loss had taken a lot out of him. Still, he didn't seem to mind my hold as I helped him into the chapel. "I want to do this right one day," he whispered.

"Right?"

"Yep. A big wedding with all our friends and the rest of the family. I want to show off my bride."

"Oh really?"

He leaned over to kiss my jaw, nibbling his way to my ear. "Absolutely. When you marry a queen, you don't hide her away. You show her off until everyone else is seething with jealousy."

Well, all right then.

* * *

The two of us walked down the aisle in T-shirts and jeans. The minister I'd found said nothing about the knives and guns strapped to our bodies, though I saw her eyes dance over them quickly. "Welcome, Ms. Marcosa. We've got everything settled."

"Thanks. I apologize for the late notice."

She smiled. "It happens more than you think. Now, who will bear witness to this union?"

Fuck, I hadn't thought about witnesses. I considered grabbing Dr. Grant, who I knew was sleeping in an on-call room a few doors down, but before I could, I heard them.

"We will."

I whipped around, eyes wide at the two disheveled men near the door. Nate and Dominic walked down the aisle, stopping a respectful distance away.

"We were going to tell you tomorrow," I promised, but both of them shook their heads.

Nate smiled softly. "We're not upset, angel. We just wanted to support you. Both of you."

"What he said." Dominic grinned at Greyson. "I like the casual look, man. It suits you."

"Don't get used to it." Grey laughed, pulling him in for a hug that I didn't see coming. The two whispered for a moment before Dominic clapped him on the shoulder and stepped back to stand with Nate.

At the minister's suggestion, I slipped off my engagement ring and handed it to Nate, while I gave Dominic Greyson's ring to hold. With everyone in position, the minister smiled at us and began.

The whole time she spoke about commitment and marriage, I looked at Greyson.

My rock. My savior. My home. I tried to reconcile the boy I'd grown up with, the one who'd brushed my hair when nobody else would and snuck me treats when I was grounded to my room without dinner. Through everything, he'd been there. He'd become my best friend, my confidant, the love of my life. One of three, but still.

He was mine and I was his. This just made it official.

When she asked if we had written our own vows, we both smiled. "I, Marianna Elizabette Marcosa, take you, Greyson Andrews, to be my lawfully wedded husband. I promise to stay and fight no matter what. To be your shelter when life gets hard and your rock when things feel unstable. I promise to love you enough for forever."

"I, Greyson Andrews, take you, Marianna Elizabette Marcosa, to be my lawfully wedded wife. I promise to be your compass when things get difficult, your home when home feels too far away, and your safe space when everything gets a little too loud. To build a life with you, whatever that looks like. Live with you, fight with you, and love you. Forever."

"The rings?"

Nate passed over my engagement ring, and I could barely breathe as Grey turned back to me with a smile so wide it stole my breath. My fingers were steady as he slipped the ring back on and brought it to his mouth for a kiss. "With this ring, I claim you as mine. My wife, my lover, my heart. Always."

Dominic passed me the other ring, his fingers dragging along my palm in support. Beaming, I took Grey's hand in mine and slid the band back where it belonged. "With this ring, I claim you as mine. My husband, my lover, my heart. Always."

A possessive thrill went through me at the words, and I wondered if I'd get over hearing them.

My husband.

"Have you decided what last name you're taking?"

"Marcosa." Greyson answered before I could, and I could feel my heart swell with happiness. Nothing about this felt real, but it was. He was mine forever.

The minister smiled again. "Congratulations, Mr. and Mrs. Marcosa. You may now kiss your bride."

Greyson moved first, wrapping one hand around my hair, sliding the other around my body until there was no breathing room between us. All I could do was drown in his kiss as he pressed our lips together.

This was a kiss of love, loyalty, and respect we'd spent decades building. It was the culmination of years spent together yet apart and a promise that we'd never have to endure that again.

It was everything.

When it was over, we went through the motions of signing the marriage certificate, and I whispered that Donnaghal and Sons had already sorted out our marriage license. The minister left, with Nate and Dominic following soon after. I'd expected them to stay with us, but other than a quick kiss to my cheek, they disappeared with happy congratulations.

Alone at last, I turned to Grey and found his eyes hot on my skin. "What now?"

He smirked and tugged me toward the first pew, taking a seat and dragging me onto his lap. "Now, I fuck my wife."

Anticipation made my fingers tingle, but the bandage on his neck held me back. Grey, who was always so aware of me, twisted like he'd lay me down on the bench, and I reacted. Hand on his neck, forcing him back until there was nothing for him to do but sit. "You're not doing anything that's going to risk your recovery."

"I'm not waiting either," he said softly. "Not when I've waited my whole life for this."

Those big hands rocked my hips, forcing me to rub myself against his straining cock. Despite the layers of clothing between us, I shivered at the feel of him, hard and ready between my thighs.

Did I really want to wait? No. That was why I'd done all of this, because I couldn't wait.

But I wouldn't let him get hurt either.

I slid off his lap, and even though I could see he was disappointed, he let me go easily. Just as he went to slide off the bench, I pulled the T-shirt off my body. "You're going to sit there and take it. I'll do all the work."

He licked his lips as I slid the rest of my clothes off, baring my skin to him and the candles. Grey's throat worked as he looked me over, nothing but devotion in his gaze. "Jesus, you're beautiful."

"Not sure we should be invoking him in his domain," I said wryly, dropping to my knees to help him undress too. I left hot kisses along his skin in places, nips and bites in others, taking my time until his cock bobbed in front of me, hard and nearly dripping.

Slipping onto his lap, letting our bodies touch everywhere, felt as natural as breathing and more erotic than it had before. "What do you want, Greyson?"

"You," he swore, lifting my hips until I hovered right above him. "Just you."

The slide onto Grey's cock was all-consuming, as was the slow, delicious pace I kept. We were connected in body, spirit, mind, and soul. The rings on our fingers and the vows in our ears. There was nothing hurried about us as we took turns touching and teasing, kissing and sucking.

"Are you going to regret this in the morning?"

"Never." I swirled my hips until he was cursing against my skin. "Are you?"

"How could I when I've wanted you forever?"

Remembering all the glances he sent my way when no one was looking and the way he supported me, even when it meant keeping him at a distance, made my heart hurt.

"I love you, Greyson. I'm sorry it took us so long to get here," I whispered, groaning when he dipped to take my nipple between his teeth.

"I don't give a shit," he promised. "I've loved you my whole life, and I'll love you through the rest of it. The rest is just noise."

The best part was, I knew he meant it. It wasn't only the pleasure talking or the way he felt inside me; it was just Greyson. Just us.

This family we were building, it started with us decades ago. Two kids who barely knew how to exist, finding themselves drawn together, bound so tightly there was no escape.

This was the culmination of our friendship and the next step toward our future, and it meant everything to know he was right there with me.

I poured all my focus into the moment. Grinding my hips, slipping my hands beneath us to play with his legs, his balls, even teasing his shaft when I moved. My teeth found purchase behind his ear and on his jaw, all the places that made him groan and stutter and beg to come. But I didn't do it alone. Grey gave as good as he got, manhandling me where he wanted, kissing and licking and never letting up.

When my orgasm exploded, it came with words ripped from my lips and Greyson's fingers on my clit. "My husband. My king. My heart."

"Only yours," he promised.

Lost in the heat, he pulled me onto him faster, rocking my hips until he was groaning against my skin. "My *reina*. My Mari. My wife."

"Yours," I promised, leaning in for another soul-searing kiss as peace stole us away. "Always yours."

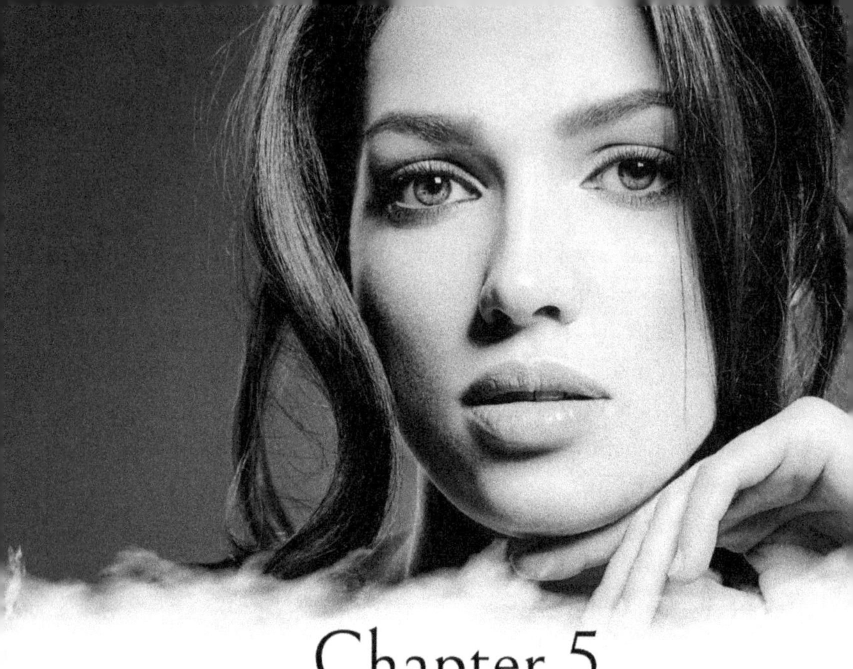

Chapter 5
Mari

It felt wrong walking into the Celestine without Greyson the next morning, like there was this voice in the back of my brain, screaming that I'd left my husband behind. Worrying that he'd be in danger if I wasn't there. Dominic wrapped his arm around my shoulder and pressed a kiss to my forehead before he let go. "He'll be fine, *mariposa*. It's only a few more days."

Two. Two more days and he'd be home. Not that I was counting or anything.

"Anything can happen in a few days," I said sharply, and Nate winced. "Shit. I didn't mean you."

"I know, Mari." He pulled me under his arm. "I guess I'm just nervous."

This would be the first time he'd interacted with my people since we'd found out he was a Beckstrom, and while I'd been stewing in my feelings about leaving Grey, he'd obviously been dealing with his own issues.

"No matter what they say, you're one of us."

Dominic's silence was pointed, but he didn't comment. Thank God. His issues with Nate were something they'd have to deal with on their own, but I'd intercede if he decided to be an asshole.

"You helped more than hurt," I promised, and Nate squeezed me.

"I don't think they're going to agree, but thank you, angel." He reeled me in for a kiss on the temple but let me go as we reached the door.

"In, out, done," I reminded them both. I didn't want us in the open more than we had to be, even in our own building. Nate's reminder of a mole high up in my organization made me antsy. They both nodded, and Dominic opened the door for us.

We'd moved the meeting to the basement, knowing the conference room was too small for an all-hands call, and I was pleased to see the room was packed already. There were my capos, their soldiers, security personnel for the bars, servers, managers, and anyone else who could make it. From my quick glance, someone from every branch of the syndicate was present.

Good. The more people to spread the word, the better.

The whispers followed us as we made our way to the front of the room, and it was obvious that everyone's eyes were on Nate. Some were antagonistic, some outright wary, but most were curious. Wondering why he was here when he'd left so abruptly.

I turned to Nate, intending to remind him that he was one of us, no matter what anyone else thought, but he didn't seem concerned. In fact, it was the most like Cash he'd ever looked. Emotionless and unapologetic. Unlike with Cash, I knew it was a protective mechanism, something to keep him separate from the reminder of his fuckups.

"Before we begin, I want to clear one thing up. Yes, Nate is a

Beckstrom, but he's still on our side." I heard some snorts in the crowd, but no one was confident enough to outright disagree. "I understand that it may be difficult for some of you to accept him back into the fold and that it could take some time. Do so at your own pace, but understand that he is a Marcosa in every way that matters, and I will not accept disrespect about him. Am I clear?"

People's eyes turned to Dominic, as if waiting to see what he would do, not realizing he was a Marcosa through and through. If I said Nate was in, he was in. Dominic's personal feelings were another situation entirely.

When no one said anything else, I decided to address the situation at hand. "As I'm sure you're all aware, Nate's defection from Cash was a surprise for the Aces. As necessary as it was, it paints a target on our backs. This war was heating up with or without him, but now it's time to discuss plans. We've already removed most of the families from the city, but it's time to move everyone else out."

"Where will they go?" someone asked from the crowd.

"The same compound as the others. There's more than enough room, and it's been protected throughout the rest of the bullshit. So far, Cash hasn't found it."

"You think it will stay that way?" I could feel everyone's eyes move to Nate. He wasn't just a risk to us but to their families, and that made my people as much of a threat as they thought he was. One wrong move and they'd string him up to keep their kids alive. Fuck.

"We do," Dominic answered. He'd been spearheading the situation, so I let him talk. He had a better understanding of things than I did. "We understand if it makes you nervous, but we've worked hard to ensure the compound is safe for your families. Nate isn't now, nor has he ever been, aware of the location. So if that's your concern, it's a moot point. He doesn't know where everyone is, and he won't."

Nate nodded next to me, perfectly comfortable with Dominic cutting him out for our people's comfort.

"What about us?" someone else asked. "Are we just supposed to let them go off alone?"

"You're welcome to go with them if you want." The shocked gasps spurred me on, and I pushed forward. "I don't intend to hold you here. It's obvious that the situation is life or death, so if you stay, be prepared for both. But I understand wanting to stay close to the people you love. The decision is yours."

There was some low mumbling as people talked among themselves.

"I want to be with my family," the first man said. "But I want to be useful. Can I help safeguard the compound while I'm there?"

Checking with Dominic, I agreed. "Of course. We could use every hand to keep the families safe."

"I can check the security system," one of Tennessee's men said. "Some of my crew will come too since their kids are already there. We'll update what you've got and set up shifts so we're monitored twenty-four seven."

More people spoke, making plans to relocate to safe houses near the compound in case of emergency, some mentioning additional houses on the way so those who were planning to stay in the city could visit, while still minimizing our movements to anyone watching. Anything to avoid the possibility of discovery. Even not knowing where they were headed, they kept trying to figure out security issues that could arise.

As more concrete solutions were created, the prouder I was of them. Of us.

Dominic slipped to my side, fingers brushing against mine. "You did good, *mariposa*."

"I did, didn't I?"

When my father had been in charge, the syndicate was

nothing more than his punishing hand, but under my tutelage, we'd become a true family. It was more than I'd ever expected, and despite all we'd been through to get here, I was grateful. I'd built something strong, long-lasting. We'd make it through this together because we'd earned it.

"What about the people who want to stay?" Shara asked once the others quieted down.

"For those who stay, businesses are on lockdown. Each one will need to figure out additional security. As for future plans? I'm not sure. Nate will be working with Tennessee and Moore to figure out where Cash will likely strike and fortify those locations. Right now, we're still the most prominent targets, but if that changes and civilians start getting hit, we'll need to consider clearing out the city to protect ourselves from federal and government oversight."

Because a bloodbath in the city was a surefire way to bring down the strong arm of the government on us. I didn't mention Two-Bit and his deal because I still wasn't sure what to think of it or how to use it to our advantage, because there had to be strings involved. There always were. Until I figured everything out, it was staying between us.

Dominic stepped forward. "Managers, run through safe house procedures with your employees. No one goes out alone or unarmed, and no one lives alone. Move to the apartments if you're out of the territory right now. We've got plenty available."

He turned and motioned to Nate, who cleared his throat and took his turn. "I'm aware no one is my biggest fan right now, but take it from me: Cash is unhinged. Nothing he does is rational, and even if he seems steady, he's not. Don't end up in his grasp. Don't get caught unawares. Don't become a target any more than you already are. The only way to win this is together."

"This is a war. Things will get worse before they get better, so make sure that you're prepared for every outcome," I said, when the whispering started up again. I stepped up so all three of us were a united front before them. "I want you to know, I appreciate everything you're doing and will do. We're stronger together as a family, and we will make it through this. Now get home and get yourselves sorted. I want anyone leaving the city to be gone by this time tomorrow. You're dismissed."

With a deferential nod, people started filing for the door. In the middle of the mayhem, Dominic slipped through the crowd, and I frowned.

"Where's he going?" I murmured. Nate's only response was a noncommittal hum, and I found him looking into the sea of people too. "What are you looking at now?"

He stared at me, deep and probing, and I felt a shiver run down my spine. The mole was here. I'd never been more thankful I'd only told a few people where the safe houses were located. Knowing that the families we'd sent out of the city to protect could be targeted made me anxious, and I knew I had to ask Nate who the mole was. I couldn't afford to ignore it anymore.

The problem was, I knew it was going to hurt. It was why he hadn't told me before. He was protecting me the only way he could. But would it really count as protection if it resulted in the death of some of my people? No. I had to ask. I had to know. Even if it killed me to find out.

Thankfully, Dominic came back with his hand planted firmly on the shoulder of a younger guy, pulling me out of my thoughts. "Mari, Nate. This is the kid I told you about, Montgomery, but he goes by Killer. He was one of Antoni's boys."

I had a faint memory of the discussion, but it had faded with the stress of Greyson's recovery. But I knew my brother's pet project well enough. "You were one of the last of his boys and the youngest, is that right?"

"Yes, Ms. Marcosa. Ma'am."

Dominic laughed, and I had to smile when the kid's cheeks

went pink. Already a killer, yet he blushed when he fumbled his words. Adorable. "Mari is fine."

"Yes, ma'am. I mean—shit."

"Relax, Killer. She's not going to bite." Dominic shook him a little, just enough to get his shoulders away from his ears. If I remembered right, the kid was alone in the world. Maybe he needed a family just like we did. A few big brothers to tease him and set him on the right path.

The way Dominic looked at him made me wonder if he'd already considered it.

Later, Mari. Expand the family later.

Smiling gently, I made a last-minute decision. "Dominic says you were instrumental in keeping him alive inside. I'd like to reward you for it."

Dominic beamed at me, and I knew I'd done the right thing.

"He's family." The kid shrugged. Humble, too. Good. We needed more men like that. "Getting out is reward enough, though."

I nodded to Dominic, who looked like he was going to burst with excitement. In our world, giving people good news was something so rare and special, we savored each moment like we'd never get another. "Mari always shows appreciation for loyalty like that. In this case, we've got a job for you. It's not common knowledge, but we've recently lost a capo. Mari's cousin will be taking the vacant spot, but that leaves a managerial position available. You'd be closer to the inner circle than most, with your own team and territory. There's room to grow from there, if it's something you're interested in."

"If you want out, that's okay too." I cut in. "You've already given so much of your life to the family, I won't be upset if you decide to leave. In fact, I'll get you set up wherever you want to go. No strings attached."

It was the least I could do for a man who'd lost his youth to my syndicate.

"I didn't know there was a new capo," Killer said carefully. Not surprising since the capo decision had been made while we'd waited for Greyson to wake up. "Would I be under his jurisdiction?"

"No. You'd be under my uncle Gabriele." I tilted my head at the shrewd look in his eyes. "Why?"

"If I'm going to take the position, I'd prefer to be under someone with enough capo experience to teach me."

Dominic and I laughed, and even Nate joined us. "Trying to take over already, kid?"

"No, but I want to do the best I can for the family. It's all I've got left."

"And we're honored to have you." The reassurance puffed his chest, and I chuckled under my breath. "Does that mean you accept?"

"Yes, ma'am. Mari. Sorry, I'll work on that."

"I know you will. Get home safe. We'll send you the information on your team tomorrow."

"Thank you, Mari. Dominic. Uh…sir." The last was said questioningly to Nate before the kid hurried out the door with a skip in his step. I snickered at the disgruntled look on Nate's face as he mouthed *sir*.

Dominic watched Killer go before turning to me. "He's young, but he'll do well."

"I don't doubt your instincts."

"That's because they're amazing." I rolled my eyes.

Finally, I turned to the only remaining people in the room. Next to the wall, Cameron was standing with no aid, though he leaned heavily on Aislynn's shoulder.

"Thought you got crutches?" I snarked.

"I did." But he wouldn't use them because it boosted his ego and his cred to walk around a week after nearly being burned alive. Fucking men.

"I'm starving. Do you guys want dinner?"

"Please. *Someone* talked so long that my stomach's rumbling." Shara nudged me on her way to the elevator, and I laughed, pulling her in for a hug. "You good?"

"I'm good. Are you?"

She peered over her shoulder at the others. "I will be."

Whatever that meant.

The rest of them decided to get their own elevator, so I took my men and headed up, but once we were inside, I noticed Nate falter. The signs of discomfort were obvious, but I didn't know why. Was it because he'd never been allowed inside the Celestine without sneaking in? Was he worried about my cousin and my friends?

While Dominic called down to get food delivered, I slipped across the room to stand next to Nate. "What's wrong?"

"It feels strange to be in here," he admitted.

"It's your home too."

"But it isn't. It's yours and Greyson's and Dominic's. Not mine."

Ah. That was the issue. He felt out of place in our lives now.

Thank God it was an easy fix.

"It's your home too," I promised, grabbing his hand and dragging him down the hall. The apartment boasted way too many rooms, but only one was left on the hallway where we slept. I pushed the door open and hauled Nate in with me.

There was nothing special about the room, other than everything being luxurious, but it just screamed Nate. Dark and peaceful. Homey, even. Deep blues and comforting greens, the faintest hint of charcoal here and there. Like being inside a forest at night. I loved it, and it was obvious Nate did too. Greyson had even managed to find a picture of Nate and his mom and set it on the bedside table.

"Grey had this one renovated for you," I said while he took everything in.

"Before I left."

"Actually, after." Nate's shocked gaze met mine, and I laughed. "He told me he was making it into a home office since things were getting dicey, but we have office space a few floors down. After you visited last time, I checked inside...and sure enough." I shrugged, because that was the only thing left to do.

"He shouldn't have," Nate whispered.

"But he did, because this is your home and you're our family. He just figured it out sooner than I did, and Dominic will too."

"I'd understand if he didn't." I knew he meant it, but there was an ache in how he spoke that told me how much he missed Dominic, how much he'd missed all of us. This wasn't the reunion we were supposed to have, with terror and worry. At least we were together.

"Well, I wouldn't," I said seriously. "The only way we survive this is if we do it together. He'll come around eventually."

We stayed in the room for a minute before I led him down the hallway, showing him the other rooms too. I wasn't sure if he'd had a chance to snoop when he'd snuck in or not. When I said that, he laughed, and I felt the fog he'd been hiding in lift a bit.

Sometime during our mini tour, the others had come up, and so had the food. With a brief kiss to the cheek, Nate headed to the kitchen to help Dominic divvy things up, but before he could even step past the threshold, Shara swung.

The loud crack forced us all into silence. I stepped forward, but at her guarded glare, I decided whatever fight that was, it wasn't my business.

"You're mad at me," Nate said, prodding his jaw. I bet he was hurting. Shara had a solid right hook.

"I'm furious. You're a dick." It was the catch in her voice that clued me in.

How had I not thought about Shara's relationship to Nate before this? They'd worked together at Gilded. She'd told me straight up that he was a good guy. It was obvious now that she'd liked him as more than an employee, as a friend—and he'd walked out on her. On all of us. Of course she'd be upset.

His infiltration of my family started with her.

"I'm sorry, Shara. I didn't want to hurt you, but I didn't have a choice." His voice was quiet, but he didn't look away. He held her gaze, even when I knew it was hard for him to do it. Nate carried so much shame for his actions, something only time and forgiveness could heal. He had mine and Grey's. He'd earn the rest eventually.

"Don't you think I know that?" she snapped, shoving her braids over her shoulder. They were a brilliant pink, and I wondered if she needed the happy color to help her bleak mood lately. "That doesn't mean I have to like you right now."

He nodded. "It won't happen again."

I knew he wasn't talking about his betrayal of her, but me, and so did she. Shara snorted. "I know that too, but I can still be mad at you."

"I'd recommend it," Dominic said.

Nate said nothing, and she huffed at him. "I hate that you're so agreeable. Makes it hard to hate you."

"Does it, though?" The barely audible whisper came out of nowhere, and I looked over to find Cameron breathing heavily on the couch with Ash at his side.

She grimaced at me, then turned to her husband. "I'll grab you a plate, babe."

Then she was gone, and it was only my cousin and me. "You know why he did it."

He settled deeper into the couch with a sigh. "I would have done the same, but that doesn't mean I have to like him."

"I trust him, Cameron."

"Do you?"

"Yes." I really did. Nate had made a mistake, but he'd done it for his mom. The only family he'd had for so long. I couldn't fault him for that. Besides, I believed he wasn't interested in doing me any harm. I had to.

My cousin stared at Nate for a while, turning away before the other man saw him. "I hope you know what you're doing, Mari."

I sighed, knowing he wasn't going to push it again. Cameron was a good soldier. He'd question me privately, but when I gave my orders, it was law. He'd do whatever I needed, and his faith meant more to me than I cared to admit.

We lapsed into silence while the others talked quietly around the table, and guilt sprang up again. There hadn't been time to talk since I'd put Joaquin down, and I hated that his death felt like a canyon between us, smaller than the one with Rafael but no more crossable. "I'm sorry."

Cameron shook his head. "It wasn't your fault, Mari."

I was the one who'd killed his father. If it wasn't my fault, whose was it?

As if he heard me, Cameron went on. "It had to happen, Mari. You have to be able to trust family, and Joaquin wasn't trustworthy. What happened was the result of his own actions."

Without waiting for me to agree, he stood, ruffled my hair, and made his way slowly to the dining room. Slumping into the seat next to Ash, he wrapped an arm around her while Shara and Dominic bickered playfully, and Nate watched with a silent grin.

Cameron was right that you had to be able to trust family, but what would he do when he found out someone else in ours wasn't trustworthy either?

Chapter 6
Dominic

ours after everyone left to take their tipsy asses home, I found myself in the gym, hands wrapped, fists blazing.

All evening, I'd been on edge. Part of it was leaving Greyson behind. Despite the fact that he was a cocky asshole, he was still family. Mari's and mine. It felt wrong to be here without him. Almost as wrong as having Nate here. This was our home, our sanctuary. He didn't belong here anymore.

Mari said she trusted him. That she'd forgiven him for what he'd done, but I hadn't. I couldn't. He'd put her in danger. He'd sided with Cash against us. I didn't think there was anything in the world that could make me forgive that.

He took a bullet for Mari. You took one for him.

But was that enough?

"I thought I'd find you here." His voice had my shoulders rising, and I threw an especially savage punch, rocking the bag back too far. I kept punching, refusing to slow my stride or acknowledge him, but that didn't seem to bother Nate. He kept stepping closer.

"Go away," I growled. Things were too on edge for him to be here. The need to beat his teeth in was hot in my veins, and if he didn't leave, I was going to have a hell of a lot to explain to Mari.

Of course, the asshole didn't listen. "We have to work this out, Dominic."

"There's nothing to work out." It was a lie, and we both knew it, just like I knew I had no choice but to forgive him someday for Mari's sake. But that day wasn't today.

He rounded the bag and held it while I let loose. It was more satisfying than I expected to hear him grunt as he tried to stay steady. "You hate me. That seems like a big thing to fix."

"Only if you stick around."

On the next punch, Nate caught my eye and held it. "I'm not going anywhere, Dominic."

I scoffed, turning away because I couldn't look at him. "Heard that before."

He sighed. "What will it take to move past this? Do you need to fight me?"

"What?" He couldn't be serious.

"If it'll help, fight me."

Crossing my arms, I twisted to face him with a huff. "Why would I do that? You'll let me win, hoping I forgive you."

"I want to earn your forgiveness, Dominic. That includes your respect. Letting you beat me doesn't get it."

Did I believe him? Not even remotely, but it wasn't a bad idea. I didn't know how Mari was going to respond, but I wanted to put him down for what he'd done. Maybe if I humiliated him enough, I'd find that I was right. He hadn't changed at all. Hell, maybe he'd leave, and we could figure out our lives, just the three of us. I didn't mind sharing with Grey anymore, though I'd never admit it.

He'd earned my loyalty; Nate had lost it.

Part of me wondered if, after it was over, I'd find it easier to be around Nate if he did stay. *What do you have to lose?*

Nothing.

"Get in the ring."

The faintest smile crossed his face, but it was gone before I blinked. "Gloves?"

"Wraps." I wanted to feel his skin break under me, but I wasn't stupid enough to risk an injury right now. Not while Cash was attempting to surround us. "Hurry up."

In minutes, we were circling each other in the ring, both ready to pounce.

Nate bounced on his toes, stretching out his body as he went. "First blood?"

Scoffing, I countered, "Tap out."

This late at night, no one was around to referee. We were counting on the other to be honorable and stop when we said. If he tapped, I'd end the fight. But Nate had to bleed for what he did to Mari. To me. If she wouldn't seek justice against him, I would.

It felt like the only way to move on.

We met in the middle, bumped fists, and jumped back. The circling continued with Nate feinting a few jabs here and there to get me to move. Finally, I saw an opening and leaped, cracking my knuckles against his cheek.

Once I started, I couldn't stop. As the punches poured out, so did the words, and we went round after round.

"You fucked up." I went for another one, but Nate blocked it, lobbing one of his own that got my ribs. He'd pulled his punch, as expected, but knowing he didn't want to injure me either made me wish I could let myself go all the way. That I could cause whatever damage I needed to get the poison out of my bloodstream.

The rage that I'd bottled up ached, and I needed it out.

As if he could see that, his next punch hurt more. He'd

stopped holding back as much. Thank God. After that, we traded blows.

"You hurt her." *Right cross.*

"I did." *Block.*

"You betrayed her." *Uppercut.*

"I did." *Left cross.*

"You betrayed us." *Block. Jab. Jab.*

Those got him, and he stumbled back.

"I did." His voice cracked, but I was too far gone to care about anything beyond the feeling of meting out justice. While he tried to gather himself, I struck him like lightning, taking us both to the floor and raining punches wherever I could hit.

Punch. Punch. Punch. "You were my brother. I accepted you because you swore you wouldn't hurt her, and look at us now. How can I trust you with her? With any of us?"

Block. Shift. Block. "You can't yet, but I'm not going to do it again, Dominic. Hell, I wouldn't have done it if I'd had a choice in the first place."

He tried to shove me off, but I held fast, hitting him in the shoulder enough to hear a small pop. Before I could grimace, his shoulder popped again. Not dislocated, but close. Too close. *Rein it in or Mari's gonna be pissed.*

"And now?" I asked, taking a second to gather my breath.

"Now I get my family back." He rolled me, freeing himself and bouncing on his toes. "You're still my brother, Dominic. You and Greyson and Mari are the only people who matter."

"I'm not your anything," I snarled, shoving to my feet and putting all the power I had into my next punch. I smashed my fist into his diaphragm until Nate's next exhale was a breathless cough.

Getting the wind knocked out of him dropped him to one knee. Even still, Nate tried to talk through the gasps. "You are, and

I'll do whatever it takes to make you see that. It's the four of us against the world."

I moved forward again, but the urge to hit him was gone. I was just tired. So fucking tired. Tired of hating him, tired of fighting against him, fighting for him, fighting myself. I knew what I had to do for Mari, but I wasn't sure how to make it happen.

Finally, I just sighed. "I don't believe you."

"I know, and I'm sorry."

"He's telling the truth." It said something about my singular focus to beat the shit out of Nate that I hadn't realized when Mari had come in. "If you don't believe him, believe me, Dominic. He didn't want to hurt us, and he won't do it again."

It was only because I was staring right at him that I saw the change on Nate's face. The way his eyes lit up and the pure joy in his smile as he whipped his head to face her. "You believe me?"

She smiled. "I do."

Everything about him screamed reverence. Respect. Adoration. It stung the part of me that still wanted that for Mari. That craved the security of giving her a family, something she'd been missing for too long. But how could I accept him? How could I just let it go?

"You trust him?" I asked.

"I shouldn't, but I do." I heard nothing but truth in her voice. "We all make mistakes, Dominic. Where would we be if we didn't have forgiveness in us?"

She wasn't talking figuratively; she was talking about herself and me. Where would *we* be if she hadn't given me another chance? When I'd been too stubborn to see that she was still my Mari, she'd given me a chance to prove myself to her. To make up for my idiotic mistakes.

At least Nate was trying to save his mother's life. I'd just been focused on resurrecting a ghost.

"I'm sorry. To both of you. To all of you." Nate's voice was sad and hopeful at the same time, and it tore me to pieces.

"We know, baby." Mari smiled at him, so sweet despite the late hour and the exhaustion I knew was dragging her down. We were making it worse for her. No. Not we. *I* was making it worse.

My girl needed stability, and so did our family. The people we took care of outside these walls. They needed a united force, and I had to be the one to give it to them. I had to choose the possibility of the future we were planning together over the potential for revenge. I had to trust that she knew what she was doing when she said she believed Nate.

I had to take the first step. "Make it up to her."

They both startled, turning toward me slowly. Mari's eyes were wide and curious, if not a little concerned. "Dominic—"

"How?" Nate asked.

"How else? On your knees, fuckboy. Best way to earn it is through orgasms. Should we say one for every omission?"

The plan formed quickly, a way for all of us to get what we wanted, and despite how concerned I was about Nate, I knew it was the right thing to do. I wasn't sure I could even go through with it, but I wanted to see how far he would go to regain his position at her side. What he would do to get back to being my friend and my brother, as he said he wanted.

"Dominic." Mari's voice had hardened, but Nate had already knelt in front of her, grabbing her hand in his. She jerked around to watch him.

"Let me do this, Mari. Let me show you how much I mean what I say."

"You don't have to, though. I know you mean it." The way she caressed his face was so painfully soft. Like he meant the whole world to her. I wasn't jealous; I was heartbroken. He'd nearly caused that softness to leave, not just for him, but for Grey and me too. He'd nearly broken her.

Focus on the now. Focus on the positive. We made it through, and she's herself again.

Pressing myself to her back, I slipped my hands around Mari's hips, loving the feel of her. Bullet wounds or not, it had been too long. "But I don't. Come on, Mari. Let the man show you he means it. Let him prove himself to us."

"Fine, but I don't think it's necessary."

I laughed into her neck. "Are you really arguing about orgasms?"

She pouted, crossing her arms just enough to prop her tits up for me. An obvious ploy, but one I didn't intend to ignore. "Yes."

"So you didn't get wet watching us fight? You don't want what we're offering?" I slid my hand into her sleep shorts, covering her pussy. It soaked my fingers, but I didn't move to do anything about it, even when she rolled her hips against me.

"I did. I do."

"Have you forgiven him so soon for what he did, *mariposa?*"

"Yes."

"Hmm. I think he should have to put that lying mouth to work. Take off her clothes, Beckstrom."

"Black," he grunted, but he did what I asked. I ripped off my shirt too, wanting more contact with my girl. When she was bare in front of us, his eyes locked on Mari's cunt like it was his favorite treat.

"See how you affect him, *mariposa?* It's the same for Grey and me. You're an addiction we just can't shake."

"Are you complaining?"

"Fuck no," Nate promised, sliding his hand up and down her thigh, but he didn't go any further until he asked me, "What now?"

"Show her what a good apology feels like."

"Dominic." Her breaths turned to gasps, her fingers digging

into my forearms when he put his mouth on her. I didn't need to watch him when all my attention was riveted on her.

The way her skin pinkened as he sucked and flicked and fucked her with his tongue. The way she keened and cried when he bit and nibbled her skin. The way she leaned into him, hand in his hair, pulling him as close as could be.

She trusted him in the most primal way you could trust another person. With her body. Her pleasure. Her soul. What more proof did I need? If Mari was willing to put her body on the line, I could put my faith in her and try to see past this, to heal so we could all move on.

Because, for Mari, I'd do anything.

Her first orgasm brought a flush to her skin that was addictive. With everything going on with Grey, we hadn't had time to connect in a bit, and even with Nate here, I was soaking in the skin-to-skin. Needing her to feel me, I rocked my hips against her bare ass, desperate to slip through her legs and find my way home inside her. But we weren't done yet.

"Again."

"Dominic," she whined, and I laughed under my breath, even as Nate and I moved away so she could breathe and decide if she wanted to keep going.

"You say done, and we stop." When she nodded, I plastered myself to her back and smiled against her damp skin. "Good girl, *mariposa*."

A look at Nate had him diving back in, and this time, Mari squirmed.

"Are you too sensitive, baby?" She mewled in my arms, clinging to me like I was her last hope of sanity. "Good. I like you best like that."

Mari's groan vibrated through me, and I lifted my hands to cage her nipple between my fingers and her throat beneath my palm. Keeping her close to my chest, I pressed hot kisses to every inch of skin I could reach. "Does it feel good to be at our mercy, baby?"

She moaned against me, those hips flying as she raced for another orgasm. I debated taking her ass, just so I could get inside her, but we didn't have lube in the gym and I wasn't going to hurt her. *Next time.*

As she writhed and rolled over top of him, Nate reached for his shorts, but I kicked his hand away. "This isn't for you, asshole. It's for Mari. Jerk off later."

He growled at me but didn't stop. The whole time he worked her up, Mari answered my every question with her favorite word.

"Do you like his tongue on you?"

Yes.

"Do you like it when you get all our attention?"

Yes.

"Are you needy for us?"

God, yes.

"Do you want my cock? Want me to stuff you full while he eats your cunt?"

Yes, yes, yes.

When I didn't move, still tweaking her nipples and biting at her neck, she whined again, and it was music to my ears. "*Dominic.*"

Yeah, I'm done being patient.

"On your back, Black. Our girl needs filling."

Nate went gingerly with a grateful smile, and I realized how much his injuries were probably hurting him. I wanted his apology, not his suffering. He didn't seem to mind too much with his face covered in Mari, though.

Our girl went to slide onto his lap, but I caught her by the waist and dropped her on his face. Nate grinned at her little squeak when she almost didn't catch herself in time.

"Show him how much you forgive him, Mari. Ride his face. Give us what we want."

"Will you forgive him if I do?" she asked, though she was already rolling those sinful hips.

"No, but it'll certainly help to remind me why I shouldn't kill him in his sleep."

She glared at me, hovering too high above his mouth, so Nate wrapped his arms around her thighs and forced her down. She squeaked again, and before she'd righted herself, I pushed her forward until she was curled over his head, palms flat on the floor. It left me straddling Nate's chest, but he didn't seem to mind, his sole focus on Mari's pleasure. He tightened his grip, adjusting so her ass lifted just enough for me to slide inside her.

Mari's pussy was a dream, as always. Warmth and wetness aside, there was a connection between us that I'd never felt with anyone else. I needed her. To breathe, to laugh, to survive. I loved her so much that I wasn't sure how to *be* without her. Not anymore.

And she needed Nate.

It was a fact. She forgave him because she needed him, just like she needed Greyson and me. I could either accept that fact and get on board—or end up on the outside of my own fucking family.

Yeah, right.

Without uttering anything but praise for her, Nate and I worked Mari over until there were claw marks in the mat, her skin was coated with sweat, and I wasn't sure if I could even breathe without coming.

"You ready for one last go, baby?" I asked, adjusting my angle so my cock hit her right where she needed it.

"No more," she begged. "I can't take any more."

"You can and you will. Last one, then you can sleep."

I saw the divots in her thighs as Nate held her close, even

when she tried to move away. I wrapped my own hand around her neck and hauled her up, letting her feel every inch of me as we took her past the point of no return one last time. She was still shuddering on my cock when I came. I'd never felt more at peace than I did when I was inside her.

For a while, there was only the sound of heavy breathing and the satisfaction of a job well done. Then she shivered, and the moment broke.

Nate and I moved Mari carefully off his face, pointedly ignoring her shaking legs. He went over to the cabinets and searched until he found what he wanted—towels. He threw one to me before he cleaned her up himself. "Here you go, angel. Let's get you sorted. You did so good for us."

Everything about the way he touched her, checked in with her, reassured her, was soft. So fucking soft. It was strangely beautiful seeing someone with so much death on his hands take care of her. Was this what it looked like when I provided aftercare? I kind of hoped so.

Fuck, I'm going to forgive him.

Grumpy about it, I threw both towels in the hamper and helped him dress Mari in nothing but my T-shirt.

Was it petty? Yeah.

Did I care? Absolutely not.

When she was clothed, I pulled her into my arms, kissing her everywhere I could reach. "You okay, *mariposa?*"

"Tired, but yes."

"Was that the best apology you've ever gotten?" I waggled my eyebrows like an idiot. She laughed, and fuck, we didn't hear that enough nowadays.

"No, but it was a very thorough one." She grinned at Nate, then me. She didn't ask if I felt better, because I think she knew I didn't have an answer to that. Not yet. Letting me come to terms with it on my own was a blessing.

She gave me another long, slow kiss before cracking into a yawn so big her eyes watered.

"Time for bed, baby." I leaned down and pressed a kiss to her lips. "Get some sleep."

"You're not coming?" Her blinks were slow, her eyes obviously heavy. Good thing I'd used the gym on our floor for once. She didn't have far to go.

"In a little bit." Though I'd made peace with my decision, I needed space and a little more time to accept that Nate wasn't going anywhere.

When he caught my eye, I jerked my chin toward Mari. "Take her up with you, please."

I wasn't one for big declarations, but I had a feeling Nate understood.

I don't trust you yet, but I'm willing to try. Don't make me regret it.

"This isn't over," Nate promised as he pulled her away from me. "I'm going to make it up to you one way or another."

Seeing how gentle he was with Mari as he swept her near-sleeping form off her feet, that was what I was afraid of.

Chapter 7
Mari

You take my family, I'll take yours.

The words dripped crimson while *Seattle General Massacre* flashed on the headline scroller as news station after news station covered the catastrophe.

Dominic and I were huddled together on the couch, watching. The longer it went on, the longer his hand on my thigh felt like the only thing keeping me from floating to the ceiling. Even Two-Bit, who sat on the love seat across from us, seemed disturbed.

The news anchor looked broken as she recited her information again. "For those just tuning in, we're covering a massacre at Seattle General this morning. According to police, the attack focused on the fourth and fifth floors of the west wing. A small group of terrorists came in quietly overnight, apparently searching for someone in particular. When they didn't find their target, they turned their attention to whoever they *could* find. One of our anchors is on the scene. John..."

They were right when they called it a tragedy. Thirteen people dead and just as many injured because Cash was looking for us. We'd been out of the hospital for less than twelve hours when he'd decided to start ripping bodies apart.

"He's devolving," Greyson said through the phone. I'd never been more grateful that he was still at the medical center instead of the hospital. The idea that it could've been his blood on the wall made me sick.

"The look-alikes?" I asked Two-Bit. His pause gave me my answer, and guilt soured my stomach.

Sending us to the medical center to recover had made sense, so I'd agreed. When Two-Bit had suggested the look-alikes taking our places at Seattle Gen, I'd agreed to that too. Anything to throw them off the scent until I was sure Grey would live.

Now, we were alive, and they weren't.

"They knew what they were getting into," Two-Bit promised. "They trained for this."

"I don't think anyone could train for my brother," Nate said from his place at the windows. He'd taken one look at the screen and promptly turned away. I didn't know how, but he knew. The moment he saw those words, he knew.

Though the news wasn't spreading it, Two-Bit told us Cash had bled out Nate's look-alike and used the blood as paint for his gruesome warning.

You take my family, I'll take yours.

We had no doubt it was retaliation for Nate switching sides, and I knew it was another weight he'd carry on his shoulders. "He's not going to stop," he said.

"Probably not," I agreed.

"What I don't understand is why he waited so long." Dominic

sat back on the couch, head tilted as he considered all sides of the situation. "It's been over a week since the wake. Why now?"

Nate grimaced. "Knowing his twisted sense of family, he was probably waiting to see if he was avenging or attacking me. To do that, he needed to know if I was dead."

"He must've followed us home. We need to double-check security at the medical center."

"The center's fine. I just checked," Two-Bit assured me. "No Aces within ten blocks of the place."

"So, how did he know?"

"He's probably had eyes on the Celestine the whole time. If he didn't before Nate defected, he definitely does now."

So, when they'd seen us come home, they'd doubled-checked the hospital and realized they'd been duped. Cash being Cash made it everyone's problem. It made sense, but for someone who was being hunted by the Feds, Cash sure wasn't being quiet with his moves. Made me wonder if he gave a fuck at all. Maybe that cartel connection of his was worth more than just drugs.

It was at the top of my list to figure out exactly who that connection was and remove him from it.

I crossed the room, slipping between Nate and the window and wrapping myself around him. "It isn't your fault."

"It is."

"Anything that happens right now is *his* decision, Nate. You can't control him."

"I should've killed him before now." When he realized I wasn't going to let him go, he squeezed me tighter than he normally would have. I didn't mind, though. I needed the hug just as much. "I should've poisoned him or suffocated him or blown up his fucking car."

"If you'd tried, you'd be dead and so would we. I'm sure Cash has contingencies for everything."

Nate didn't need to agree for me to know I was right. He

dropped his head to my shoulder, burrowing into my neck with a frustrated sigh. "He's not going to stop, angel. Grey's not here and my brother is gunning for us and it all feels like too much."

"He was never going to stop," I said softly. "Not unless we put him down. We'll get Greyson back as soon as we can, and then we'll make a plan to get rid of Cash for good."

Two-Bit cleared his throat. "As much as I enjoy the optimism, there are more urgent matters than your psychopathic brother." When he had all of our attention, he smiled uncomfortably. "I've been nominated as the messenger."

"Meaning?" Dominic asked carefully.

"The other leaders sat down with Cash as soon as the news broke. They've entered into a truce."

Shock held my tongue, but my men didn't seem to have the same issue. All three of them went off, yelling obscenities and spitting vitriol. Even Grey had his turn, cursing every single one of them to the grave and back.

I was fine to let them blow off steam, but Two-Bit raised his hand for silence. "They're scared. They can see just as well as we can that he's getting sicker and sicker. They're just trying to survive."

"They're cowards," Dominic snarled.

Seemed to be a recurring phenomenon among the men in my city.

"The deal?" I asked tiredly. I was done with all of this. I'd take Cash out, even if I did it alone, but I was going to make everyone who refused to help pay after.

"He leaves them alone, and they'll return the favor."

I expected it, but I was still frustrated. "So, we're on our own now."

"More than you think," Two-Bit agreed.

"Meaning?"

"Meaning, the Wolf is getting testy that his heir won't return home. Your uncle better figure out his allegiances before he ends up dead or replaced."

Part of me wanted to ask about his relationship with Rafael, but like the cartel leader Cash worked with, I had a feeling Two-Bit wouldn't say a word. Cousin or not.

"I hadn't realized he was still in town." We hadn't spoken since our argument. I didn't have time to coddle my grown uncle while he played both me and my grandfather.

"I'm sure he's aware, though," Nate said diplomatically, knowing I wasn't going to reach out to Rafael. "He's a big boy who knew what he was risking if he stayed in town against Emmanuel's wishes."

"Very well. I just wanted to be sure you knew." Two-Bit stood, adjusting his clothes as he headed for the door, only to stop before he left.

"Was there something else?" I asked carefully.

"We can get you in to see him."

I glanced at Nate, whose face was drawn and uncomfortable, only to find Dominic already checking on him. "When?"

"Tomorrow. I think it's best if you leave Greyson where he is. Better not to draw attention to your separation if you want him to survive."

"I'll be fine," Grey assured me. "Go ahead."

Nate took a deep, cleansing breath. "We'll be there."

"I'll send you the information in an hour. We'll stay close while you're visiting."

"That's fine. It's not like he can do anything to me now."

"Exactly." With nothing else to say, Two-Bit nodded at all of us and disappeared out the door.

When it shut behind him, leaving my family and me alone, I pulled Nate to the couch and sat down on his lap, forcing him to be still. "Are you nervous about tomorrow?"

He wrapped his arms around me carefully, keeping me close

enough to feel the frantic rush of his heartbeat. "I don't know. I don't want to see him."

Dominic cleared his throat and shifted, obviously uncomfortable. "We'll be with you the whole time. He won't get to you."

Nate's smile was strained. "I'm not worried about me, but thanks."

The three of us sat silently, watching Cash's catastrophe filter through every news station in town.

Tomorrow, we'd go see his hero in the flesh.

Tomorrow, we were having a chat with Ace Beckstrom.

Chapter 8
Nate

King County Correctional Facility was nothing but a massive square in the middle of Seattle. Nothing had changed since the last time I'd visited, which was before I'd left for the Army. It was the only comfort I had.

Without the fenced-in yard and the armed guards patrolling it, it would have looked like every other building. Instead, citizens got a firsthand look at the inmates like they were watching a fucking zoo exhibit. I wasn't inside, and I hated it.

No doubt, my feelings about the reason for our visit were clouding my judgment, but I knew whatever my father said was going to be awful. The deep pool of dread in my stomach told me as much.

As if she felt me waver, Mari wrapped an arm around my waist, giving me her strength. "You sure you're ready for this?"

"No, but we have to go in."

"He's going to do whatever it takes to get under your skin," she warned.

"I know." Ace was just as bad as Cash when he wanted to be. Occasionally, worse. My brother had to learn it from somewhere.

"Don't let him in," Dominic said. "Keep your shit together, and I'll take you to the gym later to work it off."

The offer stunned me. Dominic had been better since my apology to Mari, but he still kept his distance. I knew it was because he was hurting and that his trust would take time to rebuild, but this gave me hope.

"I may take you up on that. Thanks, man."

He didn't answer, but I knew he understood what his support meant.

"We won't leave you," Mari promised.

Grey was still at the medical center, so we were one man short, but he'd texted before we'd left to check in on me. I wasn't sure how, but these three people had become more of a family to me than the one I'd been born into—minus my mom, of course, who was apparently having a blast meeting her new friends at the facility Eagle had spirited her away to.

I couldn't get much information out of him, only that she'd bonded with a retired agent who also had memory issues. I was both heartbroken and happy to hear she was finding some joy in the situation.

Now, I just had to face my other parent.

After squeezing Mari close and dropping a kiss to her head, I straightened. "Let's get this over with."

"Say the word, and we'll leave." Mari's reassuring smile warmed me to the bones as she took the lead, leaving Dominic and me to take our respective places behind her.

Warden Michaels, whom I'd met previously, waited just beyond the door with an uncomfortable smile. He seemed the possessive type, so I assumed he didn't like us infringing on his turf. The line of guards down the hall didn't seem to have the same issue.

Half of them gawked at Dominic and me, while the other half slobbered over Mari. I got it—our girl was fine when she was strapped with weapons and any other second of the day—but it pissed me off to see them do it so blatantly.

"If you want to keep them, I'd remove your eyes from our girl-friend," Dominic hissed. When the guards darted their gazes to me, I gave them my most killer smile and hoped they read how much I'd like to rip them apart with my teeth.

Every single man found somewhere else to look.

I could feel Mari's smugness, and from the way Dominic rolled his eyes, he could too. No matter what she said, she liked us possessive. Which was good because we weren't stopping anytime soon.

The good warden cleared his throat, reaching up to adjust the collar of his pressed shirt delicately. "Ms. Marcosa. We received word from the FBI that you were coming and prepared the meeting room for you, as requested."

Mari tilted her head at the men watching the show. "Guards?"

Michaels shifted uncomfortably. "We were told not to have any inside, but I have to warn you. Beckstrom is—"

"I'm aware of what a Beckstrom can do," she assured him, sliding her hand behind her back to grab mine. A reminder that I wasn't the Beckstrom she meant, and for once, I felt it.

Cash and Ace weren't me, and I wasn't them. I didn't have to hold their sins as my own. Not anymore.

The weighted look Dominic gave me was another firm reminder. *We're your family, not them.*

I wondered if Mari would mind another man taking her name because I was ready to torch mine.

Warden Michaels looked like he wanted to argue his point again, but he finally slumped. "In that case, he's ready for you."

Lifting his arm in invitation, he walked us to a door at the end of the hall. "I'm aware you're professionals, but I have to insist that if you're going to keep your weapons, you *keep* them. I will not have an inmate getting hold of one."

Dominic smirked. "Don't worry, Warden. We won't give him a way to stab us in the back."

With an uncomfortable grunt, he knocked twice and opened the door, leaving us to our fate.

Despite the years between visits, that same sense of desperation clung to my skin the second we stepped inside the room. It seeped into the plain walls, the slick floors, the metal tables, and even the chair where my father waited in his red jumpsuit, his hands shackled to a bolt in the floor.

"This place is creepy as fuck," Dominic whispered. And I had to agree. I'd never been one to believe in ghosts, but I could practically feel the desperate specters pressing in on us.

"Desolation will do that to you," I said, finally looking at the man we were here for full on and wishing I hadn't.

It hit me then that Ace looked more like my brother than Cash did. We had the same build, though he had more muscle. His skin was darker, as was his hair, and he had a smattering of shitty tattoos along his arms. Beyond that, we could've been twins. It was like I was seeing who I would've been if I'd stayed the course and let the Aces run my life. That's if I'd managed to stay alive at all.

"Christ, it's like looking at a doppelgänger," Mari muttered.

"Just what we need. Two fuckboys," Dominic joked.

Once I got over the shock of our similarities, it was easier to see the differences. There was white in Ace's hair now and wrinkles around his face I could tell he didn't like. He'd always been a prideful fuck. The cruelty was still prevalent, the same kind I saw in Cash, plus a bit of that manic attitude the cocaine brought out in him too.

"He's juiced," I whispered to the others, and Mari hummed

under her breath, completely unsurprised. Drugs were more common in jails than most people thought. All it took was the right bribe, and you could get whatever you wanted. No doubt we had my brother to thank for Ace's recreational habits.

As the warden said, there were no guards in the room, thanks to Two-Bit's and Mari's influence, so it was just the four of us. Dominic took one look around, barely glancing at Ace before taking up a place by the door. It was not only a sign that Mari could protect herself, but a clear dismissal. Ace wasn't a threat to us at all.

The tightening of my father's mouth said he noticed and didn't appreciate it, but what else could he do when he was in chains and we were armed for extermination.

As if he realized it too, he settled back in his chair and dragged his gaze over Mari, that cruelty coming out in waves. He didn't have the upper hand yet, so he was going to push at us until he did. "Is this her, Nate? I can see why you'd falter. She looks like she'd be a good fuck. Turn around for me, sweetheart. Let me see that ass."

Apparently, I'd forgotten that Cash shared our father's need for antagonizing others. Mari sighed in aggravation while I growled, "Don't talk about her like that."

Ace tipped his head back and laughed. "Oh my God, you *do* love her. I thought Cash was kidding, but it's true. You fucking idiot."

I didn't even like the man, but hearing your father call you an idiot was always going to hit deep.

Ace didn't seem to mind my irritation, continuing to be an obnoxious prick. "I can't believe you fell for it. Love's the oldest lie in the book, Natey boy."

"Not to me."

Love was the only thing keeping me going some days. The idea that when all this shit with Cash was over, I'd have Mari and my true brothers at my side. Men like Ace and Cash, they didn't get it. If it wasn't tangible, they couldn't imagine it holding sway over them. Money, drugs, or pussy led them. Power, too. But while it wasn't tangible, you could always feel when someone had it. Emotion was something you used to manipulate others, not something you lived your life on.

Thank God I wasn't like them.

Ace scoffed. "You're wasting your time, Nate. She's going to leave you for someone hotter, richer, and with a bigger dick."

"You assume he cares whose dick she rides," Dominic drawled from where he was picking his nails with a knife. *Drama king.*

My father looked positively sick. It made me grin. "I'd heard the rumors, but I thought it was a joke. No way *my son* is sharing his woman."

"Yet here I am, with two boyfriends and a husband." Mari waved her fingers, flashing her wedding band, and Ace's face darkened.

He turned to me, dismissing her as nothing more than pussy. Fucking moron. "A real man wouldn't let anyone touch his woman. I didn't raise a cuck, Nathaniel."

"You didn't raise me at all," I countered. My girl finally dragged out her chair, sitting nice and slow and making sure to cross her legs like she was the main event of a sold-out show, while I dropped next to her. My mouth watered at how sinister she looked, and I desperately wanted this to end so I could steal her for five minutes. Twenty, tops.

"A real man understands he can't control a woman, but I understand if that's not your strong suit. It *has* been a while since you've been touched, right?"

"Less time than you'd think, and I controlled my women just fine when I was on the outside," Ace sneered. How had my mother ever liked him? It took one look in his eyes to figure out he was a monster.

"Which is exactly why I wouldn't consider you a good judge of 'real men.'" Mari lifted her hand to encompass Dominic and me before dropping it back to her lap. "The men I keep around me, they're real. Honest. Hardworking. They fight to protect their family, whatever it takes. They don't just speak, they act. You wouldn't know what a real man is because you're nothing but a man of words, Ace Beckstrom."

I'd never been more proud and horrified at the same time. She was so beautiful, but I saw my father's face twist and knew what he was going to say next. We were collision-bound, and there was nothing I could do to stop it. My only warning was a squeeze to Mari's leg, letting her know danger was coming.

Ace leaned forward as much as he could, hate blooming in his every movement. "You speak of family and loyalty and love, yet the person closest to you betrays you time and time again."

"If you're talking about my uncle, he's dead and we weren't that close."

My father's face split into an evil grin. "He may be dead, but his spawn isn't. What's that saying again? The apple doesn't fall far from the tree."

Mari gave no outward appearance that she understood what my father was insinuating—only a blankness in her eyes, like she'd shuttered all possibility of showing any emotion, that told me she knew exactly what he meant.

Cameron was the Marcosa rat.

It was the last card I'd held to my chest while I'd watched his every move. I needed to keep her safe as much as I needed not to be the reason she was hurting again. But sitting here while my father flayed her alive, I wished I'd told her anyway. Had I manned up and given her the name with everything else, he wouldn't hold this power over her. He certainly didn't deserve it.

Behind us, Dominic was an inferno of hate directed at Ace

and Cash and Cameron. God help us all if Dominic got to her cousin before Mari did.

"If you think your son's so weak, why don't you have a go?" Mari's question came out of nowhere, and my head whipped around almost before I realized what she'd said. Dominic's low growl echoed my own.

"You don't need to beg me to touch you, darlin'. I'd do it for free." Ace's smirk got bigger, though there was a piece of him that was decidedly uncertain. He'd expected her to fall to pieces at the news that her cousin was a traitor, but he didn't know Mari. She'd bury the pain until she could unleash it in private. It wasn't his to consume, nor anyone else's.

"I'm sure you would, but I'm offering for something else. You best me in a fight, you prove you're the alpha male over Nate. I best you, you give me what I want."

"Which is?"

"Information."

Ace frowned. "I won't rat my boy out."

"Then we're done here." She stood fluidly, letting her hands brush the swell of her ass like there was dirt on her pants. Ace's eyes followed her every movement, hunger growing with each passing second. It made me fucking sick.

"If I say yes, will I get in trouble for smacking my son's girl around?"

Mari laughed, the sound so fake it hurt my ears. "I'm my own woman, Beckstrom. Do we have a deal or not?"

He grinned and shook his chains. "What about these? Or do you need a handicap?"

I didn't see her move, but the door opened and a guard moved in warily. "I'd recommend you keep him—"

"Unhook the cuffs. We'll be fine."

"You heard the lady. Uncuff me," Ace jeered.

The shackles dropped to the floor, and Mari dismissed the

guard while Ace rolled his wrists, shaking out his arms like he'd been bound tight for hours. Hell, maybe he had. "If I win, do I get a taste of that golden pussy?"

"Sure."

Mari shrugged, and I growled, "No."

She ignored me. "You win, and I'll let you do whatever you want."

I'm going to tan her ass for this.

Ace grinned at me, grabbing his dick like a teenage asshole. "I'm going to take your girl right in front of you, son. Show you how a real man fucks."

I didn't realize I'd taken a step forward until Dominic hauled me back to the wall, his grip lethal on my shoulder. "Let her do this."

At first, they circled each other. Ace taunted while Mari evaluated. She ignored every word he threw at her, focusing her energy on his steps, the way he moved, and even the bullshit swings he threw her way. When he finally went for her, she was ready. His right hook was dodged and parried with an uppercut that sent blood and what could have been the tip of his tongue spilling from his mouth.

"Mari, one. Dipshit Daddy, zero," Dominic breathed, settling in for the show.

And what a show it was.

Ace roared with rage and started tossing haymakers left and right, but Mari was agile. She dodged every one, darting in for quick punches to the ribs that sent loud *cracks* echoing around the room. Where he went for maximum damage with one hit, she went for a thousand cuts.

Ace didn't stand a fucking chance.

This wasn't a lesson in humility or a competition to see who was strongest; it was a bloodletting. Mari was in so much pain, and she was using my father as a punching bag. With every punch and dodge, Ace was getting angrier, until finally, he made a fatal error. He swung for Mari's face, ducking at the last minute to reach for one of her blades. Dominic and I both grabbed for our guns, but we should've known better.

Mari spun out of his grip and kicked him in the ass. Already unbalanced, Ace went sprawling, and our little spider monkey was right there to see him finished. Mari crawled on top of him, trapping his arms at his sides, and she slipped the knife he'd gone for out of its sheath.

When they stilled, she had it pointed at his dick. She wasn't even breathing hard.

"I win, Beckstrom. Give me what I want, or I'll take your useless cock as a trophy."

Ace glared at her, ready to kill her for the embarrassment of besting him, but Mari just grinned. "Did you know they have cameras in this room? I'd hate to see the footage get leaked to the population here. What would people do if they knew you couldn't beat a woman half your size?"

She hissed through her teeth, feigning concern for his well-being, and Ace drooped. We all knew if she released the footage—if there really was any—that he'd be dead in a day.

"What the fuck do you want, bitch?"

"Tell me about the cartel."

"What about them?"

"Who are they?"

Ace's gaze flicked away for a second before returning. "Don't know. I've been in here for over a decade."

"He's lying," I told Dominic.

"Yeah, he is."

Mari pursed her lips before digging the blade in. She kept her shit sharp, so even that small of an adjustment caused enough pain for Ace to curse. "Okay, fine. I know about them, but I swear it's not much."

"Start with the basics. How did Cash get in touch with them?"

"Fate. Cash had been looking for a way into drugs, when the old leader's son got into some trouble and ended up in gen pop. I helped him out, knowing it would earn us some goodwill. At least enough to set up a meeting."

"Why them?"

"Because the Osorios wouldn't touch Seattle. Said it was a family thing but wouldn't explain. We tried everyone else, but they refused too. Said my boy was too small-time to take a risk pissing off Marcosa. It didn't stop Cash, though. Only made him more determined."

As Mari continued questioning my father, I thought about how different he was with Cash. My brother was his pride and joy, while I was a disappointment and always had been.

Why? Because I chose someone outside the two of them to trust? Because I didn't follow the same rules they did? I was still a murderer, still a man who would kill for my family. They just weren't in it.

After so many years of wondering if something was wrong with me, I finally understood.

They were two broken, damaged people who found their mirrors in each other. They'd never like me because I was never meant to be like them. I was always meant to be something more, someone better, and that was the real reason they hated me.

For once, it felt really fucking good to be on the outside.

After an hour, Mari sat back, her knife still delicately poised above Ace's dick, though his pants were cut here and there. He'd decided to fight back on some things, but Mari had eventually gotten what she wanted.

"Is there anything else we need?" she asked.

"No," Dominic said from behind us. "We've got it all."

"Good. Thank you for your time, Ace." She carefully moved off him, the knife still in hand. When she was on her feet, she gave him her back, trusting us to watch it while she slammed a hand on the door.

In seconds, the guards piled in. "Ma'am?"

"Put him in the hole."

"What? No! I helped you!" Ace screamed. Mari turned with the deadliest smile I'd ever seen. I wasn't sure what it said about me that it turned me on.

"You started this mess. You let Cash blackmail his brother until there was nothing to do but become who you wanted. It's disgusting that your own son felt so unsafe that he had to resort to killing people just to be free. You and Cash are a plague in my city, one I intend to eradicate. While he's a little harder to elimi-nate, you aren't."

She stepped closer, smirking at him. "Take a good look around, Ace. From here on out, there's no light. No sun. No inter-action besides a tray getting shoved through a slot. I'm going to keep you so isolated you lose your fucking mind."

Ace bared his teeth, fighting the guards as they clicked the shackles back on again. "Your cousin's going to kill you."

"He'll have to get in line."

We left the room to the soundtrack of his belligerent ranting. Warden Michaels waited in the hall, but we strode right past and didn't stop until we got to the car. After Dominic's quick check to make sure no one had booby-trapped it, we all climbed in.

The second the doors closed, I reached for Mari in the front seat.

"I'm so sor—"

"Don't. Just *don't*. We'll talk about this later."

She still looked as unfazed as she had in the room with Ace, but her voice was broken glass and desperate pleas. I couldn't help but obey.

Guilt forced me back to my seat and away from the woman I loved. "Okay, angel. Later."

Chapter 9
Mari

The drive home felt like hours. All I could think about was Cameron.

Sleepovers with him and Rey in Antoni's and my suites at the manse. Stuffy family dinners with starched clothes and too many drunk adults for comfort. Hiding bowls of candy in the house so the four of us could trick-or-treat safely. Birthdays where he'd sneak into my room at midnight with a cupcake he'd bought with his allowance, just so he could be the first to sing to me.

So many memories of my cousin, and most of them were good. Hell, even the bad ones had good moments.

The two of us clinging to each other beside Rey's pyre. The way they'd held me up when we burned Antoni.

The way he'd always pushed me to do more, to be better, to reach for the stars, even when I was fucking exhausted.

My whole body rebelled against the idea that Cameron would

do this, but those were my emotions talking. I had to use my brain, and I saw the truth on Nate's face. Ace wasn't lying. Which meant Cameron had.

I was destroyed. Gutted. Joaquin taught me that family didn't necessarily mean that someone was good for you, but Cameron was never supposed to be an example of that.

What did this mean for Joaquin? Cameron had been the one pushing me to make a move against his father for years, and now I thought I knew why. Joaquin had a bad habit of shoving his nose where it didn't belong. Had he found out about Cameron moonlighting as an Ace? Did he realize his son was a snake?

Did I kill the wrong man?

I wasn't far enough gone to pretend Joaquin wasn't a slippery fuck, but if Cameron was actually the one who had been working with Cash, what was my uncle's crime? Was not agreeing with me punishable by death?

The whole situation made me sick to my stomach, and I wondered if it was something I would have to atone for in the future. Maybe not for my family, but for myself.

I didn't remember getting out of the car or when we got into the elevator. All I remembered was blinking to find myself staring at the numbers, praying the damn thing didn't stop.

I didn't know what I would do if I saw Cameron. There was so much going on inside my head that I was as likely to sob at his feet as I was to shoot him. If Cameron had to die, I wanted an ironclad reason to do it. I couldn't make my best friend a widow without at least that much.

Thankfully, we made it to the penthouse unscathed, and when the door opened, I was met with a welcome sight.

Greyson grinned at me from the kitchen. "Hey, baby. I'm home."

Nothing in the world could have stopped me from throwing myself at my husband. Being in his arms felt like coming home, and when my world was untethered yet again, I needed the safety he brought me more than ever.

My men talked over my head as I focused on soaking in the comfort that was Greyson. *Inhale, good. Exhale, bad.* All my men were together again, my family intact, only to be shattered by this bullshit. It wasn't fair.

But I already knew life wasn't fair unless you made it that way, and that was exactly what I'd do to Cameron when I found my footing again.

"I missed you," I whispered eventually. My voice felt as ravaged as my soul, and I clung to him more than I had since Antoni died. When I looked up, his eyes glowed with a mixture of sympathy and rage.

"I missed you too, *reina.*"

He hauled me into his arms and set off down the hall, despite my protests. Released from the hospital didn't mean healed, but tell that to him. Finally, I let it go. Wrapped around him as tight as I could be, I let myself snuggle into the crook of his neck, desperate for a hint of that scent that was just Grey. I'd once thought if I could bottle the way he smelled, I'd never have another shitty day in my life, but it did nothing for my nerves or my sorrow this time.

I peered behind us, unsure what I'd find. Nate looked drawn, tired, and so fucking sad. Dominic looked as brutal as ever. Like he'd tear apart the building just to avenge my honor.

There was no stopping me as I reached my hand out to them. In sync, they stepped forward and held on, giving me their strength when I was feeling every brick of my life collapse. They only dropped their hold when Greyson twisted, pulling us to sit on the edge of our bed, but only long enough for them to sit next to us.

He pulled me closer, dipping his head so we were closed off to the others, lips brushing my cheek. "I'm sorry, *reina.*"

Those were the words that broke the dam inside me. Ugly sobs ripped from my chest, and I felt as if every breath was a razor blade slicing through me. My men ran their hands down my body, petting my back, my hair, my legs. They whispered to me, promising me I was safe. They were here. It would be okay.

The rat was my cousin. My best friend, outside of the men who huddled around me as if their bodies on mine could keep me intact. I couldn't understand it. "He was supposed to have my back."

I didn't realize I'd said that out loud until Nate's haunted whisper slithered across my shoulder where he perched his head. "I'm sorry, angel. I should have told you."

"It's okay." It wasn't.

I'd been avoiding the truth because I knew it would hurt. If it were someone who didn't matter, Nate would've told me right away. I'd buried my head in the sand because the fallout felt too disastrous, and now I was paying the price.

"How can I fix this?" he croaked, hands clutching at my thigh like he was worried I'd walk away.

Didn't he know I couldn't do that? I'd tried once, and look how that had ended.

"You can't. No one can." No one except the man who'd broken it in the first place.

Eventually, I'd have to accept that my cousin had betrayed me in the worst way. He needed to be dealt with and his influence carved out of the family like rotten fruit.

But that was a problem for tomorrow. Tonight, I needed something else.

I needed them.

"Touch me. Make me forget all of this."

I tilted my head, brushing my lips over first Dominic's, then Greyson's, and finally Nate's mouth. A light kiss for each of the men I loved more than anything. More than the power I held, the family I ran, or the city under our feet. They were my reason for existing, my reason to throw my shoulders back and keep going no matter what came my way.

I would succeed because it was the only way we ended happy. We fucking deserved that much, and they would be with me.

For now, I needed to feel something good. We needed a reminder that family didn't always stab you in the back.

Nate threaded his hand through my hair and pulled me away from Greyson so he could reach me. Those fathomless blue eyes swept my face like he was memorizing it. Like he never wanted to forget the moment I reached for him, and it warmed me to my core.

"Anything you need," he whispered against my lips before he closed the distance between us.

The kiss was a promise. A declaration of Nate's love and a vow to hunt down whoever harmed me. My dark knight, my quiet love.

While he kissed the brain out of my head, Grey and Dominic worked together to slip off my clothes. I didn't even realize they'd done it until four hands dropped me onto Greyson's cock.

The unexpected sensation tore me from Nate's mouth on a gasp.

"Oh fuck." It was a tight squeeze since we hadn't played first, but I didn't mind. Some nights, we sucked and teased and licked for hours, but this wasn't one of them. Tonight, I needed hard and desperate. Anything to burn away the sadness before it ate me alive. "God, Greyson. You shouldn't be doing this."

His fingers dug into my hips as he moved me. "Don't worry, you're going to do all the work."

Dominic brushed my hair back softly, his other hand pushing me down so I took Grey in inch by inch. "That's right, *mariposa*. Let us do whatever we want. You know we'll make you feel good."

I had no doubt they would, and that reminder was what let me fall into them and out of my own head. Nate was behind me, kissing my neck, rolling my nipples between his fingers, and grinding his cock into me so I could feel how much he wanted me. Greyson's eyes pinned me in place as efficiently as his hands did, while Dominic coaxed me the whole time.

Roll your hips, baby. Yes, just like that. You're taking him so good. Show us how gorgeous you are when you come, mariposa. *That's right. Give us what we want.*

The first orgasm was just as surprising as the sex had been, but no less powerful for it. It rolled through my body in a wave of warmth that thawed the chill Ace's news had set into my bones. I was so focused on how good it felt that I didn't hear anyone move until I heard the sound of a drawer opening.

"Get her ready, fuckboy."

Nate huffed against the back of my neck, making me shiver. "I prefer *boyfriend.*"

Dominic rolled his eyes, reaching in and tossing something into the air. "I prefer you do what I say."

The bottle of lube landed next to me on the bed, and I frowned. "I don't want foreplay tonight."

"I don't care," he answered.

"Seriously, Dominic. I don't want it. Just fuck me."

Dominic snatched my throat in his hand and hauled me in until we were nose to nose. "We're not taking your ass without stretching you first and using plenty of lube. It's nonnegotiable, Mari. You don't get to hurt yourself. Not like this."

Nate brushed his lips against my skin, his voice vibrating my back. "Agreed."

"Third," Grey said, hauling me in for a searing kiss. "We'll help you, but we won't ever hurt you."

Knowing they wouldn't budge, I readjusted my position over Greyson so Nate had more room to maneuver. I tried to focus on my husband, but the click of the cap and the simultaneous slide of two zippers drew my attention.

Dominic's wicked grin sent warmth straight to my pussy, and Grey groaned when I squeezed him.

"Naughty girl. Your ball and chain's trying to hold out, and you're gripping the life out of him, aren't you?"

Slicked fingers rimmed my ass, pushing in a little at a time. I enjoyed every second of Nate working me over, forcing me to stretch while I rode Grey, with Dominic's wicked words and sinful kisses keeping me distracted.

Together, the three of them pushed me into another orgasm and then another until I was no more than putty in their hands.

"She's ready."

"Yes, she is." Dominic leaned in for another kiss and disappeared just as Nate's hands did. I expected him to push inside me with Grey, but he stepped away instead, giving Dominic his place. "Wait, what?"

"I get your ass first," Dominic whispered, grabbing the lube. When he was coated, he tossed the bottle to Nate, who poured it onto his dick so slowly I was mesmerized.

My men had beautiful dicks, and I so rarely got to appreciate them the way I should. When this war was over, I was going to do something about that.

"Why do all the work for none of the reward?" I asked. Nate's crooked grin lit me up inside.

"You're the reward, angel. Right now, I need to see you. Need to show you what you do to me." He fisted his hand around his cock, stroking slowly so I had something to watch, and fuck, what a pretty show it was.

His stomach clenched as he gripped the base of his dick with a punishing hand. His jaw tightened, and his eyes were so dark, they looked black.

Fuck yes.

"Keep looking at me like that, and this is going to end quick," he warned. Grey chuckled against my neck as Dominic shoved me down to his chest.

"Yeah, Mari. Give the kid a chance not to be a two-pump chump." Dominic's low voice skated over my skin. Nate rolled his eyes but didn't argue. Not that I would've noticed when Dominic ran his cock along my ass, spreading lube everywhere he touched. He pushed at the ring of muscle, testing to see if I was truly ready, and I moaned as he did it again and again. Never truly entering me, never giving me what I wanted.

"Dominic," I begged.

"I love it when you're desperate for me." He wrapped a hand in my hair and hauled me up just as he slid inside my ass again. Only this time, he didn't stop.

"Fuck, I forgot how tight you get with two of us inside you." Grey's strangled voice came as he arched up and took my nipple in his mouth. Dominic moved his hands, one to bracket my throat again and the other to strum my clit like it was his favorite instrument.

That desperate ball of pleasure spun inside me, growing with every touch and kiss and whispered word against my skin. They wanted to distract me from the day, to make me forget about anything but them and what they could do to me, and fuck me running, it was working.

Dominic and Greyson worked me over as a team, never letting me rest for a moment, while Nate watched. Sometimes, he barked orders like *pull her nipple hard, bite her collarbone, squeeze her throat,* all the while stroking his cock until it looked so hard it hurt.

Orgasm after orgasm wrecked me until I could barely move and desperate pleas were the only words I could form. I didn't know how long it took before Dominic's pace changed, his breathing heavy on my neck.

"Damn it, I can't last any longer."

"Thank fuck," Grey breathed, hauling my hips closer and thrusting into me from below. His injuries meant Dominic had been doing most of the work for the both of us, but apparently, that didn't matter now that the end was in sight. "You feel so good, *reina*. It's been hell to hold it back."

"Come, then. All of you."

Dominic's grip on my throat tightened as he let himself loose, plunging into me so fiercely I knew I'd bruise just from how our hips connected. I didn't care, though. They could mark me until I was painted in nothing but black and blue.

Dominic was the first to go, wringing every ounce of pleasure from my body that he could before he stilled. Even though he was finished, he held himself inside me while he stroked my back and kissed my temple. "You're fucking heaven, *mariposa*."

"So are you."

I felt his grin on my skin before he gently pulled out. Greyson hauled me closer, taking my mouth in a stinging kiss. "My wife. You're so beautiful when you come for us."

"I want to do it again."

"You will," he promised. "But it's my turn now."

Unlike Dominic, Grey's orgasm was almost immediate. He'd been holding himself back, waiting for the others so we could finish close together. Even now, Dominic sat next to us on the bed, his eyes fixated on me.

When Greyson finished filling me with come, he leaned back on his hands.

Two down, one to go.

"Nate, I want you in my mouth." He shook his head, and I glared, watching as he stroked himself faster. Like Greyson, he'd waited, and if I didn't get him where I wanted him, he was going to blow on me. "I don't want a come shower. Either put it in my mouth or deal with it yourself."

"Have you always been this bossy?"

"Yes," Dominic and Grey replied together.

Nate shook his head again, this time with a laugh. "I wasn't planning to come *on* you, but I'm definitely interested in that another time."

As he spoke, he disappeared behind me, and anticipation tightened my sore muscles.

Would he take my ass? Haul me off Greyson and bend me over the bed? Would he force me to my knees and make me suck him off?

Any of those were good with me.

While I waited, Grey's softened cock slipped out, just in time for Nate to flip me over and plunge inside my pussy while I was still resting on his lap.

"Nate—"

"It's okay, *reina.* I don't mind." Grey wrapped his hands around my thighs, pulling them apart so we could all watch Nate —and fuck me, that was hot.

Dominic leaned in to toy with my nipple and run a slow, teasing hand to my clit, but once he got there, he made sure I didn't get a single break. He played it exactly the way I needed, building me up until I was crying out in no time.

"There you go, angel. One more time for us. Give us one more," Nate panted, chasing his own release as Dominic forced mine. My hands grappled to cling to something, scratching at whatever skin I could find. Anything to ride out the intense wave that took me under.

When I was almost done, Dominic moved his hand to my thigh and Nate bit down on my neck, his fingers hauling me closer as he came as deep inside me as he could get, mixing his come with Grey's.

In the aftermath, all I could hear was the roar of my pulse pounding in my ear.

My men touched me, stroked me, calmed me down until my

ears worked again. No way I could move a muscle, but I was sated and happy. What more could a girl want?

"Nothing else matters but this. Us. Our family," Nate promised against my sweaty chest. He hadn't released me yet, clinging to me like I was the only life raft in the world he could use, and when I ran my fingers through his hair, I felt the same.

"Our family," I agreed, knowing he didn't mean just the four of us. He meant Aislynn and Shara too. Moore and Tennessee. Marjorie and the people we loved more than life. They were our family, and no matter what happened with Cameron, they always would be.

When the others finally pulled away to wash off, Dominic came back quickly with a warm washcloth and slid it between my thighs until I was clean, kissing every fingertip bruise he found on the way.

No one got dressed after. Instead, we curled together, skin on skin. Greyson fiddled with the remote, and the ceiling fan above whirled to life, cooling us off. I watched in a daze as he found my favorite show and turned it on.

"Gargoyles?" Nate asked.

Dominic laughed. "Just go with it."

I tried to settle down, but reality had a way of creeping in on even the most private moments. "How am I going to tell Ash?"

It was the one thing that kept coming up when I thought about everything. How was I going to tell my best friend that the husband she'd fallen in love with was a liar? Could I tell her at all? Would Cameron hurt her to get to me?

"We're not going to do this right now," Dominic said, cutting off my protests with a firm bite to the ass. I squealed, pulling away from him, but he crawled up my side, forcing me to stay. "None of this needs to happen right this second. When you've come to terms with things, we'll make a plan and execute it, but save that for tomorrow. Tonight, all you have to do is rest with us."

So, I did. We stayed snuggled up together watching my guilty pleasure. Everywhere I moved, I had at least one hand from each of them on me, and if I got up, they watched my every step. I'd never felt more cared for than I did with all their attention on me.

None of it made my cousin's betrayal okay, but things always felt more manageable with my men by my side.

Chapter 10
Greyson

It took Mari hours to settle, and even when she did, her sleep was fitful. It pissed me off more than anything, and every time she tossed and turned, I got angrier.

Cameron had been her closest confidant, other than me, after Antoni died. She'd gone to bat for him, giving him promotion after promotion, even when the capos didn't agree. He had his own fucking territory and team, plus the ear of his don, and what had he done to earn it? *Nothing.*

Worse, he'd thrown it in her fucking face.

I just didn't understand why.

Why throw away a lifelong bond? Did he blame Mari for Rey's death? Was he angry that she'd taken over the family when Antoni died? Did he think it should have gone to him?

If so, I was going to skin him alive because I knew the capos had asked him first. Granted, he wasn't in a good place when

Antoni died—his reckless spirit had always made him harder to contain, and for Joaquin, I was sure he'd been worried his son would embarrass him. Meanwhile, Mari had always been composed. Always the first to find a solution that no one else could.

Was all this because of power? I didn't want to think ill of a man I'd known my whole life, someone I considered a friend, but what else could I do?

My thoughts drowned me, keeping me awake until I was sure I'd never sleep again, but I refused to leave Mari when she needed me. I was there for every soft whimper and agonizing cry she released in her dreams, but when I huffed and she let out a soft, annoyed sigh, I realized I wasn't helping.

She slid closer to Nate as I slipped out of bed, the furrow of her brow smoothing as he stroked a sleepy hand down her back. It killed me to go, but I couldn't always be everything to her. That was why there were three of us. Where one failed, the others succeeded.

Right now, she needed them and the rest they'd provide, and I needed to unleash my feelings before I lost my mind.

Instead of pacing outside the bedroom door like I wanted, I decided to go for a swim in the pool connected to our gym. After a quick stop in my room to change, I hauled ass over there.

The room was muggy, but the water was warm and clear. Exactly what I needed. I didn't bother warming myself up, knowing my muscles were still loose from our play earlier.

Slipping under the surface brought everything to a halt. A moment of singular peace, the same kind of stillness I felt when Mari was in my arms or speared on my cock. Like everything was okay.

I lost myself in the slow, methodical strokes of my arms, forcing my speed to be as slow as possible. I wasn't actually supposed to be doing this much activity so soon and my shoulder was screaming for me to stop, but I needed the repetition. Needed the physical action to set my brain to rights again. With every stroke, I worked through my thoughts.

What drove a person to betray their family, the people who had been there for him, regardless? Was it because of Aislynn? Did Cameron resent Mari because she'd commanded him to marry? If not that, then what?

Few things drove men like money, power, and sex. Was that it? Did he turn his back on his family for tangible yet fleeting things? Had he absolutely destroyed Mari for his own ambition? Or was it something else, something we weren't considering?

I didn't know, and there was the rub. The Cameron I'd grown up with would never have betrayed Mari. Then again, it was obvious that I didn't know him anymore. Maybe he'd been lying our entire lives. If someone wanted to deceive you, they would. There was no way to stop it.

Eventually, my body forced my midnight swim to an end, though I was no closer to figuring out what went wrong. By the time I got back to the penthouse, a pool towel slung around my hips, I was ready to crash. I passed Mari's room, heading for a shower and a change of clothes when Dominic crept out of the room with Nate close behind him.

"You okay?"

"Just needed a swim. Go back inside. I'll be there in a second."

Dominic's eyes narrowed. "How long were you gone?"

I shrugged, and they both frowned at me.

"Don't fuck up your arm when we need it most."

The laugh took me by surprise, but leave it to Dominic to make me feel like all he cared about was my fucking body.

"I'm fine. Go back in with Mari," I repeated. "She shouldn't be alone."

"She's resting, finally," Nate said, giving me a sad smile before looking down at his bare feet. "I should have told you sooner."

"Would it have changed anything?" I wondered. Would telling us have altered the destruction the news caused? Would it have ended Cameron's relationship with Cash or given Mari the peace she now desperately needed? I had a feeling the answer to all of those questions would be no. "Cameron made his own decisions. Mari knows that, and so do we. This isn't your fault."

"But I—"

Dominic cut him off. "There's no point wondering what could have been. The truth is, Cameron did what he wanted for whatever selfish reasons he had. The only thing we can do is try to lessen the fallout."

Nate seemed to waffle, wanting to berate himself more, but eventually, his resolve firmed. "What do we do?"

"Cameron's involvement means we have contingencies to make." Checking the door again, I jerked my head toward my room. I needed to rinse off the chlorine, and if they were insisting on having this conversation, they'd have to deal with my bare ass.

As expected, they each found a place to sit while I sorted myself out. "Not interested in watching me shower?"

"That's Mari's thing, not mine," Dominic answered, tossing himself on my bed. Nate nodded, finding a chair at my desk. I waited for the warning bell to ring with him so close to our most private information, but it never came. We were family. I trusted him implicitly.

"Didn't think playing hard to get was your thing, Dominic. You know you want me." I made the most ridiculous pose I could think of, sliding the towel down my hips like I was going to flash him.

I got a pillow to the face for my trouble.

"Get cleaned up, asshole. We've got shit to sort out."

At least he was laughing.

Leaving them in my space felt weird, but only because I'd never done it before. Previously, my room had been my sanctuary, but now that things with Mari were solid, her room had taken its place. This was a place I came to when I needed to be alone or to have space to think, but it wasn't my home. She was, and she always would be.

My time in the shower was spent deciding how to word what I wanted to say, and by the time I was changed and back in my bedroom, I'd figured it out. "I want Mari alive at the end of this, even if it's just her."

Neither of them balked, and I expected they'd been thinking the same thing.

"She's not going to like this," Nate warned.

"No shit." The laugh felt rusty and unused in my throat. But I was her husband, and it was my job—no, my right—to protect her.

This wasn't how today was supposed to end. I was supposed to come home to my loving wife, eat good food, drink good booze, and take her to bed with my brothers at my side. This was supposed to be a reunion for us all, and while we'd connected, it wasn't the way I'd imagined.

We'll make it up to her when this is all over, I promised myself. A vacation somewhere far away from the Beckstrom bullshit plaguing our city.

Then again, maybe this was better. A reminder of my vows that, no matter what, I would always fight for her. I would always be hers. The boys may not have stood at the altar with her, but I knew they'd made commitments to her just the same. It was obvious in the way they drifted to her, like she was the thing they orbited around. The center of their universe.

We were Mari's creatures of the night. And no one, not even her double-dipping cousin, was going to take her away from us.

"I have some people I can reach out to. But they should be last-ditch efforts," Nate volunteered. I focused on him, fully seeing the burden he carried, and wondered if I'd missed something.

Dominic saw it too and narrowed his eyes, crossing his arms

like he was protecting himself from another heavy blow. "You got something to tell us, Beckstrom?"

"It's Black," Nate corrected swiftly. There was a moment where I saw him consider keeping his secrets, but a look at Dominic—who still hadn't fully forgiven him—made the decision for him. "My contact told me it would be best if I avoided using them. The last thing I want to do is end up back in the company's clutches and away from Mari."

Dominic huffed, but it seemed more performative than realistic. Was he softening toward Nate already? It wouldn't surprise me. For all his faults, and there were many, Dominic loved his family. And whether he liked it or not, Nate was part of that family. He wouldn't have it in him to hold out for too long.

"What about the rival cartel? Would they have any intel on them?" It was the nuclear option, but Cash was years ahead of us, so we had to consider every angle.

"I doubt it, but since I'm already reaching out, I'll ask," Nate promised. "Eagle can probably get us a name, but I wouldn't hold my breath for any way to contact them. We'll probably have to figure that out ourselves."

It wasn't much, but it was a place to start. "Do it."

Nate nodded, pulled out his phone, and began tapping, though he talked while he did. "I don't know what the price is, but I'll see if I can't get a rescue option for Mari sorted out."

"Whatever it costs, we'll pay it. We've got more than enough resources to get her out." Dominic leaned against the wall.

"Not everything costs money." Nate's eyes darted to him and then back to his phone. He kept his focus on his message, but I saw the sag of his shoulders, the weight of everything he'd been dealing with.

"Are you okay?"

He looked up from his phone, surprised, and a sigh shuddered from his lips. "He's unstable, and he's only going to get worse."

We weren't talking about his friend or Cameron. This was his brother.

"We'll take care of it."

"I know we will. But at what cost?" He stared at his phone like it held everything he wanted and all the nightmares he ran from. "Will it be worth it at the end if all we have is a pile of rubble and memories?"

"We'll have Mari," Dominic said quietly. That was the only thing that mattered for us.

"Yeah, we will." Nate's lips quirked into a soft smile, and some of that torment blew away like dust on the wind. "Cash needs to go, subtlety be damned."

"The Feds have given us an out, but who knows if it'll hold up." Dominic's reminder was necessary. I'd nearly forgotten about Two-Bit's little surprise.

"Is it safe to take it, though?" We turned to Nate since he was the only one of us who'd worked with the Feds before.

"Honestly, I don't know," he admitted. "I'm not sure it matters either way. We've been playing Cash's game, hoping to minimize the casualties, but that ship has sailed. If we're at war, we need to treat it like one."

And I had no doubt he'd be the first general in line to lead our troops into battle. The fierceness in his eyes was a stark reminder that, like Dominic and me, Nate was in it for the long haul. He was Mari's champion, too, and we would do whatever was necessary to make sure she survived.

Chapter 11
Mari

"I knew that Irish fuck couldn't be trusted." Gabriele's irritated voice echoed around the conference room.

Probably would have been better to silence him, but I happened to agree. "Allying with the Irish was a calculated risk. One that's paid off immensely."

Leonardo and Mathias stared at me like I'd just lost my mind.

"How has it paid off?" Uncle Leo asked.

"We got Aislynn out safely."

Again, both looked at me so dumbfounded, I was tempted to laugh. "O'Bannon was always going to be a wild card. At least with his daughter in hand, he was supposed to be manageable."

"So, you overestimated his love for her," Mathias said plainly.

Dominic laughed. "He has no love for her."

Sad but true. Aislynn was, and always had been, a tool for her father's games.

Mathias watched me closely. "You did this because she's your friend."

"I did it because it was the right thing to do," I corrected. "Even if he betrayed us, we got more out of this alliance than he did."

Leo scoffed. "How is some fashionista princess worth more than giving O'Bannon access to our resources?"

I wasn't surprised that my uncles had counted Aislynn out without even knowing who she was, but I was disappointed. "This isn't the fifties, Uncle. Women have a place in society now. They have rights."

He rolled his eyes. "I'm talking about here and now. What tangible benefit did she bring to the family?"

Any other day, this conversation would have been maddening, but I knew that had I not made the unilateral decision to marry Cameron and Ash, we would have had it much sooner. Instead, my uncles had bided their time, waiting for the right moment to speak. I couldn't begrudge them that.

"Aislynn's power isn't in her cunt, it's in her network. That *fashionista princess* has access to all the high rollers, not just in this city, but in every other major city in the country. People with money and power and prestige. People who owe her favors, favors that are now *our* favors."

None of them seemed particularly happy, but they did seem to understand the implications of Ash's network.

Leo grunted. "What are we doing about the Irish fuck? We aren't keeping him alive for the daughter's sake, are we?"

"As I said, O'Bannon has no love for his daughter, and the feeling's mutual." I nodded at Dominic, who immediately stepped in.

"The plan is a sneak attack. We aren't giving him the satisfaction of a full-frontal war. He dies in his tighty-whities, curled up in bed beside whatever poor, unfortunate soul he's fucking at the moment."

All three of my uncles shifted uncomfortably. Dominic and I waited, knowing they'd have to wrap their heads around the situation.

One did not kill the leader of a syndicate in their home. It wasn't dignified. Normally, we earned the honor of a warrior's death, but O'Bannon could suck a dick if he thought being a two-faced asshole was getting him a grave on the battlefield.

No, he'd die screaming in his massive mansion with no one around to save him.

"He's a leader of a faction," Gabriele eventually said.

"Which is why we're intentionally taking him out in the most disrespectful way possible. He fucked up, going behind my back to Cash. The least I can do is return the favor. Or should I not show our strengths? Should I not remind the others in the city of who actually runs it? Tell me, Uncle, how far do you want this war to go? Because I, for one, want it over before we lose something we can't come back from."

"You're right," he agreed, bowing his head slightly. "Whatever it takes to end this."

Dominic ran them through the plan, and with some minor tweaking, we were in business. My uncles gathered their things, but I raised a hand before they could leave.

"One last thing before you go. Keep this to yourselves."

"And Cameron," Leo suggested.

"The people in this room only."

Leonardo's face tightened. "He's a capo, same as us. He has the right to know."

"He does, but he's grieving." I swallowed hard to ease the sorrow in my chest. I wanted to shout at them, to tell them all the truth, but I couldn't. Not without proof. "He's also healing. Until he's back on his feet, I want him left out of it. This is our fight."

I could tell they didn't agree, but the plan hinged on Cameron being unaware. If he warned O'Bannon, we were headed for an ambush we wouldn't make it out of.

"Trust me when I say it has to be this way." I'd never asked them directly for their trust. Not like this. After my killing Joaquin with no real trial, they were leery of me. I could see it in the way they shifted in their chairs, but eventually, they gave their agreement.

Relief should have filled me, but all I felt was dread.

The capos filed out as Moore and Tennessee filed in, and my chest clenched tight.

My friends sat patiently at the table, muscles taut with the tension in the room.

Whether I had evidence that Ace was telling the truth—other than Nate's agreement, of course—I couldn't leave us vulnerable. From a security standpoint, I had to tell someone. Still, I couldn't say it.

"Let me do this for you," Nate whispered. I shook my head. Cameron was my family. I would be the one to seal his fate.

"Cameron is compromised."

The words ricocheted around the room, and Moore clenched his fists together. There was a bleakness in his eyes, a desperate plea. Hope. "Blackmailed or—"

"Willingly," Nate said solemnly. It was another dagger to the heart for all of us, and Moore dropped his head to stare at his lap.

Part of me hoped my cousin wasn't at fault, but that was love, wasn't it? It always blinded us. With Nate, it had made me believe he wasn't hiding things. With Cameron, it left me clinging to the idea that this was all a mistake.

Neither was true, and yet I wasn't sure I could forgive my cousin like I had Nate. He'd betrayed me to protect his family, but *I* was Cameron's family. In blood and in heart. That should have come before everything else.

Tennessee gaped at us. "What? What happened?"

When Tennessee and Moore had fallen in love, many in the family had balked at the idea of their relationship. The mafia had always been rife with homophobia, and our family was no different. My cousin was the first man to stand at their sides and shut the others down. He was the one who battled with me to make my position clear—they were staying.

Cameron was one of Moore's closest friends. And he'd sided with Cash against them.

"How long?" Moore growled, nearly vibrating with rage.

"We don't know."

Moore stood up to pace, but Tennessee stared at the wall as if it could give him all the answers. I knew the feeling. Finally, he swallowed all his feelings down and looked at me with steely determination.

"What now?" It was clear even saying that much hurt Tennessee.

"We need to vet his people and restrict his access, but it has to be done quietly."

"He's going to know," Dominic said, spinning a pen in his fingers while he thought. "He knows everyone here, and while most of them are great liars, they're terrible actors. If he finds out too soon..."

There was no explanation needed. If Cameron found out we knew, he'd become even more unpredictable and that meant dangerous. He could disappear. That wouldn't be bad, but what if he took Ash with him? There was no doubt in my mind she had nothing to do with this, but that didn't mean that he wouldn't use her as a get-out-of-jail-free card. He knew I wouldn't do anything to hurt her.

"What about the kid?" Tennessee asked, still a little shell-shocked. "The one you brought back from jail."

Dominic nodded as he thought it over. "He's been inside for

years, so Cameron would assume any weirdness would be him acclimating to the outside again. It could work."

"Would he do it?" Dominic was the only one who really knew Killer well enough to answer that question.

His nod was firm. "Absolutely. It's pretty clear that he'd do anything for this family."

"Make it happen."

He nodded and slipped out of the room to hunt him down, leaving Nate, Greyson, and me with our devastated friends.

"We'll do our part," Moore promised, squeezing his husband's shoulder gently. "We won't let him get away with this."

I smiled sadly. "I know."

Tennessee cleared his throat. "What should we do if we find anyone in on it?"

"What you think is right. I don't need another knife in my back."

* * *

For the first time since I met him, I was grateful Sean O'Bannon was an arrogant, prideful fuck. He thought his sentries were enough to guard his home from me. He thought he was safe with Cash's men in his pocket. He thought the police would protect him.

He forgot that no one held a candle to a pissed-off Marcosa. I was like a fucking ghost in his halls, slicing through every man I saw until bodies left a trail at my feet and a wide-open path inside.

"Is it wrong that I'm turned on right now?" Dominic asked quietly as we walked up the steps and entered through the front door. Greyson shook his head at my side, but Nate's laugh buoyed me farther into the house.

The most common, critical mistake of made men was not putting a guard rotation *inside* their homes, and O'Bannon was no different. Grey and Nate each slipped down the side halls, circling back when they'd cleared the bottom floor, while I went upstairs with Dominic at my back. Normally, I'd be in the thick of it with them, but tonight was a show for those little red dots on every corner.

"Security office?" I asked quietly. The crackle of the comms unit in my ear preceded Grey.

"Dealt with. The guard was asleep at the desk anyway."

"Congrats to him," Dominic murmured. I had to agree. Everyone else died painfully, but that idiot got a peaceful goodbye out of sheer luck.

I trailed slowly down the hall, letting Dominic peel away to check rooms as we went. There was no need for stealth when the only men still alive in the house were O'Bannon and his son, and we'd deal with the whelp later.

Décor shifted from gaudy to obscene the closer we got to Sean's wing, and the amount of glitter and glitz he'd thrown on the walls made me want to gouge my eyes out. It was obvious he didn't understand the word *understated*, and I wondered again how he could be Aislynn's father. It didn't make a lick of sense.

When we found the most offensive door in the place, we paused, waiting for the others. Only when I had all of my men around me did I enter Sean's room.

A glance around showed Casanova was his only design inspiration. To avoid seeing something that would haunt my nightmares, I kept my eyes focused on the figure in the bed. Loud snores shuddered through him as he lay flat on the mattress, a sleep apnea mask fastened onto his face and the sheets dangerously close to sliding off his naked body. No one else was in the bed with him, though the used condom I sidestepped suggested he'd had a friend over earlier.

"Jesus, that's disgusting," Grey whispered, wrinkling his nose. Nate patted him on the shoulder.

"There, there, buddy. It'll be over soon."

Yes, it would.

The men fanned out around me, waiting to see what I'd do.

Originally, I'd planned to slit his throat while he slept, but I found myself curious. What would he say if I gave him the chance for last words? Would he finally be useful, or would he die a fucking idiot?

Deciding to test fate, I ripped the sleep apnea mask off his face. For a moment, nothing happened.

Then he stopped breathing.

I waited, wondering if he'd wake up, force a breath, something.

Only silence followed.

This is too easy for him, I thought, tossing the mask to the side. He didn't get to go quietly into death like his security guard. He didn't get to slip peacefully into eternal sleep.

He'd die screaming like he tried to do to me.

I reared back and slapped him, the sound echoing through the silent room, and O'Bannon's eyes shot open at the same time he heaved in a great breath.

Disoriented, he took a minute to place us, but when he did, he wasn't pleased. "What the fuck are you doing here? You shouldn't be here. Get out!"

"What's wrong, O'Bannon? Worried we'll see your dick? Don't worry, Mari's not interested in you." Nate smirked as my men crept closer to the bed, ready to hold him down the second I asked.

"I wouldn't want her used-up pussy anyway," Sean barked, scrambling until his back pressed against the headboard, the sheet clutched in his white-knuckled grip.

All three of my men snarled at him, but I held up a hand to stay their anger. "You get one chance to tell me the truth before you die."

He smirked then, though his hand shook. "You can't kill me, girly. The other leaders will exterminate you if you try."

Shrugging, I moved toward the dresser, pretending to look at the things he had on top. None of it was worth a damn to me, but people like Sean didn't like feeling insignificant. "I'll handle the others in time."

"Are you planning on killing all of us?"

"If I did, I'd be no better than Cash."

That made him laugh. "You'll never win against him. He's too smart for you."

"Only because he had a head start. Don't worry, though. We're catching up."

I twisted, and the look on my face must've given me away.

"You finally told her, huh? Good on you, boy." Sean's smile split his face, and I wanted to rip out his teeth with my bare hands the second he looked at Nate. "How does it feel knowing little Cammy doesn't want you around either?"

The words tried to twist their way inside me, but I was a block of ice. Nothing could thrive there. Not right now. "Actually, Ace Beckstrom spilled the beans."

His only reaction was a slight widening of the eyes, and I wondered if it was because he thought Ace knew nothing or because he truly didn't know who the man was.

"I'm not surprised you buddied up to a psycho, but I am curious why you'd risk your daughter's life to do it."

"You're too weak to hurt her. Besides, it's not like she was worth much."

I thought anger would sweep me away, but I felt nothing but the cold realization that this was always how O'Bannon and I were going to end.

"Aislynn is worth a hundred men. You're just too stupid to realize it." But I did, and I'd never let her pay the price for me again. "Get him down."

As one, Nate and Dominic lunged for Sean, pulling him to the end of the bed, and shoving him to the floor at my feet. While he floundered, I slipped the gun out of my holster and handed it to Greyson.

"Pin him down?" Nate asked as he and Dominic looked to me for direction.

"Put him on his knees and let go," Greyson replied instead.

"You're going to die tonight, just like this. Any last words?"

"Eat shit, cunt," Sean growled. He shoved to his feet, hands reaching for my throat, but mine caught his first. The blade slid into his skin, the slice perfect. Blood spilled down his body, splattering me in the process, and the hands that meant to hurt now reached for help.

I stepped back, letting him grasp at his throat as he fell. It always took longer than I expected for someone to bleed out, and he was no different. None of us took our eyes off him until his breathing stopped and so did the twitching in his limbs.

Sean O'Bannon, don of the Irish Mafia, died facedown on his bedroom floor as naked as the day he was born. There was no better end to a man like him.

Blood still dripped from the blade in my hands when I turned to Nate. "Where is he?"

"Two hallways down." He took charge, leading us out of the carnage and into the gaudy house beyond. It was like walking in a visual puzzle. Everything beyond O'Bannon's room was mostly unaffected, but there were dead men everywhere.

"One down," Dominic whispered.

"One to go," I answered. "Maybe."

We barely stopped when Nate indicated we'd found the right door, and in no time, we hauled a boxer-clad Kieran out of bed.

"What the hell do you think you're doing?" He was flustered out of his element, but unlike his father, he reached for a weapon immediately. Dominic hissed at him, and he snatched his hand back, never taking his eyes off me.

He knew who the real predator in the room was.

Honestly, I was glad. It boded well for me if Kieran was the smarter of the O'Bannon men since Ash obviously took the prize for smartest O'Bannon all around. "We came to tell you your father's dead."

Kieran stared at us warily. "He was fine when he went to bed a few hours ago."

Dominic grinned. "I'm sure he was."

Kieran's focus never wavered, and I shrugged. "Long live the new king. That's you, by the way."

It was fascinating, watching Kieran put away whatever he felt about his father's death in favor of focusing on his new reality. I commended him for it. That was serious leadership potential. *Should've done this years ago.*

"What about my sister?"

Greyson hummed in his throat, and I knew he agreed with me too. New to the role or not, Kieran O'Bannon was asking all the right questions. Too little, too late, but he still asked them. I gave him props for that. Still, it offered me hope that maybe Ash could have a relationship with her family in the future. If she chose to, of course.

"You sold her to me like chattel for an alliance you never intended to honor. She wasn't your sister then, just a pawn you could use. I wouldn't give her to you for all the money in the world."

It was the least I could do, knowing the devastation I was going to cause her soon enough. Aislynn was free to do whatever she wanted. I'd never force her to marry again, never push her to help me. I'd get her out of Seattle and away from this life, where she could heal and be free. Where maybe she could repair the damage my cousin caused.

We'd miss her constantly, but this life just wasn't for her. It never had been. I'd forgotten that in the carnage of Cash's war, and I regretted it fiercely.

"What do you want from me?"

"I want you to continue doing what you're doing." The words were heavy, and I saw the moment Kieran understood what I meant.

His nod was a defeated sort of thing as he stared down at his hands. "I didn't make the decision to work with Cash."

"I know. It's the only reason you're alive."

"The police are his. My father just used them to his advantage."

I'd already assumed as much, but it was still annoying.

"We'll deal with it," I said. "Right now, your only job is to tell people what happened tonight."

Kieran's face screwed up in confusion. "The other leaders won't be happy. Are you sure you don't want me to keep it quiet?"

"If I did, I would have killed you too. By all means, scream it from the rooftops. It's beyond time for a reminder that my generosity can be removed at any moment." I leaned into his space, showing him the depths of my rage. "Let them know. Let them know what happens when you come for my family."

I was fucking done. Done with Cash and playing by the rules, expecting him to do the same. I'd follow him down the rabbit hole of crazy if it meant setting my city free of him.

My men would pull me back in the end. Of that, I had no doubt.

Chapter 12
Mari

Two days later, my presence was requested in a meeting. While I wasn't sure who'd called it, it was obvious the session was about O'Bannon's untimely demise. We'd prepared for exactly this situation, but the real surprise was what waited for me when I got there.

They'd added a chair to my table.

A glance at where I normally sat showed Cash cozied up next to the other leaders as if he had every right to be there. In my seat. At my fucking table.

"Patience," Nate whispered, squeezing my hand where no one could see.

"I hope you're ready to be an only child," Dominic said back. They joked behind me, but I didn't let my expression change.

Cash wasn't going to ruin my plans.

The atmosphere was tense, no one wanting to be in the

powder keg with Cash and me when it blew. Yet, Ajilon smiled as I walked toward the only empty seat. Warily, I sat, waiting for them to turn on me. That's what this whole meeting was, right?

Kieran nodded respectfully at me, waiting until I took the chair across the table from Cash to begin. "Thank you all for coming. I know it was last minute."

"What is it, boy? We don't have time for games." Kosas grunted from where he leaned back, hands crossed over his belly. Next to him, Haru nodded, though he never took his eyes off Cash.

"No games," Kieran promised, looking around the table. "I'm here to tell you that my father is dead."

I took a sick amount of pleasure in the shock that crossed Cash's face. He hadn't been expecting that, and neither had I. I'd thought Kieran would call the other leaders the moment we left to tell them the bad news. Getting to watch it play out in front of me was better than I'd dreamed.

"What do you mean?" Cash's suspicious eyes were trained on me, and I gave him a sweet grin.

"For someone so well acquainted with death, I'm shocked you don't already know. He means Sean's gone. Sleeping the eternal sleep. Hanging with the fishes. Never to return."

Cash looked like he was about to have a coronary, and the petty part of me was entertained by that too.

"How did he die?" Ajilon finally asked.

Kieran glanced at me, and I nodded, a smug smirk trying to break free. "He was murdered at home."

Another glance at me, and it was obvious what Kieran wasn't saying. *She did it.*

Ajilon sat back in his seat, looking shocked. "I see."

The tension in the room grew thick and heavy, but I was too busy watching Cash lose his fucking mind to care.

"I didn't realize his neck would get so purple," I whispered to Nate, who smothered a laugh.

"He gets it from Ace," he whispered back, and I snorted.

"What reason did you have for killing him?"

"He was working with my enemy."

"We are all working with your enemy," Kosas said stiffly.

"I know." I smiled, loving the flinch he tried to hide. I decided then and there that my favorite part of running my own crime outfit was watching grown men shit themselves in front of me.

Cash had finally shaken off the surprise and smiled with that affable ease he'd perfected. "I wasn't aware that your current leader was so unstable."

That drew a laugh out of me. "Any instability you find is instability you've caused. Besides, I'm not the one who slaughtered half a hospital on camera." Like clockwork, Cash's eyes darted to Nate's, and the hate in them chilled me to the bone.

If Cash got ahold of him, Nate was dead.

"The others have already dealt with me for that."

"Yes, a truce to let you run amok in my city absolutely weighs the same as the loss of life you inflicted."

As usual, Cash didn't defend his actions with anything more than a shrug. "If you cared that much, you wouldn't have sent your decoys to trick me."

"The fact that I had to trick you at all is the issue here."

"Family is everything," Kosas interrupted. "While we don't condone the way Cash handled it, we do understand. Losing a brother...it had to be repaid."

"Maybe if I'd killed him, sure. But Nate chose to leave. He chose me. That doesn't require retribution."

Kosas waved his hand, brushing my thought away like a gnat he wanted dead. I should've known better than to argue with him in front of Cash. He and the others were too scared to act against Cash now that they had a truce going.

Cash grinned at the blatant irritation on my face, leaning back like he'd stolen the advantage I had in killing O'Bannon. "Are you going to allow her to run free, knowing that any minute she could turn on you next? We could put a bounty on her head. Hunt her down for sport."

When he turned to convince the others, I saw the sickness in him. The way his eyes glimmered at the thought of my death, and I wasn't the only one. My men were tense around me, but I wasn't. The not-so-subtle suggestion to annihilate me was expected, though I hadn't planned on it coming from Cash. We knew there would be consequences for O'Bannon. The others were as old-school as my uncles and wouldn't appreciate me going off book.

Ajilon shifted, obviously uncomfortable, as did Haru. Two-Bit, who'd been silent the whole time, just watched the interaction go down. *Good to know he's willing to stick his neck out for me.*

"I'm not of a mind to approve a manhunt just yet. Not until she gives us the reason she slaughtered one of our own in his bed."

"Technically, it was in his bedroom, and I'll tell you everything you need to know, but not with him in the room." I leveled one red-tipped nail at Cash, who glowered at me.

"Agreed." Ajilon practically jumped on the chance to understand, and I felt bad for worrying him. He'd been the closest thing to a real ally for ages, but he was a pacifist when possible. This situation was no longer one we could sit back and avoid confrontation on. We had to work together to take Cash down before he turned on them too.

"Remember our deal." Cash's glare burned my cheek as he stood, straightened his clothes, and walked out. The door slammed closed behind him, and everyone seemed to take a breath as he took that volatile energy with him.

Kosas leveled me with a glare that reminded me of parents and misbehaving children. "Explain."

"I suggest you check yourself, Sideris. I'm not yours to command."

"You can't even command yourself, it seems."

Instead of baring my teeth like I wanted, I sat back with a demure smile. "You have a rat."

He scoffed, rolling his eyes and looking at the others as if to say *can you believe her?*

The thump of files dropping to the table ended that soon enough.

Each leader got a massive stack of pages in front of them, the covers firmly closed to the others. Ajilon, Kosas, and Two-Bit ignored them, while Haru and Kieran brought theirs close and flipped through them. Kieran's agitated curses grew louder with every page, and the normally flappable Haru looked annoyed.

"Where did you get these?" he finally asked, pushing the file away with disgust.

"Our little Irish friend gave me a lesson before he died." It was a lie. The information came from Nate, but I wasn't going to let him become a target for the leaders and his brother.

"And you killed him for it?"

"I killed him because he was working with Cash long before your little truce. I killed him because he nearly killed his own daughter—*twice.* O'Bannon was a spineless fuck who didn't care who he allied with as long as he thought he'd survive in the end. He was a fucking cockroach, and I exterminated him like one."

Kieran shifted in his chair, clearing his throat. "I agree with Mari. My father wasn't an honorable man, and while I wish he'd gone differently, I'm not sorry he's dead."

"That doesn't change the facts," Kosas said, shoving the file away. "You killed another member of this order. There has to be some punishment."

"Correction, I killed a member of *your* order. This little tribunal of ours is a formality. *I* am the defining power in the city.

I am the leader, regardless of what that psychotic asshole thinks. These meetings of ours are a courtesy, one I've let go too long if this is how you respect me. Making treaties behind my back." I spat on the floor, the ultimate disrespect.

Kosas's face reddened, but Ajilon was the one who stood, facing off with a weariness I knew all too well. "We did make a treaty, and regardless of your reasoning, it stands. Go after Cash, and you do it alone. We won't offer any aid."

I knew they wouldn't, but it still pissed me off. Kosas decided to push the issue. "You let this go on too long, and look what happened. You should have removed the upstart the second you heard about him."

"Says the man who gave him a seat at the table," I growled.

He shrugged like it wasn't the ultimate betrayal. "We did what was necessary to survive."

"And I didn't?"

"Does it really matter?" Haru asked. "Our answer won't change, no matter how much you defend yourself to us."

"That's just it. I don't have to defend shit. I'm going to take back my city with or without you, and the second I do, I'll come for you too."

"That's exactly the kind of talk that gets you killed," Ajilon warned softly.

"Bring it on. If I'm fighting a war, I might as well deal with all my enemies at once."

Kosas scoffed again. "Your youth is showing, Mari. Don't pick a battle you can't win."

"I'm not. I'm picking a war I intend to dominate. Hope you're ready for the outcome." I stood, nodding to the folders on the table with a smug smile. "Enjoy your rodents."

* * *

I was still seething hours later. The second we got back to the Celestine, I headed straight for the private gym, and the guys settled at the wall, watching me work out my frustrations.

The rhythmic thump of the punching bag didn't help. Neither did lifting weights or running.

After who knew how long, Dominic finally dragged me into the ring with a curt, "You need to hit something."

He was right.

I rushed him, diving for his legs and twisting in time to catch him behind the knee. I pulled the punch, not wanting to hurt him, but he still went down. Before I could jump on top of him, he was up again, launching his own attack that I barely escaped. We parried back and forth, throwing punches and dodging grabs until my chest was on fire and every breath hurt. My cheek throbbed from a right hook he'd managed to land, and his lips and eyebrow were sliced and bleeding.

We looked like we'd gone through the wringer already, yet neither of us bowed out.

"Feeling better, *mariposa*?"

"Why? You ready to quit, old man?"

Dominic's eyes glinted with mischief. He dove for my legs. I jumped, but he caught my ankle in midair and, with a single jerk, dropped me to my stomach. Air whooshed out of my lungs, and I struggled to suck it back in while my body screamed, *We're suffocating!*

"Bitch move," I wheezed, rolling away when he tried to trap me. I didn't mind Dominic on top, but I wasn't in the mood to be held down this time.

He grinned at me like he hadn't just knocked the wind out of me. "We use what we've got."

"Kick his ass, Mari!" Nate yelled.

"He could use a dose of reality," Grey agreed, sharing his

focus between his tablet and us. "His overinflated ego is getting too big to share a bed with."

"Go sleep in your own room, then," Dominic challenged, twisting to glare at Greyson.

My husband grinned as I wrapped an arm around Dominic, forcing him off-balance so I could roll us. "Haven't you learned not to take your eyes off her for a second?"

Dominic panted under me, his playful glare turning molten as I took control of his arms. "How dare I forget."

With Dominic underneath me, his wrists in my hand, I felt powerful again. A different kind of power, sure, but one all the same. Warmth wrapped around me, and I couldn't help the slow grind of my hips on his.

"Don't start something you can't finish," he warned, and I licked my lips.

"Who said I can't finish it?"

"Sadly, I do." Nate slipped into the ring and hauled me off Dominic, wiggling his phone. "We've got a name."

Surprise and anticipation tingled up my spine. "Already?"

"Apparently, this guy's as big as your family." He tapped a few buttons, sharing the info with Greyson's tablet before shoving his phone back into his pocket. It wasn't much from what I could see, but it would be enough. It had to be.

Greyson ran over the info, reading it out for the rest of us. "Name's Victor Paez. He runs a cartel out of Colombia, close to the Venezuelan border. Been in a turf war with the Osorios for the last decade."

"Why?"

"Why else? Money. Power. Prestige. Take your pick." Nate shrugged, turning to Greyson. "There's a number here, but can you obtain the rest of his info?"

"If not, I know who can." Moore and Tennessee were the best people to dig up information people didn't want found, so I had no doubt he'd pass the job to them if necessary, but we all wanted to give them some space. Besides, ferreting out my cousin's helpers was more important than deep-diving into a cartel leader.

For a moment, I considered asking Rafael for his assistance, but I hadn't heard from my uncle in a while, and I was still pissed off at him for refusing to help. Was it fair? Probably not, but I felt what I felt.

"What do you want to do, Mari?"

I walked over to Nate, slipping my hand into his pocket to grab the burner phone from it. "I'm going to send him a message."

He hauled me into his body, pressing himself against my back when I twisted to face the others. "Will he answer?"

"No." Not now, anyway. We needed more incentive to coax his attention to Seattle, but we'd find it. For now, I just needed him curious. In seconds, I had the number typed in and the message delivered.

I heard we have a mutual friend. I'd love to talk green when you have a chance. –Queenie

Short, sweet, and to the point. Hopefully, it would get me what I wanted.

"Will he know it's you?" Nate asked, reading it over my shoulder.

"She's the only queen on this side of the world. He'll know," Greyson answered, snatching the phone for a once-over. He nodded once and tossed it back to Nate.

The moment Nate's hands left my body, Dominic hauled me over his shoulder, smacked my ass, and rushed toward the door. "Since that's done, we're taking a shower. Don't wait up."

"Is there room for three? I could use a cooldown, myself!" Nate called. Grey just jogged ahead and opened the door for all of us, and the stark reminder of what I was fighting for was exactly what I needed.

My family. My men. My future.

Chapter 13
Dominic

Cash's reaction to O'Bannon's death was akin to a toddler's temper tantrum. He let his Aces go wild and fell right into the mayhem. Every day, there was something new to discover. He looted businesses, burned cars, kicked down doors, and terrorized neighborhoods.

The most interesting part was he didn't just stick to Marcosa territory; he hit everyone equally. Three of Haru's businesses were demolished, and a fleet of cars went into one of Two-Bit's men's homes. He nearly blew up Ajilon's place entirely, and the bar Kosas's crew met up at was set on fire. Even Kieran's territory got trashed.

It was like Cash needed to test his little truce from the get-go, and he was giving it his all. Yet the other leaders didn't flinch. He could burn their shit to the ground, and as long as they lived, he was golden. It pissed me off.

Even if Mari wanted to put an end to things, she couldn't trust the other leaders not to turn on her the second Cash commanded them to. So we watched and waited, hoping he'd burn himself out.

He never did.

In the span of a week, he became Seattle's boogeyman. Not just in the shadows, but in the light too. People were terrified to leave their houses. The news was constantly streaming live updates, and we were getting more and more nervous glances from the rest of the country. Too many prying eyes were finding their gazes drawn to Seattle, and it made conducting business of any sort twice as dangerous.

Hence why our guest was so irritated.

Two-Bit paced the living room, tapping viciously on his phone, while Griz hung out by the door. He watched all of us like you'd watch an uncontained viper, ready to cut our heads off if we so much as twitched toward his friend. Boss? Who knew what the hierarchy really was. Nate watched him right back from where he perched on the arm of the couch beside Mari. If Griz's pinkie wiggled toward his gun, Nate would blow him away without question.

With Mari protected and Two-Bit occupied, I got to take my time and actually study him. He'd always been unassuming, someone I barely considered a threat, and it was hard to let that original instinct die.

It was automatic to compare him to Mari, though.

"He takes after his mother," Grey whispered at my side, where we stood adjacent to Mari's couch.

That much was obvious. He was light where Mari was bronzed. Their eyes, noses, and hair were completely different. Honestly, if Rafael hadn't confirmed it, I'd never have believed they shared genetics at first glance. There was something about the way he moved that reminded me of Mari, though. That self-contained strut that people who knew their place in the world had.

Mari got it from her position. Where did Two-Bit get it from?

"You think the Wolf knows about him?" I asked.

"I think he'd be stupid not to know his son procreated again."

So, that was a yes. Yet Emmanuel had allowed Two-Bit to fall into federal hands. What an idiotic decision. Then again, maybe he thought blood ties were enough to stitch his grandson's lips shut. Somehow, I doubted it. I got the feeling Two-Bit—Dante—wasn't an Osorio where it counted.

"What are we supposed to call you?" I asked randomly.

Two-Bit stopped pacing, staring at me like he didn't understand. "My name."

The eye roll was second nature. "Obviously, but is that what you'd prefer to go by, or would you prefer Dante when we're alone?"

Again, he looked like he wasn't computing what I was saying. "I've never been an Osorio."

"Neither have I, but it's okay if you want to be Dante here," Mari said.

Two-Bit looked wistful, and I wondered if anyone had ever said that to him. Rafael had kept his sons apart; it wouldn't be too out of bounds to assume that he'd told his youngest never to use his real name. For a moment, I thought he'd cave, but he shook off the emotion quickly.

"Two-Bit is my name now. I don't need you blowing my cover, so stick to that and we'll be fine."

"If that's what you want." Mari was almost gentle with him, and I wondered if part of her was aching to have another cousin so close, yet clearly out of reach. Anytime we broached the subject, she shut down, so we'd let it go. Maybe when this war was over and she had time to come to terms with Cameron's betrayal, she'd open up. For now, we'd be there for her to lean on.

Grey readjusted himself, a silent request for attention. "Just how undercover are you?"

Two-Bit's eyes flashed. "Very."

"I'm not trying to screw up your job or steal information you aren't giving. I'm just trying to understand how an Osorio became a Fed."

Damn. All those years hating Greyson, and I forgot the fucker had the same thought process as me.

Two-Bit hardened. "Because I chose to."

"You chose to turn your back on your legacy?"

He huffed. "What legacy? I wasn't raised in this world, and I certainly don't want to be here. This is the best I could do under the circumstances."

This is the best I could do. It struck me that Two-Bit might not have been a Fed because he wanted to be. Maybe we weren't the only ones cornered in a situation we couldn't control. Grey's barely there nod confirmed we were on the same wavelength.

"So you lose your name and your identity to get back at Rafael?" Nate asked. Two-Bit turned on him with a lethal glare.

"I'm not doing this because of some daddy issues. I'm doing it to take shitty people off the streets. If I lose myself in it, who cares. Whatever it takes to make a difference in this fucked-up world."

The more I watched, the more curious I was. What had his world looked like before he came to Seattle? How long had he actually been a government stooge, and had he ever really wanted to join? There was so much we didn't know about Two-Bit and so many obstacles keeping Mari from finding out, but I was going to. One day, we'd know everything about Dante Osorio—whether he liked it or not.

"If we're done discussing me, we need to talk about him." He jabbed a finger at the TV where the news was broadcasting another shot of Cash's reign of terror. "Have you considered our offer?"

Federal help and a get-out-of-jail-free pass, if we killed Cash. Yeah, we'd thought about it.

"Our goals are aligned, but I'm still feeling some things out. I can't move on Cash unless I'm sure that it's going to kill him." I knew Mari was hedging her bets, hoping Paez got in touch with us. There'd been no response to the text yet, but she wasn't giving up. The cartel leader was still our best bet moving forward.

Two-Bit watched Mari for a long moment before nodding. "Your opportunity window is getting smaller, and your time is growing thin."

My heartbeat tripped. He knew something. "What aren't you telling us?"

"The higher-ups are getting restless." Two-Bit rubbed his face, and Griz laughed bitterly.

"They're considering bringing in the National Guard to lock it down if we can't get this under control."

All four of us stiffened.

Holy shit. I knew having eyes on us would be bad for everyone, but the government locking us in with Cash on a rampage would mean astronomical levels of destruction. You didn't cage a sick, feral bear; you put it down before it killed everyone it saw.

"Jesus," Grey muttered.

"Giving Cash a captive audience will only make things worse," Nate said harshly.

"I know that and you know that, but it's all about optics to them. With the way things look now, they don't care how we fix it, only that it gets done."

"Well, make them care!" Mari snapped.

Two-Bit threw his arms out. "I can't do any more than I've already done, Mari. The truth is, Cash is outside of all of our wheelhouses without bringing a literal army into the city. He is unhinged to the point of insanity, and this type of chaos grows roots and spreads. As long as this continues, the rest of the world will see it as a weakness. A way to get at us. Your little upstart is becoming a national security problem. This needs to end, and it needs to end now."

Mari stood, toe-to-toe with her cousin, growling, "And how do you expect me to do that? You and the others are cowards. You gave him the truce. You gave him a leg up in this city. *You* did this. Why is it that I'm supposed to take care of your problem now that it's gotten out of your hands?"

"Because he came here for *you*. Because *you* should've stopped it sooner. Take your pick, Mari, but either way, you need to act. This is what being queen is. Sometimes your job is to clean up the messes that other people make. It may be fucked, but that's the role you chose to take on when you took over for your brother. So, own it. Live it, breathe it, and kill for it before Cash destroys us all."

"And will you be helping her, or is she risking her neck for your fucking gratitude?" Nate stood at her shoulder with barely contained fury. Griz straightened from his slouch, eyes alert even if he didn't move closer.

"I'm here, aren't I?" Two-Bit said. The two men stared at each other until, finally, he turned to Mari. "What's your plan?"

"Just because you're here doesn't mean the others will back us. Going after Cash right now is suicide."

"They're cowards who care more about the bottom line than the lives we're losing. Until it affects them, they won't raise a finger," Griz muttered. There was obviously no love lost between him and the other leaders. Bet he struggled to hold his tongue in those meetings too.

Mari tapped her fingers against her thigh, brows furrowed as she tried to find a solution to this fucked-up problem. When she finally settled, it wasn't happily.

"Then we force their hand."

* * *

Four hours later, Nate and I watched from a nearby rooftop as Mari knocked on the door with Greyson at her side. We'd been up there for so long, the cold had officially seeped into my bones, but I didn't waver. Not when my girl was in danger. Looking at Nate, I knew he felt the same.

"Why the fuck is he taking so long to answer?" Nate hissed.

We were both flat on our stomachs as we watched—Nate through his rifle scope and me through the long-range camera lens. He was the only real protection Mari had. We'd left Tennessee and Moore at the Celestine, still working with Killer to uncover how far Cameron's deceit went. The kid was doing better than even I'd expected. He'd given the security team three leads already, men who were more loyal to Cameron than Mari. Considering how fast he'd obtained them, I was even more grateful we'd gotten him out. He was a good man and an incredible asset so far.

"He's making her sweat." I tried staying calm, but I didn't like this plan. There were too many variables we couldn't control, and all of us were too exposed.

"What an asshole," he muttered, settling closer to the ground.

Finally, the door opened. It wasn't the housekeeper like we expected but the big man himself. Kosas glared down at Mari, arms crossed and eyes everywhere. Mari and Grey were armed, but if he notified Cash before we got them out, it was going to be a bloodbath.

Nate made a minor adjustment to the gun, humming in satisfaction when he got a clear shot. Meanwhile, I took as many photos as I could. We'd need them.

We didn't have any earpieces this time, so we couldn't hear what was being said, but I could see the smallest tension in Grey's back as Kosas and Mari talked. "He's baiting them."

Nate snorted. "He thinks Greyson's too whipped to move without Mari's say, I'm sure."

That got a smile out of me. He'd always been her steady protector, but marrying Mari had altered something fundamental in Grey. He held her a little tighter, shielded her a little more, and had a far shorter fuse than he'd possessed before. I had no doubt that if Kosas twitched the wrong way, he'd be dead before Nate took the shot. Greyson would take pleasure in eviscerating him for his wife.

Mari's shoulders relaxed, and she said something that changed everything. Kosas grew red, his shoulders shaking, hands clenched at his sides. He stepped forward, towering over Mari, and I didn't like it one bit.

Nate stiffened, and I saw his finger inch toward the trigger. "What the fuck is he doing?"

"I don't know." My fingers tightened around the camera as Kosas got in my girl's face. She stood there taking it as he yelled hard enough to spit in her face. It was fucking torture. "She better get what she needs from this."

Because if Grey didn't kill Kosas, I was going to.

"It'll work." Nate's low voice was deathly cold, and I knew he was as pissed as I was. No one disrespected our woman.

Despite how much I wanted to reach down there and remove Kosas's head from his body, I had a job to do. So, I angled the camera differently, setting the picture up so it looked like Kosas was inviting Mari in.

We were banking on Cash's hair-trigger with these photos. He needed to believe that his so-called truce was a lie and the *allies* he'd been banking on were working with the enemy.

Us.

Hopefully this would get the other leaders to pull their heads out of their asses and fight back. We needed an army, and the irony was we had one inside the city limits—they just refused to help.

The time for playing both sides was over. They either helped Mari, or they died. There was no way they could sit back and watch it happen after this. Not if they wanted to remain in power.

"I just don't want this to come back and bite us in the ass later. It's becoming a bad habit." Too many times in the last few months, history and other people's choices had made things worse. With the fuse this close to lighting, we couldn't afford another screwup.

Kosas threw his hands up and stormed back inside, slamming the door so hard we could see it tremble from where we were perched, while Mari and Grey walked back to the car. They'd drive around for a while, brushing off whatever tail had most likely watched them walk onto the Sideris compound, before circling back for us.

We stayed silent and alert as they made their way through the guards and to their car. Only when they'd driven off did we pull back and start packing everything up.

It was comfortably quiet for a few minutes before Nate cleared his throat. "I want you to know, I didn't hide Cameron to hurt Mari or any of you. I didn't want it to bite us in the ass."

Shit. I hadn't meant that to be a dig, but he'd obviously taken it as one. Sighing, I sat back against the wall of the roof, the camera bag between my legs. "I wasn't talking about you."

"You should've been. The things I hid, they had consequences."

"Everything does," I countered. "Look at why we're up here. Those idiots made a decision, and now one's going to pay with his life. That's how it goes."

"I know, I just—I needed to say that."

But it didn't seem to make him feel any better. "You know, I watched you while we visited Ace. I saw how you tried to warn her, and it wasn't the first time. Mari made the decision not to ask.

Even though I wish you'd told her, you were respecting her wishes. I can't fault that."

"I do. I should've pushed her."

Smirking, I asked, "Since when does our woman do anything she doesn't want to do?"

He laughed a little. "True."

"You did the right thing, Nate. You *keep* doing the right thing." It was uncomfortable to say it, but that didn't make it less true. Since he'd come back to Mari, he'd done everything in his power to be good for her and make up for his deceit. I couldn't fault him for that.

"I'm trying." He stared at me for a long time before turning to look at the sky. "But you still don't forgive me, do you?"

Did I?

No, I didn't, but the longer he was back, the more I understood why he'd kept his secrets. I just didn't like it. Life was all about doing things you didn't want to do, though, and I'd already decided to forgive Nate. Mari was my family, and he was part of hers. If I wanted the future I was hoping for, I had to let go of my own feelings about Nate. I had to move on.

He'd hurt her. He'd hurt all of us, but he'd hurt himself most, and that was always going to be punishment enough.

"Maybe someday," I said eventually, getting up when my phone went off. "They're on the way back. Let's go."

I offered Nate a hand up, and even though he didn't need it, he took it gladly. "I'm going to make it up to you."

As long as he kept making Mari happy, we'd be square. "I know you will, kid. For now, let's just get through this shitstorm."

Chapter 14
Mari

After our impromptu meeting with Kosas—which was as awful as I expected it to be—we went home and hunkered down for the night.

I knew that our days of peace were numbered, and it was important to me to enjoy as much time with my men as possible. Not that I was complaining. I loved being with them all the time, but these relaxing moments were the ones I cherished when things got hard. They were the seconds I fought for.

Cash wanted us dead, but I wanted to live—for them and for me.

So when they woke me up the next morning with eager faces and breakfast ready, I was both elated and suspicious. They rarely ever ganged up on me, but when they did, it was usually for my benefit.

Only, when I raised a *come back to bed* eyebrow, they laughed.

Grey slid over me, pressing barely there kisses along my skin until I was writhing. Then he slapped my thigh and slipped away. "Up, wife."

What the fuck?

Grumbling—okay, pouting—my way through a shower that no one joined me in, I came out to find clothes on the bed and breakfast made.

It wasn't until I was stuffed—and not in the good way—clothed, and shoved into the SUV that they finally let me ask, "What are you three up to?"

Dominic grinned from the driver's seat, the crooked smile that was just for me making my heart race. "We're taking you out."

"Out?" Considering what we'd done yesterday, I didn't think leaving the penthouse was a smart decision. "Is that a good idea?"

"We'll take care of you," Nate promised.

Dominic nodded. "It's time we had a little bit of fun."

Warmth spread through me at the reminder of just how *fun* they could be. Greyson, who sat next to me, laughed under his breath.

"Don't get your hopes up for that," he whispered. "You'll be disappointed."

"It's your fault I'm so horny," I hissed, but I relented when he pressed the world's softest kisses on my knuckles. "Whatever happens, I don't think I could ever be disappointed with the three of you."

"I want that in writing for the next time I fuck up," Nate joked, and even Dominic laughed.

Greyson's smile brightened his whole face, and he slid his hand onto my thigh, letting it rest there. As we drove, I watched the city I loved.

There were hints of Cash everywhere. Boarded-up windows and people rushing to get inside, but I was stamped all over the city too. My businesses and men patrolling the streets, the faint hints of my family crest in bricks and cement sidewalks. But the biggest indication that Seattle was still mine was the hope. For every person rushing into their home, there were ten more walking casually on the street, trusting that I'd keep them safe.

Knowing I'd die to do so.

No matter where we were going, if all I got out of the day was that desperately needed reminder, I'd be pleased.

It wasn't until we pulled past the copse of evergreens that I realized where we were, and adrenaline rushed through me.

Grey and I didn't take vacations, but when the city got too loud, the cabin was where we went. It wasn't a safe house per se, but it was as close to off the grid as we could allow it to be. We hadn't been in months, despite how much we could've used it.

The cabin was big enough to house all of us, though it was definitely rustic. We hadn't wanted to do more than basic renovations to it. After all, we'd purchased it under more than a few layers of protection, so no one knew it was ours. Bringing contractors out would've ruined that.

I'd thought about what it would be like to have all of us here, to spend a week connecting in whatever way we needed—mostly, naked. It made me nervous that we'd come to our little hidey-hole right now, though.

"Has something happened?"

"No, *reina*." Grey squeezed my thigh in reassurance. "Nothing's going on."

"Are you sure?"

Dominic slid out of the car, opening my door and leaning into my space to press a kiss to the corner of my mouth. The click echoed through the car as my seat belt slithered back to its resting position, Dominic's hands firm on my hips. "I promise everything is okay. Just come with us."

All I needed was Nate's hand and I'd be—oh, there it was. He snuck it onto my knee like he knew I needed the connection.

Looking between all three of them, I sighed. "Fine, but if you're lying, I'm not fucking any of you again."

Dominic threw back his head and laughed. "Whatever you say, baby."

With another squeeze of my hips, he helped me out of the car, letting me slip under his arm so I was plastered to his side. Being close to my men had become my safe place. Touching them, a balm to the anxiety and stress that Cash's bullshit forced me to carry. A buoy for the weight of the world on my shoulders.

It was like being in their presence made everything better. I never wanted that to change.

Fuck, I'm a sap for these men. Gross.

Dominic towed me to the back of the car, where Greyson and Nate opened the liftgate, pulling out case after case.

Unexpected joy shot through me when I saw what they were. "Wait. Are we shooting?"

Nate's easy smile told me I was right, and I tried not to squeal with joy. I was a mafia queen.

I did not squeal.

How long had it been since I'd gone to the shooting range, not just to keep my skills up, but because I wanted to? I used to go all the time. It was a good stress-reliever on days when I couldn't handle my body being hurt any more, but I hadn't been since—fuck, how long had it really been?

The last time I remembered was when...Rey was alive.

The answer came to me with a sad pang of loss. *Too long, then.*

I missed him so much in that moment that I couldn't breathe. Then I thought of what he'd say to the three men who walked with me to the range we'd set up farther into the woods.

He'd love them.

He'd already been a huge fan of Greyson's, constantly telling me to wife that man up, and I remembered the long looks he'd give

Dominic when no one was looking. He was the first to realize we'd been something to each other when we were young.

Then there was Nate. I wasn't sure how Rey would react to his family, but Nate himself was a shoo-in. My cousin had been a sucker for men devoted to their partners, and it was clear that Nate was mine in every way. All Rey ever wanted for me was happiness. Joy. Love. All things I didn't think I'd ever get. All things my men gave me in spades.

So yeah, Rey would've loved them, and in turn, that made me love them more.

Dominic bumped me with his hip. "I hope you don't mind, but we figured the four of us could all use the time away."

He had no idea.

I leaned up to press a kiss to the underside of his jaw. "I couldn't have asked for a better day."

"Don't say that quite yet." He squeezed my shoulder, pressing a kiss to my temple before shooting a wicked grin at the other two. "I thought we'd make it interesting."

"We are not having sex with guns," I said clearly.

Look, I didn't yuck anyone's yums. I knew better than most that the underworld was full of people willing to do lots of things, but that was one I couldn't get behind. Gun safety had been drilled into my head too early in life to think of them as anything more than a weapon. Kudos to those who could, though. They were living on the wild side.

I just wasn't willing to use a sex toy that could end me before I came.

Nate grunted. "I don't love the idea of sex around so many weapons either."

"Agreed," Dominic said easily. "Though I'd be willing to try anything once."

He dipped his head again to whisper ideas against my throat, and I couldn't tell if it was what he said that turned me on or just having him so damn close. I pushed him away with an exaggerated eye roll, though I was smiling when he reeled me back into his grasp.

"I was actually thinking about a little wager with our newest companion."

"Me?" Nate's wide eyes looked confused and honored at the same time.

Fucking adorable.

"Yeah, you. I was thinking we'd have a shooting contest. You win, you choose the tattoo I get. I win, I choose the tattoo you get."

"You want me to give you my tattoo virginity?"

Dominic's face twisted so hard I bit into his chest to hide my laughter. He yelped and bit back, snagging my neck with a quick nip that stung so good. "Not like that, you asshole. I just think if you're going to be part of the Mari Marcosa fan club, you should have a bit of ink."

My heart skipped at how casually he said it, like he wasn't offering Nate the biggest fucking olive branch after everything. The sheen in Nate's eyes said he knew exactly what was happening and that it meant so much to him.

"You don't have to do this," I told Nate. "I'll still love you even if you never get a single tattoo."

He looked down at his arm with a frown. "It's not that I don't want one. I've just never had anything I wanted to get."

"Then don't take the bet," I said with a shrug. "No one deserves to take any part of you that you're not willing to give them."

For a moment, his eyes were so utterly devastated that I wanted to take back what I'd said, until he reeled me in and kissed me. "I love you."

"Love you too."

When he smiled again, it was the real deal, and when he looked at Dominic, I saw the gratitude. "I trust you."

Grey laughed. "With this, I probably wouldn't."

"Rude." Dominic turned back to Nate with an admittedly feral grin. "Best two out of three."

"Deal."

Greyson was unanimously voted to be the judge as he could be trusted to stay neutral, whereas I, apparently, would be easily swayed. My obvious offense, and threat to shoot Dominic for even suggesting it, was another point in their favor.

Before the boys started their competition, we decided to just relax and shoot. Our version of a warm-up. It was only fair since who knew how long it had been since Nate had actually shot a gun. Dominic grumbled about giving him another advantage on top of his training, but he agreed when I reminded him that he was the one who'd decided on a competition with a sharpshooter in the first place.

Hard to argue with that logic.

For a while, there was no conversation, just the muted sounds of our shots behind the earplugs I wore. Every shot, I pictured Cash's face on the target. The man who had taken my brother and cousin from me, who had threatened my home, my livelihood, my safety, and everyone I loved. Who'd ripped the one ally I'd thought was unreachable from my grasp.

I let myself imagine killing him over and over and over, and even though it wasn't real, it helped. The ball of anger wound tight in my gut unraveled just a touch, and by the time I was out of ammo, I felt lighter than before. It wasn't much, but even the smallest change made a big difference.

When we were all warmed up, Greyson walked off to set up the targets for the competition, while Dominic badgered him about making them perfectly even. Meanwhile, Nate pulled me between his legs so we could watch them bicker.

"You okay?" he asked, kissing the side of my neck before laying his head on my shoulder. I liked the ease in it, how right it felt for our bodies to be so close. Leaning in, I let myself just *be* with him.

No pretenses, no life or death, no trouble around us. Just me and my man.

God, it felt good.

"Yes."

Nate's hands, which had been loose on my hips, tightened and pulled me back farther until I could feel every part of him.

"How do you feel?" I asked, grinning when his huffed laugh sounded deliciously pained.

"I think you can feel it for yourself. I'm hard as a rock from watching you," he admitted. "I've thought it since the day we met, but you look so good with a weapon in your hand."

I admit it, I preened. Compliments were not something I had to work for often, but compliments from my men just hit somewhere different. Namely, between my legs.

As subtly as I could, I ground myself into Nate, and he groaned deep in his throat. "What are you doing?"

"Nothing," I said innocently.

"Am I supposed to believe that?"

Dominic whistled, gathering our attention, and I gave Nate's cock one more rub before jumping up. "Believe whatever you want, baby. Don't you have a competition to win?"

I gave him a flutter of my oh-so-innocent eyelashes. When Nate stood, he moved carefully around me like I was about to explode. "Why do I feel like you're up to something?"

Because you're not an idiot.

"I would never." I didn't even try for innocent, just grinned and watched that suspicion bloom thick in his eyes.

"Right."

As my men discussed the rules, I sat by the car, plotting. By the time Greyson sat with me, I knew exactly how I was going to enact my plan.

"I want Dominic to win," I told Grey.

"Then he better shoot well." When I said nothing, he looked at me with suspicion. "I'm not going to throw the competition because you want me to."

What the hell?

"I didn't ask," I growled, more than a little affronted.

I was a criminal, yes, but even I believed in fairness. I just happened to believe it was better at my hands than someone else's.

Grey set his hand on my thigh, squeezing when I refused to look at him in favor of watching Nate and Dominic set up their guns. They'd decided on three rounds, three guns, with the targets moving farther away each time. The last shot required a rifle, which felt like a mistake on Dominic's part, but since they hadn't asked my opinion, I didn't offer it. He'd figure it out himself.

"I didn't mean it like that," Grey said softly. "I'm sorry."

I knew he didn't, but I wasn't going to let the chance go by.

"Apologize by helping me."

I didn't need his help to enact my plan, but I wanted it. Half because it was payback and half because I still felt his lips on my skin from this morning.

"Nate agreed to this, knowing Dominic could win. He offered up his skin, and I want to see if he'll really go through with it." Mostly because I knew Dominic. Whatever tattoo he was planning, I'd like.

"What's your plan?"

"A little reminder of what's to come. Mainly, me."

When Grey looked over at me with a wolfish grin, I knew I'd won. "Come here, wife."

Hell yes. Nate was going down.

Chapter 15
Mari

Greyson pulled me between his legs like Nate had. As the other two began their first round, he unbuttoned my shorts just enough to wedge his hand into my panties. Since this wasn't about fucking or teasing me mercilessly, he just sank his fingers inside me, forcing a gasp out of my throat right as Nate took his first shot.

It went wide.

He flipped around, gun pointed down, and immediately scowled. "Should have known you wouldn't play fair."

"I don't know what you're talking about," I breathed as Grey's palm ground against my clit. "I was horny, and Grey was available."

Nate lifted an eyebrow. "Is that so? Your greedy little pussy decided it couldn't wait ten fucking minutes?"

I shrugged, arching into Grey as he drove his fingers in deeper. "What can I say? You handling weapons makes me hot."

Nate's eyes flared, and he stepped toward me until Dominic's shot broke the tension.

Dead center.

"One point for me," he said gleefully. His eyes were smoldering over Nate's shoulder, even as he gave me a thumbs-up.

Nate glowered, but I refused to back down. If he really didn't want the tattoo, all he had to do was say so, but he wouldn't. He was in this, just like we were.

The moment stretched as he moved his gaze to where Grey touched me, where my hips were writhing, where I felt so wet, I was nearly dripping. I could almost hear his thick swallow as he tore those eyes away.

Nate's jaw was tight as he stepped back into position, lifting the next gun with precision. With his own special form of skill, Greyson twisted his fingers, hitting that spot that made me cry out.

"That's it, *reina*," he crooned in my ear. "Give him all the noises you can."

As Grey started fucking me faster, the only sounds around us were the wind brushing through the trees, the birds chirping, and my indecent moans.

Nate's shot cracked through the air before hitting the target. Dead center.

Motherfuck.

I bit my lip, wondering if it was even worth it to keep going, when the man in question turned back to us with an unrepentant grin. "You'll have to try harder than that, angel."

He sounded cool and collected, but his eyes were locked between my thighs like he could see through the fabric, and I wanted more. I wanted him to lose control. I wanted to win.

Game on.

Dominic took his shot. Too high.

They were tied.

At my disappointed sigh, Grey chuckled. "Come on, baby. Show them what you can really do."

I don't know what he did, some twist of his fingers or shift of his hand, but the orgasm that had been steadily creeping suddenly crested. I was so surprised, I yelped, digging my nails into his thighs and grinding on him until the only thing keeping me steady was his hand on my pussy.

It was so intense, I had to shut my eyes. I didn't know what happened with Nate's last shot until he cursed.

Wide again.

"Motherfucker." He put the safety on and set the rifle on the table. At his side, Dominic's hooded gaze was focused on me, not the target. He just stood there, watching me writhe.

"Take your shot, asshole," Nate snapped. His body trembled, but it wasn't rage. It was need.

Deep, feral, and desperate enough to raze a city.

The moan crept out of my throat before I could even think about it.

Dominic shook as if coming out of a trance, twisted to lift the gun, and fired. He barely had a chance to aim, but there was something about the way he stood that told me he'd done it.

I was right.

Dead center.

Dominic won. *I won.*

Nate stalked over to grab me by the throat, tilting my head up so I could see his face. He yanked me out of Grey's lap and into his arms, keeping that hand around my throat.

"You cheated," he growled at me before twisting back to Grey. "And you let her."

"She wasn't part of the contest, and there were no rules saying she couldn't interfere," Grey corrected.

"Some rules don't need to be stated," Nate argued.

"All rules should be stated beforehand."

There was some standoff between them, and I ran my hand up Nate's chest, bringing his face closer to mine to cut it off. "Let me make it up to you."

His eyes pinned me in place as he pressed his very hard cock into me. God, I wanted it inside me. "How do you plan to do that?"

I bit my lip, knowing exactly what to do. "Come find out."

Nate glared at me, heat and interest pooling in his eyes. He let go of my throat, just to latch on to the back of my neck instead. The way he held me was pure ownership. What did it say that I liked it as much as I did?

Twisting a finger into the loop of his jeans, I tugged him closer.

"Pack up," I told the other two, towing Nate behind me to the sound of Dominic's playful complaints. I whipped open the car door and shoved my captive into the back seat. Thankfully, the SUV had enough room that I could kneel between his legs.

He stared down at me, eyes blown with desire and voice raspy. "You think a blow job is going to make up for some shitty-ass tattoo?"

I felt every word thrum through me like an electric charge, practically vibrating across my skin as I ran my hands down his thighs. When I got close to his dick, he grabbed my wrists, halting my progress.

I liked that he was fighting me on this. We'd had a lot of me fighting, him bending lately. It felt good to be the one on my knees.

Leaning forward, I pressed a soft kiss on his clothed cock, enjoying how his hips kicked up at that small touch. His hands released me almost without his volition, and I took that as consent to move forward. I undid his jeans until I could see his cock pressed against his briefs. My mouth watered at him hot and hard and ready for me. "You know I'd never allow that. It'll be a tasteful tattoo. Promise."

I figured Dominic wouldn't do anything too embarrassing, but I'd have Grey make sure of it, just in case. Nate hummed, running his hand through my hair and lifting his hips to help me slide his jeans down, revealing muscles and all that bare, naked skin. "You always take such good care of us."

Why did that light me up inside? Why did I need him to tell me I was doing a good job?

Because this matters, my brain whispered.

It did. *They* did.

I'd never been in an actual relationship before them. Casual sex and long-term hookups, but no love. No commitment. Now, I was married to Greyson and committed to the other two. New or not, this was huge and real and the one thing in my life I was wholly unprepared for. I needed to know that I wasn't fucking this up.

"I'm trying."

"You're doing." Nate's correction made me smile, but I wanted to focus on the task at hand.

He was barely out of his briefs before I was leaning forward for a slow lick along the underside of his cock.

"Fucking Christ," he whispered, one hand tight in my hair while the other fisted against the seat.

I didn't even get him completely in my mouth before a throat cleared nearby, and we both turned dazed eyes to see Dominic and Greyson with half the cases loaded in their arms.

"Is this a party or a show?" Dominic asked.

"A show," Nate growled, turning back to me. He curled his hand around my neck and jaw in a possessive grip. Those eyes, dark blue and desperate, held me captive. "This is for us. Right now, you're mine and only mine."

Um, yes.

Even though I'd just come, my panties were soaked, and I shifted, trying to get some friction on my clit and knowing he wouldn't let me.

"What do you like, Mari? How do you want to take me?"

It was a struggle to breathe through the arousal, let alone think, but I did. I had to. We'd never actually talked about my limits, and he needed to know them. Nate knew me so well and we'd been through so much, I sometimes forgot we were still new to each other. "You can pull my hair and fuck my face, but don't shove me onto your cock. I don't mind choking, but I like being able to pull away."

"I can hold you still, then? Keep you exactly where I want you as I use your mouth?"

Oh God. "Yes, please."

"Fuck me." His cock jumped in my hand, and I stroked it absently. "Tap my hips twice if you need me to stop, even just to breathe. I don't want this if it's going to hurt you."

"I'll tap out if I have to."

"I know, angel." He ran his thumb across my lower lip. "Now, be my good girl. Make it up to me and suck me off."

With Nate's hesitation gone, I dove onto him, alternating between shallow bobs and deep, sucking pulls. Twirling my tongue around the width of him while I stroked what I couldn't reach with my mouth. I needed him to lose his mind and he was right there with me, but I knew the control was a lie.

I moved because Nate let me. I took him because he wanted me to, and when he was sick of giving me even a hint of control, he framed my cheeks and took. Those powerful muscles rippled as he flexed, lifting his hips off the seat until they pressed tight against my face, using my mouth for his pleasure. Over and over, he gave me all he had until everything narrowed down to this. Us.

He split his time between praising me to the sky and back, chanting my name, and saying *mine, mine, mine* like he needed the world to hear it. Maybe he did. Maybe he needed to claim me just as much as I needed to claim him. That deep-seated desire to brand my name on his skin so no one could look at him without understanding who he belonged to.

Maybe that was why I was so dead set on the tattoo. It was my way of tying him to me forever. Ink on skin. Permanence in the most deliciously painful way.

When his thighs tensed under my hand and he squeezed my throat, I knew what he was planning to do.

He panted, chest heaving as he stared down at me. "You ready?"

Since I couldn't move, all I could do was nod and groan around him, making him hiss.

"Good girl." Then his hips were snapping harder, and it was all I could do to breathe through my nose as he took and took and took. "I can feel myself inside you, angel, and it feels so fucking right."

When he came, it was with his dick as far down my throat as it could go and a groan that flooded my panties. Before I could finish swallowing, Nate hauled me off my knees and halfway onto the seat. His big hand slipped between my legs, and a hard yank had my shorts in tatters before he pulled me up and impaled me on his cock.

I immediately cried out. Going from empty to so fucking full was an adjustment, but I wanted it. I wanted that struggle to fit him inside me, the tension of fighting for every inch as his hands shoved me down.

By the time our hips were flush, I was moaning his name like a prayer.

"Holy shit," someone whispered, but I didn't look. There was no one else right now.

The clap of Nate's palm against my ass was its own gunshot as he urged my hips higher, faster.

"That's it, baby. Ride me." I was already so close I could feel myself rippling around him, clenching, pulling him tighter inside me. "God, yes. First that mouth, now this pussy. You're such a good girl for me, angel."

On and on, he whispered into my ear, his body relentless as he worked me over. I'd never felt more frantic. I needed this. Needed him inside me where I could keep him, always. When I came, I dragged claw marks down his throat and shoulders, needing that visceral reminder of this moment and telling him so. He groaned, hips thrusting to meet me as he came again.

Afterward, he didn't pull out, and I didn't get up. I just sat there on his lap while we regulated our breathing together.

"Did I make it up to you?" I finally asked, and he laughed, making the both of us groan.

"Yeah, baby. That more than made up for it."

"Thank God. I'm not sure we could take another episode of that show."

A pack of baby wipes landed on the seat beside us, and I looked over, startled to see Dominic and Grey still there. When Dominic caught my eye, he winked. "Great show, *mariposa*. Next time, you'll have to invite us."

Grey shoved him away with a playful grimace and eyes full of love. "We'll let you two clean up."

After a serious look at Nate, Greyson shut the door and locked us in our own little world.

Nate pried his hands off my hips, brushing sweaty hair out of my face. "Are you okay?"

Admittedly, it was hard to focus when my whole body was thrumming from my orgasms and...were my ears ringing?

"Come on, angel. I need words. Are you okay?"

"Yes."

"Are you sure?" He looked away, and the concern was so heavy, it hurt my heart.

I pressed closer, draping myself over him. "I'm sure. I loved this. You don't need to worry about me."

"Yeah, I do."

It was that simple for him. He cared for me, so he worried.

He'll never love anyone else like this. The thought came quick and heavy, but it rang with truth. There was no one else for Nate but me. We'd fought for each other, shoved and pulled our way back from the edge.

No one would give him what I did, just like no one else could give me what he did. The chance to be both parts of ourselves. The killer and the man, the one who gave so freely and took so beautifully. The woman and the queen, who wanted to save and be saved.

He was mine. All mine.

And I was his.

After cleaning us off, Nate dug into one of the bags in the back for a new pair of shorts for me, blushing when he threw the ripped ones away. It was so sweet, it made me laugh. When my voice came out hoarse from all the ways he'd made me his, he laughed too, and the world felt brighter for it.

"Where to now? Back home?" I asked when I was dressed.

I tried to move to the other side of the car, but Nate hauled me back to the seat beside him with a hand on my hip. "You stay here."

Well, okay then. I grinned at him, wrapping my fingers around his and sinking into his chest when he threw his arm around me.

"We gotta go back to town," Dominic said as he hopped in and started the car, Grey following soon after. "Nate's appointment is in an hour."

"My appointment," Nate said slowly, glaring at me with suspicion.

I lifted my hands in surrender. "I didn't even know we were going out today."

Dominic laughed at the obvious skepticism. "I didn't know who'd win, so I let them know it could be either of us when I called to make the appointment."

Nate rolled his eyes before relaxing back in his seat, giving my hip a light slap. "Come here."

My smile grew, and I leaned against his chest, happy to snuggle while we had time. As soon as the car started moving, the orgasms caught up to me, and I yawned wide enough to crack my jaw.

"Sleep, angel. We've got you." Nate's soft voice was the last thing I heard before I dozed off.

The nap was short-lived but so needed, especially when Nate woke me up with a searing kiss.

When we got inside the local shop, he seemed happy with the flash sheets and workbooks of all the artists, even if he didn't know which one was his. When the artist called him back, I went with.

"I'll hold your hand the whole time if you want," I promised.

He grinned and kissed me lightly. "I'll be fine, Mari."

In fact, he didn't need me at all.

The instant he saw the tattoo, while I was distracted looking somewhere else, he kicked me out of the room, forcing me into the lobby of the shop Dominic had closed down for us. "No peeking, angel."

Sitting idly wasn't my style, but I tried. It got harder when Greyson and Dominic decided they wanted tattoos too.

I wanted to be annoyed with waiting so fucking long, but I was riding the high of the day. Being together, coming so hard I nearly blacked out, connecting with my men. Hard to be irritated after a day like that.

When the buzzing stopped and they finally called me over, I practically skipped to the back of the shop.

The second I got a look at the tattoo, I knew why I'd pushed so hard for Nate to get it. I had no doubt Dominic had chosen it for me.

I hadn't realized Dominic and Grey were getting matching ones, though.

It took effort to swallow back the tears that sprang up at the sight of three identical black-and-gray crowns on their chests, right over their hearts. It was their own way of committing to me, to our little family, and I adored them for it.

"I love them," I said quietly, my voice thick with tears and all the happiness I couldn't quite contain. I huffed a laugh as Greyson hauled me into a hug, pressing kisses against my head.

"We love you, *reina.*"

Dominic smiled softly at me before holding out a hand to Nate. "Consider this your official induction into the fan club, Black. Welcome home."

Nate stared at him, eyes heavy with the same feelings that ran through me before he shook that hand and smiled. "So glad to be here."

Chapter 16
Mari

I knew Cash worked quickly, but I was still in bed with Nate when the phone rang less than a day later.

"We need to meet." Kosas sounded more subdued than he'd been when I'd shown up at his house. He'd been nervous then, eyes darting back and forth on the street like he was expecting an Ace to show up and kill us both. Hell, maybe he was. I had no idea what the terms of the truce with Cash were. When I'd suggested he reconsider it, Kosas nearly spat in my face before slamming the door on us. Rude, but not a shock.

Still, I didn't think he was calling because he'd seen the light.

My stomach twisted, even as I responded calmly. "Last we spoke, you told me to get lost. What's changed?"

"Everything."

One weighted word and I knew I'd meet him. I heard more than just exhaustion; Kosas sounded bleak and desperate. If I didn't get to him now, Cash might reel him in too far for me to ever pull him back.

"Beanistry, one hour."

The local coffee shop was as close to neutral territory as I could guarantee at the moment. Kosas grunted his agreement. "Don't bring your entire army."

Scoffing, I went to the closet and pulled out clothes and weapons. If he wanted to meet, there wasn't time to argue about this. "I don't leave the house without my men."

Nate grumbled about being woken up as he got ready behind me, rummaging around in the dresser where he kept his stuff, despite his room being down the hall. I refused to tell him or the others how much I liked having their things in my room. It made it feel so much homier.

"I'm not asking you to come alone. I just—I need this to stay between us for now."

Again, he sounded cagey and uncomfortable. "We'll see."

When I hung up the phone, Nate was pulling a shirt over his chest. The tattoo was covered with Saniderm, but I could still see the vague outline of my crown on his skin and I liked it.

"Stop looking at me like that when I don't have time to fuck you."

"Who says we don't have time?" We definitely didn't.

"I do. Need to head over to Beanistry and scope it out. Make sure it's not a trap for you."

Humming, I pulled him in by the hips and laid a kiss above the tattoo. "I like this."

Nate wrapped a hand in my hair and pulled my head back so he could give me a kiss that made me weak in the knees and wetter than I should've been. As if he knew what he'd done, he smirked. "Show me how much you like it later."

"I will."

By the time I was done, I'd have that man covered in my marks.

With the two of us grinning, he let me go. "You want Dominic for this?"

Knowing whatever happened was Cash's fault—and not wanting Kosas to transfer the blame to Nate—I nodded. "Please."

Thankfully, he wasn't upset. Just pressed a kiss to my forehead. "I'll be watching. Be safe, angel."

"You too."

When he was gone, I slipped into the new outfit and grabbed a few weapons I could easily hide. The point was to look as unarmed as possible, to remind Kosas I didn't consider him a threat. Until I found a real way to end this war, mind games were all I had, and I was going to play to the very end.

We made a quick stop by the office floor to give Greyson a heads-up—he'd met with Killer, hoping to touch base before anyone else was awake, lest we make the wrong people suspicious. He gave me a stern warning to watch my back and a smack on the ass that made Killer's whole face turn red before I left, glaring him black and blue. Dominic took one look at my face, wrapped an arm around my shoulder, and laughed himself silly at the kid's expense until I elbowed him in the diaphragm.

I felt much better after that.

The drive was short, and even though the hour wasn't up, I wanted to get there before Kosas. As we pulled in, my phone buzzed with a message from Nate.

He's already inside. No signs of an ambush, but we'll keep watch.

I knew he'd grabbed Moore and a few others for additional eyes, so if he said it was clear, I believed him.

Turning my phone off. Call Dominic twice for emergencies.

Got it. Love you, angel.

Love you too.

Relaying the relevant parts of the conversation to Dominic, I was more than comfortable leisurely hopping out of the car and strolling inside.

Beanistry was a quaint seaside café that smelled heavenly of fresh-brewed coffee and homemade pastries. The tables were scuffed and the leather chairs had seen better days, but the interior was warm and inviting despite the obvious use. Exactly the opposite kind of place I normally met people in the underworld.

"I'll get you a drink and check the place out," Dominic whispered, kissing my cheek before making his way to the counter. Not a problem since I'd already spotted my target.

Kosas sat at a table in the farthest corner of the café, his back half turned to the wall, staring down into a cup of coffee like he'd never seen it before. When I got closer, he looked up, and my blood froze.

I'd never seen someone look so empty before.

"You're early," I said carefully.

"He killed them." Fuck, even his voice was empty. The words sank into my skin, but I ignored them. I had to.

Sliding into the chair, I made sure my entire back faced the wall. Last thing I needed was a bullet or knife in the back.

When Dominic sauntered over with our drinks, he slid his chair next to mine and slung an arm over the back of my chair.

"We're good," he whispered, and I picked up my cup, comfortable now that he'd confirmed we weren't about to end up at the center of a bloodbath.

"Killed whom?"

"My son and daughter-in-law."

Tyrone and Chloe. The coffee in my mouth turned to ash, and I struggled to swallow it. Dominic rested his hand on my shoulder where Kosas wouldn't see, giving me strength when guilt tried to drown me.

We'd known this was a possibility. Cash wasn't going to let this go without a fight, but we'd assumed he'd go after Kosas himself, not the family. We assumed he'd play fair.

Stupid Mari.

Kosas cleared his throat, though his entire being vibrated with agony. "He said he saw pictures of us meeting. Thought I backstabbed him. Said he'd lost trust in me, so I was going to lose something important in return. He shot them in their home, just watching a movie on the couch. The only good thing was they didn't see it coming. Just there one second, gone the next."

Every broken word slid into my skin like a dagger, but I took it all. I'd made this call, and despite losing two good people, I stood by it. The leaders needed a wake-up call, and even though I'd started this, I wasn't stupid. Tyrone's time was always going to be limited because Cash was always going to use him against Kosas. We just pushed him to do it sooner rather than later. Chloe, though. As she was someone I'd considered a friendly acquaintance, her death stung.

"I'm sorry for your loss. They were good people."

Kosas shifted, his face changing from blank to enraged. "Cash needs to pay for this. He took my boy. He took my daughter. They were trying for a baby. Tyrone wanted to go home to Greece and retire early so they could have a normal life with their kid. Said he'd already seen too much fucking war in all of this. I was gonna let them go. I *should* have let them go. He deserved more than he got." His voice was thick before he stopped himself, taking a long drink of coffee to clear it. When he spoke, it was so quiet it was almost impossible to hear. "You were right. Cash was never going to leave us alone. The truce was a lie."

It was, but no one should've learned this way. I knew all too well how much losing family killed the soul. Forcing my thoughts away from Rey, Chloe, and Tyrone, I kept my mind on the prize.

Defeat Cash, save the city. A few precious lives to protect hundreds of thousands. That was the price I'd paid, and I wouldn't let their sacrifice be in vain.

I'm sorry.

Leaning back in my chair, I forced my face to look sympathetic yet distant. I had to regain what ground this shitshow with Cash had made me lose. The city needed a strong leader, and Kosas was primed to put me right back on top where I belonged. It just sucked that it had to be this way.

"You gave Cash power in the city that he didn't need. Now, you need to take it back."

"I can't."

"Why not?" When he didn't answer, I continued. "He's got you leashed so fucking tight, you're choking and can't even feel it. The longer you hesitate, the more he wins."

He huffed into his cup, looking truly broken. "What do you want me to do, Mari?"

"Get revenge."

His head whipped up, eyes blazing as they watched me. "How?"

"Help me convince the others to join us."

"No. Just us."

I knew the spirit in him, the vengeance that crawled through his skin like acid, but he had to look beyond it. You couldn't win a war without using your brain. "You and I aren't enough to take him down. To be honest, I'm not sure that we'll be able to oust him even if we all work together. He's got roots so fucking deep here, I'm not certain we'll ever get him out, but we have to try."

"I just want him to pay for what he did to my family."

"He will, *if* you help me."

Kosas sighed, but I could see he was on board. "They won't agree."

"Then they'll die, at my hands or Cash's. But with you on my side, they're more likely to listen."

His sigh was weary and grieving. "I'll call a meeting."

"Today."

"Today," he agreed as he stood.

Before he turned away, I called out, "I'm sorry for your loss."

"So am I." Kosas's shoulders slumped. "I'll be in touch."

When it was just Dominic and me, he wrapped his arm around my shoulder and forced my head to his chest. "You did the right thing, *mariposa*."

"I know."

All was fair in love and war. It didn't mean I had to like it.

* * *

Hours later, I strode into the meeting room with my men at my back.

The last time we'd been there, Cash had been in my seat, playing fake king. It was nice to see my place waiting for me again.

"Gentlemen."

"If this is a ploy to speak about the truce, you're wasting our time," Haru said. Not much of a talker, but he was always quick to get to the heart of things when he did.

"We're not going to change our minds, Mari," Ajilon agreed, not unkindly. He seemed tense, eyes darting around. I wondered how much Cash was tormenting him out of view.

"I have." Everyone's attention snapped to Kosas. He cleared his throat, staring down at his fingers. "My son and his wife are dead. Cash killed them."

Two-Bit's eyes narrowed, and I was struck by how good of an actor he was. "Why?"

"He thought I was meeting with Mari behind his back. Didn't even ask if it was true, just broke into their home and slaughtered them."

Ajilon murmured a prayer under his breath while Haru stared at Kosas long and hard. "Were you?"

"No." There was a world of grief in that one word.

He wished he had been. At least then, his family would've died for a good cause. It was always harder when deaths were senseless. Those were the kind you couldn't come back from.

A tap of my fingers against the table drew everyone's attention to me. "I went to see Kosas, to try to get him to reconsider the truce. He refused, but it got back to Cash."

The accusations in their gazes were easy to read.

You did this. You killed them. You'll get us killed too.

The worst part was, I couldn't refute any of it. I *had* done it. I'd gotten Chloe and Tyrone killed, and I'd do it again if it meant this war was over before we lost even more.

Did that make me a bad person? Probably. But Two-Bit was right. Sometimes rulers had to make decisions others couldn't to protect their territory and their people. What was unfathomable to them was another day's work for me. I'd forgotten that in the mayhem of Cash's infiltration, but I wouldn't forget again. I'd damage my own city if it meant the cockroach would be squashed with it.

Lifting my chin, I stared them all down. "You offered Cash a truce, and he broke it. Are you going to let it slide, or are you going to help me punish him?"

Unsurprisingly, Kieran was the first to offer support. He'd learned immediately that I was no longer playing games when I'd woken him up still warm from his daddy's blood. "I'm in."

"You know my answer," Kosas said quietly.

Two-Bit looked at Griz, then back at me with a sigh. "It can't be worse than what's happened. The Vipers are in."

All that was left were Haru and Ajilon.

My old friend stared out the window. "It's obvious we made a mistake with Cash. He was never going to leave us alone."

"Does that mean you're in?" Grey asked.

Ajilon nodded. "This city has been my home for a long time. I won't see it go to a madman."

And then there was one.

"We can't piss off a hornet. We either kill him, or we die trying." Haru's steely expression gave nothing away, but there was more tension in him than I'd ever seen.

"We won't," I promised. "When it's time to take him out, it's him or us."

With a steady nod, he agreed, and a wave of relief nearly bowled me over.

I did it. I finally got them on my side. Part of me was pissed it had taken so long, but I didn't care when it got me one step closer to eradicating Cash and his Aces.

We're coming for you, asshole.

Two-Bit leaned back in his chair. "I'm assuming you have a plan after all this."

"We attack," Nate said.

* * *

Kosas glared at Nate, and once again, I was glad I'd brought Dominic to meet with him earlier. It was clear that the sins of the brother were getting laid at Nate's feet. With a snarl, he twisted to glare at me. "You expect us to fight with your fuckboy at the helm?"

"No, I expect you to fight under me, but you have to admit Nate's a good asset to have."

"If he doesn't stab us in the back the way he did his brother," he muttered.

Deep breaths, Mari. He's grieving and lashing out. Even so, it was hard for me to rein in the urge to put him in his place for good.

"I'm going to give you that one shot since you've had a rough day, but I won't have anyone talk shit about Nate. Certainly not in my presence."

Kieran shifted uncomfortably in his chair. "We're aware of your feelings for him, but how do we know he's loyal? He doesn't wear your mark."

"Yes, he does."

Without my asking, Nate stripped off his tee, tossing it on the table and baring the tattoo on his chest. Dominic pulled the collar of his shirt down low enough to see the top of his crown, while Greyson carefully unbuttoned his shirt to flash his as well. The leaders watched warily as my men stood there, proud and unashamed.

It hit me again, with the three of them sharing their marks like it meant everything to them, how much I loved them. How devoted they were to me. *How fucking lucky I was.* I'd do whatever it took to make sure they didn't regret choosing me.

Nate stepped up, planting his palms on the table and keeping steady eyes on Kosas. "I'd die for Mari. Almost did, in fact. Can you say the same when you ignored her warnings? Or do you not agree that your son would still be here if you had listened when she was speaking?"

I expected Kosas to rage out, as he often did. Grief was an uncertain thing, and I didn't want Nate getting caught in the crossfire. Instead, Kosas dropped his head, and the guilt in that one motion nearly undid me.

"Nate," I said quietly. Regardless of how much I agreed with him, I was not going to rub salt into that wound, especially when we were the ones who had exacerbated the issue. I had no doubt

Cash would have gone after their families sooner rather than later, but that didn't mean we hadn't pushed him over the edge.

I barely heard his resigned sigh before he took another approach. "I know my brother, as much as I can know someone as unhinged as Cash. I'm helping whether you like it or not, but let me be clear: your trust isn't important to me. Mari's is. If you want my help, you have it. If not, then we'll do this without you."

The rest of the leaders looked at me, and I backed him up. "I agree with everything Nate said. He's our best shot at catching Cash off guard. If you don't like it, you can leave. But make no mistake. If you walk out of this room, you're my enemy as well as Cash's. I don't have time for hurt feelings and scared men. You're either with me, or you're dead. Choose."

I let them sit in silence, giving them one final chance to leave. I wouldn't stop them, wouldn't even hunt them down right away. They'd spend the rest of their lives looking over their shoulders until I finally decided to put them out of their misery.

Truthfully, I didn't want to do it. I wanted them to join me. I wanted my city put to rights and Cash's influence burned out of the core of it.

Finally, Kieran looked at each of the others before turning to me. "We follow you."

Thank fuck. I smiled. "Let's get to work."

Chapter 17
Nate

Hoping to deal Cash a blow he couldn't come back from, we decided on a three-pronged attack. Guns, money, and drugs, all struck simultaneously. Granted, he could get more guns and money eventually, but it would take time, and the loss would be a hit to his reputation.

The real prize was going to be the drugs. If we took out his stash house, we made him look incompetent to Paez. Losing the drug money route—and the cartel's favor—would not only be crippling; it would be deadly. You didn't lose the cartel's product without forfeiting your life, and Cash knew it. It would throw him off guard, and while we were certain he'd panic and get more dangerous, he'd also be more likely to slip up and lose control of his people.

Exactly what we needed.

My body buzzed, and adrenaline rushed through my veins as I

tried and failed to calm myself. For the first time since this had all started, it felt like we were landing a solid blow against my brother, and I needed it. Mari needed it.

The city needed it.

Ready or not, here we come, fucker.

"Position check. Green team in position." Mari's voice crackled over the comms unit. The stash houses were all separated, but only by a mile or two each. She and Dominic were leading Kosas and his men to the money stash, and fighting my instinctive need to be by her side was hell. I hated being separated from her, but we'd made the decision together that keeping me from the group was the best call. We wanted to avoid giving the Aces a bigger target if they caught on to what we were doing early, and having Mari and me in the same group was waving a bright red flag in front of them.

I hated it, though.

"Black team in position," Haru's quiet voice said. Along with Two-Bit's men, the Yakuza leader had a contingency of Marcosa men and Greyson himself to keep them on their toes while they went for the guns.

"White team in position," I said, desperately wanting to hear Mari one last time.

I'd been saddled with Ajilon and the Irish fuck about four miles from where Mari and Dominic were at the farthest stash, and I felt every foot separating us acutely.

Focus.

Ajilon didn't speak to me, only talked quietly to his men while keeping a keen eye on the horizon. Kieran gave me a wide berth, and I didn't blame him. He might have agreed with our killing his father, but he knew one wrong move and he could be next. Or, he would be if we didn't need him. But since our ragtag team was going after the thing Cash loved most, Kieran was safe. At least until we found the dope.

The warehouse was deserted. Windows were broken and graffiti was everywhere, but there was something ominous about it. Something that screamed *stay away*. I had no doubt that anyone who stumbled across it would beeline right back to where they came from.

I couldn't wait to burn that shit to the ground.

"Get in, get out, and stay clean," Mari said firmly, and I sent up a silent prayer that our family would make it through this unscathed. "On my mark."

As one, we lifted our guns, and I forced the part of me that worried for my people into the back of my brain. Fear could come later. Right now, it was time for a reckoning.

Falling into that familiar headspace was like settling back into my skin. I'd forgotten how much I liked it.

"Three, two, one. Mark."

We surged forward as one unit, our steps quiet and our guns silenced. Everyone focused on getting as far inside the warehouse as we could before the alarm went out.

The first set of guards got broken necks before they even realized they were being invaded, and the second set fell just as fast. The sounds of quiet breaths, grunts, and pained yells came over the comms, but I tuned them out. I couldn't help anyone if I was dead, and getting distracted was a surefire way to end up six feet under.

"Outside's clear," Kieran muttered, head swiveling as we took in the empty landscape. "Cash doesn't have much protection here."

"He does. They're just inside." He stared at me, and I shook my head. "He wants this place to look abandoned. Armed guards roaming the grounds will give the opposite impression."

I was tempted to ask if Kieran had men guarding every building in his territory, but it wasn't the time. Not to mention, I wasn't sure if I liked the asshole. No use giving him free advice if we were going to kill him later. Then we'd have to work harder.

Once the grounds were clear, we waited just long enough for our men to surround the building before setting up next to the door. "Breaching in three, two, one."

Kieran and I moved in sync, opening the door and diving on the two closest men. Stealth had its place and we were working hard to maintain it, but eventually, we were going to lose the element of surprise. I just hoped we cleared the warehouse before someone called in the cavalry.

Ajilon moved to my other side, sandwiching me between the other two leaders, and I fought down the anxiety curling around my shoulders. They weren't stupid enough to plan a hit on me right now, were they?

No. Mari made it clear that she'd kill anyone who came for me.

I didn't like it though, and the small smirk on Kieran's face said he knew it.

Cheeky fucker.

Ajilon lifted his gun, taking out two snipers from the rafters before ducking behind a stack of crates to get two more. We'd put silencers on the guns, but anyone who knew what to listen for would be able to identify the muffled sounds.

"Clear the building," I said.

With a nod, Kieran directed half the men to fan out and clear the left side of the building while we took the other half to the right.

Although I'd never been in the warehouse before, I knew what to look for. Neurotic or not, Cash was a creature of habit. He liked his drugs to be well-hidden yet easily accessible to him. When we found the office, I knew exactly where to go.

The coat closet looked normal until I peeled away the back wall.

"I fucking hate rabbit holes," Kieran muttered. "How likely is it he's got men down here?"

"He'll have two, but no more."

That got me twin frowns from him and Ajilon, who kept position by the office door. "Why not?"

"Because that means trusting them not to take his drugs, and he no longer does." After the issues with Cooper and Renaldi, Cash had taken his drugs underground. He kept the actual stashes separate from the cut houses to avoid any more *incidents.*

I couldn't do much while I was with him, but making Cash paranoid enough to give us this chance to go after him was worth every day in that hellhole. It had taken time—*so much time*—but I'd slowly dripped information into my brother's ear related to my "suspicions" about his dealers and the men he used to keep the drugs safe. He wasn't even mad they were stealing his money—he was *pissed* they stole his dope.

Cooper and Renaldi had been strung up by sunrise, and the cut houses were disbanded by sundown. An entire system destroyed in a day.

"Green team, cleared." Mari's voice came as I took my first steps into the darkness, and I let out a relieved breath.

"Black team, cleared." Grey's response a second later was another weight off my shoulders.

"White team approaching the stash," Ajilon answered quietly.

The three of us crept through the tunnel, keeping our steps light and our guns raised. Who knew what nasty surprises Cash had waiting for us.

The first came when we hit the end of the tunnel and peeled the next wall back. Bright light blinded us long enough for someone to send a punch to my jaw and another to my gut. I ducked out of the way, blinking fast to get my eyes to adjust again. I was still seeing shadows when I shoved up from the ground and rammed myself into the stomach of the guard who'd come after me.

Gunshots exploded in the hidden basement, and I grunted as my ears rang. Thank God for ear protection. Otherwise, we'd have been screwed.

We tumbled over each other, trading blows and hissed curses until I got an opening and took it. He feinted to the left, hoping to distract me for an uppercut. I mirrored him, letting him take the swing but dodging at the last second. Instead of punching him, I took a knife from my belt and buried it in his neck. Warm blood coated my skin as I twisted the blade, making sure it was a kill shot. The last thing we needed was him surviving and coming back for us.

"Did you have to make it messy?" Kieran asked, brushing some of the splatter that had gotten on his clothes. "I almost made it out of here clean."

"What can I say? My girl likes me in blood," I said flippantly. Mari's irritated grunt hit my ears, and I grinned. She was going to kill me later.

Worth it.

Finding nothing in the dead man's pockets, I was about to stand, when the hairs on the back of my neck stood up. Reaching for my gun, I spun, only to come face-to-face with the barrel of another. Before the Ace could fire, his head jerked back almost at the same time I heard the depressed air of the silenced shot.

Twisting, I found Ajilon standing there with a grim look on his face as his men swarmed the hidden room the final guard had come out of.

"Thank you."

"I did it for Mari." After getting confirmation that everyone was dead, he gave the update. "White team, cleared."

"You find the drugs?"

"In sight." We stared at the massive stack of cocaine bricks in the center of the room. It was more than I'd ever seen at once before, even with Cash's penchant for the drug. Easily millions of dollars' worth of product that we were going to steal. Yeah, he was going to be pissed.

There was a moment of silence before Mari's voice came down the line. "Any losses?"

"None on our part," I said, knowing she needed reassurance as much as I did. "You?"

"Two of Kosas's men got shot, but they'll live. Everyone else is fine."

"Same here," Grey said.

"Good." Her voice held a wealth of relief when she finally answered. "Get everything loaded and rendezvous at the docks in an hour."

"You got it." As the other teams signed off, Ajilon started barking orders, but I held up my hand. "Wait."

Pulling out my phone, I made sure to take a full video of the drugs as well as take a ton of pictures. I'd learned a long time ago that you never knew when you might need evidence, even if it was just to piss off my brother when I got the chance.

"All right, we're good." With a nod, I let Ajilon get back to work, setting up some of the men outside to watch for any incoming trouble, while the other half pulled open the loading doors and began stacking bricks of coke inside the trucks. Leaning against a wall, I kept a vigilant eye over it all, making sure no one made a move I didn't like.

It was interesting to see how Ajilon's and Kieran's men looked at me. The former's just looked wary, while most of the Irish looked like they were going to shit their pants when they caught my eye. I had a feeling our little break-in had earned us quite the reputation. Not that I minded. If it kept Mari safe, I'd kill every last one of them without question.

We had the warehouse cleared in less than thirty minutes and had more than enough time to drown the building in gasoline before setting it on fire. There was something cathartic about dropping one of my father's lighters and hearing the *whoosh* as the flames ate the old building. Seeing Cash's hard work burn, his drugs stolen, his men dead—it was all so much better than I'd expected.

Take that, asshole.

Despite the others clearing their areas first, we were the first to make it to the docks. Micah let us in, sending us to the still-damaged area where Cash had set up a bomb for Mari. Ajilon and Kieran sat along the boardwalk while I paced, desperate to see my family now that the work was done.

They were five minutes late, but Greyson had texted that they'd run into an accidental police blockade and had to go around.

No biggie, but there was nothing from Mari.

Then they were ten minutes late. At fifteen, I was going out of my skin.

"You're going to give yourself a heart attack if you don't calm down." Kieran stared at me like an animal in the zoo, his fingers twitching toward his gun.

"Pull that on him, and there won't be enough pieces of you to feed to the sharks, O'Bannon."

I whipped my head around, and I was rushing for Mari before I even realized I was moving. Every worst-case scenario flashed through my brain as I crossed the distance between us, but she seemed unharmed. I'd find out for myself in a moment, though.

The second she was in reach, I hauled her into my arms, burying my face in her neck. "Thank fuck. I was worried."

"I'm fine, Nate. Just got caught in some traffic." Her hands petted my hair as she whispered soothing words until I was ready to let her go. Even then, she couldn't move far. I was clinging to her too hard for that.

"What, no hug for me?" Dominic joked, only to laugh when I hauled him in for a hug too. Like Mari, he gave me a pat on the head before shoving me away. "Christ, we were gone for a few hours. You have abandonment issues."

"You have no idea," I muttered.

When Greyson walked over to us two minutes later, he got the same treatment, though he didn't seem surprised at all. He even gloated that he got a longer one because he'd thought to text that he was going to be late. Fucker was just trying to start shit with Dominic, but I didn't even care.

Once my family was in sight, I finally felt like I could breathe again.

Mari settled into a chair at my side, letting me hover without complaint before turning her eyes to the other leaders. "Tell me everything."

Two-Bit described their attack on the gun warehouse, followed by Dominic explaining the money run. When it was our turn, Ajilon stepped in, though he didn't mention killing the final guard. Interesting.

"Once your boy got his pictures, we loaded up quick. Burned the place down behind us, as requested."

Mari's hand clenched in mine, but other than that, she looked unaffected by it all. After she triple-checked the trucks herself, Micah and his men picked up the keys from Dominic and drove them away.

Mari turned to us, more relaxed than I'd seen in weeks. "Thank you for tonight. I'm hoping the blow to Cash's reserves is as big as I think it is."

"What's next?" Kieran asked.

"War. Get your families out of the city tomorrow. Seattle's officially a powder keg, and we just lit the match. Literally." With another grateful nod, she let them go. Well, all except one. "Kosas. A word."

He turned back to us, his brows drawn in confusion. "Is there a problem?"

"No. I wanted to tell you the money is yours."

Shock rocked him back. "What?"

"The money is—"

"I heard you. I just don't understand why."

Mari glanced out at the water, taking her time before she turned back. "I can't bring your family back, and even though I know money won't help ease the ache, it's something. Keep it, burn it, give it away. I don't care, it's yours."

"The others won't like this."

She shrugged. "So, don't tell them."

His stare was probing as he looked for whatever trap he thought she'd hidden in the offer. He found none. "Why are you doing this?"

"Because Tyrone and Chloe deserved better."

This time, Kosas watched the water before answering. "Thank you."

"Thank me when it's over and Cash is dead."

His lips tipped into the faintest smile. "I'll do that."

The four of us watched him walk away, shoulders heavy with grief. Only when he was out of sight did Greyson lean over and press a kiss to Mari's temple. "You did a good thing, *reina*."

I could tell she didn't agree, but she didn't argue either. "Can you two go get the car? I want to go home, and I'm too tired to walk."

"I can carry you," I offered. She patted my hand but looked pointedly at the others.

"Anything you want, *mariposa*," Dominic said, swooping in for a brief kiss before hauling Greyson along with him. He immediately started telling Grey about all the kills Mari made and how badass our woman was, making me smile as they disappeared around the corner.

When they were gone, she turned to me with brows raised. "Pictures?"

I felt my cheeks flush a little at the stern tone and straightened my shoulders. *I will not be embarrassed about this—or turned on by how hot she is when she's firm with me.* "They're just in case."

"Show me." Pulling out my phone, I loaded the video and pictures I'd taken, letting her see the images. It didn't take a genius to notice her brain was whirling, trying to figure out how to make sense of everything. When she'd gone through all of them, she handed the phone back to me, one photo still on the screen. "Send that to the burner phone."

I forwarded the picture, then leaned over her shoulder to see what she was doing. She huffed but still smiled as she typed out a message to Paez.

I've got something of yours. Ready to talk yet? –Queenie

"Are you sure baiting him is a good idea?" I asked.

"No, but that's all we've got right now. We need Cash neutered, and this is one step to getting it done."

Nodding, I rested my head on hers for another minute, just needing to feel her against me.

Mari's okay. She's safe. We're all safe.

And Cash would be reeling from what we'd accomplished. Not too bad for a night's work.

When the SUV pulled up, I opened the door and held out my hand. "Let's go home, angel."

Mari grinned, letting me pull her close for a kiss. "Absolutely. I think it's time to celebrate what a great night we had."

Her eyes glittered as she climbed into the back seat and beckoned me to follow. I had my shirt off before the door closed behind me.

Oh, hell yes.

Chapter 18
Mari

The night of the raid was our last night in the Celestine. Making moves against Cash was always going to be dangerous, but the added instability of my own family made it even more necessary for us to have a place to disappear to. A place that no one knew about.

We moved around here and there for a week, staying in safe houses Greyson had set up so we didn't shine a spotlight on our new place. It was only because of luck, a shit-ton of money, and Greyson's extraordinary multitasking skills that one of the new houses we'd bought was finished in time.

I knew how stressful it'd been for him, but honestly, he was the only person I trusted with the project—and for good reason.

He'd absolutely nailed it.

The outside of our new home looked like a massive Craftsman, but the inside was a completely different story.

"There's a gym at the far end of the first floor, an indoor and outdoor pool so we have all-weather access to the water and hot tubs to soak our muscles away."

I could get behind a nightly hot-tub routine, and Dominic's waggling eyebrows said he was down for completely different reasons.

Grey led us to the garage. The place was big enough for all of our cars and then some, but I knew his smile was for something else entirely. He took us to the far wall, where a massive cabinet loomed.

"Are you getting interested in car restoration? Because I'm not sure I need to see all the tools required." I eyed the metal monstrosity like it was going to fall and crush us, even knowing Grey would never let that happen.

"I'll leave that to Dominic." With the handle in his palm, Grey slid his finger across the metal, revealing a hinge lever where the lock should've been. He pressed his thumb down, and a flash of green preceded a faint click. I watched in awe as the cabinet doors opened.

"Why do you have a fingerprint scanner in the garage cabinet?" I asked, only to get the answer when Grey stepped inside the cabinet and, after another scan of his thumb, shoved the back open. "A rabbit hole?"

He nodded. "It's an escape route first and foremost, but there's something else I think you'll like more."

Grey held out his hand, helping me down the stairs even though I was perfectly capable of doing it myself. I had a feeling he just wanted me close. When we hit the bottom, he flipped a switch, and light surrounded us, showing me a—

Oh my God. "Is that what I think it is?" There was no hiding how excited I was.

"If you think it's an indoor shooting range, then yes." Grey's grin was so pleased, I couldn't help but smile back.

"How the fuck did you manage that?" Nate asked as he stepped farther into the basement.

"This place was built by rich preppers, so it already had the bones of what we needed."

I didn't remember anything in the real estate listings about preppers, but I'd been distracted and angry. They could've said Willy Wonka built the place, and I wouldn't have batted an eye.

"We renovated some of their bolt-holes and created plenty of places to hide weapons caches and even disappear, if needed. I can't tell you how many panic rooms I found before we came across the second basement, but the moment I saw it, I knew exactly what I wanted to do."

Grey moved along the walls, showing off hidden cabinets and running his hand lovingly over the surfaces. "We reinforced the walls and soundproofed them, so we can shoot whenever we want without worrying about the cops showing up. Plus, we know we won't shoot a pipe or something by mistake. The far wall has an extra escape hatch for emergencies, too."

He showed it to us, though I hoped we'd never have to use it. Nate immediately agreed it was a good idea, but Dominic frowned. "Why so many ways out?"

"In case we get infiltrated," Grey said easily. When Dominic kept staring at him, he sighed. "The fire got to me. I want to be sure Mari can get out easily."

"Even if it means adding extra entry points to staff?"

Grey shook his head. "There's no way into the house without being in the system, and I coded the damn thing myself. No one's getting in or out without my say-so."

"Okay, Big Brother. Take it down a notch," Dominic joked. Grey ribbed him right back as we made our way back inside the house.

Even though I'd already seen it, the shock was still present. I'd lived in luxury my whole life, but that was my family's home. My father's design choices were everywhere. Beyond the Celestine, this was the first home that was ever truly mine—*ours*—and it showed.

Grey had taken the same color scheme as Gilded—the burnished gold and dark reds mixed with black and charcoal—and made the house inviting and sensual. It looked like a place the queen of the underworld would live with her devoted guards.

Staring at the sunken living room with couches I knew we'd be living on one day, I leaned up to kiss his jaw. "This is perfect, baby. Thank you."

Grey didn't gloat often, but he was firmly in gloating territory now. "Anything for you, *reina*."

"This is definitely not a kid-friendly house," Dominic muttered as he pulled open one of the gun vaults behind a massive painting of flowers and four ethereal figures twined together in bliss, and he surveyed the machines with a whistle.

I raised a single eyebrow in his direction, even if he wasn't looking at me. "We aren't a kid-friendly family."

Anxiety snaked through my belly fast and hot as I worried if that was going to be a deal-breaker for Dominic. He knew I didn't want kids; they all did. We'd talked about it, so why the fuck was he bringing them up?

Dominic's head jerked up, and he winced at whatever he found on my face. In a heartbeat, he had me bundled up in his arms, face buried in my neck. When he spoke, his breath warmed my skin. "I wasn't saying it because I want them myself, *mariposa*. It was just an observation."

"So, you don't want them?" I had to be sure. We could get through a lot, but a disagreement over whether we had kids was absolutely not one of them.

Thankfully, Dominic's voice was firm and honest. "No. I only want you."

"Good. Let's keep it that way."

"You got it." He pressed a hot kiss to my mouth and smacked my ass before darting away from me and up the stairs. "Show me my room, Jeeves."

Greyson rolled his eyes, but his smile was broader than it had been in a while. He liked having all of us under one roof, and he especially liked that he'd been the one to make it happen.

Nate held a hand out to me, wiggling his fingers, but I shook my head. I wanted to go up on my own, take in the sights and smells of the house in peace.

And God, did it feel peaceful.

When all this is over, this will be our home. What a good incentive to get rid of Cash.

My dawdling meant I was the last to make it upstairs, so I'd lost my men. The house was big, but not unnecessarily so. I eventually found them, only to see Dominic darting around, digging in drawers and peeking in closets, while Nate and Grey talked quietly to each other in the hallway. I followed behind, enjoying the curved edge of the house, and found four identical bedrooms leading to a massive window in the hallway. It was all beautifully done in tasteful colors so perfect for each of us that it wasn't hard to see whose was whose.

Dominic poked his head out of the room in the middle with a grin. "I want this one."

"That's Mari's." Greyson's voice held no room for argument, and it made me smile. I'd bet money it was the biggest, too.

Unexpectedly, Dominic nodded. "Now the orgy-sized bed makes sense."

Wait, what?

I stepped closer to see, only for Nate to grab me around the shoulders and haul me into a hug. Other than a kiss on the head, he didn't seem inclined to do anything now that he had me, and I wondered if he was feeling a little unmoored here. We'd bought this home without him in mind. Did he worry he'd been forgotten in the mayhem?

Grey lifted a finger and pointed to the rooms in order. "Me, Dominic, Mari, and Nate."

"Why are you on the end?" Nate asked. "I assumed you'd want to be closest to Mari."

"I'm the first line of defense. I figure I'll be in her room more often than not, but if something happens, I want to be between it and her."

"And me?"

I knew what Nate was asking, and I clung to his arm, giving him whatever strength I could.

Greyson watched him steadily. "You're the last line of defense. If we go down, I know you'll get her out."

Dominic nodded, and I held my breath as I felt Nate's heart pounding behind me. When he swallowed, it was thick enough to hear. "I don't take this for granted."

This. Our family. Their trust.

Grey softened, coming over to clap Nate on the shoulder. "I know."

Dominic rolled his eyes like the giant teenager he truly felt like sometimes. "We get it. You're happy to be home. Can we move on already?"

Nate laughed, squeezing me once before he hauled me over his shoulder so fast I lost my breath. I lost it even more when his hand slipped between my legs. "I want to see this orgy-sized bed."

Boosting myself up, I could see how excited the other two were as they stalked behind us. Dominic crept closer, holding my chin in his hand while he laid another kiss against me.

"We're going to make you scream our names, *mariposa*. It's the only way to christen these walls."

Twisting my fingers into his hair, I bit his bottom lip. "I can get behind that."

* * *

It was dark by the time the doorbell rang. All my men looked as deliciously mussed as I felt, their hair in that just-fucked tangle that always appeared more artful on them than the rat's nest I ended up with.

"Put a shirt on!" I snapped when Dominic slipped on his jeans and went off to get our dinner without even bothering to button them. All it would take was one slight adjustment and his dick would be hanging out for anyone to see.

Oh, hell no. That's my cock.

He turned back, eyes full of mischief when I growled. "And if I don't?"

"I'll superglue the fucking thing on you."

The longer he stood there, the more I realized he was going to do it anyway, and I did not want whoever was out there ogling his half-naked body. The jealousy I thought I'd kicked reared up, but it was tempered by a fuck-ton of possession. These men were mine. They each had a tattoo to prove it. I wouldn't allow him to flaunt himself to some random bitch on my porch.

"Put on the fucking shirt before I have to gouge the poor delivery driver's eyes out for looking at what's mine."

He grinned, sauntering closer to brush his lips against mine. "Am I yours, Mari?"

"That tattoo on your skin says yes. Don't fight me on this, Dominic."

"But it's so much fun." He snatched the shirt Nate threw at him out of the air and slipped it on, winking at me when he was covered. "I like it when you're possessive, *mariposa*. Keep it up."

"You won't like it as much when I chain your ass to my side."

"Oh, kinky."

I tried to throw something at him, but he was too far away. Asshole definitely had a bounce to his step when he left too.

I was grumbling when the others closed ranks around me.

"Come on, baby. Let's get some food." Nate wrapped an arm around my shoulders, while Greyson grabbed my hand, his fingers playing over my wedding ring as we walked downstairs together. By the time we made it to the spacious kitchen, Dominic had unloaded our order.

Dominic, Grey, and I had been fine with eating whatever we had, but apparently, Nate had a tradition he wouldn't budge on. Hence the insane number of pizza boxes on our counter.

He slapped the island beside him, and I jumped up, watching their eyes darken as Grey's T-shirt stretched across my thighs. He sidled up to me, twisting the hem in his fingers.

"Gotta say, I like you in my clothes, *reina*."

Considering it was all I was wearing, he'd better. Smiling coyly, I wrapped my hand around his neck and drew his mouth down to me. "I like being in them."

"You just proved you're a possessive wife, *mariposa*. Can we eat now? Someone made me work hard earlier, and I'm *starved*."

I brushed my lips over Greyson's and twisted to glare at Dominic. Smart man that he was, he held out a slice of pizza as a peace offering, though we both knew I'd heard what he'd said.

"You're lucky you're cute and I'm in a good mood."

"I know." He grinned and hopped up on my other side, leaving me boxed in between my men. Exactly how I liked it.

We ate in relative peace. Smiling, laughing, poking fun at one another. It was nice. Restful, even.

How often did we get a moment to just exist with one another? Hardly ever.

Even when things with Cash were slow, we had businesses like Gilded and Wicked to run. The world didn't stop turning just because we were in a war. Honestly, without Shara, we would've been fucked. She deserved two raises for everything she'd done to keep us afloat while the boys and I were occupied. Still, this was nice.

As always, the real world had a way of intruding on our peaceful existence.

I was halfway through my third slice—foursomes burned a shit-ton of calories—when Nate's phone rang. My food stilled in midair.

"Cash?"

He shook his head. "Paez."

Well, shit. Lunging for a napkin, I wiped off my fingers and answered the call but said nothing. He'd called me; he could start the conversation.

When he finally spoke, I got the impression that my silence amused him. "Interesting picture you sent. It certainly got my attention."

"Good. I hoped it would provide context for the request I'm about to make."

"What is that, little queen?"

I let the nickname go. I'd started it by calling myself Queenie. Besides, men with as much power as Victor Paez got off on making other people feel small. They needed the ego boost to feel alive, and I wasn't concerned enough about my ego to worry about his attempts to squash it.

"Slow your supply."

My men slid closer but didn't try to add anything or involve themselves in the conversation. They knew I'd tell them later.

Paez paused, and I got the impression I'd surprised him, though I doubted he'd show it. "Why would I do that?"

"Because your mule is about to die."

"I have others who could take his place in a heartbeat. There wouldn't even be an interruption in the flow of things."

At first, I thought he could be just as terrible as Cash, but something about the way he said it didn't feel genuine. It felt like he was testing me.

"Maybe, but with all the attention this one's garnering, I'm not sure it's a great idea to start over in my city right now."

The words were a warning and a claim. *This is* my *territory.*

There was a beat of silence, then low laughter. Oh, goodie. I loved amusing men.

"You know, I heard about the hidden Osorio. The little princess they allowed to live out of the roost. I thought about finding you more than once, but I wasn't sure if it would end the war between your grandfather and me or make things worse."

Whether he would've killed me or kept me he didn't say, and I wondered what he'd think if he knew there was a lost prince out there, too. Would he feel the same about Two-Bit?

"There's no love lost between Emmanuel and me," I said. Grey's brow ticked in annoyance, and I grinned, knowing he hated being out of the loop for even a second.

Paez grunted an agreement. "Maybe not, but I doubt he'd have let me live if I'd come for you. Family is the most important thing to Emmanuel."

I played with the hem of my shirt absently as I spoke. "You know him better than I do, but let's agree to disagree. Besides, we're not talking about my grandfather."

"No, we aren't." Paez sighed, and it was an oddly vulnerable sound. "I'll admit, I'm a little leery to continue sending product, considering how much publicity your city is getting right now. It's certainly not doing me any favors."

"It's only going to get worse," I said.

"No doubt. I've never known someone as headstrong and psychotic as Cash."

"Then why work with him?" It didn't make any sense to me. The second a pusher got hooked on the product they were supposed to sell, they were useless to the person pulling the strings. If they loved the high more than they feared for their life or respected you, they were too unpredictable to live.

Cash had far surpassed that level in his addiction, so why was he still alive?

"He's good at what he does."

"And money talks," I guessed.

"Exactly."

"Will money get you to agree?"

"No."

"Why not?"

"I won't take yours when I'm not sure you have enough to afford me."

I could never work another day in my life and still die with enough money to make my imaginary great-grandkids trust-fund babies. No way I didn't have enough to pay off Paez. He just wanted something else. "What will you take?"

"For starters, I want the drugs you stole back."

Easy enough. "Only if you sell them somewhere else."

"Are you negotiating with me about my own product?"

"Yes. We both know that in our world, possession is the law. If I had the balls and ability to steal it, it's mine."

"True enough." He laughed again, and I was woman enough to know it was a good laugh. Low and slow and easy on the ears. Like he knew what I was thinking, Dominic dropped a possessive hand on my thigh. *Now who's a possessive husband?* "Fine, I'll move it somewhere else."

"Thank you," I said. I even meant it.

"Don't thank me yet. I want a deal."

Yes! Sitting up straight, I shoved Dominic's hand off and refocused. "What are the terms?"

"I will help you with your little problem if you allow me to use your city as a funnel when it's all over."

I stiffened. I wanted to get rid of coke; he wanted to add it.

Despite how much I wanted Cash out of the picture, I knew I couldn't agree. Not when I wasn't sure if I was trading a cockroach for a dragon.

"With the eyes on my city, I'm not sure that's a good idea."

"What if I gave you a year's reprieve as a good-faith measure?"

It was certainly better, but not great. I didn't *want* drugs anywhere near Seattle, but I wasn't sure I could keep them out. Not when I hadn't eradicated them in the first place. I looked at each of my men, and the loyalty that stared back at me gave me the courage to do what had to be done.

They trust you, Mari. Don't let them down.

"It's a good offer, but I can't accept. Our ambitions don't align when it comes to our positions on drugs."

My men smiled back at me, pride evident in each of their faces, and it solidified that I'd done the right thing.

"You love your city. I respect that. My offer stands."

Shocked, I reared back. I'd expected anger, outrage, threats, and blackmail, not acceptance. It was too good to be true, and I'd learned that meant it would probably kill me down the line. "Why?"

"Because you seem like a good ally to have."

I didn't even try to hide my snort. "More like, because you're at war with my grandfather and I'm good collateral."

"He's at war with me."

The distinction was so clear, I was surprised I hadn't noticed it before. What had put them at war with each other? Was it something like the battle with my father, where Victor Paez had taken something that Emmanuel Osorio thought of as his, or did Paez have something that Emmanuel wanted?

"You know how to reach me if you change your mind. For now, I'll slow my supply to your city. You have two weeks to sort out our little friend before it's back to business as usual."

It wasn't much, but I had to hope it would be enough. "I appreciate it."

"You should. Keep in touch, little queen. I'm curious to see where you go from here. Perhaps this will be the beginning of a beautiful friendship."

The line went dead before I could answer. Good thing too, since all I could think was, *God, I hope not.*

Chapter 19
Mari

With the bullshit truce and the raid taking my focus, I'd put off thinking about Cameron as long as I could. It wasn't that I was naïve and praying things were different; I just needed time to process and space to readjust my thinking.

This was my cousin. The one man in my family I trusted above all else, and he'd taken that trust and pounded it into the dirt.

Still, I didn't know how to handle him. Did I torture the information from his lips or kill him quickly? Did I string him up as a warning to the others in our family to toe the line or hide his indiscretions in case it made me look weak?

I needed outside opinions on the situation. I needed clarity.

I needed Shara.

That was the easiest part of the decision. My men weren't pleased at my leaving the house with a target on my head, despite the fact that Shara's apartment was as fortified as the Celestine. If it weren't, I would've moved her ages ago. Still, they insisted on shadowing me to the apartment and searching it before I went in.

We're not going to risk your life over something as small as checking a few rooms.

Well, when they put it that way.

The trek to Shara's took no time at all, and I was still trying to piece together how I wanted to say things when the door opened. Only, Shara wasn't the one answering it.

"Rafael?"

Getting caught off guard was the worst possible scenario, but I just couldn't wrap my head around my uncle being in Shara's apartment. Why was he here? Where was she? Had he hurt her? If so, there wasn't a single thing he could do to save himself from my wrath.

"Come inside."

Immediately, I bristled. "Pretty sure you can't invite people into my space."

Breathing came easier when Shara hip bumped him out of the way, her beaded braids clicking together as she did. She grinned at our shell-shocked faces, but her smile faded to apprehension and discomfort fast. Yeah, something had definitely happened.

"Are you okay?"

"Fine," she whispered, glancing back at Rafael before turning resolutely to me. "Definitely hard, though."

Fuck, I'd completely forgotten how much Rafael looked like Antoni. Shara had only met him once, and it had ended with her running away. I couldn't imagine how she felt trapped in a room with him.

"Whatever happened, you don't need to—"

"Get away from the door," a voice snapped. There was so much aggression there, I stepped closer, ready to put my body between Shara and whoever it was, yet all she did was roll her eyes.

"Don't bark at me, Christian."

"Who the fuck is Christian?" Dominic muttered. He'd plastered himself to my back the second *Christian* spoke, and I could feel the press of his gun against my ass. At least, I was pretty sure it was his gun.

"*Querida.* Listen to him. He's trying to help." From the living room, a man came toward us, hands up in surrender. I moved closer to Shara, but she shook her head. *I've got this.*

Okay, then.

"Helping doesn't mean commanding, Adrien."

"You're right, *amore*, but Christian isn't used to someone fighting him. He'll get better, won't you, *hermano*?" Adrien glared into the shadows of the room, and a low chuckle answered.

"*Claro que sí.*" *Of course.*

Smiling, Adrien turned back to Shara, stepping closer so he could coax her out of the doorway. "Now that's settled, can you move away from the door, please, *querida*? Let us keep you safe."

I'll admit, I was distracted by the pet names. Hearing my brother's fiancée called darling and love was beyond unexpected, but what came next was almost worse. Most people looked at Shara and saw a sweet, meek woman, but I knew she had a backbone of steel beneath her skin. She wouldn't have lasted so long with Antoni otherwise. Needless to say, it was odd to watch her melt for this man I'd never met.

She let him take her hand and tow her to the other side of the room, waving us in once she was out of the way. Warily, I entered, though I never took my eye off the men I didn't know.

My own men stayed close, no doubt with hands on their weapons. Well, all except Greyson, who stepped forward. "We need to clear the apartment."

"It's clear," Adrien said.

"We'll check for ourselves, thanks."

The warmth with which he looked at Shara blinked out, and he frowned. Only when she tugged his hand—and attention—back to her did it return. "Let them do whatever they need."

Adrien looked at her for another second before checking with the man still hiding in the shadows. When he got whatever confirmation he wanted, he nodded to us. "We'll stay right here."

He sat next to Shara and kept their hands together, fingers interlocked, while the other lay flat on his thigh. The position screamed *I'm not a threat*, and I didn't believe it for one second.

Only when Dominic came back with a curt *All clear* did I finally ask, "Who are you?"

Rafael stepped up to make introductions. "Mari, this is my son Christian. Your cousin. Adrien is his second. Boys, this is Marianna Marcosa and her men, Dominic, Greyson, and Nate Marcosa."

Nate, who had taken Dominic's position at my back, preened at the name, and I made a note to ask if he wanted to take it permanently. It was something I'd already planned to do but hadn't had the time to check with him about. With the final battle coming closer every day, we needed to take the wins we could, and if Nate wanted my name, I'd give it to him.

Christian stepped out of the shadows, and I twisted to keep him and Adrien in sight. He saw my adjustment and smirked just a little. "*¿Qué tal, prima?*"

How are things, cousin? I honestly didn't know how to answer that anymore and only partially because I wasn't sure if I liked him.

This day's gone to hell in a handbasket, thanks for asking. That would be a greeting to remember.

"I wasn't aware your son was in town," I said carefully, making sure I didn't reveal Two-Bit to Christian. We didn't need the family drama.

Christian answered. "We've been keeping an eye on your girls. Good thing too, considering that *cabrón* nearly snatched them."

I twisted just enough to look between him and Rafael, but I couldn't see many similarities between them. Christian was a few inches taller than me, dark hair and deeply tanned skin, yet he had the strangest eyes. Almost colorless. The longer I looked, the more I realized they were similar to Two-Bit's. I nearly said as much, but remembering what Rafael had said about his son's opinion of his younger brother, I kept my mouth shut.

Then what he said registered.

"Did you say *them*?"

Footsteps padded from the hallway where I knew Shara's spare room sat unused. Except it obviously had a new tenant. Aislynn's face was drawn, arms wrapped around herself as a shadow deepened along her jaw. Someone had hit her. Rage flared through me as the light winked against her wedding ring.

If Cameron had hit her, he was going to die slowly and painfully. He'd be begging for me to end him before it was over.

A soft hand settled on my clenched ones, and Dominic's whisper trailed over my neck. "It wasn't him. We have eyes on him."

Relief hit me straight in the solar plexus, only for dread to follow just behind. I'd come to talk to Shara because I wasn't ready to see Ash yet. How was I going to explain that her husband was a liar and a traitor? How could I destroy her happiness when I was the one who pushed them together in the first place?

Fuck.

"What happened?"

Shara huffed. "We were out getting lunch when they cornered us. Clocked Ash good before I even knew they were there. They were about to stick us with something when these two swooped in."

She rolled her eyes at Christian, but I could see her fondness for Adrien a mile away, and I didn't understand where it came from. She'd mentioned dating again but never followed up with anymore information. Had she downloaded an app and landed on him? No, that was too coincidental. It had to be something else. "You've met before?"

"He was a dancer at my bachelorette party." Ash waggled her eyebrows, and mine rose to the ceiling even as my breaths tightened at the way she grinned. *She won't be smiling like that for long.*

"I assume that was planned." I narrowed my eyes on Adrien. There was no chance in hell I believed he'd been there by coincidence.

Shockingly, Shara answered. "It was, but he told me before anything happened."

"What?" Christian and I said at the same time, though he was obviously more irritated than shocked.

Adrien shrugged, keeping Shara's hand tight in his grasp. "I didn't want to lie to her."

"So you outed us to—"

Christian was going to say *an enemy*, but we weren't really adversaries. We weren't allies either.

"No, I outed us to Shara. Just her." The haughty tip of his chin screamed *I don't regret it*, and I had to say, it was nice to see someone fight for Shara again. The faintest color in her cheeks meant she agreed.

A part of me hated seeing her move on because it meant that Antoni was really gone, but she deserved happiness. If my brother had had one last wish, it would've been that. So, I took the grief that tried to swallow me and let it go.

It was time to live again, and if Adrien made Shara happy—and the glimmer in her eye said he did—then who was I to stand in the way of that?

"Where are the men who attacked them?"

"Dead."

"Where were you?" Grey asked Aislynn, and I knew he'd send our own men to make sure the scene was clear and the girls had gotten out fully unscathed. I didn't want either of them to end up in jail again.

Only when we verified with one of our men patrolling the area that everything was sorted did we move on.

"What happens next?" Shara knew things with Cash were getting bad. I'd been begging her for ages to leave the city. She had family in another state she could visit, places that Antoni had set up for her to be safe, and that was what I needed—for her to be safe while I took out the threat to our existence. I couldn't handle it if he went after her or Ash to get to me. Not again.

"We should put them in a safe house." It didn't escape my notice that Christian said *we* or that he hadn't moved his eyes off Shara once. Rafael had mentioned she was Christian's type at Ash's wedding, but I hadn't really thought much about it. Now it was glaringly obvious that my cousin was interested, and I didn't know what to think about that.

Greyson, focused as usual, nodded. "We have plenty of places to hide them."

Adrien cleared his throat. "It would be better if they were somewhere even you couldn't find."

My laugh sounded on edge even to me. "You're out of your mind."

Christian shrugged. "Maybe, but I wouldn't scoff at the offer outright."

"What exactly are you offering?"

"Safety for both of them."

I waited for him to continue, but there was nothing. No stipulations, no rewards for him. Christian was prepared to give them sanctuary indefinitely with no payoff for himself.

"Why?"

He stared me straight in the eye and refused to answer, but I had a good idea of what—or who—had influenced the decision.

Christian wanted Shara, and from the surreptitious glances she was giving him, she was just as interested. When I peeked at Adrien, he looked between them and gave me a big grin. Yep, Shara was going to end up with a little family of her own, just like I had.

Shaking my head, I looked at my friends. "What do you think?"

"I'm fine." Shara shrugged, trying to play it cool like she wasn't drooling over the men, but Ash shook her head.

"I'm not going anywhere without Cameron."

Fuck. My heart squeezed, and I knew there was no avoiding it now. Aislynn had to know.

Turning to Shara, I gave her my blessing. "If you're okay with it, get your stuff packed. I want you out of the city by dark."

She nodded, sweeping me up into a hug. "I'll be okay."

But would I be when it was over?

I clung to her, stealing her strength to get me through this talk. "Love you."

"Love you too."

Twisting to Rafael, I pinned him with a glare. "I'm trusting Christian because I still trust you to a point. I expect you to make sure that trust isn't misplaced."

Translation, if your son or his second hurts my friend, I'll kill you, them, and everyone you love.

"They'll both be perfect gentlemen," he promised with a hard look toward them. Adrien laughed, but I saw Christian bristle, and I filed it away for later.

The three men stepped into the hallway where the bedrooms were, leaving Ash and Shara with us.

"I just have to grab my bag, and then you can take me home."

"Aislynn..." I grabbed her hand, stopping her from leaving too. "We need to talk."

"What is it? Is something wrong with Cameron? I knew I shouldn't have left him—"

"It's not that." I sighed, running a hand through my hair and realizing I just had to come out with it. Spill the secret into the air and hope to hell it didn't blow up in my face. "Cameron's working with Cash."

Ash froze like I'd pressed pause on her before she pursed her lips. "Did *he* tell you that?"

"No. Ace did."

"Ace?"

"Nate's father."

She frowned. "Who's to say he wasn't messing with you? Lying to get you to kill the only person left in your corner?"

Nate cleared his throat, dragging our attention his way. "I saw him. All the nights he went to see Cash, I was there."

"Prove it."

He pulled out one of his phones and dropped it on the table. "Check the photos."

Aislynn's hand shook when she grabbed it, though her brow was an angry slash that slackened with every swipe. By the time the phone slipped from her fingers, she had tears in her eyes.

"I don't believe you," she whispered, but it was a lie. I could see the devastation in her expression. She believed it; she just didn't want to.

"Ash." My voice broke, agony invading my chest when I reached for her, and she slapped my hand away.

"No! I don't believe him. There's no way Cameron would do this to us." She turned away, breathing deeply. When she faced me again, the faint shimmer of tears in her eyes was gone, replaced by fierce determination. "He loves you. He loves *me*. I can't—I won't believe this."

I reached for her again, but she was already sinking down on the couch, dropping her head in her hands and whispering to herself over and over, "It can't be true. It can't."

Slipping onto the couch beside her, I wrapped an arm around her shoulder. "I'm so sorry."

Again, my voice broke, and this time, she broke with me. My heart cracked at the gut-wrenching sobs, but I didn't move a muscle. Ash had just had the ground ripped out from under her. I'd be her rock until she could stand on her own two feet again.

Her teary eyes lifted, focusing on Nate. "Did he—was he cheating? At the parties, I mean."

"No. He never touched anyone else."

She shuddered in my arms, and I could feel her sad relief. It killed me that she was worried about that, but then again, why wouldn't she be? If he could lie to and deceive me, was cheating all that unfathomable? Was it really so farfetched to wonder?

"I'll take you for an STI test, if you want."

"Now?"

"Dr. Grant will meet us at home."

Her nod was hesitant, but she seemed steadier with the news that she'd get what she needed soon. After one more hug, Ash stood, wiping her cheeks with angry swipes. "I need to hear it."

"Hear what?"

"Everything. I need to hear it all from his lips."

I winced. "We can record—"

"No. Use me." She glared down at me, but I knew her anger wasn't directed at me. "We both have things we need to hear from him, so use me to get his confession. I'll play along however you need until we get what we want. Then I'm done."

I felt the finality, her desperation to leave this world behind and start over. Living with O'Bannon hadn't broken her, but loving a liar had, and it killed me. *I never should've asked her to do this.* Knowing that I'd caused one of my best friends to suffer was agony. I didn't know if it was possible, but if I could grant her a normal life, I would. She'd more than earned it.

"That could work," Nate said, sitting next to me and rubbing a hand along my back. "He won't be expecting Ash to work against him."

"It may take a few days," I warned. "Can you handle being around him until then?"

"You know the house I grew up in. I'm a very skilled actor."

I hadn't; I just hated that she was falling back on who she was then to survive in my family. It wasn't supposed to be this way, but it was, and we had to make peace with it or suffer worse. "Okay. We'll get him."

With another nod, Aislynn left to get her bag and recenter herself before walking back into the lion's den. The only reason I was okay with her going was because Cameron was injured and she was on guard. If he went for her, I had no doubt she'd shoot to kill.

I was still staring down the hallway she'd disappeared into when Rafael came back out to the living room. He seemed older than he had before, wearier too. "Are you okay, Uncle?"

He smiled, but it was a little lost. "As much as I can be."

"And the Wolf?"

His mouth tightened. "The same."

So, no help there. Walking to the windows, I gazed down on the city I loved, wondering if I had to make a deal with the devil to save it. The reminder of my newest not-quite ally, not-quite enemy sent my thoughts whirling.

I had a cartel expert in front of me. It was time to use him.

"What do you think of Paez?"

I appreciated that Rafael took the time to consider the question before answering. "He's ruthless, but aren't we all? If you're asking if he's a good man, I'm not really sure anyone with the power we have is, but he's certainly not the worst. Why?"

"He offered me an alliance."

Again, Rafael thought about it. "Maybe it's a good thing."

"Why?"

"The Wolf won't help you, Mari. Not unless you back him into a corner, and I wouldn't suggest that. Regardless of his motives, Paez would be a good ally to have."

"Will it make more problems for you if I do align with him?"

"I'm not sure it matters. You're not an Osorio. Right now, that's a blessing."

Again, I got the sense that he was fighting more battles than one. Two-Bit's warning flashed in my mind, and I decided to repeat it. "Careful, Uncle. That sounds a lot like treason to me."

"Maybe that could be a good thing, too."

Hope and caution warred inside me. I wanted to believe that Rafael was changing his mind, but I knew I couldn't count on him. Not yet.

Aislynn came back with her purse and a blank face that made my chest tight. Turning back to Rafael, I smiled grimly. "Let me know what you decide. In the meantime, I expect your son to keep Shara safe."

"She'll be well cared for with Christian and Adrien," he promised.

"Good. We'll speak soon."

"*Sí, tesorita.* We'll speak soon."

With Dominic and Greyson guarding Ash, Nate took his place at my side. Just like Kosas, he was steering clear in case Ash placed Cash's sins at his feet, and I appreciated it, even if it killed me to see him do it.

"Where are we going now?" he asked.

"We've got a rat trap to construct."

Chapter 20
Mari

Knowing the only way we could keep our advantage was to bring Cameron to us, I used makeup to enhance Aislynn's bruises from the attack, making it look worse than it was before we took her to a random apartment in the Celestine, careful not to let anyone see us.

The room had to look as unidentifiable as possible, so we chose an empty unit and stuck her in the closet, tying her up before we took a ton of pictures.

After we snuck Ash into the shower at our place and back to her apartment with a warning that we would keep one of our closest people nearby if she needed help, we waited. It took a few days to find the right place for the showdown. The night before, we pulled a silent, angry Ash out of the house for an "all-nighter at work" and set the first leg of the trap.

The second happened the next day. We waited to send the

text until we were in place, making sure there was no possible way Cameron could ambush us.

I stared down at the clone of Cash's phone, the picture of a wide-eyed Ash making me anxious, even knowing it wasn't real. "Are we sure this is a good idea?"

"It's what Cash would do," Nate promised.

I knew that. I really did. Maybe a part of me was still rebelling against the idea that someone I trusted could have betrayed me like this, or the reality that I'd put Ash in harm's way. Either way, I felt uneasy about the whole situation, but as with everything else Cash started, I knew the only way it ended was if I finished it.

So, I clicked send.

And we waited.

Not for the first time since this godforsaken war had started, I found myself praying. *Please reach out. Call me. Tell me she's missing. Ask for my help. Please don't let this be how we end.*

As the minutes dragged on, the silence of my phone was too much, my heartbeat too loud. *Call me. Call me. Call me.*

When the phone finally buzzed, it wasn't mine. It was Cameron.

> I'll be there. If she's hurt, I'm going to make you pay, Cash.

The confirmation that he knew the number killed me. But what was worse? My phone never went off.

Every minute felt like torture as we waited. But as each one passed, something in me shifted. This trap wasn't to convince me anymore. The moment he decided not to let me in on his plans was the moment I realized he'd really done it.

This was for Aislynn.

My men and I were spread out across the warehouse, covering all the exits, while Tennessee and Moore watched from a nearby rooftop. We'd been in the building all day, but I didn't want to be caught off guard.

When the sound of tires on gravel hit my ears, I checked my phone before turning it off. No texts from the security team meant he'd come alone, no bombs that they could see. Guns and knives, we could handle. Anything else would be a problem in this small of a space.

A door slammed open, the echo ricocheting around the warehouse. Then my cousin's voice followed, wrecking me all over again. "I want my wife." When no one responded, Cameron growled. "Did you hear me, Cash? I want my wife!"

Again, silence, and I felt his rage grow. "Where are you, motherfucker? Come and face me. Unless you're too much of a coward. Is that why you took my woman? Because you're afraid?"

"I can assure you I'm no coward," I said, finally stepping into the light.

Cameron's eyes widened, a flash of fear taking over before he schooled his expression. "I'm so glad you got my message. Have you found Aislynn yet?"

He sounded so sincere, but we both knew there were no messages, no texts, no calls, no carrier pigeons. Just lies upon lies leaking between us to spread on the floor.

"Mari, have you seen Ash? Cash has her."

"He doesn't," I promised.

"I don't understand. Did he text you too?" Again, he faltered, and at his uneven gait, I looked down to see the cane in his hand. I hadn't even realized he'd walked in with it.

The fire had been weeks ago, but because of his injuries, his healing had been slow. For weeks, I'd been killing myself over it all, but now I was glad. This would've been much harder if he was in fighting form.

"No, I didn't text her." Nate stepped out from behind his pillar, hands casually in his pockets.

Cameron's eyes narrowed as he looked between us. "What the hell, Mari? Did your boyfriend take my wife?"

"Thought you said Cash did that?" I asked easily.

My cousin's face froze as he tried to figure out how to get out of the mess he'd made. "I mean, that's who I assumed."

"You seemed pretty positive when you walked in shouting his name. How'd you know it was Cash who took her in the first place?"

For a split second he hesitated, motionless, as if he realized he'd let slip something he shouldn't have. "Who else would it have been?"

"Who else, indeed? Can I see the message?"

Cameron dug the phone out of his pocket and held it out to me. With every step closer, I felt my men getting tenser and tenser. I could practically feel the trigger beneath my finger as they kept him in their sights, but I didn't flinch. There was nothing my cousin could do to hurt me anymore.

Taking the phone, I didn't look at the message. Instead, I nodded to Nate. "Call him."

Cameron's eyes darted between us as I moved back, putting space between us again. "What? The message is right there. You just have to—"

I held up a hand, cutting him off. "Call it, Nate."

He slipped the clone phone out and hit a few buttons until ringing echoed around us. There was nothing but the sound of it for a second, until my cousin's phone went off in my hand. I didn't bother answering, just held it up for him to see.

He went pale, but he stayed where he was, even when I continued. "You knew it was Cash texting because you've worked with them before."

"I haven't." When I rolled my angry eyes, he doubled down. "Seriously, Mari. Look at my phone. You won't find any messages. No phone calls either."

"I have no doubt you covered your tracks, but you forgot about one important thing."

"What?"

"Not a what, a who." When I flicked my gaze to him, Nate grinned, and Cameron's fists clenched.

"Are you telling me you believe that backstabbing asshole over me, your cousin?"

This time, I laughed in his face, and he jerked like I'd smacked him. "You would too if you'd seen the proof I have, *cousin*."

"What proof?"

"Messages and phone logs. Videos, voice memos. You name it."

After we'd taken the pictures, Ash had gone to our guest room to rest, and I had finally asked Nate to show me everything. He had so much evidence, there was no way to refute it. I only wished I'd been brave enough to ask sooner.

Cameron swallowed, but he still fought to convince me. "They were all faked. Every single one of them."

A grim smile split my lips. "Of course they were."

I tossed Cameron's phone to Greyson and watched as he slipped it into his pocket. Whether it truly had anything on it or not, we'd find out later, but for now, I had more important things to focus on.

Behind Cameron, his wife peered out from behind her own pillar. We kept her closest to the door so she could run if there was a problem, but I hated that I'd get a front-row view of the devastation to come.

"Why did you come here?" I asked, knowing she needed the answer.

"I came for my wife." Ash's relief was palpable, even as Cameron relaxed where he stood. Now that his secret was out, it was obvious he wasn't going to fight us. He wasn't the type to go down swinging with his fists. Not when he had more than enough ammo in his head for a kill shot. "Did he even have her, or was this some trick to get me out in the open?"

Her, not Ash. Interesting.

"Would it have mattered if he had?"

He shrugged. "It's hard to get people to trust in you when you can't even keep your own wife safe."

"So you're not here because you love her."

Aislynn jerked with his disbelieving huff. Anger made my limbs tremble, and I watched the boy I grew up with, the man I thought I'd known, take off the mask he'd obviously been wearing.

"Of course not. You're the only one stupid enough to fall in love with your spouse. They're bargaining chips, Mari. Tools to get us where we want to go. That's all."

I got a firsthand view of the unfathomable sorrow on Aislynn's face, and even though I hated myself for it, I knew this was only the beginning. The worst was yet to come.

Nodding slightly to Nate, I kept my eyes on my cousin as Nate crept up on Cameron's other side. Before he could react, my man pistol-whipped him, sending him to the floor unconscious.

Ash gasped, her hands covering her mouth in shock. Even from afar, I could see how they trembled, and I hated that for her. Hated that I'd been a part of damaging her like this.

Stepping closer, I tried not to let the way she stumbled back affect me. "Are you all right?"

It didn't take a genius to see she was destroyed. Her lips trembled and her knuckles were tight as she twisted her hands together. She looked down at my cousin with love and loathing mixed in her eyes. Then she wiped it all away, hidden beneath her own mask. She was distant and aloof, beautiful even as she fractured. This was the Ash who'd been a mafia princess. This ice queen was O'Bannon's spawn, and it broke my heart that she was hurt enough to fall back into that person again.

Clearing her throat, Ash wiped the tears off her face. "He

doesn't love me. He never loved me. He kept me close because it was easier to keep me safe if I was sitting happily at his feet. I was nothing but property to him, just like my father."

She ghosted a hand over her belly, and I wondered if she felt as sick as I did at just how wrong we had been about Cameron.

Even though I agreed, part of me had to try to reason with her. "We don't know that."

"I do," she said firmly. "I've grown up with men like him my whole life. He's just exceptionally good at hiding himself, but now that I know, I can see the rot." She stared down at him for a moment longer before stiffening. "I need to go. Do whatever you want to him. I don't care."

As she turned away, hustling out the door to her car outside, I realized I was no closer to figuring out what to do with Cameron, and that was a big problem.

Chapter 21
Greyson

We took one car with Cameron hog-tied and stuffed into the trunk and didn't split up until we got to the Celestine. Nate and Dominic took our prisoner to the basement, while Mari and I took the elevator to the top floors.

"Do you think she's here?" Mari whispered as we got closer to Aislynn's apartment. It would never be Cameron's again.

I didn't, but knowing Mari wouldn't rest until she tried, I simply shrugged.

The door at the end of the hall seemed innocuous, plain even, but not knowing what lay behind it made it all the more sinister. What had our friend been through with her husband? What had he done to her besides make her fall for a lie?

I didn't know that either, and it roiled my stomach.

"Won't know until we try." Mari drew in a deep breath and knocked.

No response.

After a minute, she knocked again.

Still nothing.

"Do I keep pounding on the door until she opens up, or do I give her space?"

Mari sagged against me, and I tucked her into my chest. When she hurt, I hurt, and she was fucking hurting. "I can't answer that, *reina*." I ran a hand over her hair, loving how she leaned into the comfort—if only for a minute before steeling her spine.

"We'll keep checking on her. Text Moore and Tennessee. We need them to keep an eye out. Have them let me know when she comes back, if she's left at all."

Nodding, I steered her to the elevator with one hand and relayed the message with the other while we rode down in silence.

With one step out of the doors, cold air seeped into us from the underground basement. Part of me wanted to grab a jacket for Mari, and the other embraced it, knowing we wouldn't be cold for long. Interrogating warmed the body fast, even if I wasn't the one doing it.

In the time it had taken us to run our errand, Nate and Dominic had strung Cameron up, suspending him with chains wrapped around one of the ceiling's steel beams. His legs barely held him, and the grimace of pain told me he was still suffering from the injuries he'd sustained in the fire.

Now that I thought about it, had the fire been part of the plan all along to throw us off the scent, or had Cash gone off book? Thinking back, I recalled Cameron had been enraged at the situation. He'd nearly died—his *wife* had nearly died—but knowing that Ash's safety was more for his image than anything else, I could see how the rage had been manufactured in places. I was nearly feral at the idea of Mari getting caught in that fire.

Dominic, Nate, and I took our places behind Mari. This was her show; we were just the silent supporters.

The two cousins silently watched each other. I wondered what Mari saw when she looked at her cousin's face. Was it the boy she'd grown up with—or the man who'd betrayed her? Maybe she was one of the unlucky ones, and it was both. How would she handle the punishment in that case?

A glance at Nate and Dominic showed the same worries on their faces, but before I could sink too far into the concern, Mari spoke. "I figured it out, you know."

Cameron just watched her. He didn't fight the chains or try to defend himself. He knew he'd been caught. He knew it was over. When Mari took the knife Nate handed her, Cameron didn't even flinch.

She stepped up, slicing the shirt off his chest with careful motions as she talked. "I had Moore look into your comings and goings over the last year, though I'm sure it was longer. Honestly, I'm surprised I missed the signs, but when we knew what to look for, we found everything I needed. Going out late, sneaking around, showing up places you shouldn't have been. Not to mention all the fuckups that made things difficult. The people trying to rob Gilded—hell, even the raid on the club—was your doing. You scanned your ID card less than an hour before the cops showed up and slipped out the back before anyone noticed."

Her fingers clenched with anger, and I wondered if she was fighting the urge to hit him. Shara had been in jail, in danger, because of him. That rankled Mari. Her pride was tightly tethered to keeping her people safe, and he'd preyed on that.

The first swipe of the knife was shallow, barely enough to draw blood, but paper cuts always stung something fierce, didn't they? Cameron still didn't react, and I saw how much it pissed her off in the tension of her shoulders.

"Mari." I wasn't going to let her cousin goad her into killing him.

She was too far gone to listen, though.

She swiped again, this time cutting deep enough for rivulets of blood to leak down his chest. Cameron's only reaction was a soft hiss.

"All those nights you said you were following your father, you were really meeting Cash. Nate said the compound was one big party. It's always easier to get people to agree with you when they're drunk and high, living the good life, right?"

Another swipe, this one from hip to hip. She was close enough to his pelvis that he tensed automatically, but he still didn't respond, and I felt Mari's satisfaction like my own.

"Joaquin was a good scapegoat," she admitted, and for the first time, a flicker of something flashed on Cameron's face.

Guilt.

He felt guilty that his father had died in his place. It was almost gratifying to know he wasn't a robot. I knew Mari felt the same on some level, but even if she hadn't killed Joaquin for supposedly working for Cash, he would have died eventually. Mari wouldn't have been safe as long as he was alive, but it would take her time to see that side of things. She would, though. We'd make sure of it.

Tapping the knife on her leg, she paced. "What I keep racking my brain trying to figure out is what you possibly could have wanted that I didn't give you. You had power, prestige, and more money than God. Beyond that, you had the ear of the queen of this city, and you had a beautiful, kind wife who loved you. Yet you went behind my back. For what? What was so damn important that you had to throw away thirty years of memories and every ounce of trust I've ever given you?"

"Are you sure you wanna know?" Cameron asked, though it was more tired than taunting. "It won't make things easier for you. It won't make any of it better."

"Nothing will make it better, but I deserve to know," Mari countered.

Cameron sagged in the chains, but I kept my narrowed gaze on him. He was too good of an actor for me to believe he had any remorse. When he lifted his head and forced those rage-filled eyes on Mari, I knew I was right.

"It should have been mine."

Mari paused. "What?"

"Everything. After Antoni died, it all should have gone to me, but it didn't. Rey never wanted to lead. He was always content in second place. I wanted what was rightfully mine." Cameron shook his head, that rage morphing into something deep and ugly as he spoke.

"At first, I let it go, thinking either you would fuck up and they'd kill you, or you'd give up and they'd hand the city over. Then you fought back. You kept fighting, and when you settled into your skin as you did, I realized it was over. You would do whatever it took to keep what was now yours: the city, the power, the money, the throne. I thought I could accept you because you were so much better at everything than I'd expected, but the anger just kept growing. How could they bow to you when I was right here? When Cash made me an offer, it was easy to take it."

Easy to betray a lifelong bond. For power.

The saying was true; absolute power corrupts absolutely. Except in Cameron's case, it was the thought of it that turned him against his family. Disgusting.

There was another edge to the jealousy that I couldn't quite pinpoint, but it wasn't my place to ask. This was Mari's show, her need for closure and clarity. I was just a witness. I could only see a sliver of her profile, but the tension in her jaw was hard to miss. "What about Aislynn? Why manipulate her?"

"It's like I said, she's mine to protect. I hated you for giving her to me at first. I didn't want another spoiled mafia princess, and there were times when I genuinely thought about wringing her neck. Then I realized that, with her, I could take the O'Bannon territory too. All it would take was a little engineered luck."

The implication slithered under my skin. *Holy shit.*

Mari stared at him, but I could tell she wasn't really seeing him. She was seeing the monster she hadn't realized he was.

"You were trying to get her pregnant." It was the first time I'd spoken, but it had to be said. The evil had to be purged before any of us could move on.

Cameron tried to shrug, but his position made it impossible. "She's my wife. Babies are part of the deal."

"She loved you, and you used her." Mari's voice held a grave-yard of memories, the destruction of the last good thing she'd ever thought about her cousin laid at her feet.

Cameron huffed. "If she does, then she's a fool."

"No, you are. She would have given you everything, and you spat in her face."

He grinned at her, and I finally saw how unhinged he was. "All's fair in love and war, Mari."

"Are we at war, cousin?"

"We've always been at war," he spat.

"Why is that?"

This was it, the real truth of why he'd done it, and I had no idea what he'd say.

That hatred was there, desperate to break free, clawing its way out in the vitriol of his words. "Because since the moment you were born, you have taken things from me. Men who should've been *my* allies willingly swore to you instead—my brother, my cousin, even Greyson."

Shock rocked me, though I fought not to show it. I was his excuse, but why? He'd never been interested in my friendship. Or maybe he had, but my bond with Mari and Antoni was too tight from the beginning. Maybe that was why he'd lost himself.

"When you walk into a room, people gravitate toward you like you're the sun, and everything else gets blotted out by your presence. Perfect, precious Mari. Rey knew it. Antoni knew it too. Hell, Nate nearly died trying to get back to you because he knew it. You are a force to be reckoned with, and for so long, I haven't had the power to fight back."

"And now you do." Mari's voice was cold. Empty.

"Now I do."

"You went to Cash out of jealousy. You sided with him like a child desperate to cling to his toys." Mari scoffed, twisting around like she couldn't stand to look at him anymore. "You would've made a pathetic king."

He'd kept cool the whole time, but his eyes flared at her scathing remark. "I sided with Cash because I wanted my birthright. The one that you stole straight from my waiting, bleeding hands. You're too soft to rule, Mari."

"I've held the city for nearly a decade, but that's not enough." My love laughed, and the sound was so bitter and acrid, it stung my throat. "I shot your father in the head, and you're telling me I'm too soft."

"You're weak, Mari. You've always been weak. You want bonds and loyalty and respect. You want *family*, but that's not meant for this world. Not when it breeds selfishness and greed."

"You're right. I have been weak. It's time to rectify that."

Before he could even blink, she twisted and sent a hard kick to his ribs. The crack echoed through the room and dug its way into my brain. My wife looked fierce and formidable, all that sadness buried deep behind the queen she was.

She took out every bit of her frustration on her cousin until she was shaking with adrenaline, soaked in sweat, knuckles and knife dripping blood. Cameron looked almost unrecognizable as he sagged on his chains. Only when his eyes closed did she step back and walk away without a word. I nodded to Dominic and Nate, knowing they would sort out a watch schedule for

Cameron. Until Mari decided his true punishment, every breath he took would be monitored.

She waited for me in front of the elevator, her fists and jaw clenched so tightly, her body shook. Even with all that anger, she said nothing until she was sure we were alone.

"He's right."

"About what?"

"That I'm weak."

"Mari—"

"I don't know if I can kill him, Greyson." She said it so quietly, I almost couldn't hear, but I did and it broke my heart. So much grief in those few words. So much agony.

So much self-hatred.

"So, don't."

Her head jerked up, and she looked at me through clouded eyes. "I can't let him live, Grey."

"Says who?"

"If the family finds out—"

"You *are* the family," I told her, trapping her face in my hands when she tried to look away. "No, listen to me. You have been so worried about the uncles for so long that you have been tiptoeing around them. This is *your* family, Mari. *You* are the queen. *You* make the decisions. If you decide that he lives, he lives. End of story."

Anyone who had another opinion could form a line, and Dominic, Nate, and I would take care of it. We would be her soldiers, protecting her will with our lives.

"What am I supposed to do, just stick him in a hole somewhere and watch him rot?"

"Why not? Cameron's done, Mari. If he escapes, the family will hunt him down. If not, he'll die alone. It's a lose-lose for him, regardless."

She shook her head, but I could see the idea worming its way into her brain. Exile didn't have to mean mercy. "If he dies, that gives Ash closure, a way for her to move on."

"He doesn't need to die for her to live again," I said. "Start with divorce papers. If she needs more than that, we can reevaluate. There's no need to rush."

Mari leaned into me, pressing a kiss to my jaw. "Thank you."

"I'll always have your back, *reina*."

We were inside the penthouse, though we hadn't moved beyond the foyer. She slipped her phone from her pocket and made the call.

"Donnaghal and Sons. How can I help you?"

"This is Marianna Marcosa. Get me Laidan."

"Of course."

In less than ten seconds, Laidan answered. "Ms. Marcosa."

"I need you to draft divorce papers and have them delivered within the hour."

"For you?"

"My cousin, Cameron, and his wife, Aislynn. They have no children and no shared assets, so you can use a basic divorce decree, as long as Cameron walks away with nothing."

There was a pause during which I wondered if Laidan would ask the questions she was obviously thinking, but I should've known better. She had been trained by the best, and Ronan would never ask anything that wasn't necessary. "I'll have them for you in twenty minutes."

After hanging up, Mari held the phone out to me. "I need a shower, and then we're going to start making things right."

Twenty minutes later, Mari was clean, and the divorce papers were in hand. Thirty minutes later, we were back in the basement.

Nate and Dominic had given Cameron a cursory first aid check for the worst of the damage, but beyond that and the cage he'd been shoved into, he was otherwise exactly as we'd left him.

He lifted dull eyes up to Mari as she nodded for Nate to open the door. Dominic stood close, ready to end Cameron if he went for our woman.

"Back again so soon?" Cameron taunted, but he'd already lost his spark. Hard to stay confident when you're bleeding out on your knees in a dog cage.

Mari smiled. "I decided I want one more thing from you before I'm done for the night."

She tossed the manila envelope by his knees, but he didn't pick it up. "What's this?"

"Divorce papers."

His eyes shifted subtly, but I saw the menace in them. "I won't sign them."

Mari shrugged. "Either you sign them of your own free will or I force you to, but either way, I'm giving Aislynn what she wants."

Cameron cocked his head. "She asked for this?"

"She wants to be free of you."

His hand slid carefully to the envelope, and he stared down at it. The papers crinkled. His hands clenched. I darted forward, but Mari was faster, plucking his hand from the envelope and anchoring it to the floor with her knife before he could do the damage he so obviously wanted.

Cameron clenched his teeth, hissing through them, but that was the only sound.

Mari leaned closer, putting pressure on the knife. "Sign the papers, or I start cutting off body parts."

"How will I sign if you take my fingers?"

"You only need one hand to write, and we're all here as witnesses. I'll make it work."

The knife wiggled farther into his hand, and Cameron sneered at her. "Why not just forge my signature? You wouldn't even have to fight me on it."

"Making you sign it is part of the fun. You think that Ash is yours, just another piece of property to add to your extensive list.

So, I'm going to make you sign over everything you've earned to her." He flushed with anger as Mari's smile grew. "She'll get every car, every house, every red, bloodied cent you've ever made. She'll be free to leave the country, to disappear off the face of the map. To remarry and shower her new husband with all the riches her former one gave her. You'll give her the freedom she's always wanted, exactly as a good starter husband should, and you'll do it right in front of me."

By the time she was done, her cousin vibrated with anger, and Mari obviously enjoyed getting to poke at him. "Sign, Cameron."

"I'm going to make you regret this."

This time, when Mari laughed, it was light and carefree. "You have no power to do anything but take what I give you. Now, *sign.*"

He took the pen she held out carefully, signing so hard he nearly ripped the paper. After checking that he had every signature and initial required, Cameron shoved the papers away.

Mari grabbed them, stopping only to hand them back to me before standing. Dominic stepped closer, waiting for Cameron to retaliate, but he didn't. He just watched her with hatred until she was nearly to the door.

"She'll never be free of me, you know. Not where it counts."

Mari looked over her shoulder as Nate locked her cousin back up. "Maybe not, but this is a good start."

Then we left him there to rot, alone in the mess he'd made.

Chapter 22
Mari

As soon as Cameron signed, I slipped a copy of the paperwork under the apartment door in case Ash was still there. The others went to Donnaghal and Sons to file. I let Laidan know I wanted the divorce finalized immediately, and she promised she knew exactly who to call to make it happen.

With any luck, Aislynn would be free again soon. Maybe it would be the kick-start she needed to begin again. To heal.

Fuck, I hoped so.

When we finally got back to the new house that night, I lay in bed. Not sleeping, not resting, just existing with my men pressed around me.

Tennessee had texted sometime between my getting the divorce papers signed and our arriving home with an update I didn't like.

Ash never returned to the Celestine. She didn't answer any

calls or texts. I even resorted to sending emails to her work address. Still nothing. She was a ghost.

The only thing keeping me from tearing the city apart to find her was Rafael. He promised he was watching her, that she was safe but needed to be alone. I didn't like it, but I had to respect her wishes. She deserved the chance to process however she needed.

I wasn't sure how I'd react in her place. Finding out my husband had manipulated me into loving him, that he'd made plans for the future, knowing he didn't give a shit about me—that would destroy me. And that was without the knowledge that he was intentionally trying to impregnate her to steal her birthright too.

Fuck, I didn't want to see the damage that bomb would cause.

After an infuriating text exchange with my uncle, during which he refused to send even a proof-of-life photo, I video-called Shara. She'd been close to my cousin too and she needed to know, but telling her was brutal. I could have called before we caught him, but Christian and Adrien had been moving her to the safe house, and I wanted her to have time to settle in. Selfishly, I also wanted a break myself, or maybe I just needed the answers he gave before I told her.

Even if I didn't want it to, time always passed, no matter how much you wanted to hide from it.

Recounting everything Cameron had said to me was heartbreaking, and we were both quiet and numb after. I was just grateful that even though Shara could see how destroyed I was, she didn't push me to talk yet, letting me stare out the window instead. We sat in silence, two people who'd lost someone they considered family, grieving together. No words of condolence or anger. Just quiet pain shared among women who'd seen too much of it.

Eventually, I sighed and turned back to the call. As expected, she watched me patiently.

"I don't like this," I said for the hundredth time, and we both knew I wasn't talking about *him.*

"Neither do I, but she needs time to lick her wounds. Considering what you just said, I'd say she deserves it."

"He's not dead." *Yet.*

I was still unsure what the best punishment for my cousin's betrayal would be. Did I kill him and end his existence and my suffering, or did I put him somewhere no one would find him, forcing him to live his life knowing he'd lost everything to me *again?*

What would give me more satisfaction? What would give Aislynn the closure she needed?

"Her husband was a fraud and a traitor to the both of you. She's just got to come to terms with that, and it could take her a while. All we can do is be there for her and support her."

Shoving my hands through my hair, I sighed. "I shouldn't have pushed her into this."

"You couldn't have known."

"I was being selfish. I didn't want O'Bannon to have Greyson, so I shoved her at Cameron instead. I put her on this path because I didn't want to lose him."

"Of course you didn't. He's your husband."

"Now, but he wasn't before. Before, he was just my second-in-command and the man her father wanted her to marry."

Shara frowned, obviously not liking my train of thought. "She wouldn't blame you for keeping Greyson, Mari. Everyone could see that he matters to you. Honestly, I'm just shocked it took this long to wife him up."

She *should* blame me. I'd ruined her life.

"This is a blip," Shara said gently.

But it was more than that.

It was so obvious how much Cameron meant to Ash. When I'd told her that O'Bannon was dead, she didn't even flinch. In fact, she'd told me *good riddance.* When my cousin had broken her heart, she'd fled.

He'd manipulated her, convinced her to love him, to plan a future with him—all while knowing he didn't give a shit about her. That was bound to create such trust issues that I wasn't sure she'd ever recover from, and it killed me.

Aislynn O'Bannon had only ever wanted three things in life: her business, her freedom, and the love of a good man. Knowing she'd had that last one under false pretenses was going to cause shock waves I wasn't sure we could help her through. I didn't want to lose her to the darkness of his treachery.

Shara sat forward, pulling my attention back. "It'll take time, but she's strong enough. She'll make it through, and we'll help her. But right now, she needs to be alone."

The only thing Ash was asking for after everything was space, and as the person who'd put her on this path to heartbreak, I had to give it to her. I didn't have to like it, though.

"How are you?" I had to change the subject before I lost my mind. "How's the safehouse?"

"It's good." Shara smiled. "I'm actually enjoying myself."

"Enjoying yourself...or enjoying Adrien?" There was no need to be coy with Shara. We both knew what I was asking, and as expected, she laughed.

"Both."

"You like him?"

"I've liked him since the moment I set eyes on him," she admitted.

"And Christian?"

She squirmed a little, and I laughed, enjoying how uncomfortable she looked. "Is it weird?"

"What, that you're attracted to him?"

"He's your cousin, Mari. He's Antoni's cousin."

Understanding softened me. "He wouldn't be upset with you.

Antoni would have wanted you to follow your heart, wherever that led. He wasn't the type to hold you back just because something wasn't *normal*." When she didn't respond, I asked, "Is it a problem for Christian?"

"I haven't asked," she admitted.

I heard a world of unspoken things in her words. "Are you scared too?"

Shara had lost the love of her life, and she was watching her best friend lose hers too. It wouldn't be out of bounds to assume the idea of diving into something new would terrify her.

"He's just so...infuriating." She growled in frustration, and I bit my lip to keep from laughing again. "Seriously, he's so hot and cold all the time. Sometimes he stares at me and I think he's mentally undressing me. Other times, I'm pretty sure he's skinning me alive."

"Are you being annoying?" One thing that people didn't know about Shara was she lived to irritate her men. She used to drive Antoni crazy, poking at him, doing everything she shouldn't, until he finally snapped.

He'd grab her by the neck, haul her over his shoulder, and disappear out of the room. We wouldn't see them for at least two days, and no one went into their wing of the house for fear of needing to bleach their eyes.

"Of course not. I'm a lady." She huffed, and I rolled my eyes. Like I'd ever believe she was prim and proper.

"Maybe he's just not used to sharing," I suggested.

That made her tap her long nails on the counter in front of her. "That's what Adrien said, but I'm not sure I believe it."

"You think they've shared before you?"

"Better not have," she snapped before taking a calming breath. It was the first hint of jealousy I'd noticed her show in a while, and it was nice to see her care enough about someone to bring that out again. "I don't see why sharing would be an issue. If you really want someone, you do what it takes to get them. Even if it means sharing with your bestie."

True, but... "The men in our world would not do well with sharing. They want what they want, and they'll take out anyone in their way. You know this."

"Yeah, I do. It still sucks, though. I wish he wanted me enough to try."

The conversation was hitting closer to home than I expected. Cameron thought of me as an obstacle in his path to greatness, and all I wanted was for him to love me enough to try to be on my side again.

I swallowed thickly as irritation bloomed in my chest. What the fuck had I ever done to him except exist? It was bullshit for him to blame his shortcomings on me. I had been a little girl—the *only* little girl on the compound—and as hard as the men in our family were, they were also fathers.

They saw young me as someone to dote on when the urge struck and nothing more, but all he saw was one more person to split the gold with.

"Are you okay?" Shara asked, soft understanding on her face.

"I think I hate him," I admitted. When she nodded, encouraging me to continue, I did. "I spent my whole life putting him on a pedestal as one of my closest allies, my best friend, and he never felt the same. I'm so sick of men thinking it's okay to use and abuse women's feelings to get what they want. I mean, Christ. Do they think we'll just lie down and take it?"

There was so much bubbling inside that I realized it wasn't just my cousin I was mad at; it was Joaquin too. It was the remnants of the anger I'd felt toward Nate and even Dominic when he'd first come back. I thought I'd worked through it, but some still remained and that pissed me off.

"Cameron probably assumed you'd never find out, or if you did, it would be too late to do anything."

Light from the coffee table stole my attention, and I stiffened as Cameron's phone rang. Grey had downloaded the files on it right away, and while he was digging through them, I'd kept the phone close, waiting for Cash to reach out. Even though it irritated me that my eyes kept straying to it, I couldn't seem to put it too far out of my reach.

"Hey, Shara. I gotta go."

"Okay. Be careful, babe."

"You too. I'll call you as soon as I can."

"Don't worry about me. The boys are taking good care of me." She waggled her eyebrows and gave me an exaggerated wink.

Grateful for the tension-breaker, I grinned. "Don't forget—no glove, no love."

She barked a laugh. "You know I have stock in condoms. Talk soon."

With another quick *love you*, we both hung up.

Tossing my phone to the side, I moved to the other. The text from Cash was two sentences that boiled my blood.

> You're late. Where's my intel?

And there it was, a blatant reminder of just how far Cameron had fallen. His treachery infuriated me, jolting me into action before I could overthink it.

> Sorry to say, your little mouse got caught in a trap. Seems you'll have to find another.

I wondered how long I'd have to wait for a response, but Cash texted almost immediately.

> Is that you, little queen? Have you stolen one more thing from your cousin?

> No, I've stolen from you. He's just an added bonus.

> Enjoy my leftovers. I've got enough intel to get to you if I want, but I'm enjoying our game too much to end it at this point.

> It's so fun watching you squirm.

> I hope you're still saying that when I kill you.

I gritted my teeth and sent back one more message before breaking the phone in half and throwing it to the side.

> If you want me, come and find me.

* * *

As usual, I sought solace in the gym. I spent some time with a heavy bag and then realized all I wanted to do was run. I had just done my fifth mile when Grey rushed in.

A quick tap to my phone paused my music, and I pulled out the earbud. "What's wrong?"

"You should see this."

Grabbing a towel to wipe my face, I followed him through the house to his office. As with the rest of our new home, Greyson had taken his time to make sure the room was perfect for his needs. He'd set up multiple massive work desks, each with their own docking station so he could manipulate whatever tech he was messing with, but the highlight of the room was an entire wall of monitors that he could move around at will.

He tapped on the keyboard, and the main screen changed. It took only a moment for me to realize what I was seeing.

"Is that the penthouse?"

It was almost strange to see the Celestine again, not to mention the psychopath stalking through it.

Grey nodded. "He broke in five minutes ago."

My eyes lifted in surprise, and I watched, detached, as Cash destroyed our suite.

He threw tables and broke chairs. He took a bat to the TVs and pissed on the couches. That wasn't even mentioning what he did when he found my room. Grey and I were silent as he went batshit on our former home.

Knowing I'd pushed him to it, if only to prove to himself that he had a leg up on me, I let it happen. No use losing good men when he was throwing another temper tantrum. It was all stuff that could easily be replaced anyway. When he disappeared into the bathroom, I looked at my man. "Find out how he got upstairs."

"Already on it," Grey said. "He could have duplicated Cameron's keycard access."

"I thought we blocked his access to any floors but his own?"

"We did, but Cash could've forced the stairwell open."

Humming, I decided that made the most sense. "Any casualties?"

"None."

"Security?"

Grey pulled up another screen, and we watched as the security team lined up in front of the penthouse. Cash paused his destruction, cocking his head like a golden retriever hearing his favorite squeaky toy. By the time security broke down the door like a SWAT team, ready and willing to take Cash dead or alive, he was already moving.

Knowing Nate had climbed from the roof, I wondered how Cash was getting out. As my men filtered into the apartment, we watched as Cash slipped out a window and disappeared from the frame.

"Did he climb down?"

Grey switched camera views to the blind spot Nate had manipulated to get to me. "Looks like he parachuted."

Are you fucking kidding me? "I thought people only did that shit in movies."

"Apparently not."

Sure enough, Cash was already halfway down the block, his body completely covered by the fabric of his parachute. The little psycho didn't seem to care that any malfunction could've meant his death. His unpredictability worried me. How did we beat someone who didn't give a shit if he lived or died?

"Fucking Beckstroms."

Grey laughed, and we watched as our men cleared the penthouse before surveying the damage.

Too bad the parachute didn't fail. Even as I thought it, I knew our story would end in bloodshed and pain. That was fine, though. No matter what it took, I intended to be the last one standing.

Chapter 23
Nate

"We need to evacuate the city."

Since Cash had broken into the Celestine, we'd agreed to leave the new house only if absolutely necessary, so all four of us were crammed inside the security room for a video call we'd been dreading.

The room was a smaller version of Greyson's office, with walls packed with monitors and enough desks for each of us to have one if we chose. This time, we crowded around Mari while her capos filled three of the screens, each showing various levels of disbelief and shock.

A heavy moment of stunned silence descended on the meeting.

Mathias cleared his throat when it was clear no one else was going to speak. "How are we supposed to do that?"

Mari shrugged, fingers tapping on her leg. "Tell the press

there's a gas leak or a landslide. Say a potential tsunami's coming in. Hell, tell them the fault's rumbling and we're about to get a catastrophic earthquake. I don't give a fuck how you spin it. Just get the civilians out of Seattle."

"You say that like it's easy," Leo countered.

"I'm aware of the difficulties, but we don't have the time to worry about them. Between the three of you, I'm sure you can come up with a way to make it happen."

It was more than clear that the capos didn't share Mari's conviction, and I could understand why.

Seattle had a population of over 700,000. Even though we'd already moved a ton of people out of the city, there were still hundreds of thousands of citizens to remove and no place to put them. The compounds were secure, but most were already at capacity. The extra men we'd sent recently were a good protective measure that seemed to be working. Not a single hint of Cash catching wind of the safe space, which I knew gave us all some relief.

But that didn't mean we could afford to send more people there. The larger the group, the higher the risk my brother would find our little hideaway, and the second he did, it was game over.

"What about the clubs?" Gabriele's obvious change of topic was probably for the best. Mari's teeth were starting to grind. "We've got them on a skeleton crew right now, but—"

"Shut them down."

"For how long?"

"Until Cash is neutralized."

Gabriele's eyes widened, but he didn't voice his shock, unlike Leo, who huffed loud enough for us all to hear. "We can't shut down the clubs. It will destroy our income and probably kill the economy."

Mari's glare was hot enough to melt metal. "Better the economy than the people who support it."

An irritating *click, click, click* came from Mathias's screen, and he winced when he realized we could all hear it. "Can we afford to close everything?"

"That's a lot of money to lose," Gabriele agreed.

Grey leaned forward. "We've got enough to keep us going for a little while, but it would be in our best interest to end this soon. Once we rebuild, we have plans to recoup any losses we incur."

The idea of going bankrupt was terrifying, but I knew better than to doubt Mari. If whatever she had planned didn't work, Grey's plan would. We'd be back on top before anyone noticed we were floundering. That was only *if* we ended up financially fucked.

"Not everyone can afford to leave," Gabriele said.

He wasn't wrong. I had no doubt in my mind that anyone Cash could hurt would die screaming. He'd do it just to draw Mari out. In fact, I was surprised he hadn't already. Then again, he'd tried to kidnap Aislynn three times, so maybe he just hadn't been able to get hands on his preferred bait.

"I have calls in to get help for the people who actually need it." When they still looked unconvinced, she sighed. "Look, I understand this is a lot to take on, but we don't have a choice. We've gotten lucky with the body count so far, but it's only going to rise. The best thing to do is get anyone nonessential out of the city. Any of our people who want to leave can go without punishment—we don't need to worry about someone going AWOL on the battlefield—but there's no guarantee of their position when they return. Anyone who stays better be ready to give their life for the cause."

Leo leaned forward. "Some of our men are cowards. If you give them the chance to leave, they will."

"Some will," Mari agreed. "There will be more who stay, if only to say they were here on the ground when we stomped out Cash's influence."

"You have that much faith in your men?"

"I have that much faith in myself. If I'm a good leader, my men will rally. They'll fight behind me, not because they're being commanded to, but because they know it's their duty. Anyone who runs now is a chickenshit who doesn't deserve to live under my banner. Not all men can be counted on during times of war. It'd be best if we get them out before they fuck us over."

It was obvious they both respected and resented Mari's opinion.

"We'll give the word," Leo promised.

While he and Mathias got to work on their phones themselves, Gabriele leaned closer to the screen. "About the evacuation notice. I've got a friend who has contacts in the news centers. He can probably help us out."

Mari blinked at her uncle, her voice low and dubious. "A friend."

"Yes." Gabriele's face stayed unmoving while his ears grew red.

Mari hummed under her breath, fingers tapping along her leg again. "This friend of yours got a name?"

He swallowed, looking away for a split second before turning back. Mari didn't push, though I could tell she wanted to. "Do you trust him?"

"With my life." Those three words held so much longing that it sent goose bumps over my skin. Whoever the guy was, Gabriele had more than friendly feelings toward him. Feelings I doubted he'd shared with anyone else.

Looking at Mari, I wondered what it would be like to have to love her in the shadows instead of out loud. What would it feel like to see my angel and not be able to touch her or kiss her or show anyone what she meant to me?

Torture. Pure and simple.

Nodding at Gabriele, Mari raised her voice, pulling the others back into the conversation. "Gabriele's agreed to contact the news. He'll feed them some bullshit story to get everyone moving."

"Are we sure this is a good idea?" Leo asked, finally tuning back in. "Widespread hysteria is a beacon for the government to swoop in. We can't afford for them to cause more chaos right now."

"We've got the government handled," Mari promised, a wicked gleam in her eye.

The capos didn't seem convinced, but they were less uncomfortable than before. Hard to disagree with Mari when it was clear she wasn't planning to let it go. Greyson and Dominic rolled their eyes at how easily they changed opinions, and I had to agree.

Not only was it annoying, it was a problem. Weak men at the helm of an organization would put the whole thing at risk. Mari was a force of nature, but if the men who led her armies weren't, we were all doomed.

Should we talk about replacing them when Cash was taken care of? According to Grey, they'd been in power since Mario was alive. They'd been his right-hand men, his brothers-in-arms and blood, but that was a long time ago. Things had changed. The *world* had changed.

While Gabriele was committed to Mari, the others were a fight when she needed them to listen. That didn't even touch the fact that they'd actively tried to remove her from her position.

Family or not, they were a risk to her authority and her life.

Yeah, we'd definitely be considering some new blood around the table soon.

Killer seemed like a good start to me. The kid had done well during the Cameron situation, and he'd gotten his territory under control and thriving quicker than expected, even with the Aces interference. He was young and loyal, smart and open to new ideas and ways of thinking. Even though he'd spent years in jail, he had street smarts that had already paid off in droves.

He'd make a good capo whenever Mari was ready to take the leap.

After a short discussion, the capos were handed orders to create small diversions that would amplify the story Gabriele was going to spread. The city didn't need more damage, but it was necessary to get people to evacuate.

With plans made, it was time for the worst part of the meeting.

"Before you go, there's one more thing to discuss."

After considering all sides, Mari had decided to tell the capos what she'd discovered. They needed to know Cameron wasn't coming back, but she also needed to quash any ideas that she was a threat to their safety if they found out on their own. We didn't need them taking justice into their own hands or removing her from the picture if they thought Mari was cleaning house. I just hoped they took it well.

Dominic and Grey didn't budge from their positions against the wall, but I felt their tension. We all knew that if the capos handled this poorly, we'd have another fight on our hands. Mari didn't want her remaining uncles to die, but we'd bury them ourselves if it kept her safe. No fucking way were we going to war, just to get shot in the back by those assholes.

Gabriele, Leo, and Mathias sat back in their chairs, watching Mari warily. Still, she didn't speak. When she cleared her throat for the third time, I realized it wasn't an intentional pause. She didn't want to tell them.

I couldn't imagine how hard this was for her. Her hesitation was all it took for me to slide my hand onto her shoulder. I wanted to be there for her, to give her whatever strength she needed to get through this, and thankfully, it worked.

She took a deep breath, her fingers brushing mine. "Cameron is no longer with the family."

There was a moment's pause before Gabriele crossed himself and Mathias cursed.

Chapter Twenty-Three

"He's dead?" Leo swallowed hard.

Mari stared him down, her face disturbingly blank on screen. "He's a traitor."

Utter silence.

"Was there proof?" Mathias asked, only to shrink when she glared into the camera. "Not that we don't believe you, but I think we would all feel more comfortable with evidence in hand."

Though they'd argued earlier, it was clear Mathias was trying to keep the peace with his request.

Mari didn't respond, just watched until he squirmed in his seat. After a minute, she waved Greyson forward. With a few clicks, he was sharing the screen of his tablet with everyone. All the screenshots of conversations we'd found on Cameron's phone, plus the photos and videos I'd taken at the clubhouse, right there for all to see.

"He's been meeting with Cash for a long time," I said carefully, not knowing if I had a right to speak at all. When Mari sent me a grateful smile, I continued. "He gave up the intel Cash used to kill his brother, among other things."

The news was something Mari herself had asked about after taking time to think about Cameron's confessions. Cash had already taken credit for the attempted hit on her, but how else would he have known where she'd be? She'd only told the most important people in her life.

My confirmation had nearly devastated her all over again, but she stayed strong, knowing we were going to end Cash and spend the rest of our lives making Cameron wish he'd died too. It was the only retribution I could offer her.

Gabriele crossed himself again, and Leo turned away, swallowing hard against the sheen in his eyes. According to Mari, everyone had loved Rey. He'd been the bright, smiling joy of the family, and it was obvious his loss was still painful to everyone he'd loved.

"Will he die?" Mathias eventually asked. He seemed as weighed down as the others, his head shaking with disbelief. He didn't attempt to argue Cameron's innocence, and I was grateful. No doubt Mari wouldn't handle that well.

"Not until Aislynn has had time to digest and say what she needs," she said.

"He'll be imprisoned indefinitely?"

"For now." Maybe forever.

He nodded. "What about Cash?"

"We've got weapons shipments coming in bulk over the next few days. We'll need any help you can spare to make sure it's all checked and accounted for. With any luck, we should be moving on him as soon as the city's clear."

"How soon?" Gabriele asked. His eyes glittered with something that looked an awful lot like rage to me. I hoped he stoked it, held it close to his heart, and nurtured it, so that when we went to war, he was ready to explode and take out every Ace he met.

Mari glanced between Grey and me, knowing we'd been handling most of the shipment details for her. "Within two weeks."

Probably sooner.

"Who will take Cameron's place?"

It was the least of our worries, but I could understand why Mathias wanted to know.

Mari sighed. "As of right now, I have no plans to—"

"It should be Nate." All of us turned to Leo with varying levels of shock, me most of all.

"What the fuck?"

Whoops. Didn't mean to say that out loud.

Leo glared at the screen—likely at me, which was exactly why I didn't understand the nomination. The man barely tolerated my presence. "If you're serious about having him in your life after this is over, he needs more power than your bodyguard can have. He needs to add to your reputation. He can't be seen as the one you picked for love. He must be as ruthless as you are."

How the fuck was I supposed to do that? How were any of us supposed to add to Mari? She'd been ruling Seattle for so many years alone. She didn't need us to ramp up the reputation she'd built by herself. If people thought she wasn't scary enough on her own, they were fucking stupid and deserved what they got.

The annoyed grunts of Greyson and Dominic agreed with my point, but Mari didn't notice. She tapped her fingers on the table, though I could tell it wasn't in annoyance. She was considering what he said.

"Nate has his own reputation."

"His mercenary days help," Leo admitted. "But being a Beckstrom is going to lose him credit."

"I'm not a Beckstrom," I interrupted. "Technically, I'm a Black."

"Technically, you're still not a Marcosa, and that's a mark against you."

Well, what the fuck was I supposed to do about that?

I was about to say as much when Gabriele cleared his throat. "It might be better to table this discussion until things quiet down."

Yes. Solid suggestion. Let's go with that.

"Agreed." Mari shoved the chair back, and the others followed. "I'd like you all to make it known that Cameron is no longer with us, but leave out any details beyond that."

"You're not telling the rest of the family what he did?" Mathias asked, holding his hands up when she glared at him again. "Just asking."

"I'm choosing to keep certain information that could destabilize my organization to myself, and I expect you to do the same. It does no good to tell anyone we had a fox in the henhouse for so fucking long, and I can promise if word gets out, I'm coming for you three first."

With solemn nods and promises to keep their mouths shut, they exited the video chat.

The sudden silence was jarring. It left too much room to think.

Me. Capo.

What an awful idea.

Mari twisted in her chair, watching me warily. Seriously, though. What the hell was Leo thinking? I couldn't run this family. I'd been actively working against them for *years* before meeting Mari.

I was not a good choice for capo.

"Why not?" Mari asked.

Shit. I didn't mean to say that out loud. I half hoped not answering would make her back off, but I should've known better. Mari didn't back off for anyone.

"Seriously, you're as loyal as they come."

I swallowed. "I wasn't always."

"Here we go again." Dominic rolled his eyes, but he, of all people, should have understood my hesitation. I hadn't always done what was best for Mari.

"You were loyal when it counted," he said, daring me to argue.

I couldn't, so I didn't. "It's a bad idea."

Mari stepped into me, and I wrapped my arms around her automatically as she scraped her fingers along my shirt. "Would you hurt me again?"

"Of course not."

Dominic nodded behind her. "Lie?"

"No."

"Betray us?" Greyson asked.

"Never," I growled.

"Exactly." Mari ran her hand along my cheek, smiling when I

rubbed it against her. "Leo knows this. He sees you making up for your mistakes. They all do, and they know whose side you're on."

"Yours. Only yours." It was a promise and a devotion in one.

Mari's smile widened. "I know."

"Great, we all know you're part of the family. Can we move the fuck on?" Dominic griped, shaking his head as he walked out. "Fucking guilty consciences."

Greyson smothered his laugh but nodded to me before dropping a kiss to Mari's head. "We'll see you later."

We stood there, wrapped around each other for a moment before I had to say it. "It's an honor to be chosen as capo, but I'm not sure it's the right thing for me."

"We'll discuss it after your brother's dead," she promised, pulling me down for a filthy kiss that promised a world of pleasure in the near future.

Well, if she was going to distract me with her body, who was I to say no?

"What else do we need to do today?" I palmed her ass, lifting her onto the desk to prove just how devoted I was. She'd slipped on a sundress earlier, so I shoved it up to her hips, enjoying the scrap of pale blue lace covering her pussy. "Christ, you're beautiful. And I'm hungry."

I'd already knelt and started pressing kisses to her inner thighs when she finally answered. "All I've got planned is sending some emails and setting up a meeting."

My brow rose when I caught her eyes glittering with mischief. "What kind of meeting?"

"Nothing much, really." I gave her my best *I don't believe you* look as I pulled the lace down her legs, and she laughed, wrapping her fingers in my hair and pulling me straight toward her glistening cunt. "We're going to make a deal with the devil, baby."

Chapter 24
Mari

W e exited the car to a line that twisted around the building, everyone desperately waiting to see if their names were on the list for Gilded's final night.

The club was shutting down indefinitely for *unexpected repairs,* and it wasn't the only one. Wicked was undergoing renovations due to a faulty water line that didn't exist. We'd even had some of the smaller businesses take time off. It felt like running away, but it was the only option to keep people safe.

Giving Cash fewer targets to fixate on was in everyone's best interest.

The club was still as beautiful as ever. Deep pomegranate walls and brushed gold everywhere. Still the crown jewel of my empire. Cash's previous attempts at destroying it had been weak, but he'd attempt it again before this was over.

Just being here made me jumpy, though that wasn't the only reason.

"Everything's going to be okay," Nate promised, pulling me closer with a hand on my hip. I wasn't so optimistic.

Dominic, who was holding my hand on the other side, squeezed my fingers in silent support.

We'd all dressed up for the night, and I knew we looked incredible as a group. Greyson's sapphire-blue silk shirt complemented the black suit he'd paired it with, while Nate had stuck with an expensive emerald-green T-shirt and a pair of ass-hugging jeans. Dominic's style fit somewhere between the business and casual they sported, with dark-washed jeans and a blood-red button-up that made his eyes molten. It was very bad-boy chic.

They looked fucking edible, and I rubbed my legs together as the first kernels of heat warmed me.

What I wouldn't give to take one of these men to the bathroom for a little distraction.

Dominic squeezed my hand again, though this time, he took the opportunity to look me over.

I'd stuck with a dark purple dress that cinched tight at the bust and waist and flared around my thighs. It looked whimsical until you saw the very occupied thigh holster. I'd paired it with heeled boots, knowing they'd be easier to run in later if necessary.

"Have we told you how beautiful you look?" he asked as he bit his lip, clenching my hand tighter. "I want to sink my teeth into you."

Um, yes. Now, please.

He chuckled under his breath when he heard my sharp inhale, but he pulled me forward before I could say as much. Rude.

"Your booth, ma'am." Dominic's bow was over-the-top dramatic, and I rolled my eyes.

"Get in." I shoved him down, making sure I gave his ass a nice tap as I did. Nate and Grey smothered their laughs, but Dominic's eyes were burning when I took my seat beside him.

The U-shaped booth was darker than the others in the club and sectioned off by the guard standing close by. The low table in front gave us space for drinks, which appeared without asking, but didn't disrupt the view—the whole point of the booth. From here, we could watch the entire club, from the front door to the side stairs. It was obvious that this booth wasn't for just anyone—no reservation sign needed.

They each took one side of the booth, leaving me in the corner between Dominic and Nate, but I didn't mind. I downed the first drink fast, ordering another before the empty glass had even hit the table. Our server scurried off, returning with my drink and disappearing when Greyson waved him away with a curt, "That'll be all, Jimmy."

"I wanted another," I protested.

"After the meeting."

The argument was right there when Dominic squeezed my thigh. "You can't be drunk when we meet your cousin."

What the fuck?

"Who said I was getting drunk?" Really, they should've known me better than that. As anxious as I was to get things dealt with, I was neither stupid nor suicidal enough to drink my way through a meeting with the Feds. "It was just to calm my nerves."

Working with the man made me itchy.

Nate hauled me into his lap and kept me there with a palm to the hip, glaring at Dominic when he tried to steal me back. Wrapping his free hand around my throat, Nate tipped my head back until it hit his shoulder and he could whisper freely against my neck. "I get that you're stressed, but we all agreed this is the right move. Are you having second thoughts?"

"No, I'm just not sure I trust them." I didn't just mean the government either. Two-Bit might've been blood, but he was still an unknown factor, and I didn't like that we were heading into this situation without a good read on him or his intentions.

Nate hummed against me, his palm sliding over my hip until it wedged between my thighs. He was so close to my pussy that I could feel the heat of him through my panties even though he wasn't touching them. Goddamn, I was too wound up for this. "Whatever happens, we'll figure it out together. Stop stressing."

"How long until they get here?" I asked, swallowing against the pressure on my throat. Greyson's eyes glittered. He knew exactly why I asked. "Twenty minutes. Maybe less."

Thank fuck.

The way the booth was lit meant we had almost complete privacy. Sure, people could look over and see something if the light flashed just right, but no one was stupid enough to watch us outright. They didn't want to draw my attention by looking too long at something that wasn't theirs. We could do anything we wanted, and I knew just how to spend our wait.

I let my legs fall open a little, hoping to force Nate's hand right to the apex of my—

It disappeared from between my legs, only to smack hard against the outside of my thigh. "What do you think you're doing, angel?"

"Yeah, Mari. What are you doing?" I'd twisted so Dominic was right in front of me, elbows on his knees, drink dangling in his fingers, and those eyes burning over my body. He took a sip, tongue darting out to capture the last drop that escaped when he lowered it again, and I felt like I was dick-drunk.

I wanted them, needed them to fill me up the way only they could. I was desperate for their touch and the way they fed me reassurance through it.

My men were the only ones who could ground me, and I needed it bad.

"I just— I want—"

The need inside me mixed with my stress until I knew I couldn't explain it out loud. So, I showed them. Latching on to Nate's hand, I slid it between my legs and rolled my hips, but he snaked an arm around me to hold me still. Frustrated, I growled, trying to wiggle myself against his cock, to find friction—fucking *anything*.

Nate smacked me again. "Keep squirming and I'm going to give you something else to occupy your mind...and your mouth."

From the other side of the booth, Grey laughed. "That's exactly what she wants."

"Is that so? Do you need me to take the edge off, angel?" Nate moved his hand, rubbing the damp fabric between my legs just enough to tease at giving me the friction I craved before moving away. I whined, chasing the touch before I realized they were laughing.

"I swear to God, if someone doesn't fuck the nerves out of me..." That frustration grew until I was digging my nails into Nate's thighs. Jeans or not, he was going to feel that later.

"Pretty sure that's not how you ask, *reina*." Grey stood, checking his watch again as he moved around the table to get to me. "We don't have time for all three of us to fuck you. Nate's already got you on his lap. Dominic?"

"You play. I'll join at the end."

"Perfect. Are you ready, wife?"

Grey's grin was damn near feral as he slipped my thighs over Nate's arms, forcing him to hold me open. "Your turn."

Nate's laugh skated down my neck, quickly followed by his lips. "No problem."

"Show us how ready she is. Fuck, you're so perfect, *mariposa*." Nate hiked my dress up around my hips, and Grey threw my panties to Dominic, who tucked them into his pocket with a wink. "Saving these for later."

The part of me that knew she was about to get two dicks didn't want to be greedy, but I shut her down quick. "You're not going to fuck me after the meeting?"

Dominic's eyes glittered as he watched me pout. "Depends. Show me how good you can be for your husband, and I'll think about it."

Why was that so hot?

Grey tapped Nate's knees, spreading his legs so he could kneel between them. "We have to make this fast."

"Okay." I was still frantically nodding when I fisted his hair and pulled his mouth to me.

His warm breath against my desperate skin was everything, and when he slid a flattened tongue across my clit, I nearly screamed. He slipped two fingers inside me, groaning at how soaked I was as he worked me over exactly how I wanted. "Were you needy, *reina*? Were you over there squirming, desperate for our cocks?"

Nate laughed against my shoulder. "Of course she was. She's got us so addicted to her taste, it's only fair."

Dominic nodded, grinning when Grey's contented hum vibrating along my clit made me writhe. Nate and Dominic took turns whispering dirty things, while Grey worked an orgasm from my body that nearly stole my sight.

I was still coming down from it when a cock slid into me. "I thought we had to be quick," I panted.

"Trust me, I won't last long." My vision cleared enough to watch Greyson trap his bottom lip between his teeth, eyes furrowed in concentration. "Fuck, I love when you're like this. Swollen and needy and dripping down my balls. I'm going to smell like you for days."

More like forever.

I tried to speak, tried to tell him I liked him like this too, but all that came out were one-word sentences.

Harder. Deeper. More. Please.

But Grey didn't need more than that. He'd always known exactly what I needed and played my body like he'd memorized every cheat code to it. When I came again, it was with his name on my lips.

Grey eased me through the orgasm, pumping into me with slow, hard rolls of his hips that felt so goddamn good. It was like the climax that never ended. I tipped my head back, and I tried to keep my body from shivering when movement to the side of the booth stole my attention.

In the shadows, a man watched us with wide eyes and trembling fingers. He looked like he wanted to run just as much as he wanted to touch himself. Like he knew we were the last people he should be peeping on, but he couldn't look away.

My pussy clenched. Something about the lust and fear on his face turned me on. "Grey."

"That's it, baby. Tell us who's inside you." He shuddered through his orgasm, neck straining in release.

"No, *Grey*."

His eyes, which had been focused on where our bodies met, immediately lifted to mine. As soon as they did, his attention shifted to where I was looking. I could tell he saw the man too, when his fingers clenched on my thighs. "We've got a watcher."

Nate's head barely moved, but the little voyeur's face drained. He dropped his drink on the nearest table and hightailed it out of the building.

Dominic laughed, but it was tainted with something unhinged. "Good riddance."

Grey slipped out of my body, tucking himself away as I whimpered, but I wasn't empty for long. Nate lifted me enough to notch himself inside before he let go and dropped me on his cock. Gravity meant I took every inch of him at once, and it sucked the air from my lungs. "God, you're so big."

"That's it, baby. Stroke his ego." Grey winked when Nate

flipped him off, which only lasted until I laughed. Then both of us were too busy moaning to care what the others did.

And they were plotting.

Greyson had moved over to Dominic's side, and they were whispering over the former's phone while I adjusted to Nate. I felt a little pain, but mostly a lot of pleasure.

"What're you doing over there?"

"You're not keeping her entertained enough, Black," Dominic teased, and Nate lifted me up and dropped me right back on his cock, watching me squirm when my ass met his hips.

It felt so good when he did that. Borderline too much, but my men made the hurt feel good. And the show of strength when he picked my whole body up like that? Mini orgasms, I swear.

"Don't worry about them." Nate forced my legs wider with his, giving Dominic and Grey a full view of him inside me. "They're just taking care of our unwanted guest."

The watcher.

Oh shit.

"You think he liked what he saw, angel? Liked seeing this perfect pussy stretched around our cocks? I bet he heard the way you begged for more too. Our filthy queen."

"Yes," I breathed, unsure how I felt about it. On the one hand, I liked the idea of being caught. On the other, I didn't want anyone but my men seeing me vulnerable. It felt wrong. I was theirs.

Nate's laugh drifted over my lips when he hauled my head back again. The movement caused me to lift on my toes. Exactly what he wanted. As I held myself above him, Nate fucked me from below, making sure I got every inch of him as he did. "Good. Everyone should have a memorable last moment on earth."

"What?" I was too focused on the building sensations in my core, desperately reaching for the pleasure just out of reach, to understand what he meant.

"You think we're going to let him live after that? He watched our woman come. Saw this perfect body spread out for us." Nate leaned back just as Dominic reached over and smacked my clit so hard I folded in half.

Goddamn.

He gripped my chin, hauling me back up again.

"No one gets to see you but us, *mariposa*, and they certainly don't get to survive if they do."

I knew I was fucked up when my pussy clenched at the thought of them murdering a man for that, but whatever. Nate cursed under his breath, shifting just enough that he slid over my G-spot with his thrusts. "She liked that."

Dominic's smile was pure male satisfaction. "Of course she did. Our Mari likes when we go dark for her. Don't you, baby? It gets you hot."

"Yes." He rewarded me by running his knuckles across my clit, and my legs shook.

Nate lifted my pelvis higher, holding me exactly where he wanted until I dug my fingers into his hands. No doubt everyone in the club knew what we were doing, but I didn't fucking care. I wanted them to know. Wanted them to see these men worship me.

Wanted to show the world that they were mine. All mine.

"That's it, angel. You're almost there."

I was. My body was tense, poised to fall over the cliff the second they told me to.

"You're such a good girl," Nate whispered. "Now, come for us. Give your men what they want. Squeeze me dry."

And I did.

Head back, chest heaving as I screamed their names. Nate kept his pace until I sagged in his lap, then he slammed me down, forcing me to grind on him until he came so deep inside me, I wasn't sure I'd ever get him out.

"Fuck me, that was amazing." He pressed a kiss to my temple.

"A solid 9.5." Dominic came over and hauled me off Nate's lap despite both our protests, spreading me out on the booth between them. I'd barely settled before he was climbing over me, stroking his cock. "You look freshly fucked, *mariposa*. I can't wait to add to it."

"I thought we didn't have time for you all to fuck me," I snarked, though it faded when his tip nudged my clit. It was so oversensitive, I twitched, but God, I wanted him to touch me anyway.

He smirked, grinding into me a little harder. "We don't."

While I frowned, Dominic kissed my nose before sitting back on his knees. He looked so imposing up there, completely dressed, with that big cock in his hands. He looked like he was ready to ruin me, mark me, make me his.

I wanted it so bad I could taste it.

"Don't get come on her dress," Grey warned, but Dominic's smirk deepened.

"Trust me, I won't."

He stayed like that, poised above me, hitting my clit with every stroke until his rhythm changed. His teeth were bared, forearms tense as he stroked harder and faster, bringing me with him.

I couldn't see anyone but him until Greyson cleared his throat. "Two-Bit said they're two minutes out."

"Almost there. Come with me, Mari."

That was the easy part. I was holding it off until he was finished. Reaching between us, I palmed his balls, rubbing them as best I could. "I need you to come, Dominic."

"Don't worry, baby, I'm already there. It feels too good when you touch me like that." He groaned my name as he slipped his dick between my lips, painting my clit with his come before lifting up just enough to bathe the rest of me in it too. By the time he was done, my entire pussy was coated in him, and he looked feral at the sight of it. I wanted to be mad because he'd just created a huge fucking mess, but I'd never felt quite as desired as I did when all three of them zeroed in on it. Even though we didn't have time, I slid my fingers between my legs, swirling them around before popping them into my mouth to taste all of our releases combined.

"Jesus Christ," Nate grunted, readjusting himself behind me.

Dominic grinned. "Fuck, you look beautiful covered in me, *mariposa.*"

"One minute out," Grey said tightly. He didn't even attempt to fix his dick. Just watched me with eyes that said we were doing that again.

Sighing, I pushed Dominic back so I could swing my legs around and stand. "I need to run to the bathroom."

Dominic looked behind me and shook his head. "We don't have time for that, *mariposa.*"

"I'll be quick."

"No."

"No?"

"You heard me."

"Oh shit," Nate whispered. Grey just laughed.

"I must've heard wrong. I'm going to wipe off *your* come. I'll be right back."

Scoffing, I stood, only for Dominic to stand with me. He wrapped his hand around my throat, forcing my body into his. "No, you're going to do as you're told."

What the actual fuck?

I narrowed my eyes, and Dominic tightened his grip just enough to keep me silent. "Sit there and wear our mess happily, or as soon as our guests leave, I'll have you licking it off the booth."

There was something about Dominic bossing me around that hit me straight in the libido. Fuck me.

I shivered, and he ran his lips along my neck. "Are you going to listen to me?" When I still didn't answer, he bit the soft skin and my whole body jerked.

Chapter Twenty-Four

"I'm not wearing panties," I whispered.

"I'm aware. Keep those gorgeous legs closed so no one else figures it out." Still holding me captive, he forced me back into my seat, following me down to whisper against my lips. "Be a good girl, and I'll fuck you to sleep when we get home."

Oh, hell yes.

He smiled, kissed me hard, and sat down beside me while my whole body buzzed.

Nate shifted in his seat with the tiniest frown.

I bumped his shoulder. "Problem?"

He huffed, but the grin threw off his moody vibes. "Just thinking that I'd have come somewhere else if I'd known that was an option."

I scoffed while Dominic fucking preened. "You need to get more creative than that, Black."

Jesus Christ. Men.

"Oh, trust me. I'm plenty creative." The way Nate smirked at me made my entire body flush in the best of ways, and the smirk only got bigger when I refused to look at Dominic.

"We'll finish this later. They're here."

Game time.

I was still trying to find a position where I wasn't sitting in a puddle of come when Two-Bit and Griz came over. My cousin still looked as stoic as always, but he had an added tightness around his eyes that made me wonder how much trouble Cash was getting into that we didn't know about.

Grey and Nate patted them down, even going so far as to dig through the leather bag Griz carried. They took the guns they found and slid them onto the table, promising to give them back when the meeting was over.

I squirmed again, trying to ignore the very wet feeling between my thighs, and Dominic dropped his hand on my thigh, stilling my body with a single look.

Right. No wiggling.

He'd have me ass-up, tongue-out the second Two-Bit left if I didn't knock it off, and I wasn't willing to test just how clean our crew kept things.

"Do you want a drink?" I asked, beckoning the Feds to sit.

Griz looked like he'd order a drink, but Two-Bit shot him a look before turning to me. "We don't want to be here too long. You said you had an answer for us."

We'd talked in circles until deciding we were taking the deal. Working with the government felt fundamentally wrong in ways only someone who'd been raised in the criminal world would understand, but it was the best option we had. We weren't spending the rest of our lives in jail for Cash. "Before I say anything, I want assurances."

Two-Bit nodded to Griz, who slipped a stack of papers out of the bag he carried. I didn't bother to read, sliding them over to Greyson. We all sat quietly while he sent pictures of the pages to Laidan, who was on standby with Ronan, before reading it over twice himself. He was about to go through it a third time when my phone rang.

Laidan.

"The deal's good. Immunity for any actions that get Cash out of the picture. Obviously, they're not putting *kill the asshole for us* on the contract, but the vagueness works in your favor, especially since it doesn't actually have a time limit. It could even be said that your get-out-of-jail-free card is indefinite."

My eyes moved to my cousin. Two-Bit stared back at me, and I couldn't be totally sure, but I got the idea he'd worded the contract intentionally to give me some extra wiggle room, and I appreciated it.

"They even added monetary compensation for any losses you suffer, also vague, so I can probably get financial retribution for any buildings destroyed *and* loss of life."

The stipulation was one we'd added after talking to Two-Bit the first time. I hadn't been sure the government would agree, but apparently they didn't mind paying us to murder Cash. Nice.

Laidan's voice dropped. "There are some clauses about potentially being a part of stings for other organizations, but they made it clear that your involvement would be surface-level and your name would never be linked to their investigations. Beyond that, it's what we expected. You do the dirty work, and as long as you keep the drugs out of Seattle, you're free and clear."

"I understand. Thanks for your help."

She laughed. "You're paying us more than enough for an after-hours phone call. Good luck with the Feds. Call us when it's over."

Ronan Donnaghal had called his entire family to Ireland, planning to hunker down out of the country while I waged war. I didn't hold it against him. If this was anyone else's battle, I'd have slipped my family onto a jet and stolen away in the night, too.

Sadly, a war wasn't won without its general.

"Fly safe."

Hanging up, I looked straight at Two-Bit. He had endless patience most days, but he was too wired for that now. "Well?"

"You got a pen?"

His shoulders dropped as he reached into his pocket and tossed the pen to me. "You're doing the right thing."

"I'm doing the only thing," I corrected, signing the pages before handing them to Grey to photograph.

He slid them back over to Griz, with Laidan's card on top. "Our lawyer is expecting it immediately, and they better match up."

"They'll have it by the end of the night," Griz promised.

Mari

"No one can find out about this." Even though I knew we both had a lot to lose if our agreement got out, I still had to say it.

Two-Bit shoved his hands into his pockets. "The powers that be are well aware what'll happen if they let our involvement with you slip." Namely, my death. "They don't want someone worse taking over."

"As long as they stick to their terms, I'll stick to mine." I wasn't hopeful that the government would actually do what they promised, but that was my burden.

Playing spy would save our skin now, but who knew if it would damn us in the long run.

This better be worth it.

Chapter 25
Mari

I was checking over quarterly profits for the club inventory when the alarm beeped. Pulling up the security system on my phone, I verified it was my guest, hit the button for the garage, and locked down the office. By the time I made it to the garage, Aislynn was wringing her fingers by the hood of her car.

She was too pale, hair hanging limp. Her normally bright eyes were dull and sunken, with heavy purple bags underneath them. The worst part was how hunched she was, a hand wrapped around her torso like she was trying to protect her soft spots.

Where just last month she'd been glowing with love, now she was an imitation of herself.

It made me hate Cameron even more, especially because I wasn't sure how to act. If I tried to hug her, would she rebuke me? Did she want comfort or support, or would she prefer it came from someone other than me?

Maybe I was an unfortunate reminder of the mistakes she'd made—the mistakes we'd both made. Knowing that, I wouldn't want to hug me either.

We stared at each other, the distance a chasm, until her eyes welled and a tear tracked down her cheek.

"Fuck it." My long strides meant I wrapped her in a hug just as the sobs started. The thing no one told you about friendship was that when their hearts broke, so did yours. Seeing Ash, I knew this was no different. Every shuddering gasp dug a little deeper at my heart. She twisted her fingers in my shirt, holding me to her. Eventually, it became less of me holding her together and more about the two of us connecting in a way that I hadn't realized I needed.

I needed to know that she didn't hate me for my cousin's actions. That she could look at me and see past the blood I shared. I had to know that our friendship could survive the chaos he'd wrought. When Ash hugged me back, I knew we'd be okay.

This might be a roadblock, but it wasn't the end of us.

"I'm sorry," I whispered, though the words didn't feel like enough.

"You didn't know," she whispered, holding me tighter than before. "I know you wouldn't put me in this position willingly. Plus, you're making it better. Thank you for the divorce papers."

"They aren't enough."

"They're a good start, though. Having them with me, knowing I'll be free of him in every way soon... It means a lot." Ash looked away like she was embarrassed. "Sorry I snotted on you."

Snorting, I wrapped an arm around her shoulder and steered her inside the house. "You can snot on me anytime."

"Gross." Her wrinkled nose disappeared as she took in the new space.

It was so interesting watching someone else look at our home for the first time, but the smile on her face was a sight for sore eyes.

"It's beautiful, Mari."

"It's all Grey's work."

"No doubt." She laughed, but I didn't mind. We all knew Greyson was better at decorating than I was.

Things were slightly more comfortable as I walked her through the house to the lounge we gravitated toward most. The area was sunken in, giving it a cozy feel despite the high ceilings. Grey had bought a massive couch with plenty of corners to snuggle into while we watched the television hung on the wall. A shit-ton of blankets were in a huge basket near the fireplace, and the room had big windows we could open to look out at the back-yard whenever we wanted.

It was the perfect rainy-day spot.

Bonus, it was close to the kitchen, so we'd have easy access to Amara's snacks once she was home.

I curled into my favorite corner of the couch with a blanket on my lap, tossing Ash one too. "How are you doing?"

For a second, I thought she was going to lie, maybe try to pretend that she was doing great. Then she sighed, her body drooping into the cushions with a soft huff. "Awful. I feel stupid and foolish. Childish, even."

"Ash—"

She held up her hand. "I don't want to discuss it. You asked and I answered, but I don't want to talk about it now. I need time to get over it all."

It was the only thing she'd asked for since we'd found out, and even if I hated it, I couldn't tell her no. "Of course."

She cleared her throat, shifting on the seat before turning to look at me with a renewed vigor in her gaze. "Rafael said he has a safe house I can use."

"That's good." If Rafael offered a safe house, it meant that he knew he could actually keep her alive. "He won't do anything to hurt you."

"I know. That's not what I want to talk about, though." She cleared her throat, and my stomach dropped. "I'm going away for a while after this."

Oh. It wasn't that I wanted to keep her in Seattle—though I did—I just couldn't guarantee her safety anywhere else.

Has she really been all that safe here?

No, she hadn't. Fuck. "Where?"

She blew her hair out of her face, and I realized she needed a trim. Another thing about Aislynn that was off. She never let her hair go too long without professional styling. "Anywhere. I just need to heal, and I can't do it here, where there are memories of him and me."

And you.

She didn't have to say it.

I swallowed thickly, knowing she was trying to be honest even when it hurt. "Wherever you want to go, I'll make it happen," I promised.

She nodded, though I didn't know if she realized she was doing it. It was more of an impulse to soothe herself. "I just need a restart. To reinvent myself somewhere new where no one's ever met me. I need to wash myself clean of all of *this.*"

"You deserve it."

I was mentally sifting through places I could send her—resorts with on-site spas and massages and celebrity-level therapists who could take care of her and help her get her mind right—when the doorbell rang.

Ash stiffened at the sound, not blinking when I pulled a gun from under the table. She'd had to jump through hoops just to get inside the gates. No way I'd invited anyone else over.

Typing out a message to the boys, who'd left to check in with Moore and Tennessee now that they'd finished their sweep of Cameron's men—and to give us a little privacy—I let them know we had a guest.

My phone immediately started vibrating with texts, but I set it to silent and reached under the side table, pulling out two more guns and handing one to Aislynn. Her body shook, but her hand was steady as she checked it over before chambering a bullet.

Once she was armed, I dragged her with me to the pantry. "Stay back here until I say otherwise. If you hear gunshots, there's a small catch on the side wall that will take you to the underground portion of the garage. Right behind the Lucky Charms."

"Is that an Irish joke?" Her voice was tight, even with the attempted humor, and I flashed a smile her way.

"Dominic picked it."

That got an actual laugh. "Of course he did."

Our unwanted visitor rang the bell again, and I sucked in a breath. "Remember, stay here."

Even though I didn't want to leave her, I trusted that she could take care of herself. Once I was in the hallway, I pulled up the security cameras and swore, shooting off another text to my men, who'd flooded the group chat while I was busy. Slipping the still-vibrating phone into my pocket, I opened the door to the one man I'd never expected to see on my doorstep.

Victor Paez.

"Hello, Mari."

I was devoted to my men, but even I could admit that Victor was handsome.

Tall, dark, and dangerous, but the laugh lines on his face screamed that he could enjoy life with the best of them. Expensive clothes covered a body I was almost certain was as fit as my men, not that I'd find out. And that voice—dear God. He wasn't as old as I'd expected him to be either. Probably close to forty if he hadn't already hit it.

Hot or not, he was a snake in the grass, and I wasn't a fan of serpents.

I leaned in the doorway, making sure to keep my body between him and Aislynn. "There a reason you're here?"

"Figured it was time for us to talk face-to-face."

"Last I checked, I didn't invite you to my home."

He shrugged, but I could see that he was enjoying that he'd thrown me off. Asshole. "Yet here I am."

In other words, I'm not leaving. Well, fuck him for deciding that.

"Now's not a good time."

"You have a guest. I'm aware." When I raised an eyebrow, he almost smiled. "I wouldn't be very good at my job if I didn't know absolutely everything going into a situation."

He was Moore's occupational wet dream. "Your security team must love you."

"They certainly appreciate my efforts to stay safe."

For some reason, it made me chuckle, but the sound of Ash's footsteps behind me quickly wiped that away. "Is it safe to come out now?"

"No," I said, frowning when Victor responded, "Yes."

When I glared at him, he raised his arms to his sides. "I promise I'm not here to hurt either of you. I really do just want to talk. Feel free to search me if it will make you more comfortable."

Aislynn was at my back already, so I could either do what he was not-so-subtly suggesting or slam the door in his face and kiss my one chance at getting his help goodbye.

Fuck this.

"Eyes on him," I said.

"Got it." From the corner of my eye, I watched Ash lift the gun. Victor didn't seem nervous that two women were holding him up, but he did trail his eyes over my friend. In fact, the entire time I frisked him, he kept his focus on her.

Not good.

Victor's body was stacked with muscles that weren't too

obscene, which I got a serious feel for as I checked him over for weapons I didn't find. I almost wished he had some so I could kick him out without feeling a sliver of concern for how he'd react. Frankly, the way he was eye-fucking Ash was making me uncomfortable.

She was just getting out of one train wreck of a relationship. She didn't need another, and cartel men were far worse than mafia men. They took possessive to a whole new level. Crossing my arms, I jerked my chin at her to lower the weapon. "He's clean."

Victor frowned. "I told you, I come in peace."

"We're not really trusting men right now, so your word doesn't mean shit," Aislynn said caustically, dropping the gun to her side, though she didn't take her eyes off him, and not for the same reason he couldn't stop watching her. There was a boatload of mistrust in my friend's eyes.

"Is there a reason men are persona non grata at the moment?" When she didn't automatically answer, Victor stared at her, and I watched Ash struggle to hold still. I wasn't on the receiving end of that look, and even I felt how penetrating it was. Like he could peek inside her brain and see all the gory details of her marriage written out for him to read.

I shivered.

The motion caught his attention, and he blinked, pulling himself out of whatever moment they were having. With one last look at her, he turned back to me. "Could we take this inside? Like you said, my security team appreciates my ability to minimize the danger in situations they can't join me for, and I'd prefer not to take a bullet to the head right now."

There was no way we were being watched unless he'd brought Cash to my doorstep—in which case, I'd kill him myself—but he wasn't the only one uncomfortable with a conversation on the porch.

Keeping most of my attention on him, I looked over at Aislynn. *You okay with that?*

She shrugged. *Does it matter?*

Yeah, it did. If she wasn't comfortable with him coming inside the house, then he wouldn't be allowed in. She'd earned more than that small concession.

"We should get inside," she said softly. The haunted look as she passed reminded me that she'd been caught unaware and attacked by Cash three separate times. I planned to make him pay for each one.

Victor stepped forward, only to stop when I barred him with my arm. "Make one wrong move and I'll be down an ally."

"Of course. Thank you for allowing me into your home." He inclined his head before stepping fully inside the house.

"I doubt we could've stopped you," Ash mumbled, though there was a teasing grin on her lips.

"Likely not, but I appreciate the hospitality anyway." I shut the door as he turned to Ash and held out a hand. "Victor Paez, and you are Miss...?"

Considering he already knew I had a guest, I had no doubt that he knew who Ash was and that she was technically a Mrs.

That haunted look returned, and she crossed her arms awkwardly, rubbing her bare ring finger. "Aislynn O'Bannon."

Victor studied her finger absently, and I was sure I was right. He knew everything there was to know about Ash. The silence held us for a moment until he softened his voice. "I apologize if I've made you uncomfortable since I arrived."

"You didn't. Life did."

With nothing else to say about that, I motioned to Victor first. "Formal sitting room is over there."

He seemed amused but didn't contradict me as he walked ahead of both of us.

This was going to be a shitshow.

Chapter 26
Mari

Greyson planned the parts of the house we'd use most to be comfortable and soothing, but he also knew we'd likely have to entertain guests here at some point. So, he'd set up the first rooms in the house as my formal *Queen of Seattle* rooms.

Places that my people could come for official reports, spaces where allies could come to negotiate, all while being completely closed off from our actual home since the entire building was locked down with state-of-the-art security.

People couldn't piss under our roof without us knowing.

It was fucking brilliant, especially because he made it very clear with every piece of furniture and décor that people weren't encouraged to hang around. The walls were bright, sterile whites to match the most expensively bland fabrics imaginable.

The chairs were all hard corners, the lounges had stiff cushions, and not a single throw pillow was in sight beyond the couch

Ash and I headed to. It was softer than the rest, which made me itch just looking at them, but not by much. Again, anything to remind people to leave as soon as possible.

Victor settled onto the most uncomfortable couch known to man, sprawling like a king on someone else's throne. Knowing there were no weapons on his half of the room was the only thing that let me relax into the couch in front of him.

Aislynn sat, wiggling in place with a grumbled, "Christ, these are awful."

Victor's laugh was barely an exhale, but I saw the way Ash's lips tipped before they immediately dropped again. More evidence of the scars Cameron had left.

Not wanting to drag things out, I turned back to Victor. "I'll be honest, you seem far happier to see me than someone who just lost part of his business should."

He laughed again, much louder this time. Not sure I liked making him laugh as much as Ash did. "Cash was already cut off before you took the coke. Although, I think that helped you in the long run."

"You'd already cut him off?"

That didn't make any sense. Why would he cut off a man he'd already admitted was a cash cow? No pun intended.

I sounded exactly as mistrustful as I felt, and Victor heard it. "Cash wasn't as sneaky as he'd hoped. The rumors of him lacing the coke, losing it, snorting it—all of them found their way to me. It's bad form to fuck with a product when someone else's name is on it, and I'm particularly attached to my reputation. So, I cut him off. According to my intel, what you confiscated was the last of his personal supply."

If that was true, Cash had been stealing far more than even I'd suspected. The pictures Nate took—I blew out a breath. "That doesn't exactly tell me why you're here."

Victor leaned forward. "I'm here because I want to reiterate in person that my offer still stands."

Help removing Cash for the ability to import coke into Seattle. Which wasn't ideal, especially considering I had a federal contract buried in a safe somewhere on the premises, prohibiting that very thing.

I hummed under my breath, wondering if there was a way to leverage his help without ruining the immunity of sorts that I'd already secured.

Importing was the biggest incentive for Victor to work with me, and even if it wasn't something I was interested in, it was something I could work with. Greyson would know how to ferry the drugs to some other city if we had to, but with the watchful eyes of the government on us, I couldn't guarantee smooth passage the way I normally could. We'd already shut down the docks to regular shipments because we didn't trust Cash not to bomb it again.

Truthfully, we were hemorrhaging money at every turn. I had plenty, but there was only so long I could float the business from my personal accounts before things got dicey.

I had to keep Victor on board.

"What I'm about to tell you goes no further than this room."

He immediately shook his head. "I can't promise that. I need to be able to tell my second, at the very least."

Thinking back on the information we had on Paez and his second, I considered it. Maximoff Vega came from generations of Bratva soldiers. No doubt he would've joined too if not for his father meeting his mother in Colombia. Nine months later, he was born, they were married, and his father had left the home country for warmer shores. According to the intel, Victor's second was an asshole of extreme measures, but he took his word seriously.

"Promise me that your second will keep this to himself."

His nod was immediate. "I swear. Maximoff will keep it

quiet." I wasn't sure I believed him, but did I really have another choice? I had to tell him or risk the Paez cartel gunning for me when this was over. "My contacts say the Feds have a vested interest in the outcome of what happens with Cash. Even when this war is over, they're going to be watching me closely. There's not going to be any importing available until they find someone else to stalk. And even when I can import, I won't be able to distribute without tipping them off, and neither of us wants that."

It wasn't quite the truth, but it was as close to it as I was willing to get without promising to push drugs in my city. Truthfully, I thought he knew as much too.

Victor's eyes narrowed, and he seemed to war with himself, but finally, he nodded decisively. "I understand not wanting to put your people at risk. Perhaps there's something I can have in return."

His eyes drifted to Aislynn, and anger surged through my body so fast, my fingers tingled.

He wanted me to offer up my best friend as part of the contract. Whether as collateral or a body to warm his sheets, my answer was the same. To some leaders, giving away one of their people would be nothing, but I'd already asked too much of Ash, and she was still paying the price. I wouldn't do it to her again.

"I don't sell my people," I snarled. "You need to leave. Now."

Victor paused for a moment, letting me reconsider, but when I stood with crossed arms, he nodded to himself. "I understand."

He hadn't even finished standing when Ash's voice rang out. "Wait."

The determination pouring off her struck like a stone sinking in my stomach, and I fisted my hands. "You don't need to do this," I whispered so only she could hear. "I'll find another way."

"We don't have time for another way anymore. You obviously need his help, or you wouldn't have let him in." When I still didn't respond, she gripped my forearm. "Will it end this?"

Truthfully, yes, but I wasn't going to tell her that. "The answer is no, Aislynn."

"It's not your decision," she said firmly. "With my father, I didn't have a choice. My place was at the altar. Even with *him*, I knew it was my only way out, and I don't regret it. This time, it's my choice. I *choose* to do this for you and for our family and for the city we both love."

"You've done enough. You've been through enough."

Ash rolled her eyes. "I'm not going to fall in love with him."

I saw the way Victor flinched behind her before he schooled his face into something neutral.

Fuck, I did not need my best friend getting tangled up with a cartel leader. "Mari, if we say yes, we have a chance to negotiate terms we both want. If we say no and have to crawl back for help later, we're fucked."

Meaning, he could ask for her anyway, and I wouldn't have room to refuse. Fuck.

"I don't want you to do this," I admitted.

"I know, but it's done. What's one person in the grand scheme of things?" Ash asked.

The words hit me directly in my chest. Hadn't I just said that as I watched Kosas grieve his son and daughter-in-law? Two people I'd put in danger to end this war. Being willing to sacrifice his family while refusing to risk my own felt too hypocritical to condone.

"I'll be fine."

"If you're not, they all die."

"I know." She smiled before turning back to Victor, who watched her with what I could only call admiration. "I'm married."

He didn't even glance at her ring finger. "You're a hostage, not a whore."

There was no doubt he was borderline offended at the idea

that he'd use her like that, and it increased my opinion of him. I knew some made men didn't care about things like consent. That Victor did was an unexpected boon.

I sat back down on the couch next to Aislynn as she squared off in her seat. "What are the terms?"

Victor watched her with something verging on obsession, the way a king coveted what he wanted to own. It didn't ease my nerves at all. "Room and board. Money to spend. Freedom within reason."

"For how long?"

"A year."

Ash's eyes widened almost imperceptibly before they shuttered, and I wanted to end the negotiations now. My skin was itching with the need to do *something*, and I felt terrible knowing that I couldn't. I'd never felt more helpless in my life, and I'd watched my men get shot.

This is her choice, I reminded myself. Didn't mean I had to like it, though.

"Can you promise my safety?"

Victor's glare was icy, making me realize just how warm it had been before. "Of course. I wouldn't bring you to my home if you were in danger."

"Your home?" For the first time since she'd decided, Aislynn looked uncertain. She probably assumed she'd be in some apartment somewhere, locked far out of sight as the timer counted down, but I had no doubt Victor would keep her underfoot as much as possible.

He pulled out his phone, scrolling through it quickly before walking around the coffee table. I was tensing to shove myself between them when he dropped to his knees at her feet. No doubt my mouth was wide open, but what else was I supposed to do?

Ash hadn't released the gun in her grip. This powerful man

was giving my friend all the power in the world to end him. Happily, it would seem. It was nearly unheard of.

"I have an island just outside of Colombia. It's private and secure, with only my most trusted staff. You'll live there."

"Alone?"

"No. You'll never be alone." It should've felt threatening, but his gaze and voice were soft as he set his phone on her lap, his thumb swiping across her knee. More of a lover's promise than anything else.

I wondered if this was what Antoni and Shara had looked like when they'd met. Not quite love at first sight, but an unexpected connection forged in a single night. Did Ash feel that same draw? If she did, it was obviously reciprocated, unless he was as good an actor as my cousin. The way Aislynn shuddered made me wonder if she had the same thought.

Victor flipped through so we could see pictures of beautiful white sand beaches and clear blue water. Big trees and incredibly colorful flowers everywhere. It was as close to paradise as I could imagine and not far off from where I'd planned to send her when this was all over. He let her look over everything twice, even showing her pictures of the staff, which he tilted just far enough that I could see too.

Eventually, Ash handed the phone back. "It's beautiful."

"The perfect place to heal." There was a heavy weight of promise in his voice, and when Ash turned to me, it was with more hope than I'd seen since she'd found out about her husband's deceit.

Fuck, if he can give her that peace back, I may end up doing something I shouldn't. Like trusting the guy.

Victor moved to the windows on the opposite side of the room without a word, offering us as much privacy as he could, knowing he wasn't allowed to leave my sight.

"You're going." I had no doubt in my mind. Unfortunately for me, I also had the feeling this was the best decision for her.

Ash must've seen my acceptance, reaching for my hand with a tentative smile on her face. "Seriously, Mari. I want to do this. I need to." Her voice dropped, eyes darting to Victor, only to swallow when she found him already watching. "I need a redo."

"You're not marrying him," I grumbled, knowing there was no way I would deny her after everything. She laughed, and the sound was so shockingly bright that I smiled.

"Of course not, but he is pretty to look at."

She wasn't wrong. Hell, maybe she'd have some fun on that island when all this was over. Maybe she'd come back stronger than ever.

It's one year, and you have enough money to buy a plane. Let her go.

"I'll ensure your safety," I promised. Though, truthfully, the hostage deal Victor was offering was pretty good. I'd know for sure once he sent over the paperwork. Still, Ash had to know I'd always have her back.

She smiled. "I know. You always take care of me."

I didn't feel that way, especially not when I walked over with a hand out to Victor Paez and gave him my best friend. "Deal."

"You won't regret this."

Joke's on him; I already do.

"Let's hope not." As he started to pull away, I tightened my grip and pulled him close. "If you hurt her in any way, I will wipe you, your bloodline, and any man loyal to either from existence."

"I don't doubt it, but you have nothing to worry about." He looked over my shoulder at Aislynn with a softness he hadn't earned. "I'm going to take very good care of her."

I wasn't so sure about that, but I'd be watching either way.

All I could do was hope Aislynn made it through in one piece.

Chapter 27
Greyson

Mari hadn't stopped moving since Ash got in the car with Paez. He'd given her a day to sort out her affairs before coming back to the house with his entire security team in tow.

We'd all tensed until he explained that he wanted to get Aislynn out of the city before Cash realized he could come for her again. Paez wasn't going to let her be a target anymore.

I watched the words land hard for Mari, but she didn't disagree. Instead, she hugged Ash while the rest of us piled her bags into one of the armored SUVs Victor brought.

After giving our own goodbyes, we surrounded Mari, watching somewhat helplessly as Ash was escorted to the car by Victor's second. She was about to slip inside when he leaned close to whisper something that made Ash's whole face turn red and not in embarrassment.

She'd snapped back at him so fiercely, Victor himself had separated the two with a stern glare at Maximoff. Apparently, whatever he'd done didn't sit well with the boss.

The taller man huffed but backed off, circling the car to slide into the driver's seat while Victor smoothed Ash's ruffled feathers. While I didn't like my friend unhappy, I was thrilled to see her fighting back. It was the most fire we'd seen in her in a while.

Unfortunately, it only set off Mari's protective instincts, and she'd been pacing ever since they turned out of the drive.

"You're going to wear a groove in the hardwood," Dominic said before chomping down on an apple.

Mari whirled on him, glaring as if she could wish him to the nine circles of hell. "Is that your way of telling me to calm down? Because my best friend just willingly walked into a cartel's arms as a hostage. I think I have the right to be upset."

"Which she chose to do." When she growled, Nate crossed his arms. "None of us said you couldn't be upset. We're just not going to let you hurt yourself in the process."

"How is walking in the kitchen hurting myself?"

"You haven't slept since Ash made the deal. Haven't eaten much either." It was all booze and caffeine. She was going to pass out soon. I stepped closer, rubbing my hands down her arms. "I'm aware you know this, but we're in the middle of a war, *reina*. Ash is safer with Victor Paez than she is with us right now, just like Shara is safer with Christian and Adrien. I know you don't want to believe it, but it's the truth."

She sagged, her mind finally accepting that she couldn't fight this. "What about Victor's second? Every other text from Ash is about how they're arguing already."

Nate rolled his eyes. "Maximoff's a dick, but we have to trust Victor to keep him in check. If he can't, no one's going to do business with him again. Besides, I gave her a few burner phones so she can call if she needs help."

He wasn't wrong. If Victor let something happen to Aislynn, especially by his own men, he'd lose a lot of the power he'd amassed. Hard to trust someone was a strong ally when they couldn't keep their own men in line. It was why we'd kept Cameron's involvement with Cash a secret.

"What about when he's not looking?" Mari asked, and I knew she was calming down, albeit against her will.

I ghosted a kiss over her temple. "We have to trust Ash to keep herself safe. She made the deal. She bears the consequences."

Nate pressed against Mari's back, nuzzling her neck. "You can't take the whole world on your shoulders, angel. It's not good for you."

I hummed my agreement, which was apparently not a good idea. She twisted out from between us with a glare, pointing at all three of us. "Don't gang up on me right now. You're supposed to be on my side."

"We are on your side. We're just trying to take care of you." Dominic snatched her by the waist and hauled her into his lap, holding her there even when she clawed at him. "Tell us what's really going on?"

He was so soft with her that it was no surprise when she melted. She popped her lip between her teeth, chewing it anxiously. "What if they snap and kill her? Not Victor, but the rest of them."

"They're not going to risk your wrath, and they certainly won't risk the Osorios' wrath. Just because he doesn't like you doesn't mean that the Wolf wouldn't go to war for a perceived threat against you. Ash is as safe as she can be with them."

Mari's shoulders lost a bit of tension as she realized that was true, but she was still gnawing her lip. "They don't even know her. What if she needs something or gets sick? Are they going to take her to the doctor?"

I pulled out her bottom lip, swiping it with my thumb. "Victor promised safety, a roof over her head, and money to spend. We have to assume that also includes health care, but I'll check if you'd like."

"Please." She gave me big doe eyes, and I grinned. Didn't she know I'd do anything for her?

I shot a text to Victor, knowing Mari needed to have it in writing or she'd never relax.

> Mari wants to know if Ash will be provided adequate health care while she's in your custody.

He texted back immediately.

> We have an on-site doctor who is a general practitioner and a gynecologist. We're also close enough to the other islands that a day trip for a different doctor isn't a problem.

After repeating the messages to Mari, I raised the phone. "Anything else you want to know?"

She gnawed on her lip again, sagging a little deeper into Dominic's arms so he was holding instead of restraining. "I just want her to be comfortable."

Reaching over, I brushed the hair out of her face, cupping her cheek. "I'll make sure it happens."

Since I'm sure Ash is going to try to be as unobtrusive as possible, here are some things you should know. She loves breakfast foods but won't eat them in the morning. Her favorite candies are those butter mints you get at restaurants sometimes. She hates olives but will eat tomatoes like apples if they're ripe enough. She always sleeps with the window open but likes three blankets on top of her, no matter what the temperature outside is. If allowed, she'll fall asleep at her sewing desk—which I highly recommend you build for her so she's occupied while she's there. An entire room would be better, but I'm not sure what your space situation looks like.

With the text sent, I checked my email, letting Dominic and Nate soothe Mari on their own. I'd check in with her later, but I knew they were on edge about her right now.

As I went to put my phone down, it vibrated with a call. Waving the device at Dominic so he knew where I was going, I stepped through the French doors at the rear of the kitchen and onto the back porch.

Rain poured across the yard with a sudden storm, and I slipped into the corner where everything was quieter. I could've taken the call inside, but I didn't want Mari to be concerned when we'd finally gotten her to breathe. "Paez."

"I just got your list."

He sounded...abrasive. I didn't know Victor well enough to know what kind of mood he was in, so I kept my tone neutral. "Mari suggested I send you some things to make sure Aislynn is comfortable during her stay."

"So, this came from her?"

"The list itself or the specifics?"

"The specifics."

"No, those came from me."

"How do you know so much about Aislynn?" he asked tightly. I probably would have assumed it was a casual question if Mari hadn't told me all about how he'd looked at Ash during their little chat. Suddenly, the abrasiveness made sense. The whole conversation screamed jealousy. My phone beeped with a notification, and I debated checking it, but I figured a text from one of our men could wait. Mari needed this reassurance. Another followed right after, but I left that too.

"Greyson." Victor's voice pulled me back to the conversation.

"We grew up with Aislynn," I finally said, curbing the shit-eating grin that tried to cross my lips.

"Is that so?" Again, he tried to sound relaxed when he was anything but, and I couldn't help myself.

"It is. There was talk of an arranged marriage at one point, but Aislynn married Cameron instead."

By now, I was taunting him, but it was too fun not to. It gave me an immense sort of pride to hear the way he ground his teeth as he asked, "Did that bother you?"

I could kind of understand why Dominic liked fucking with people so much.

"No," I said sincerely. I could practically feel his frustration through the phone, so I decided to let him off the hook. We didn't need him taking his frustrations out on Ash. "I'm married to Mari, and even if I weren't, my soul's always been hers. Aislynn was never even an option in my mind."

"I see." Victor blew out a breath. "Thank you for the list. I promise to make her as comfortable and safe as possible while she's in my care."

"Please do. Mari is protective of her friends, and I would hate to see what happens if anything goes wrong."

His grunt made it clear he understood the implied threat.

The thought of letting it go was swiftly beaten out by my need to meddle. Fuck, Dominic really was rubbing off on me. Gross. "Whatever happens between you and Ash stays between the two of you, but when I tell you that woman deserves to be treated like a queen, I mean it. Listen to her always, and fight for her every chance you get."

"I already said I'd treat her with the utmost care. Why are you telling me this?"

For so many reasons, none of which were my place to tell him. As a man loving a powerful, independent woman in a world that didn't like them, I needed him to know that Aislynn wouldn't be easy.

She was a mafia princess—and a damaged one at that. If he wasn't ready for that, he'd better not start anything with her. She deserved better.

"I have no doubt, but what will you do when your desire to care for her contradicts what she says she wants for herself? Will you be there for her even when she says she doesn't want you? Because she will. A man's pride can only take so many hits before it falters. How long will yours hold out?"

Paez said nothing, though I wasn't expecting him to. As long as he heard me, *really* heard me, that was what mattered. "Let us know when you need us."

The beep of a dropped call came before I could respond. Slipping the phone into my pocket, I decided to take some time on the porch. The smell of rain and fresh beginnings seeped deep into my body, reinvigorating me. It'd been a long few days and an even longer few months. War was on the horizon, and I needed every bit of strength and fortitude I had to ride it out with Mari.

One day soon, Cash was going to die, and our family would finally be safe. I knew it.

We just had to hang in a little longer.

With one final breath of storm air, I slipped back into the kitchen, expecting Mari and finding...no one. Two shirts were on the floor, and I assumed Dominic had taken her upstairs to get her mind off things. My cock stirred as I contemplated joining them, only to die a painful death the second I heard Mari scream.

I snatched my gun from the holster on my waistband and ran for the stairs, grateful that I was still in bare feet so I didn't slip on the slick floor.

"Security room." Dominic's voice stopped me, and in seconds, I'd redirected.

Finding Mari unharmed curbed the initial impulse to start shooting. I took one step inside the door and stopped. It was like I was unable to move farther as I watched the chaos unfold.

One of the walls had a twenty-four-hour feed to the compound just outside of Seattle, where we'd sent the Marcosa families. It was essentially a few neighborhoods locked inside a guarded gate line. The whole area was well-maintained and touted as one of the most exclusive neighborhoods in the suburbs, but no outsiders could get in, regardless of how desperate they were.

Normally, it was just a single screen on the wall, something I checked twice a day to make sure everything was going well. I had daily chats with the men stationed there, and true to their word, they'd fortified the security and added more watch shifts so every square inch was covered. Nothing strange had ever happened on the feed.

Not until now.

"Enlarge the picture and end it here," I rasped, pointing to the largest single screen I had. Since he was behind the desk, Nate's fingers flew to do what I asked. Finally, the picture pulled up where I wanted it, and we watched the loop of all the cameras on the property.

Mari stood behind him, one hand clutching her throat and the other shaking over her mouth. Her eyes were wide and darting everywhere.

"What's happening?" I asked, but I knew.

There was no way to look at the footage and not understand what was taking place.

The first camera in the loop was the front gate, which was nothing more than a pile of rubble with arms and legs askew underneath. Mari made a noise in the back of her throat, and I crept closer even though I didn't want to.

The next camera was the road leading into the compound. Usually it was empty, with a few cars passing here and there as they went to nearby towns for supplies. Now, there was an entire convoy lined up, every door wide open, leaving no doubt they were empty.

The third, fourth, and fifth cameras showed the main streets of the compound, the barracks, and the medical center. All of which were smoldering husks.

Cash had taken out the strongest members of the compound first—the soldiers—so there was no one left to defend the others.

He was going to slaughter our most defenseless people while we watched.

"The kids," Mari croaked. "We have to go get the kids."

"There are escape tunnels," Dominic promised. "Ones they can automatically detonate once they get to the other side. It'll be impossible for Cash to follow."

If they made it to the tunnels at all.

I rushed to one of the other computers and raced through my systems to find what I needed. "Looks like the hatches opened twenty minutes ago." Typing some more, I heaved out a breath. "That gave them ten minutes before the Aces hit."

It wasn't a lot of time, but our men promised they practiced their drills daily. In all likelihood, as long as they were close to a tunnel, most of our people would survive. It was the ones who weren't that were the problem.

We watched as a team kicked in the door of a house and stormed inside in an uncoordinated jumble. I could practically hear the yelling, cheering, and taunts through the screens, even though there was no audio. I'd never been more grateful for that oversight. The last thing Mari needed was to hear these people scream in her dreams every night.

Even now, she was pacing again, pulling at her hair.

"We have to go. We have to save them." Her eyes were wild as she looked at us, and I could see her pulse thundering in her neck.

The compound was an hour away by car on a good day. With the weather, it would be double, even if we drove like maniacs. We could've gone by helicopter, but flying in the storm would put us in more danger.

"Mari—"

"I know." She swallowed. "I know."

There was nothing we could do.

"Well, I don't. We can't just sit here." Nate growled.

"I already called in every reinforcement I had close by, but they won't make it in time," Mari said softly, her voice catching in the end. She was trying so hard to keep herself level, but this was too much for any of us. "If we can't be there to help or join them, the least we can do is bear witness."

Nate looked so fucking lost that I wasn't surprised when Mari slipped a hand over his shoulder. He grabbed it immediately, clinging to it like a life raft.

Finally, I stepped all the way into the room. Dominic's body was so tense, his knuckles were white, and I could see the imprint of his teeth on the outside of his cheek. Nate seemed like he was barely breathing. Mari looked like she was torn between having a breakdown and breaking the world.

"Whatever we do, we do together." I pressed myself to Mari's back, wrapping my arms around her shoulders and keeping her close. Dominic gripped one of her hands, while Nate trapped the other over his heart.

Together, we watched as the Aces burned our safety to the ground and prayed for the survivors we hoped we'd find.

Chapter 28
Mari

Six families died in the Aces carnage. Dozens were injured, not to mention the number of people who were displaced. I called Two-Bit and told him to pull some strings and get them all to safety before I made his life a living hell. He did, and it was the only thing letting me sleep at night.

It could've been worse, but that didn't negate the losses.

So many unnecessary losses.

I was grateful that the people who'd died did so quickly, grateful that they didn't suffer more, but even that didn't feel right. They shouldn't have died at all.

None of this should've happened.

Standing there with my men, watching the chaos in the home my husband had made for us, I felt something inside me break. Something I wasn't sure I'd ever be able to get back. Part of me wondered if my people were even safe with me at all, while another part wondered how anyone with a soul could watch children flee in terror and laugh about it the way the Aces had.

And they had. They'd taunted and teased, tormented the people I'd moved for their safety, and then they'd slaughtered them.

I'll kill them all.

I spent every waking moment watching and rewatching the footage, noting which Aces did what and how much pleasure they took in it. Which ones disappeared over the walls of the compound, never to return. We'd hunt them down eventually, but for now, the ringleaders were first on the chopping block.

I'd decided that no one who'd ever worn Cash's banner was safe.

I was still face first in the footage when I got a text that changed everything. I barely took time to gather my men and change my clothes before I stormed into my father's mansion, fresh rage stoked in my heart. It wasn't hard to locate the man who could have ended this so long ago if he had put his petty vendettas aside.

He was sitting in my fucking seat, after all.

The Wolf looked the same, like nothing could touch him, and that pissed me off. My people were dirty and bruised and bleeding, and this fucker had the audacity to call a meeting in *my house* wearing thousand-dollar shoes?

He had a death wish. Plain and simple.

"Last I checked, it's a form of respect to let a territory leader know if you're entering their city."

"I'm just crossing through."

"Doesn't change the protocol."

"Oh, get off it," he spat. "I'm not here for you, Marcosa."

Dominic growled under his breath at the disrespect, but he stayed where he was even though I knew he wanted to beat the shit out of Emmanuel.

Get in line, babe.

Christian stood off to the side, blocking the couch where Adrien and Shara sat together, the men very obviously on guard and ready to make a move if any of the Wolf's men so much as looked at Shara wrong. Adrien leaned over, whispering in her ear as he squeezed her thigh reassuringly. Her eyes flashed to me and she smiled, but it wavered at the edges.

I didn't like that at all.

The door opened, and everyone stiffened as Two-Bit stomped in. Christian, who'd lifted his gun at the newcomer, curled his lip at his brother. Suddenly, I could see the resemblance between him and Emmanuel. Did I look like that when I was disgusted? Fuck, I hoped not.

Our friendly little Fed kept his distance from everyone, choosing to lean against the wall closest to the door. Maybe he was hoping for a quick getaway.

"Dante. I'm glad you made it."

Two-Bit's lips tightened at the name, but he didn't correct it. "I didn't have a choice."

"Of course not. When your grandfather calls, you come."

"Of course." He gritted. "What's this about, Grandfather?"

Emmanuel turned away. "I'm here for my ungrateful heir."

It was then that I noticed Rafael standing behind him with crossed arms and a tight jaw.

"Did you really need an audience for that?"

"Apparently so, since my son likes to ignore what he's told."

I rolled my eyes, which was apparently the wrong thing since Emmanuel snarled, crossing the room to grip my chin tightly between his fingers. "Has he helped you, Marianna? Is your little vendetta why he refuses to come home and do his duties?"

"You better take your hands off her, old man." Dominic took a step forward like he was going to rip my grandfather away, but I lifted a hand to stop him. All three of my men—plus Two-Bit—had guns trained on him, but this was between Emmanuel and me.

How could a man who was powerful be so fucking weak?

Holding power was one thing, but withholding it to the detriment of others was another. Emmanuel Osorio had no backbone—no soul—and he wasn't someone I would bow to. I might have needed his help before, but now that I had the Paez cartel in my pocket, the Osorios were obsolete. Which meant there was no reason for me to answer.

He shook me with his hold, bobbing my head like a rag doll, and that rage in my chest grew. I'd had enough.

Wrapping my fingers around the Wolf's wrist, I kicked him in the knee and twisted, holding his arm in my grasp. He snarled and snapped, but he still dropped to the floor like anyone else. The sounds of guns lifting filled my ears, but I didn't take my eyes off my grandfather. "If you were such a powerful leader, *Wolf,* you could've kept him under your thumb easily. Don't blame me because you're too old to control your men."

A noise made me look toward Two-Bit to find him nearly smiling. He wiped it away before I'd even fully registered it, but I'd seen it and so had the Wolf.

Emmanuel was vindictive; anyone with half a brain could see it. He could blow us away with a wave of his hand if he wanted to —and he wanted it. No doubt he was weighing the pros and cons of his decision when Rafael spoke.

"Yes. You asked if I've helped her, and the answer is yes."

Emmanuel hissed, turning toward his son, and I let him go, stepping away and closer to my men. As I did, the Wolf's goons lowered their weapons, though they still eyed us warily.

Emmanuel panted angry, heaving breaths. "You admit it, then? You disobeyed my direct orders and helped that—"

"Watch it."

"Yes, and I'd do it again." Rafael lifted his chin at his father but made no move to attack or protect himself.

Anger rolled off the Wolf in waves, and he bared his teeth at his son like he was seconds from shifting his skin and taking his bloody pound of flesh. Was this how he'd gotten the name *the Wolf*? If so, it was fitting.

"You're no son of mine. Certainly no heir."

The room stilled, everyone seeming to hold their breath as the implications hit us at once.

If Rafael wasn't the Osorio heir, who was?

"Grandson." Emmanuel turned to Christian, and my heart pounded in my ears. I'd come here not sure what to expect, but watching Christian ascend wasn't it. "My grandson's trained his whole life to lead, and now it's time to see what he's made of. Will you be the heir your father couldn't be?"

There was no show of pride from Christian. No puffed chest and blinding smile. He stood there like it was just another day, instead of the most monumental moment of his life. "I will."

Two-Bit didn't move beyond the smallest sag in his shoulders. If I hadn't seen relief in his gaze, I'd have assumed it was disappointment. I imagined that was intentional on his part, needing to balance his life as Emmanuel's grandson and his world as a federal agent. *Fuck, that's got to be tough.*

Emmanuel smiled and clapped Christian on the back, lifting the mood.

That was it. Rafael was out and his son was in, but what did that mean for our tentative alliance? What would he do if Emmanuel asked him to hand over Shara? Would he hurt her as a way of proving his own loyalty?

I glanced at Grey, who obviously shared the same concerns, then over to Nate, who was closest to Shara. If a fight broke out, he was our only shot at getting her out safely. His head dipped in the slightest nod, drawing Adrien's eyes.

The turmoil in them made my chest tight. His loyalty was split between his boss, his friend, and Shara. I didn't envy him one bit. When Christian's head was bent with Emmanuel, Nate snatched Shara just as Adrien pushed her off the couch. It was barely a movement, but I saw it. Knew he'd helped us because Shara didn't stumble once.

He'd told her to get ready because he *couldn't* guarantee her safety anymore.

Fuck.

Emmanuel didn't care what we'd done, but Christian looked ready to burn us to ash.

"Let her go, cousin," he said with quiet menace. To the side, Two-Bit straightened, and I wondered if he'd intervene if his brother came for me.

"When I know she's safe," I promised. Nate moved behind me, so Shara was pinned between our bodies, giving her a human shield. I didn't give a fuck if that made her a target right now. If Emmanuel tried to use her as leverage, I'd kill him and deal with the consequences later. All being cautious had gotten me was a city in chaos and my friends disappearing before my eyes.

Shara leaned into me for a moment before her hand squeezed mine twice.

Trust me.

We'd come up with the nonverbal sign ages ago, when Shara had just figured out who Antoni was—who we all were. She hadn't been born into this life, and it had taken some adjusting for her to learn the right kind of self-preservation when confronted with Mario's versions of testing her and the unfortunate situations that being in the underworld brought.

I squeezed back, promising not to fly off the handle, but I was still tense.

Was this a trick? Did they plan it ahead of time? What did she know that I didn't? Because she knew something. Whatever it was, it would come with time. For now, she was safe, and that was what mattered.

Christian glanced at Shara again before stepping forward, waving his big arms toward my couches like he owned them. "Why don't we sit?"

"I don't need to sit," Emmanuel huffed, though I noticed he was still favoring the knee I'd kicked. A vicious smile lit my face, and he glowered at me.

Christian turned back to him with a congenial smile. "Grandfather, there are things that you should know about this war of Mari's before you turn her down again."

I wasn't planning to ask Emmanuel to join me again. Not when I'd given him the chance to help already. Especially not when I'd made other arrangements. I wasn't sure if Paez would work with him, regardless, even if the Wolf agreed, so what else was there to discuss?

"By all means, have a seat. That knee looks bad."

Christian's look of admonishment was easy to read. *I'm trying to help. Don't make things worse.*

I wasn't entirely sure they could get worse at this point.

The Wolf sat next to his newest heir, with Adrien standing sentinel behind his friend. Shara nudged me in the back, pushing until she and I were seated on the final love seat, my men spread around us.

"There, now we can have a conversation like civilized adults," Adrien said with a smile. Shara rolled her eyes next to me, but I could tell she was amused.

Again, she squeezed my hand. *Trust me. Trust us.*

Well, my cousin hadn't earned my trust beyond keeping her safe, but Shara had earned it in droves.

"Why am I really here?" I asked. "Because if it was just to see Rafael's downfall, I could have stayed home for that."

Emmanuel opened his mouth, probably to snap at me, but

Christian cut him off. "I've had word that you're working with the Paez cartel to get rid of your little problem. Is that true?"

Two-Bit froze, and I realized that having him here while I discussed this was a really bad idea. I'd just made a deal with the Feds, and now he had proof that I wasn't going to follow through with it. Fuck, what a mess. "It is. We've come to an arrangement."

Apparently, this was also news to our grandfather because the Wolf stiffened and turned a look of betrayal so much fiercer than anything he'd ever given Rafael on me. "You would partner with my rivals? Is there no family loyalty?"

Images of the compound filtered through my head, and I had to let go of Shara for fear of breaking her fingers as I clenched my fists. "We *did* show loyalty, remember? We came to you first. We asked for help, and you spat in our faces. You made it clear that I wasn't an Osorio, not by blood or claim, and my war wasn't yours. So, what's stopping me from working with Paez when he's willing to give me what you never will?"

"Blood is bullshit. Family is what matters, and you've made it clear you're not our family." Dominic rested a hand on my shoulder, and I could almost feel Nate and Grey nodding.

"She's right. We haven't shown her our loyalty, so how can we expect hers?" Emmanuel turned away, whispering fiercely to Christian, who took it all in stride.

I could see a hint of the leader he would become. Formidable, fair, calm under pressure. I felt a strange sort of pride in my chest that I refused to acknowledge as I watched him own his birthright. If he could get rid of Emmanuel, I had no doubt the cartel would flourish under his leadership.

Emmanuel was grinding his teeth loud enough for us to hear when he begrudgingly asked, "What kind of arrangement did you make?"

I shrugged. "I'm not sure that's any of your business."

It was actually kind of fun watching that vein in his head pop out.

Christian smiled to himself and sank a little deeper into the couch. "I assume Victor doesn't want to lose Seattle's importing capabilities. Chances are, he gave you his army for that alone." When I still didn't reply, he nodded to himself. "What if we offered you the same deal? Our help for the ability to import what we need through your docks."

"Why would I need you when I already have him?"

That smile turned into an infuriating smirk that I wanted to smack off his face. According to Shara's scoff, she did too. "I think we both know you need as much help as you can get. Cash's forces are far more widespread than you assume. It'll take months to eradicate him on your own. Months that you don't have, especially when the cost will be lives you won't spare. We'll help remove the cockroach in return for the same agreement you gave Paez."

I was going to tell him to fuck off when Shara squeezed my hand again. *God fucking damn it.* "It's something to consider."

"No," Emmanuel said. "I want more."

"Of course you do," I scoffed. Men like him always wanted more just to prove their dick swung farther. "What do you want in return?"

"Marriage."

Chapter 29
Mari

Marriage. God help us all.

My men stiffened behind me, and Shara felt like a statue at my side, but I didn't move a muscle beyond casually slipping my left hand—and my wedding ring—beneath my thigh. How they hadn't seen it, I wasn't sure, but there was no way I was showing that card yet.

"Pretty sure marrying cousins went away with the monarchy. You're handsome and all, but you're not my type."

Christian's lips tipped into the smallest smile, while Adrian tossed his head back and laughed.

Emmanuel smirked. "Not your cousin, his second."

Adrien's mouth snapped closed, and Shara snarled under her breath. This time, I squeezed her hand. *Trust me.*

She squeezed back, but I could tell she wasn't pleased. I wouldn't be either if someone tried to marry off one of my men.

Oh, wait...

Pasting a smile on my face, I said, "While Adrien seems nice enough, I can't accept."

"Why the hell not?"

"I'm already married." Lifting my hand into the air, I wiggled my ring finger.

"Who?" Emmanuel glared at the men behind me as if he could get rid of my husband by sheer will alone. I didn't even have to look to know all three of them puffed up at the challenge.

"Doesn't matter. The point is, I'm unavailable. And if they should die, I'll take the black."

Widows weren't uncommon in mafia life, and it was a sign of great honor and respect for a woman to wear black during the grieving period. Custom dictated that most widows remarried, but the ones who took the black never remarried. Never moved on. They were committed to their husbands beyond the grave.

I'd always thought that if Lucia Ricci had lived a different life, she'd have taken the black for Dominic's father.

I knew I would.

There would be no other loves for me if my men died. They were already more than a lifetime's worth, and I would be content living out my days in remembrance of them.

Shara leaned in, resting her cheek against mine so she could whisper in my ear. "Let me do it."

Fuck me sideways, it was like Aislynn all over again.

"Before you refuse, you should know I'm already in love with Adrien. Marrying him isn't exactly a hardship since I already said yes."

Looking into her eyes, I saw strength and resolve, tempered by a lightness I hadn't seen since Antoni was alive. She really did love Adrien just as much as she loved my brother, and this was likely the only way she could have him. Emmanuel or Christian would marry him off if I didn't help her.

By agreeing, she could finally marry the man she wanted. She could move on in the way I knew she'd been dying to for years.

That it would clear the city of Cash at the same time was a boon I couldn't ignore.

"I don't want this to be like Cameron," I admitted.

"It won't be. Adrien's... He's amazing, but he's also real. He hasn't lied to me, and he's proven it. I know that means nothing to you, but I'm asking you to trust me. I know what I'm doing." When I nodded reluctantly—because what else could I do? —she straightened in her seat. "I'll do it."

Christian's jaw clenched, while Emmanuel looked at her like she was roadkill. "What use is a friend with no power to us?"

"Shara is my sister in all but name, and if we'd had even a few more months with Antoni, she would've been that too."

"Ah, this is the would-be fiancée." Suddenly Emmanuel's gaze was far more appraising.

"Yes."

"Fine, she'll marry—"

"Me."

Adrien started and Shara clenched her fists at her sides at Christian's interruption, but neither of them spoke, so I did.

"No." Marrying her to Adrien because she was in love with him was one thing. Marrying her to Christian was another.

"Yes," Emmanuel said, jumping on anything to make me uncomfortable. Dick. "Your sister will marry my heir."

He grinned at my unimpressed look, but my focus was taken by the two men beside him. Adrien glared at his best friend like he was ready to fight to the death. I couldn't see Christian's face well, but he maintained a haughty air that said he was baiting his second.

If you want her, you'll have to get through me. It made me like him less and Adrien more.

Adrien slid his eyes to Shara, and only when she shook her

head did he back down, though there was no doubt he was going to make Christian pay. As my cousin twisted back to us, Adrien watched Shara with a look of such stark devotion and possession that it made my skin tingle.

"Jesus," Nate whispered behind us, and it made me laugh.

Shara's firm nod pushed me to answer, though it pained me to do it. "Agreed."

Emmanuel and I stood, shaking on the deal before he turned to Christian with a grin then looked at Two-Bit. "Congratulations, boys."

What the hell is he— No.

My stomach dropped. It didn't make sense at first, but Two-Bit was here, when he'd otherwise been separated from Osorio business. Why else would Emmanuel have invited him unless...

"You made them co-heirs."

Emmanuel's smirk got bigger. "I did."

Christian's head snapped toward him. "What? When?"

"No," Two-Bit snarled.

"Now, and yes. My grandsons will take over for their father." He sent a disapproving glance toward Rafael, who stood with his mouth open in shock. "You'll both marry the girl."

Every part of me wanted to pull Shara away, not willing to let her get involved in what was bound to be a brotherly shitshow, but she held firm. "Okay."

I could practically see Two-Bit's mind whirling, trying hard to come up with a way to get out of being pulled further into the life he clearly hated, but there wasn't one. He'd come to the meeting, and even if he hadn't fully agreed, he'd shown his support as an Osorio. Just being here, he had signed his name on the dotted line. Unless he gave up pretending and told them all the truth, he was going to rule at his brother's side whether he liked it or not.

While everyone was still scrambling, I knew I had to figure

things out fast. "The wedding will have to wait until after Cash is gone."

"No," Emmanuel and Christian said at once, though I had a feeling it was for very different reasons.

"Yes. Consider it a show of good faith that you'll actually be where I need you."

Emmanuel's shoulders tightened, but he didn't disagree, which meant Christian wouldn't either.

"It'll take two days to get my men here."

Which meant that was all the time I had to come up with a viable plan. "We'll be ready," I promised. Greyson was already on the phone, whispering to Victor. When he nodded my way, I knew we'd make it. It would be a tight timeline, but we'd pull it off.

For a chance to destroy Cash for all he'd done, I'd do just about anything.

With a clap on Christian's shoulder and a few whispered words to a pissed-off Two-Bit, Emmanuel swept out of the room, taking his guards with him.

Like an unspoken decree, no one spoke until the cars left the drive, and even then, we waited for Nate and Adrien to scan for and remove the five listening devices they found in the room and adjoining hallways. By the time they got back, Two-Bit looked ready to disappear into the wall, and Christian was practically vibrating.

"We're clear," Adrien said, Nate nodding his agreement.

Christian stalked over to Shara until they were pressed together, framing her face with his hands. "Are you sure you're okay with this?"

Even though the room was cleared, he barely spoke over a whisper.

She curled her hands around his wrists. "I already agreed."

"You agreed to marry Adrien. This changes things." He sent a dark look to Two-Bit, which he returned.

Shara huffed and pulled Christian's focus back to her. "It changes nothing. If Mari trusts him, I trust him. Besides, *you're* the one who changed things."

"Don't worry, *amore*. We'll be talking about that later." Adrien's glower was impressive, but Christian didn't seem to care. He pulled Shara in until he could press his lips to her forehead. "You're too trusting, *mi sol*."

Her cheeks flushed at the name, but he was already turning to his brother.

"What the hell are you doing here?" Two-Bit stared Christian down, and again, I could see the resemblance. Mostly in the eyes. They looked less like their father and more like each other. It was a little disturbing. "My presence was requested."

I could see Christian tensing up for a showdown, and when Shara sent me a pleading look, I waded in. "Did you know what he was going to do?"

Christian shook his head, running a hand through his hair in agitation. "I knew he was going to remove Rafael, but the rest was a shock."

"How'd you get him to work with us?" Grey asked Christian, coming back over now that his phone call was done.

"I reminded him that you may be Mario's daughter, but plenty of people know you're Bianca's too. If we let you fall, it looks bad on us."

"He helped because his reputation was on the line." It should've annoyed me, but I'd made peace with Emmanuel. One day, he'd die and be out of my hands. Until then, I'd pretend he didn't exist. "If you decide you want to speed up your transition to power when this is all over, let me know."

Adrien laughed and Shara's shoulders dropped, especially when he lifted an arm for her. She sped across the room and snuggled into his side as he kissed her temple. They were so wrapped in each other, whispering with their mouths almost pressed together, that they didn't see the way Christian watched her like she was the most coveted thing in his life.

Or the way Two-Bit looked like he'd rather throw himself in front of a moving bus than take a single step closer to her.

I chose to believe it was because he didn't like being commanded to marry and had nothing to do with Shara herself. If that wasn't the case, we'd be having a very serious conversation soon.

Christian, however, decided the conversation was due now.

"I don't care what the old man said. If you hurt her—"

"I don't even want her. I'm certainly not going to hurt her."

They stared at each other like they were playing chicken until, finally, Christian scoffed, walking away with a look that promised death if he'd lied.

Through it all, Christian didn't once look at his father.

After a brief chat, Shara skipped over for a hug and a promise to video-call soon before she grabbed both Christian's and Adrien's hands and swept them out of the room. Poor bastards stared at her like she was the only star in the sky, and I was kind of excited to see if she could truly find the level of happiness I had with my men.

With Christian gone, Two-Bit seemed to relax more, although he didn't look at Rafael either. "You're working with Paez?"

Shit. I was hoping we wouldn't have this conversation today. "I am, but I'm not going to let him distribute in the city."

It was technically within the lines of our deal, even if it didn't honor the spirit of it, and he knew it. I thought he'd be angry, but instead, there was a hint of humor in his eyes. "Why am I not surprised you worked a deal like that?"

He wasn't talking about the one with the cartel.

My shrug was automatic. "What can I say? It's a gift."

We watched each other for a moment, two people who had secrets that could destroy the other's life. All it would take was choosing to let those secrets loose, and everything would be destroyed.

I'd be in jail.

Two-Bit would likely be dead.

It hit me that his little secret would spell death for more than just him if he wasn't careful.

"Keep her out of the mess. Please."

His hands clenched. "I'll do what I can to do right by her."

"That's all I ask. For the record, I'm sorry about today."

That he'd been dragged into the life he'd fought so hard to avoid. That he'd been gifted a marriage he didn't want. That his existence was going to be even harder now because of all of it.

And that I'd be just another opponent if his actions caused Shara harm.

"I know you are." He shook his head with a faint smile. "See you soon, Mari."

"Good luck."

He walked out with a nod to my men, leaving just us and my uncle.

"Are you okay?" I asked.

Rafael stared at the door with the kind of acceptance that said he knew nothing would ever fix the way he'd fucked up. With his father. With his sons. He was on his own for the first time. I wondered how that felt. "I am. I should have done it sooner. For Bianca and for you."

But he wasn't okay. Walking away from his birthright would never be easy, but he'd done it for me, and I was grateful. So, when he turned to me and asked if I needed another sharpshooter, I accepted.

I had a feeling I'd need every man I could get.

Chapter 30
Mari

Emmanuel eyed Victor the moment he arrived. Everywhere he went, Emmanuel followed, and despite Maximoff glaring daggers at the other don, he never let up. It only got worse when the meetings started.

Every time Victor suggested something, the Wolf shot it down. If he offered help, Emmanuel always offered more. Seeing the interactions in person, I agreed more with Victor's assumptions. Emmanuel was at war with him, and he was being a petty bitch about it.

"This is ridiculous." Dominic leaned back against the wall next to me, wearily watching the two men butt heads. I had a headache from all the testosterone pumping through the air and was *this close* to losing it from hunger alone.

Male posturing was going to take me out long before the war could.

Being stuck in a room with two warring cartel leaders was the epitome of stupid, but not for the reasons I originally assumed. After hours of trying to plan and getting nowhere, I was ready to shoot them both, damn the consequences. The only thing holding me back was Greyson absently playing with my fingers where they hung between us. "This whole meeting is a dick-measuring contest," Nate muttered.

Eagle snorted next to him. "No fucking joke."

Somewhere in all the chaos of sorting orders and preparing for battle, the black ops agent had slipped into the house and hadn't left. Not that I minded. He brought all sorts of friends with him— ones who owed Nate favors—and they'd gone to work immediately. Soon, we had a network of people hunting through my city, with tools even Two-Bit couldn't comprehend.

It made me nervous. The mercs were for life. That Nate got out was a miracle, and I didn't want to fight another war when this one was over. I'd cornered Eagle yesterday, and he'd been very clear when I asked if the *company* was going to come after my partner again.

From where I stand, we're just removing some trash from your house like any good friend would. Nothing more, nothing less.

I was grateful for small mercies.

His team preferred to handle their own accommodations, and thank fuck for that. Both cartels had come through majorly, and we were swarming with bodies sworn to the cause. Every spare room in the Marcosa mansion was being used to house the Paez cartel, and the Celestine was overrun with Osorios.

Emmanuel hated that Victor was treated to the place of honor in my home, even one I didn't use anymore, but he didn't say it outright. We all knew things would've been different if he'd put his pride aside when I'd first come to him. Now, he could stew in it.

Whatever space wasn't turned into overnight bunkhouses was

weapons storage, and we'd converted the basement into our war room, which was currently filled to the rafters with people.

We'd long since run out of seats, but the leaders and their seconds were huddled closer to the center of the room while everyone crowded in to see the projected map of Seattle on the wall.

The other territory leaders didn't offer to house any offshoot guests, but then, they were busy gathering their own men.

The night Emmanuel agreed, we'd sent out the call.

Meeting in two days. Be ready.

Now, everyone was here, weapons prepared and timeline set, yet we'd gotten exactly nothing done because of my grandfather.

I was sweating my metaphorical balls off with so many people around. The air was so thick with the scent of people that it nearly made me sick, but I didn't mind. I was this close to finally getting rid of Cash. I had every territory leader in the city watching me, the government at my back, a group of fucking mercs ready to kill at my order. The only thing standing between me and the freedom my enemy's death would grant me was Emmanuel Osorio's fucking pride.

Pride that I was ready to destroy if he didn't shut the fuck up and let us get on with it.

Patience, Mari. It'll be over soon.

Couldn't come fast enough.

Sighing, I tuned back in as Victor calmly explained his plan to bomb three of Cash's safe houses as a distraction. We'd already decided on an extended version of the three-pronged approach from the stash house raid. We'd send the distractions in first to draw out the Aces before sending a second wave to decimate the rest.

"That's a stupid idea. Why bomb the safe houses when there are plenty of buildings he could be hiding in?"

Victor sucked in a deep breath, obviously trying to calm

himself. "As I've said twice now, if we want to get Cash, we need to remove his army from consideration. He won't be distracted by the safe houses, but they will. They know they're on borrowed time. If we destroy their chance at escape, they're going to scurry."

"We don't want them. We want the ones who stay," Emmanuel pushed.

It was obvious Victor's patience was thinning. "Yes, but in order to get to them, the weak ones need to run. Why waste the bullets and risk our men if we don't have to?"

"If your men can't handle the trials of war, they shouldn't be here."

"Says the man who was picked last for this ragtag team." Grey huffed.

Emmanuel twisted to bite his head off, and I was done.

"Enough."

The room fell silent. Victor quietly sat, ceding me the floor while the Wolf stayed on his feet. Christian stood behind him, eyes tight with warning while Emmanuel's flashed with ire. "You don't command me, Marianna."

"Yet here I am, doing it anyway."

"I'm trying to help."

"No, you're nitpicking Victor because of some bullshit grudge. I'm not sure if you're doing it to hide that you don't have any ideas of your own or if you're just that invested in irritating the shit out of all of us, but we don't have time for this. I don't have the patience to deal with your forever-and-a-day grudge when the people of my city are in danger. Either offer up a suggestion, or sit the fuck down."

Emmanuel glared at me as if he could set me on fire with his mind and my men stiffened, but I didn't care. He could hate me all he wanted if it meant we got somewhere.

Christian cleared his throat, stepping forward to take the heat off Emmanuel. The other man slumped into his seat like a petulant child. "Do we have enough supplies to widen the first wave? Maybe we could hit another of his buildings that's not a safe house."

I looked at Victor, who nodded.

Finally, a fucking compromise.

Hallelujah.

Greyson looked over the inventory list of everything our allies had brought, weapons I'd imported specifically for this war, and a whole host of things we hadn't been expecting.

After he'd done his calculations, he nodded. "We could reasonably add a location to the first wave. I'd keep the initial teams light, though. We're aiming to remove any runners and take out as many active men as possible so they can't become reinforcements when the bigger launches start."

"These are the buildings we've had under watch." With a few clicks of the mouse, Eagle drew circles around ten buildings throughout Seattle, addresses we'd gotten from Two-Bit after the meeting yesterday.

Agreeing to play spy for the Feds was already paying off. We'd received more information than we'd expected with the addresses of Cash's most-used hideouts. Not to mention the weapons. We didn't want to tie Two-Bit to the information, so we'd given it to Eagle, who had no problem lying to the other leaders about where it came from. Not that anyone questioned it in the first place, but we had it covered in case they did.

The moment they arrived, we sent the mercs to play spies and gather more intel, and it was going well. Though no one had found Cash yet, I was still hoping we'd have a solid lead before we went in blind. I wanted him dead.

"We've got a running tally of everyone coming and going over the last day, so by the time we're ready, we'll have a good idea of how many people to expect at each place." He typed again, and each circle got a staggering number next to it. Even with the additional help, we barely outnumbered the Aces. *Where's Cash been hiding them?*

I bit my lip. "How can you be sure your tally's correct?"

Eagle dug into the backpack at his feet and tossed something at me with a grin. I caught it, scowling at him when I realized it was a pair of very expensive infrared goggles.

Specifically, *government-issued* infrared goggles.

"I've got three men on each building who rotate the count every hour. The others confirm the number with those before we get the total."

"Margin for error?"

He shrugged. "I padded each one by ten, fifteen if the building's bigger. The probability of reinforced basements on some of these is pretty low, but it isn't zero."

"Where the hell did this guy come from?" Christian asked, his narrowed gaze tracking between the merc and the goggles I still held.

"Old friend," Nate said easily.

Christian watched him carefully. "Is that so?"

The sarcasm was duly noted and unappreciated.

"Nate used to be a mercenary."

Apparently, that was news to most everyone in the room. I watched as all the big players' eyes sharpened on my man and frowned. Maybe Leo's assessment wasn't as off as I assumed.

A problem for another time. Once the war was over and I'd had about a month to relax, we'd get to work on revamping Nate's reputation in the city. Make sure everyone knew he was a badass in his own right.

My phone buzzed as they talked about the toys, and I took it out, hoping it was one of the scouts with good news. Rafael's name was an unexpected surprise, as was his text.

He's taken your club.

Which one?

The name flashed on my screen, and I wasn't even surprised. Now that I thought about it, it made all the sense in the world. Dominic's eyes drifted to the death grip I had on my phone, and he straightened. Nate and Greyson followed suit, and it was Nate's movement that caught Eagle's eye. "Something to add?"

"I just got word that we need to add a building to the tally."

Emmanuel scowled. "The others have been on watch for the last day. Adding another so late means we're likely flying in blind."

"We have the goggles, and I have enough men to add one last observation group." Eagle shrugged while the Wolf scowled.

"I'm not risking my men."

"I don't expect you to." I handed my phone to Dominic, who moved through the crowd and stole the laptop temporarily, typing *Black Team* over the address. No way anyone else was taking that building but us.

Because Cash had taken Gilded as his final stand.

It wouldn't have even been hard to do. Our men were either readying for war or gone. I'd left the businesses locked and armed, but I didn't need guards on buildings. I needed them in the streets. All Cash had to do was break down the door and take it.

Part of me hated the idea of him sullying the crown jewel of my empire, but it felt right that he'd done it. This was a full-circle moment. Our story would end where it truly began.

"What the hell is that?" For his part, Emmanuel just looked confused, and I realized that he'd kept his position because he was too big to go to war with. In the event that Paez retaliated, the Wolf didn't have the strategic knowledge to outlast him. He'd die screaming, and everything he worked for would be gone.

Hopefully my cousin was smarter than his predecessor.

"My club."

Kosas stood immediately, knowing it was too good of an opportunity for Cash to pass up. "I'm with you."

Two-Bit nodded. I still wasn't sure how I felt about the Vipers coming to war with us, knowing there were more Feds than criminals in their ranks, but we didn't have a choice. Leaving them out was going to put a target on Two-Bit's back when the dust settled, and I'd signed my soul away to make sure that didn't happen.

We finalized the plans quickly after that, ensuring who would ride the first wave and who was on the second. We even kept behind our best pinch hitters, knowing there may be a need for a third wave to extract us. We worked together to make sure every group leader had sufficient ammo, knew their exit strategies, and had access to more help if required. Field medics would be stationed as close as we could get them to the blast sites without endangering them, and we'd managed to secure a fleet of ambulances for transport to the medical center at the university after it was over. Seattle Gen was still recovering from Cash's massacre.

Victor offered himself to my group, even as Maximoff's face twisted like he'd eaten something sour. The other territory leaders followed, though we decided that we weren't going to have all the big bads in one group. Better to spread us out. Victor demanded we stay together, and I knew it was, in part, because of our deal with Ash. He felt obligated to keep me alive because he had her, and I respected that.

Emmanuel was the only one who hadn't offered men, which wasn't surprising. Christian stepping in to do it, however, was.

"I'll go with you."

"Absolutely not." Emmanuel's outrage traveled across the room, but I didn't care. The only way for the two factions to play nice was to ensure that they both had stakes in the game. With the Paez don and the Osorio heir in my party, there wouldn't be any issues with friendly fire.

"Actually, I'd feel better if Christian was with us," I said. The

Wolf geared up to argue with me, but I held up a hand. "He'll be as safe as possible."

"He's my heir." He said it like Christian's death meant more than everyone else's, and it pissed me off.

"Get over yourself," I snapped. "Everyone is at risk with this mission. Your potential loss isn't greater than ours just because you raised him higher than the rest of the army."

Done with whatever bullshit he was going to spew, I turned back to the rest of the crew. "You've all got your orders. Go home. Fuck your partners, kiss your kids, and go to bed early. Tomorrow's going to be a big day."

The war was ending, one way or another.

* * *

My men and I went home after that. We showered quietly, dressed in comfy clothes, and found our way to the den. Someone put a movie on, but none of us were watching it. We were focused on one another. Hands roaming softly, not for sex but for comfort. Remembrance.

Nate kissed my forehead where I was sprawled across his chest, hand outstretched for Dominic, while Greyson rubbed my calves. "Love you, angel."

"Love you too."

This was the feeling I wanted to take into tomorrow. Being so fucking loved I couldn't stand it.

There was something else I wanted to take with us, though.

Nudging Grey's thigh, I looked pointedly under the coffee table where I'd stashed my surprise earlier. His eyes twinkled as he saw the box, and he pulled it off the floor before snatching me from Nate's grasp and bringing me into his. It wasn't just because he wanted to touch me, though he did that too. The move gave me the best view of the other two men.

The box slipped into my hands, and I was surprised to find Dominic eyeing it warily. "What's inside?"

"A bomb."

His brows flattened. "Not a good time for jokes, *mariposa*."

Rolling my eyes, I pushed it into their waiting hands. "Open it and find out."

They looked at each other, making Grey laugh behind me as one hand toyed with my wedding band, but eventually they opened it.

Two rings sat nestled in the silk, polished to a shine and untouched. I'd been waiting for the right time to give them to the rest of my men, but I'd realized earlier that was a mistake.

I should've done it the second Nate came back.

I should've given Dominic his ages ago.

Fear was a powerful motivator. It held you back from going after what you wanted.

Well, not anymore.

Nate's eyes widened, and he turned to me, speechless. Dominic, on the other hand...

"No."

I huffed. I knew he'd freak out the most. "Dominic."

"No." He shoved the box at Nate and crossed his arms like if he didn't touch it, the ring didn't exist.

"We aren't saying goodbye. This isn't over," Dominic growled, and the others crossed their arms in agreement.

"It's not goodbye. It's the start of forever."

"Then it can wait."

"No, it can't."

"I don't want this because of tomorrow, Mari. I want this because *you* want it. Because you want me in your life—"

"Forever."

Nate's voice was so fucking soft when he said it. He'd slipped his ring out of the box while I was distracted by Dominic, twisting the metal until he saw the engraving.

"Yeah," I whispered. "Forever."

Dominic reached for the other ring with shaking fingers, twisting until he saw his engraving too. I saw the flare in his eyes when he read it for the first time. "Everything."

Because he was my everything. Just like Nate. Just like Greyson.

My home. My peace. My love.

"I'm not doing this because we might die tomorrow. I'm doing it because we deserve to live. You deserve to know how much you mean to me. These are not a pity gift for the afterlife, Dominic. Not when you should've been wearing them all along." He still didn't believe me, and I crawled into his lap, taking the ring and slipping it onto his finger anyway. "I've had these for ages, and it's time for you to have it. I *need* it on your finger tomorrow."

"Why?"

"Every time you take out an Ace, I want them to know you're mine. That you're doing this for me. For us. For the city and the people we love. For our family. Cash thinks that love is bullshit and people are expendable. We're going to show him that he's wrong. But mainly, I want you to wear it for me. Because I love you, and I want everyone to know it." I ghosted my lips over his. "Say yes, Dominic."

"Do I have a choice? You already put it on me." He sounded annoyed, but his lips were twitching.

"No, you don't. You don't really want one, though."

That got me a smile, and he swooped in, kissing me until he'd stolen every breath from my lungs. "Nah, I think I'm perfectly fine where I'm at. Love you, *mariposa*."

"Love you too."

With another kiss and a pat on my ass, he gave me over to

Nate. I straddled his legs, giving him a peck before starting. "Nate—"

"Yes."

I laughed, joy bubbling when the others laughed with me. "I didn't even ask yet."

"You don't have to. My answer's yes. It's always been yes for you."

It had. Even when the universe had us on opposing sides, Nate had always been mine. Mine to have. Mine to hold. Mine to keep.

Forever.

He held up the ring and kissed me as I slipped it on his finger, our lips writing vows so soft and sweet they buried themselves in my soul.

When we parted, he wrapped a hand in my hair to keep me close. "We're going to make you so fucking happy."

"You already do."

"Now that we're all wifed up, how do we want to spend our last evening?"

"Actually, I have one more gift."

Dominic rubbed his hands together. "Who's it for?"

"Nate."

Dominic pouted, but Nate reared back, surprise obvious on his face. "Me?"

"You."

His hands flexed on my hips. "I want everything with you."

I smiled, knowing my last gift was going to rock him even more. "I want to give you my name."

Nate froze. He didn't move, didn't breathe, didn't even blink. It was like his whole body shut down for the two seconds it took him to understand what I said. Finally, he heaved in a huge breath that did nothing to ease the uncertainty on his face. "Why?"

"Because you've earned it."

"I haven't—"

"You have," Dominic said.

They stared at each other for a long moment until I turned Nate's gaze back to me. "You were a Beckstrom when you had to be and a Black when it suited. Neither was really your choice, but this is. Be a Marcosa because we want you to be. Your mom won't be here forever and I know that kills you, but we're your family too. Take my name because you want it, because you choose us."

After another long moment of silence in which I wasn't sure if I'd overstepped, Nate launched himself at me, pressing kisses all over my face until I was howling with laughter. I pushed on his shoulders, both of us smiling so hard our eyes creased. "You haven't responded yet."

"I'd be honored, angel."

"Fucking finally. Now we don't have to hear any more *I'm a terrible boyfriend* speeches." Dominic rolled his eyes, even as he smiled. "Congrats on being official, brother."

They hugged, clapping each other on the back before Nate turned to Greyson and did the same. Then they all turned to me, hauling me back onto the couch and into their arms.

I burrowed between them as they bickered about what show we were going to start when this was over and who got to sleep next to me tomorrow, and I knew the fire in my chest wasn't going to ebb.

Tomorrow, we'd take the war to Cash, and we'd win because, with them by my side, I couldn't lose.

I wouldn't.

Cash would die because I wasn't giving up the happiness I found with these men. After everything the universe had put me through, I'd fucking earned it.

Chapter 31
Dominic

Faint wisps of sunrise lit up the night sky as we gathered our forces in a parking garage a few blocks from Gilded.

We'd decided to hit the Aces early in the morning, when most people had finally passed out from partying. Nate said that dawn still had some stragglers awake, but they were half in the bag and unlikely to be much of a defense. The men Cash had at Gilded would be different, but at least the other teams would have an easier route to success.

Mari greeted Victor before moving to do the same to Christian. Their low conversations couldn't be heard, but I knew Mari. She was checking on her girls. She wouldn't be able to focus if she wasn't sure they were okay.

Kosas settled quietly next to where I leaned on one of the SUVs. "Are you sure you want to stay with us? We'll have a target bigger than the state on our backs."

It was a risk to have us all together, but it was one we'd had time to accept. Mari had taken some convincing, but she knew we wouldn't back down.

She'd go into this fight with all of us at her back, or she wouldn't go in at all.

After that was settled, we spent our time focusing on contingencies to keep ourselves safe. The four of us were a bigger target when we weren't spread out, so we needed to mitigate the increased danger. Weeks of late-night talks had finally led us right back to the beginning.

Separating into smaller groups meant the others could be used as bait. We couldn't afford to stretch our resources even further for a hostage rescue. So, we'd stay together, end Cash, and get out alive.

It was almost strange that the day was finally here, but I was ready.

Ready to wake up tomorrow to a Cash-free world. Ready to watch the stress of his existence wash off my woman's and my brother's backs. Ready to begin our fucking lives together—the family we'd lived, breathed, and bled for.

Today would be filled with carnage so tomorrow could be brighter.

I couldn't fucking wait.

Kosas grunted, which I took as a yes to my question. As I looked at him, it was almost hard to see the man he'd been a month ago. His cheeks were hollow, his eyes dead. There was some life to them, a pit of vengeance buried and waiting to burst out, but it was fleeting. There was no more righteous anger, no more jokes, no more laughter. He was empty, and my stomach sank with the realization that, for him, this was probably a one-way ticket to the afterlife.

He had no one to come home to. Nothing to fight for. He was going into Gilded with us, but I knew in my soul he wasn't coming out. Standing taller, I held out a hand to him. "May this balance the scales."

Pain trickled through his gaze. "They'll never be balanced."

He left without another word, but it wasn't long before someone else took his place.

"You look good in black, Killer."

The kid rolled his eyes, but I meant it. He looked like he was meant to be in tactical gear. A general in the making. Once he'd gotten out of jail, he'd thrown himself into work with a zest for life that I couldn't believe, and every day he got better. If he kept it up, I could see him leading his own family or maybe even taking over ours when we were ready to retire.

Not that I'd told Mari yet.

"Are you ready for this, kid?"

"Absolutely. Anything for the family." I looked him over, trying to pick out a chink in his armor, but I found none. He believed every word he said, not because it'd been drilled into his brain but because he was loyal. Indoctrination could only get you so far, but faith like this—in Mari and our family? That shit would take us to the moon.

Just like I did with Kosas, I held out my hand. "We appreciate having you with us, Killer."

He stared for a moment before finally taking it, giving me a hearty shake. "There's nowhere I'd rather be."

I believed him.

Mari waved him over, and he nodded one last time before he entered the circle of generals. They'd all been briefed already, but Mari wanted to make sure everyone knew their individual parts. We'd gone over ours in the car, so I took my time watching her in her element.

Hair braided down her back, black tactical gear surrounding her body, weapons absolutely everywhere. She looked like a wet dream, but it was the look in her eyes that made me hard.

Fierce. Determined. Ready to slaughter anything between us and our future.

Yeah, that was the good stuff.

"Are you going to eye-fuck her all morning?" Nate asked, standing on one side of me, while Grey mirrored his position on the other.

"Could you blame me if I did?"

He hummed, which was obviously a *no*.

"Is it done?" I breathed, not willing to let even a word get to Mari.

Nate dipped his chin. "Eagle will get her out if things go south."

"Where?"

"Colombia. Christian has agreed to keep her out of Emmanuel's sight if the worst happens."

"Probably because of Shara," Grey mused, but he seemed more relaxed knowing there was a way out for our girl if everything went wrong. Truthfully, so was I.

I wanted to stay by her side always, but I preferred she lived, even if she was alone.

The fear of what would happen to Mari if things went sideways didn't go away just because we had an exit plan for her, but it did ease a little, knowing Eagle and his band of psychos would get her out if Cash won. Made it easier to focus on what we needed to do.

"We stay together. No one gets separated, and none of us dies," Grey said. "Mari won't survive it."

Nate and I nodded. Grey was right. There was only so much a person could go through without losing their humanity, and Mari was already at that point. Losing us would tip her over the edge.

Our girl looked over, and even though she softened at the sight of us, her eyes glimmered with a vengeance that the world would lose her to. But that was only *if* we died. So, we just wouldn't.

We'd stay alive and make Mari the happiest woman in the world.

All we had to do was defeat an army to make it happen.

No big deal.

* * *

We decided to split Black Team in two, putting our family as part of the first wave of attacks in hopes that Cash didn't fortify himself against us more than he already had. Kosas immediately stepped up, offering himself and his men to break in, which meant it was likely going to be a lot bloodier than expected.

The second wave—with Victor and Christian—would come soon after. We also kept a third recovery team nearby to help in case of evacuation or in case Cash tried to run again. Sharpshooters, including Rafael, already lined the closest building, ready and willing to take out every Ace who stepped outside the club.

This was all going to be fast movement with heavy impact. We needed plenty of eyes to make sure no one slipped away. If they sided with Cash, they were dead. End of story.

Opening the back of the SUVs, we all armed ourselves quickly. We all had comms units in our ears so we could talk once we breached since our plan had a tighter timeline than all the other hits.

We needed to be inside—having taken out some men already —when the rest of the first wave crashed into the Aces. Cash would likely lock down the club the second he got word. If we could get to him while the rest of his forces went after the second wave, we were pretty sure we could end this quick. Or, as quick as killing a psychopath could be.

Mari looked us over, triple-checking that we had everything too but moving back to check in one last time with Christian and Victor. "Give us ten minutes, and then go."

They nodded, and we skirted around the building.

Two minutes to get to the club. Eight to get inside.

No fucking pressure.

We stuck to the shadows and alleys as we wound our way toward Gilded, expecting to find the Aces guarding the perimeter.

Nothing.

That wasn't suspicious at all.

"Mari..."

She glanced my way with a frown. "Tell the others."

"Almost to the basement door. No signs of guards outside. Any movement on your end?"

I waited a second for confirmation, but none came.

"Repeat. No guards outside the basement door. Anyone have eyes on an Ace?"

Still nothing.

Mari frowned, taking over. "Black Team Two? Black Team Three? Birds? Anyone copy?"

"No signal. He's got a jammer," Grey said, waving his phone. Which meant the comms units were useless.

Well, fuck. That made things complicated. We had no way to tell the others what we were seeing, so we were all going in blind.

Let's hope it's not like this everywhere.

Pocketing the earpiece, I stayed low and forced my focus here and now. The other teams weren't my problem. Surviving was.

"We stay together," I said again, making sure Mari heard me. There would be no running off to kill Cash alone. We did it together, or someone else could take the fucking shot.

"Together," she promised.

We'd intended to use the fingerprint scanners to get inside since there was no way Cash could override them, but he'd apparently found a work-around.

Security systems needed power to run. We had a generator, but since the club was typically guarded, we didn't have it set to kick on automatically. Which meant, when Cash had cut the power, he'd gotten access to the club without a fight, and now he'd manually locked the doors.

A feat Greyson was obviously pissed about. He grumbled under his breath about what he was going to do when this was over until Mari snapped, "Fix it later. We've got to get in there."

Thankfully, the basement had its own separate backup, so it still needed a fingerprint to enter. Mari laid hers down until the light glowed green. As soon as we were all in, we let the door shut. First order of business, providing an entrance for the others.

We took the stairs up quietly, only stopping to make sure the basement was secure again. When we hit the top, we angled for the back hallway where the bathrooms bracketed an emergency exit, but we'd found our first snag.

The hall had a single guard who was dozing when we cleared the top stair. The creak of our boots against the wood woke him fully, and he opened his mouth to yell out. Nate surged toward him, clapping a gloved hand over it and slipping a knife into the guy's throat. He was too focused on suffocating to care about us anymore.

Grey opened a nearby storage room and helped Nate lay the first Ace down before hustling over to ensure the emergency exit stayed open. It took some clever work, but he got a knife wedged in there so good, we'd have to replace the whole damn door to get it out. "Let's go."

Mari and I took point, rounding the corner quickly, which meant we got a face full of knuckles when we ran into a duo of guards who were far more alert than the last. I ducked out of the way, but Mari took a fist to the cheek. Her quiet *oof* pissed me off, and I grabbed my guard by the throat, plunging the blade into the same place Nate had. I wanted him dead so I could take my time with the other guy, but when I turned, Mari had his mouth pinned closed with her own knife.

"You shouldn't have touched me."

The Ace dropped to her feet, and she stepped over him, letting Nate and Grey drag the bodies to the closet again. We weren't trying to hide our entrance; we just wanted to get closer before Cash found us. A person only had so much energy, and if we used all of ours before then, we'd be dead.

We took out six more Aces by the time my watch vibrated with a warning. I lifted one finger into the air.

One minute until the second wave.

We had to find Cash before we lost him in the mayhem.

The main room was littered with dozens of Aces. They sat around the tables smoking, drinking all the second-tier booze— probably because the top-shelf shit was gone—and playing cards. Most of them looked half smashed, and the others were openly snoring in their seats.

How the fuck was this the army that had nearly taken Seattle?

"Jesus," Mari whispered, and I just knew she was thinking the same thing.

Nate winced. "They're better when they're sober."

Didn't we all know it.

The reminder of what had happened at the compound stole my breath, but I kept my focus. "Let's check the office."

We crept down the side hallway, clearing the storage rooms as we went, but we found no one else.

An eerie feeling prickled through me, and I strained my ears for the noise from the main room again.

It was so goddamned quiet.

The hair on my neck stood up, and my gut rolled with the need to run. *Get the fuck out of here.*

I tried to tell everyone to back up, but I had no chance before the wall exploded inward.

The explosion was small, so while it took us off our feet, it didn't do much else beyond spraying us with a shit-ton of debris. At least, I thought it didn't.

The floor rumbled, and I shoved Mari into Nate, pushing them to the edges of the room. With her safe, I reached for Greyson, but I was too late. The floor gave way as the fabric of his shirt slipped through my fingers. "No!"

"Greyson!" Mari yelled his name, desperation ringing through my ears even over the sound of gunfire.

The cavalry had arrived. Thank fuck.

We still didn't know where Cash was, but we'd figure it out. He wasn't getting out of here alive.

More gunshots fired, and I realized that the "sleeping" men probably hadn't been sleeping at all.

Definitely a trap, which means the floor situation is too.

"Stay back," I ordered, happy to see Nate holding Mari back. "I'll get him."

I felt her eyes on me as I climbed down the fucking landslide, but as long as she stayed there, I was fine with it. I wasn't going to let her fall into the pit and be lost herself.

The floor looked to have collapsed about one story down, to the storage part of Gilded's basement. The debris had made a slope we could use to climb, thanks to part of the floor staying mostly intact. The rubble was from the rest of the floor crumbling. Thankfully, Grey had fallen onto the rubble and not the other way around, so it was easy to see him. Not as easy to get to him and probably a bitch to get him out, but we'd manage.

He was on his back, panting at the ceiling when I finally got to his level. "Up you go, big boy."

"That's what she said," he huffed, rolling to his side so he could get back on his feet. His teeth were gritted, but I didn't see any glaring injuries.

"You good?"

"Perfect. Get me up there."

I went first, stopping often to make sure he was still behind me. Our palms were scraped, blood oozing between the small cuts, but we kept pushing. The higher we got, the slower I went, making sure I was there in case his hands slipped. I'd push the guy with a hand on the ass if it meant we got out of the hole sooner.

Gunshots were still ringing out, people screaming, but the hallway was quiet. Maybe because they knew there was no exit over here.

I didn't breathe as I climbed out of the hole and threw a hand down for him. It took Grey a second to shift his hand so he wouldn't fall when he let go, but eventually, he tossed himself forward and grabbed me. Greyson's grip was strong as I hauled him out of the rubble, breathing heavily once we were on mostly solid ground. When he finally stood, it was with one arm wrapped around his ribs. I hoped his body didn't have any serious damage. We were shit out of luck if so.

Broken ribs, we could handle. Punctured lungs, not so much.

"Quit it, mother hen."

"Jesus, I'm just making sure you're not dying."

"*Aw*, I knew you loved me." He pushed my hovering body away from him, giving me a shit-eating grin.

Should've left him in the rubble. No good deed goes unpunished. "Mari would've been sad without you, that's all."

"Sure, sure." His smile didn't fall as he dug his spare gun out of its holster. "Let's get back to our girl."

Only, when we turned around, we found nothing but dust.

No Mari. No Nate.

Fuck.

Chapter 32
Nate

One second, we were watching Dominic haul Greyson out of the hole, and the next, we were flying.

Or, more accurately, falling.

"I wasn't aware there was a trap door in the bar," I groaned.

The sounds of men screaming and random pops of gunfire above us would hide our yells, so no way the others could hear us down here. Wherever the hell *here* was.

"There isn't one," Mari said.

"What?"

"We don't have a trap door in the bar."

"A serious oversight on your part."

We both jerked at Cash's voice, though Mari was quicker to get on her feet than I was. She had her gun up and pointed at him before I registered she'd moved at all.

Cash clicked his tongue like a disapproving father. "Better put that down. Wouldn't want the whole place to blow."

He tipped his head back, that manic fire that preceded his worst plans obvious, and my eyes widened. He'd taped a fuck-ton of explosives to the far wall, more than enough to level not just the building but the entire street.

"Are you fucking stupid?" Hauling myself to my feet, I kept my body between him and Mari.

"One stray bullet and we're all dead." Mari shook her head.

Obviously, I'd forgotten that my brother hadn't been a rational person in a long time. All he did was shrug. "I'm ready to die today. Are you?"

Not a chance, but with bullets flying around upstairs, we needed to get this done and get the fuck out of the club before it blew.

Mari stared at the wall before carefully handing her gun to me then stripping off the rest and laying them at my feet. After that, she moved to the knives.

I looked between her and my brother, finding him doing the same with his own cache of weapons. "What the hell are you doing? Put those back on."

Cash had spent most of his adult life strung out, but he was still bigger than Mari in every way. Her training meant she could take him, but it wouldn't be pretty. Far easier just to shoot the fucker and move on.

"I'm ending this."

"Not like this," I begged. "Just shoot him and be done."

"I'm not blowing us all up."

Cash had positioned himself right in front of the explosive wall, and I had no doubt he'd do his best to stay near it throughout the fight. Mari was right; one stray bullet and we were all done.

"You too, little brother. Weapons off. I promise it'll be a fair fight."

Not a fucking chance.

Mari didn't even glance at me. "Do it, Nate."

"This is a bad idea." I still did it, even when my stomach was screaming at me. Who was I to decide how Mari got her revenge? Who was I to take this away from her? If she wanted to inflict pain for all she'd suffered, that was her right.

I didn't fucking like it, though.

"I'll let you keep one knife each," Cash said, kicking his own pile away.

"Deal." Leaning into me, she whispered, "Trust me."

I did. It was Cash I didn't trust, and for good reason.

We all checked one another for weapons, making sure no one had more than the one allotted knife before I took my place at the wall. It felt wrong to watch, knowing Cash was going to hit Mari. Wrong to stand aside and let her take the hits I knew she needed to feel.

This was her atonement, and even if I didn't think she needed it, it was obvious she felt she did.

They circled each other, both testing the waters, trying to find the other's weaknesses.

Finally, Cash grinned. "Fuck it."

His first punch grazed her temple, throwing her off-balance just as much as his body weight did, but she kept her feet. Shoving at him, she went hard, trying to get at any soft spots she could find.

Eyes, neck, diaphragm, balls. Whatever she could reach, she went for.

Mari unleashed on my brother, but his eyes were glittering. He enjoyed having her in front of him. Enjoyed seeing how much he'd pissed her off. That rage fueled him as much as the madness did. It made him cocky.

Too cocky.

A solid kick to his wrist knocked the knife out of his hand, sending it careening into the shadows. Cash lunged for the pile, and Mari followed. She blocked him from the other weapons, slowly backing him into a corner that was too small for his big frame. It limited his movements to defense only, while Mari had the freedom to attack as she saw fit.

And she did.

She snapped his head back with a punch to the neck, following it with one to the throat. While he was bent over gasping, she sent her knee to his ribs until they cracked too.

Over and over, she beat him until he was down on one knee with an eye swelling shut and no way out.

Mari had Cash trapped, and he knew it.

Which was why he raised a gun he must have hidden somewhere and shot at me.

Instinct had me on the floor before the sound ricocheted around us, and the bullet dug into the wall close to where I'd stood.

Thank fuck it's not the wall with explosives.

I tried to call out to Mari that I was okay, but she was already whipping around, my name on her lips.

I got a firsthand look as Cash jumped on her, watching in horror as he took her down.

They rolled, Mari trying to get the upper hand before a loud *crack* stopped her. Her voice was tight with pain when he wrenched her knife away from her now-limp arm. It too went into the shadows, and then it was just the two of them. But while Mari had done some damage, Cash still had the use of both his hands. She didn't.

She fought to get some space between them, fought to have some breathing room, but it wasn't working.

Go to her. Help her. Kill him. But she didn't want my help. My desire to keep her safe warred with her desire to free herself from Cash's demons, and I wasn't sure what the best decision was.

He had to die, but it had to be the right way.

Somehow, Mari got the space she wanted and rolled out from under him, getting to her feet on wobbly knees. She was breathing heavily, obviously hurting and down a fully functioning arm. She needed a fucking weapon.

"Don't," she croaked, seeing me reach for the pile. "Let me finish this."

He stalked her steps, punching every which way. He cracked her in the head again, and she was disoriented and stumbling on her feet. I could see her blinking hard, trying to remember what was around so she could decide where to go.

That's it.

I only had the one knife on me, and I wasn't going to let it go to waste.

Throwing was out since they were moving too fast and I didn't want to hit Mari, so I crept up behind them, blade at the ready, and waited. My body swayed as I lightly followed Cash's movements until I found my moment.

When he dodged one of Mari's punches, I sank the knife deep into his shoulder.

He roared, twisting until he could shove a blade of his own into my leg. The pain stole my breath, then expanded when he ripped it out and did it again. Blood poured down my leg, and I wondered if he'd hit the artery, but I doubted it. He could've, but it was more than obvious Cash preferred to play with his food. "You should've stayed out of it, little brother. Now I'm tired of playing."

Mari was weaving on her feet when he backhanded her into the cement wall, her good hand too slow to protect her head. The crack echoed through the room, sliding into my bones in a way I knew I'd never be able to unhear.

Mari's body wobbled, then dropped to the floor with a thump.

She didn't get back up.

Oh God. Please, no.

Chapter Thirty-Two

"Mari?" I whispered, coughing as the dust from the wall got into my mouth.

"Mari," Cash mocked. "Your girl's dead. Good riddance, too. The bitch made this fucking impossible."

I didn't listen to him, didn't look at him. I couldn't turn away from Mari.

How still she was.

The blood pooling beside her head.

Was her back even rising?

You can't be dead. You can't leave me.

"You shouldn't worry about her, brother. Her death was quick. Yours is going to be a lot more painful."

He came at me, hands flying and mind fully engaged. That was the thing about Cash. He could be manic at times, but he was determined. If he set his sights on something—taking the city, killing Mari, destroying me—it would require a force of nature to stop him. His hyperfocus was unmatched when he wanted it to be.

Right now, his hyperfocus was on removing me from the playing field.

Which was good, because mine was the same.

We battled each other with heavy blows and harsh kicks. Cash threw taunting words too, picking at wounds he knew would hurt any other day.

Today, I was numb.

Mari still hadn't moved.

I threw myself into the action, dodging a kick to the ribs and delivering my own to the dick. Fighting dirty probably wouldn't get me much respect right now, but I didn't really care.

He'd hurt my Mari.

My angel.

She was on the floor bleeding because of him.

She'd lost her brother, her cousins, her family because of *him*.

I wasn't going to let this moment go to waste.

She'd have her vengeance, even if it came through me.

"You're going to regret that," I said carefully.

"I doubt it, but let's see what you can do, little brother." He rushed my legs, hauling me into the air and dropping me hard. Something popped, and I wheezed with the effort of drawing air. *Ribs. He fractured my ribs.*

Probably worse than that, but I wouldn't know until I got an X-ray.

Blinking hard, I tried to force my lungs to suck in a breath, but he'd knocked the wind out of me.

No matter, breath would come eventually. I just had to stay alive until then. Mari needed me to finish this.

Cash didn't have the same idea. He pulled my head up and smashed it back down on the floor below us. I groaned, feeling skin split and blood pour. Head wounds were notoriously heavy bleeders, so I couldn't be sure he'd done lasting damage.

Feet planted on the floor, I rolled us, tossing hard blows to his ribs as I went. For every injury he gave me, I'd give him one back. Cash landed on his back much softer than I had, already on the offensive. He slid his knees up to keep me from pinning him and swung an elbow at my nose. The crack made my eyes water, but I doubled down, punching every exposed area I could. Finally, he got his legs in a place where he could kick my chest, shoving me off him long enough to get to his feet.

"You were always weak," he taunted. "Too weak to lead, too weak to live."

"Yet here I am, alive." My leg lifted into a roundhouse before I'd even consciously thought it, taking Cash straight in the jaw.

"For now." He grinned, blood dripping from his mouth. "Not for long, though."

Being a merc had taught me a lot about defeating my opponents. How to watch their bodies for what they'd do next, how to get in their heads and throw them off their game. How to hunt down my prey.

This was the culmination. Cash's death would come from the monster he'd made.

How fitting.

We battled until we were both sweating and exhausted. Every move I made, Cash blocked. Every punch he threw, I swerved. Despite my training and the age gap between us, we were too similar. But Cash had one thing on me.

Unpredictability.

Just as he was swinging a serious left hook, he dropped to his knees and sent it toward my legs instead. His punch landed square at the bend of my knee, and it took me out. I wasn't on my back for a second before he sprang and laid into me.

Every punch had a different reminder.

"Poor little Nate with his fucked-up mom and his dead girlfriend. *I'm so sad. Everyone around me dies.* You could've been a hero. You could've ruled this fucking city at my side, but instead, you chose *her.* Was it worth betraying your brother?"

"Yes," I hissed.

His eyes tightened, and he moved, trapping my arms between his legs and my own body so I couldn't get them out. Couldn't defend myself as he wrapped his hands around my neck and squeezed.

This wasn't the gentle choke of two brothers horsing around; this was stealing the breath from my lungs. Killing me slowly and painfully.

There was no mercy in suffocation. No mercy in the panic that came when air wouldn't.

This was Cash's final torture. "I always knew you weren't fit to be my brother, and you've proven me right time and time again. But this is too far. *She* is too far." He shook my head, hands tightening their grip. "You're a pathetic excuse for a Beckstrom."

"Good thing I'm not a Beckstrom," I spat. "I'm a Marcosa."

That was the ultimate sin to my brother. Giving up my name, my birthright, for *her*.

He couldn't allow me to survive the disrespect.

Cash bore down on my neck with nothing but rage and death in his eyes. That was fine. My reason for living was gone anyway.

Black spots danced in my vision, slowly crowding the world until all I could see was darkness. I tried to extricate my hands, tried to shift so I could get him off my chest, but there was no freeing myself. I was going to die with him in front of me.

Fuck that.

I tried to turn my head just a little. I didn't want to die with my brother's face in front of me. I wanted to see Mari.

My girl.

My angel.

The love of my fucking life.

I wanted to look at her as the world went black and acknowledge that I had been a lucky bastard to have her in my life.

To hold her. Kiss her. Comfort her.

To get her back when she could've walked away for good at any time.

To die wearing her ring, carrying her name—which was more than I'd ever thought I'd have.

So, I fought Cash's grip enough to twist my head so I could leave this world with her face in my mind.

Only, she wasn't there.

Before I had a chance to wonder where the hell she'd gone, someone appeared behind Cash.

Blood dripping down her face, skin exposed in all the spots her clothes were torn, and a look of pure rage on her face, she'd never been more beautiful.

My Mari.

My angel of vengeance had come to take her pound of flesh.

Chapter 33
Mari

The tackle was off-kilter because my head was fucking killing me, but it did the job. Cash flew off his brother, my weight taking him to the floor. It wouldn't have worked if he hadn't been distracted, but it didn't matter. Nate's pained gasp was music to my ears even as my skin scraped against the rocks.

Peering over, I saw him blink, saw him try to focus, and told myself that was enough for the moment. *He's alive. Now, get to work.*

Pushing through every ounce of pain, I fought to get to my knees at the same time Cash struggled to his. A moment of stillness lingered as we looked each other over—weary and bleeding—and I knew we had the same thought.

Only one of us would leave this room. Only one could survive. And I knew exactly who it would be.

I threw myself at him, knowing that I had to make him

unsteady if I had a chance. He was weak without the coke, and he'd obviously hit his head at some point. If I could wear him out before I got too tired to fight, it was over.

All I had to do was finish him first.

My fist glanced off his jaw, and he threw another punch at me that clipped my injured shoulder. But I was already dipping, already shoving the bottom of my foot into his knee. It crumpled, but he kept his feet.

Lucky bastard.

"Come on, queenie. Show me what you've got." His lips tipped to one side, even as his leg tried to give out on him, and I almost laughed in his face at how fucking pathetic he was, trying to play the big man right now.

Men like Cash were so cocky. They thought brute strength would get them what they wanted, but longevity was the real key. He could beat my ass into the ground, but I could outlast him in the ring. And that was exactly what I'd do.

We circled each other, but he never made the first move. It was always me taking a swipe before retreating. Me who forced him to use his energy.

Almost like he wasn't sure he could handle me anymore.

I liked that.

"What's wrong?" I taunted. "Struggling to know what to do when I'm not tied up like a fucking present?"

Cash's eyes narrowed. He didn't like when I talked back. Didn't like when I made him feel like less than a man.

Well, joke was on him because he was less than a man. Anyone who preyed on kids and attacked innocents was nothing more than scum. An infestation I was all too happy to wipe out.

When he still didn't move first, I laughed. "You're fucking pathetic, Cash. Can't handle a woman if she's not unconscious first. Can't run a business without snorting half of it. Can't be the leader of your family without your little brother messing things up. You're a fucking waste. An old man too focused on power to realize what you stole was never yours to begin with."

Red muddied his face even below the dripping blood, and the vein in his forehead pulsed heavily. "You fucking bitch."

"Wow, so creative," I deadpanned. "Try harder next time, yeah? A third grader could insult me better."

"I'm going to keep you alive just so I can fuck you in front of your weak little boyfriends, and then I'm going to pass you around to my men. Doubt you'll be talking so much when they're done with you."

"So your men are the real threat. Good to know." His jaw popped and he clenched his teeth, but I didn't let up. "As for my men, are you sure you want me to compare you to Nate? Because he's been fucking me so good, I'm not sure you can compete. I certainly haven't heard good things. Having trouble lately?"

Egotistical men were hard to hurt. In their minds, they were too big to damage. Too powerful to injure. But their pride? That shit was an Achilles' heel. Find the right button, and they went down.

Fun fact, prolonged cocaine use caused sexual dysfunction. It had only taken Nate one call to confirm with one of the girls the Aces passed around.

Cash couldn't get it up.

I could admit it was a low blow, but if exploiting Cash's impotence got him to show me his neck, I'd do it every goddamn time. Whatever it took to slay the dragon.

Also, he fucking started it.

Cash's chest heaved, eyes wild with anger at just the mention of his little problem. When I lifted a hand and made my little pinkie wilt like a dying daisy? That was the final straw.

His roar echoed around us as he charged, throwing punch after punch. I dodged most until he finally landed one straight to my jaw. He'd put his whole weight into it, and the force of the collision of his fist to my face tossed him backward. He tried to correct himself, but he was still wobbling when I saw my move and took it.

Bending my knees, I bolted for him, dropping my uninjured shoulder just in time to take Cash off his feet. His head cracked against the rock, and he groaned, struggling to right himself. To come back up for more.

He was mistaken. There would be no getting up for him again.

Pouncing on him, I knew this was it. My moment, my second of divine retribution. All I had to do was take it.

And take it, I did.

Using Cash's disorientation to my advantage, I trapped him the same way he'd trapped Nate—arms clenched between my thighs—and let myself go. My knuckles were already split, so the blood pooling on his face was a mixture of us both, but I didn't stop, grateful I'd been taught to fight with both hands.

"You thought you beat us. You thought you won, and here you are, sniveling under me like the coward you are." The next punch hit him in the throat, and the sound of Cash gasping was so satisfying I wanted to do it again.

Go slow. Make it hurt. Do it for everyone you've hurt.

Crack. Crack. Crack. "That's for Mama Ophelia. Kosas's family. Sabine."

Crack. Crack. "For Aislynn and Shara, whom you've terrorized." *Crack.*

The last punch threw me off-balance, and I nearly unseated myself. My hand landed on a wedge of rock that fit perfectly in my palm. A sign from the gods.

Nate called for me as I hefted it above my head.

It was time to end this, once and for all.

"This is for your brother, who spent his entire life being tortured by you." My muscles bunched as I threw myself into the hit, cracking Cash's cheek. *Smash.*

"For Greyson and Dominic, whom you nearly killed." *Smash.*

"For Antoni and Rey, whom you *did* kill." *Smash.*

I held the rock above his barely breathing form while my own chest heaved. "And this? This is for me. Rot in hell, you fucking asshole."

The sound of the rock taking the last bit of Cash's life would forever be ingrained in my memory. I could live to be a thousand and never forget. It was the sound of the restraints he'd shackled me in breaking, the sound of my city getting its freedom back.

It was the sound of living.

I dropped the rock to the side, sitting back on my haunches and just breathing. Blood speckled my body, making my skin tight as it dried, and my arms felt *this* close to giving out. But my heart? That was lighter than a fucking feather. Nate scrambled to my side, hauling me closer and checking over every square inch of me for injuries. I wasn't sure he even saw Cash anymore, he was so focused on me.

"Fuck, I thought I lost you."

"I'm okay."

He didn't answer, his big hands cradling my head as he took in what had to be a nasty cut. The backhanded blow had rocked me, but it had really been just a glance. "Where else are you hurt?

"Nate."

He couldn't hear me, too focused on pulling at my shirt so he could check my sides, my arms, my hands. "I have to see where you're hurt, angel. Is it your arm?"

Pretty sure he's in shock. I tried again. "Nate."

He shook his head, reaching for my buckle without a thought beyond making sure I was okay. "The others are coming soon. They'll get us out of here—"

"*Nate.*" He finally looked at me then, and I clutched his hand. "He's dead. Cash is dead."

"What?" He turned to the corpse beside us and stared at it in confusion. People often thought the nightmare ended when the demon died, but it was more difficult to recognize the end when you'd been trying so hard to survive the middle. The closing of a chapter felt as impossible as flying to the moon in a hot-air balloon.

But when it hit, it was euphoric.

It took Nate touching Cash, feeling for himself that he had no heartbeat, for him to realize it was truly over.

"Cash is dead." Those three words preceded the most beautiful smile I'd ever seen. A laugh crept between Nate's lips, and he didn't even try to stifle it. "He's dead. *He's dead!*"

Even with his voice raspy, eyes bloodshot, and a ring of purple creeping around his neck, Nate looked lighter than I'd ever seen him. It was as if his brother's death had stolen back the weight that hadn't been his to carry. He looked relieved and resolved and... free.

Nate looked free.

He hauled me into his arms and kissed me until we were both panting for air. "You did it."

"We did it," I corrected. "How does it feel?"

"Like I'm a new man." He nuzzled my nose with his. "Your man."

"I like the sound of that."

"Good, because I've decided I much prefer being a Marcosa to being a Black. You're stuck with me." He didn't let me respond before he wrapped a hand around my neck and took my mouth again.

My body hurt and Nate looked like he was barely upright, but clearly, neither of us cared because we did it again. We smiled and laughed and kissed, and when the frantic calls of our names got louder, I wanted to cry because there they were. My other men. Probably bruised, maybe even broken, but they were alive.

We were alive.

I couldn't say the same for everyone else, but my family had survived, and that meant everything to me.

"What are we going to do now?" Nate whispered, and I grinned.

The war was over. We'd won.

Now, it was time to live.

Chapter 34
Mari

T*wo weeks later*

It still hadn't hit me that Cash was dead.

We'd hauled his body from the wreckage and had Dr. Grant ensure that there was no coming back, then we'd burned him to ash.

If there was anyone who could come back from the dead to haunt us, it would be that annoying asshole.

Nate had nearly crushed my good hand while we watched, but that was fine. He'd just lost a brother after nearly losing his life and me. If he needed to squeeze me too tightly for a while, I could deal. As long as he was here.

My right arm was broken, which was beyond inconvenient. I

also had a concussion that took a week to heal and more cuts and bruises than expected. Nate had fractured ribs, which meant he was wrapped like a mummy until they healed. Greyson and Dominic were bruised, which they took great pleasure in teasing Nate about. Grey's other wounds were relatively superficial, *thank God*, but Dominic had nearly torn his left ACL fighting while Nate and I were with Cash. The strain was hard on him, but far better than surgery.

Christian ended up with two new bullet holes that Shara had berated him about over the phone for almost twenty minutes. Two-Bit had a graze on his forehead, another on his shoulder, and a through and through on his side. When I asked what happened, the brothers were cagey as fuck, so I let it go.

Not my circus, not my monkeys. God help Shara with those two.

Victor survived as well with nothing more than some bruised knuckles and a black eye. Maximoff looked as fresh as a daisy when it all was said and done, which was beyond creepy. Who walked out of a battle clean? Especially when I *knew* he'd killed at least four people.

Not everyone was as lucky, though. Our side of the battle lost a lot of men, but Cash's lost more.

Everyone, in fact.

After the initial waves that killed most of their comrades, the remaining Aces fled. Rafael and Eagle each took teams to hunt them down. Since they were too stupid to truly hide, we rounded them up fairly fast and gave them a proper burial.

Sea creatures loved to eat dead Aces.

After they were gone, we'd realized just how much damage Cash had done to the city—which the war had obviously made worse. We had our work cut out for us, but with Two-Bit's help, we'd get the city back to normal within the year.

He'd survived, as had the other leaders who'd come with me.

Well, except Kosas. One of the Aces who had killed his son got a lucky shot to Kosas's stomach. It wasn't enough to save the guy, but it was enough to ensure Kosas died with him. His nephew was due to arrive in the city next week to take over his territory fully, and from the few interactions we'd had over the phone, he seemed smart enough. As long as he stayed on my good side, he'd be allowed to stay.

Cash had shone a light on my failures, making it obvious I'd been too lenient with the other leaders. I blamed most of it on grief, but that wasn't the only culprit. Thankfully, it was an easy fix. All I had to do was explain to the other leaders that if they crossed me even once, they were dead.

Everyone fell in line when they realized it was their head on the chopping block.

Without the weight of Cash and the Aces hanging over us, the air smelled sweeter. Though, that could've been the victory high I was still on.

Christian, Two-Bit, and Shara were set to be married.

I was at the Marcosa mansion, which I'd decided to turn into a base of operations for the recovery efforts for now, though who knew what it would be next. My capos and I were discussing recovery payments for families who'd lost someone in what we were calling the Battle of Seattle when the text came through from Killer.

The package is loaded.

Perfect.

Waving the phone to my men, I left Greyson to take over and made my way to the driveway.

Three white vans were parked outside the mansion, all with the same fake construction logos on the sides. In the middle, the door was open, giving me a perfect view of my cousin strapped down to the seat.

Cameron was pale and subdued, though he had an almost feral edge to him that I knew came from his solitude. There was a reason solitary confinement was a punishment in jail. Loss of human interaction had a way of making even the sanest person lose their mind.

That edge took over when he saw me in front of him. "What is this, Mari?"

Pasting on a smile was easy. I loved seeing my enemies on their knees. "Aw, you didn't enjoy your ride? I thought you'd like some fresh air after being cooped up in the basement for so long."

He snarled at me, struggling with the straps that held him down.

"Give us a minute, Killer. My cousin and I need to talk."

He was years younger than both of us, but the way he glared at Cameron as he walked away gave me the shivers. How interesting.

When it was finally just the two of us, my cousin glowered at me. "Are you here to gloat?"

Actually, yes. "Thought you might like to know it's over. Your boss is dead."

"He's not my—wait, Cash is dead?"

"Him and everyone who worked with him."

Except for you.

I didn't have to say it for it to be true.

Cameron swallowed, suddenly much less aggressive. "What are you going to do with me now?"

"Nothing."

His brows furrowed in confusion. "What?"

"I've thought about killing you, but why waste the bullet?" I leaned in with a wicked smile. "Instead, I'm going to strike you out of the record books. Scour your existence from the planet. No matter how hard anyone looks, they won't find a single mention of Cameron Marcosa anywhere. You'll be a ghost."

"And Aislynn?"

"Already on the way to her new home, exactly like she wanted."

God, I loved the way his face turned red. "She's still my wife."

I smiled viciously. "Didn't I tell you? The divorce went through. Ash is officially a free woman again."

"Marcosas don't divorce."

"My father did, and now, so have you. Trust me, it's kinder than death. Although, she did get everything you own, so maybe not."

"Where is she?"

"Somewhere you'll never find her. She's got a real army to protect her now. Men who will die at her feet to keep her safe. Between you and me, *whew*, they're gorgeous. Even if she still wants you—which she doesn't—she has no use for you. Not with them around."

"You can send her to the ends of the earth, and I'll still find her. She's *mine*, Mari."

"She was, but the moment you betrayed her, you lost any right you had to her. You lost the most precious thing you've ever owned—although, we both know you didn't really own her at all. I hope the memories of what you almost had keep you warm at night. I hear it gets cold in the desert."

"Desert? What the hell are you talking about?"

I stopped Killer's slow roll of the closing door and smiled at Cameron. "Since Ash has gone to her new life, I thought you'd like the same. I hope you like snakes, *cousin*."

One of the things I'd asked Greyson to do sporadically throughout my reign was buy up property in other places. Places no one else wanted to go. Places that could kill the wrong person living there.

Cameron was destined for one of those places.

If the heat didn't kill him, the scorpions might.

Killer had volunteered to be the driver for this portion of the trip, despite how fucking long it was going to take to get there and that he'd been injured. He'd taken two bullets to the left leg with the second wave, but Dr. Grant swore he was recovering fine.

"How's the leg?"

"Healing." When I stared at him, hoping for more information, he shrugged. "There's nothing else to say."

"You're limping."

He immediately straightened. "I can do my job."

Shaking my head, I laid a hand on his shoulder. "I didn't say it because I doubt you. I said it because I want to make sure you're taking care of yourself."

Uncertainty flickered in his gaze before he dropped it. "Thank you. I'm fine most of the time. Hauling him around put some additional strain on it, is all."

I frowned at the white van. "He wasn't cooperative?"

Killer shrugged. "I wasn't expecting him to be."

Yet he'd still gone along with it, knowing he was at a disadvantage because he wanted to do right by me. The more I learned about Killer, the more I liked him. Always the first to offer his help and the first to throw himself into the line of fire to protect other people. Loyal and steadfast and fair with everyone, even when they looked down on him for his age.

Exactly the type of man I wanted at my table.

"Come see me when you get back. I think I've got a promotion that's perfect for you."

In the days following the battle, Nate had pulled me aside and begged me not to make him capo. It was an honor, but he didn't want to handle his own men or have his focus pulled, and he didn't care what other people thought of him. As long as he was protecting me, he'd be happy.

Of course, I agreed. Now that the other leaders were aware of his history, I wasn't concerned about Leo's warning. If Nate needed to prove just how scary he was, he would. I just wanted Nate happy, and if that meant shadowing my every move, I could deal.

The door slammed on Cameron's screaming, and I laughed. It paid to know someone's biggest fears.

Killer tucked his head, but I saw his grin too. He was just as happy to see my cousin disappear. He might've been young, but Montgomery had a loyalty streak a mile long.

"Sedate him before you go. God knows you don't need to listen to him bitch for twenty hours."

"I think I'll let him scream himself hoarse first."

"That's fine. Get a move on, though. I want him out of my city by sundown."

"Yes, ma'am. Uh, miss. Mari. *Fuck.*" My head tipped back as I laughed, and Killer's relieved chuckle followed. "I'll text Dominic when we arrive at the house."

He waved a hand, rounding up the rest of his men. The door to the mansion opened behind me as the crew slid into the vans. I felt my men as the engines turned over, felt Dominic wave to Killer as they pulled out. He wrapped me in a hug, kissing my temple softly.

"He's gone," I whispered.

"He is," Dominic agreed. "How do you feel about that?"

"All's well that ends well."

Honestly, I was happy Cameron was gone. Happy to have him out of my life and away from Aislynn. Happy to be free of his memory. The pain of his betrayal lingered, but I knew it would fade eventually. Knew that one day, I'd look back on him and feel nothing at all.

I couldn't wait.

"Exactly." He squeezed me tight then shoved me away playfully. "Now, go wash off the stench of desperation. We're taking you out."

"Where?"

"Little Sal's, of course."

I gave all three a kiss, squealing when Nate's hand clapped my ass. "Get moving, angel. We've got plans."

Stepping back into the hall, I peeled off my shirt, dangling it in the air. Their eyes darkened as they watched the fabric fall from between my fingers. "What happens if we're late?"

"Someone wants to play," Greyson mused.

"Then let's play." Dominic smirked, whipping off his shirt too. "We're definitely going to be late, *mariposa*."

They moved as one, but Grey was the one to swoop me into his arms, grinning down at me with more love than I'd ever known was possible. "Couldn't help yourself, could you?"

"Why have three men if I have to hold myself back?"

With a bark of laughter, he lifted me over his shoulder so I could watch Dominic and Nate stalk half naked behind us.

Thank God we'd taken the back stairs so no one could see us. I didn't want to know how I'd react if another woman saw my men like that, because *goddamn*. They looked good. I was going to say as much, but instead of smacking my ass as I expected, Grey slipped his hand between my legs. "Never hold back, *reina*. We love you just as you are."

And they showed me exactly how much they loved me in the shower.

We were definitely late for dinner, but I didn't care. I loved time with my men, and now, I got to love them forever.

•••

The End

Also by Janie Crouch

All books: https://www.janiecrouch.com/books

HEROES OF OAK CREEK

Hero Unbound

Hero's Flight

Hero's Prize

GILDED EMPIRE (as MJ Crouch)

Broken Crown

Damaged Kingdom

Fierce Monarch

Vicious Throne

ZODIAC TACTICAL

Code Name: ARIES

Code Name: VIRGO

Code Name: LIBRA

Code Name: PISCES

Code Name: OUTLAW

Code Name: GEMINI

NEVER TOO LATE FOR LOVE (with Regan Black)

Heartbreak Key Collection

Ellington Cove Collection

Wyoming Cowboys Collection

Holiday Heroes Collection

RESTING WARRIOR RANCH (with Josie Jade)

Montana Sanctuary

Montana Danger

Montana Desire

Montana Mystery

Montana Storm

Montana Freedom

Montana Silence

Montana Rain

LINEAR TACTICAL (series complete)

Cyclone

Eagle

Shamrock

Angel

Ghost

Shadow

Echo

Phoenix

Baby

Storm

Redwood

Scout

Blaze

Hero Forever

INSTINCT SERIES (series complete)

Primal Instinct

Critical Instinct

Survival Instinct

THE RISK SERIES (series complete)

Calculated Risk

Security Risk

Constant Risk

Risk Everything

OMEGA SECTOR (series complete)

Stealth

Covert

Conceal

Secret

OMEGA SECTOR: CRITICAL RESPONSE & UNDER SIEGE
(series complete)

Special Forces Savior

Fully Committed

Armored Attraction

Man of Action

Overwhelming Force

Battle Tested

Daddy Defender

Protector's Instinct

Cease Fire

Major Crimes

Armed Response

In the Lawman's Protection

About the Author (Janie Crouch)

"Passion that leaps right off the page." - Romantic Times Book Reviews

MJ Crouch is the alter ego of USA Today and Publishers Weekly bestselling author Janie Crouch. Her books have won multiple awards, including the Romance Writers of America's coveted Vivian® Award, the National Readers Choice Award, and the Booksellers' Best.

After a lifetime on the East Coast, and a six-year stint in Germany due to her husband's job as support for the U.S. Military, Janie has settled into her dream home in Front Range of the Colorado Rockies.

When she's not listening to the voices in her head—and even when she is—she enjoys engaging in all sorts of crazy adventures (200-mile relay races; Ironman Triathlons, treks to Mt. Everest Base Camp...), traveling, and hanging out with her four kids.

Her favorite quote: "Life is a daring adventure or nothing." ~ Helen Keller.

facebook.com/janiecrouch

amazon.com/author/janiecrouch

instagram.com/janiecrouch

bookbub.com/authors/janie-crouch

www.ingramcontent.com/pod-product-compliance
Lightning Source LLC
Chambersburg PA
CBHW060851210726

48293CB00006B/1759